Lena Diaz was born in Kentucky and has also lived in California, Louisiana and Florida, where she now resides with her husband and two children. Before becoming a romantic suspense author, she was a computer programmer. A Romance Writers of America Golden Heart® Award finalist, she has also won the prestigious Daphne du Maurier Award for Excellence in Mystery/Suspense. To get the latest news about Lena, please visit her website, lenadiaz.com

Nicole Helm grew up with her nose in a book and the dream of one day becoming a writer. Luckily, after a few failed career choices, she gets to follow that dream— writing down-to-earth contemporary romance and romantic suspense. From farmers to cowboys, Midwest to *the* West, Nicole writes stories about people finding themselves and finding love in the process. She lives in Missouri with her husband and two sons and dreams of someday owning a barn.

UNDERCOVER REBEL

LENA DIAZ

SOUTH DAKOTA SHOWDOWN

NICOLE HELM

MILLS & BOON

First Published in Great Britain 2020
by Mills & Boon, an imprint of HarperCollins*Publishers*
1 London Bridge Street, London, SE1 9GF

Undercover Rebel © 2020 Lena Diaz
South Dakota Showdown © 2020 Nicole Helm

ISBN: 978-0-263-28022-7

0320

MIX
Paper from
responsible sources
FSC™ C007454

This book is produced from independently certified FSC™
paper to ensure responsible forest management.

For more information visit: www.harpercollins.co.uk/green

Printed and bound in Spain
by CPI, Barcelona

UNDERCOVER
REBEL

LENA DIAZ

Thank you to all the wonderful readers enjoying this series, especially those who have sent me emails and messages about how much they love this special family of law-enforcement heroes. I hope Ian's story warms your heart and leaves you with a smile on your face.

Chapter One

Ian spotted his target in the back-left corner of the truck stop's massive parking lot, parked sideways as if poised for a quick getaway. Two empty spaces separated the white panel van from a garish bright yellow semi, one of dozens of rigs parked along the chain-link fence. He couldn't help rolling his eyes at the cliché of bad guys in a panel van. Just once he'd like to come up against his prey driving something more original with a cool factor, like a sports car, or even a blacked-out Suburban if they had to go big. Then again, a fancy car would attract attention, and attention was the last thing they wanted. It was the last thing *Ian* wanted.

He hunched his leather jacket against the cold wind blowing down from the Tennessee side of the Smoky Mountains and started forward. A glance to his right revealed the fast-food drive-through was already beginning to bustle with people looking for a quick, easy supper. Harassed-looking moms and dads in SUVs placed their orders, kids in the back yelling, laughing or crying through the open windows. None of them seemed to notice what was *really* going on outside the reach of the restaurant's neon glow. Few people ever did.

Rigs belched smoke behind the restaurant, pulling up

to lines of diesel fuel pumps that seemed to go on forever. Others parked to catch a few hours of sleep before getting back on I-40 to head into nearby Gatlinburg or some other destination. The occasional achingly young woman or man hopped in and out of the various sleeper cabs, sometimes pausing to grab junk food right alongside the soccer moms and dads inside the restaurant. And no one thought twice about it. Which was why business thrived out here. Just not the kind of business most of the decent people in this part of Tennessee knew about. Or the average person in hundreds of other towns just like this one.

Sometimes Ian wondered why he bothered to fight anymore. The odds were overwhelmingly against him. More often than not, his missions ended in defeat rather than victory. But every time he was on the verge of quitting, the memories would slam into him. Dormant grief and anger would work their way through his system like banked coals igniting into a dangerous wildfire. And then a name would prick his conscience.

Willow.

That was his battle cry, a reminder of his greatest failure, the reason he persevered even when the odds of making a difference seemed pathetically out of reach. But it was a newer name that pushed him forward tonight—*Maria*. Although he didn't know her, his friend and neighbor Shannon did. And the word on the street was that the men he was about to meet knew Maria too.

But they weren't her friends.

Ian sent up a silent prayer that Shannon would be uncharacteristically patient, that she'd stay in his car as she'd promised when this opportunity came up. They'd been on their way to a pizza joint when the long-awaited call had come in. If he'd taken the time to drive her home, he'd have missed the meeting. And neither of them had been willing to risk that.

Up ahead, a twentysomething skinny white guy with dark greasy hair and ragged jeans waved at Ian from near the van's front bumper. The kid had dubbed himself Wolverine. But something more passive, like Archie or Howard, seemed more appropriate. He didn't exactly inspire fear. But he did have his uses—like setting up tonight's meeting.

"Hurry up, Ian." Wolverine wrung his hands and glanced at the trio standing beside the van's closed sliding door. "The boss doesn't have all day."

Ian kept his steady, unhurried pace. It gave him time to size up his adversaries. According to Wolverine, their names were Butch, Jagger and Axel. Ian would bet the .357 Magnum Ruger GP100 that he'd left in his car for Shannon's protection that those monikers were just as fake as Wolverine's. But unlike Wolverine, these men's nicknames fit them perfectly. And they didn't give the impression that they were the least bit worried about Ian's size.

At six-one, his height tended to be an advantage when facing an opponent. But it was his powerful biceps and muscular physique that usually gave him the intimidation edge. His leather jacket, spiky black-and-blond hair, and dragon tattoos peeking out from his neck and wrists completed his street image. But the bulked-up men calmly watching him approach had Ian thinking he should up his reps at the gym. A lot. If things went south in the next few minutes, he might end up in the fight of his life. And that was only if they didn't kill each other in a shoot-out first.

"Lose the shades." The biggest of the three gave the order. His red hair and pale, freckled skin probably got him teased when he was younger. No one would make that mistake now. He could have been the Incredible Hulk's younger, less green brother, with a carrot top.

"And take your hands out of your pockets." That from the middle guy. Ian half expected the dark-skinned giant to pull a sword from behind his back and go all day-walker on him like Wesley Snipes in the *Blade* movies.

Ian kept his hands in his pockets. He didn't take off his shades. He looked to number three and jerked his head toward his fellow thugs. "I get the Incredible Hulk and Blade. But who are you supposed to be? Captain Jack Sparrow, on steroids?"

Jack's eyes widened, and he looked to his boss as if to take his lead on a response. Ian chalked him up as a minion, like Wolverine. No one important. He focused his attention on the other two. It was Blade who straightened, tossing his dreads and baring his white teeth like a hungry pit bull. First lieutenant, then, the main man's bodyguard. Definitely important. And dangerous.

"You think you're funny or something?" Blade flexed his fists at his sides.

"What are you doing, Ian?" Wolverine sounded like he was ready to faint. "You tryin' to get yourself killed?"

Zeroing in on the one he'd come for, Ian stopped three feet away from Hulk. He kept his left hand in his jacket pocket wrapped around the butt of his second-favorite gun, a Glock .22. Not as powerful or impressive-looking as his .357 revolver, it had the advantage of holding more rounds with less recoil. And it fit perfectly in his pocket. He could take out Blade and Jack without even pulling out the gun. But it would ruin a really nice jacket.

He stared directly at Hulk. "This macho drama is great if you're trying to intimidate some green kid straight out of high school. But I'm not green, and high school was a long time ago. My buyers are impatient for some fresh product. I was told you were the guy who could get it. Either show me what you have or my money and I go elsewhere."

"Ian, man. You're blowin' it." Wolverine sidled closer to Hulk. "You need to show some respect and—"

Hulk held up his hand. Wolverine slunk to the front of the van again. Blade had moved forward when Ian had. But he stepped back at his boss's signal, looking none too happy about it. Jack's eyes seemed to bulge from their sockets as he glared at Ian. Apparently, he wasn't a fan of Captain Jack Sparrow. That alone had Ian wanting to knock some sense into him.

"How fresh are we talking?" Hulk's voice was deathly quiet, his dark gaze riveted on Ian.

"I don't make deals with people I don't know." Ian slowly and deliberately pulled his right hand out of his pocket, then held it out toward the leader. "Ian Savage."

Hulk eyed his hand for a long moment. Time seemed to stand still as Ian waited. In his peripheral vision, he watched for sudden movements from the others, calculating distances and reaction times as he sifted through various possible scenarios.

"The name's Butch." Hulk finally grasped Ian's hand in a firm handshake. When he let go, he waved toward his lieutenant. "That's Axel, and over there is Jagger." The corner of his mouth lifted. "But I kind of like Blade and Sparrow. Might have to borrow those." He chuckled and reached into his pocket.

Ian tensed. Butch noticed and hesitated. He mimicked

Ian's earlier slow, deliberate movements as he pulled his hand out of his pocket, revealing a stack of photographs.

"Product." Butch's mouth curved into a lecherous grin. "The freshest around. Your buyers have any particular preferences, fetishes?" He fanned out the pictures like he was playing poker, and held them up in the air. "Redheads, blondes, brunettes. Tall, short, skinny, fat. I've got 'em all."

Ian flicked his gaze over each of the pictures. None of them matched Maria's description or had the tattoo on her neck that Shannon had told him about. "Got any Latinas? Dark hair, dark eyes? Curvy?"

Butch shrugged, his smile fading. "I got a few. But they're older, more…experienced. I thought your buyer wanted fresh."

Ian made a quick course correction, forcing a grin as he worked to keep his worm on the hook. "The Latina would be a bonus, for me."

Butch laughed, biting at the bait again. "If we deal, maybe I'll throw *two* Spanish beauties in just for you. What about your buyer? What's his preference?"

"Young," Ian said. "*Very* young."

"A man after my own tastes." He winked.

The urge to slam the butt of his pistol against the pervert's grinning mouth was nearly overwhelming. Instead, Ian schooled his features into a bland expression that gave nothing away of the turmoil inside him.

Butch pulled a smaller stack of pictures from his other pocket and made a show of licking his lips before turning them face out. "Young enough for you?" His brow arched. "I mean, for your friend, of course."

Bile rose in Ian's throat. The girls in the photographs didn't look old enough to be in high school. Two were prepubescent. He tightened his grip on the pistol in his pocket. One little squeeze and he could rid the world of this piece of garbage. But that wouldn't help the victims in those photographs. Until he knew where they were, he had to treat this animal like a human being.

Forcing a conspiratorial grin was beyond Ian's abilities. "How fast can you deliver?"

"A couple of hours. If the price is right."

Disappointment shot through him. He'd hoped the victims were close by, maybe hidden in the back of one of the big rigs. The whole mission could have been resolved in minutes. The young girls—none of them were old enough to be called women—could be rescued from this scum's depraved clutches and given a new chance at the life they deserved. Instead, he'd have to keep up the facade a little longer.

He held out his hand to take possession of the photographs. "I need a closer look before I choose."

"They're all A1 prime. I take good care of my girls." Another lascivious grin. "You pick the ones you're interested in. Then we talk price and delivery." Butch stacked the pictures together and held them out.

"Ian? Ian, is that you?" a man called out from behind him.

Ian froze. *No.* Of all people to recognize him from his other life, why did it have to be *him*? He was going to ruin everything.

He reached for the pictures.

Butch snatched them back, and suddenly Ian was looking down the bore of a pistol.

Chapter Two

Ian bit back a curse. "What are you doing, Butch? You threaten all your potential buyers?"

He'd been close, so close. He *needed* those pictures. He *needed* the trust of this monster pointing the pistol at him. And now a chance encounter with someone from his *other* life was jeopardizing months of undercover work, and the anticipated rescue of Hulk's young victims.

"You a cop, Ian?" Butch's knuckles whitened on the pistol grip. "'Cause that guy calling your name smells like a cop to me. You trying to pull something?"

Ian leaned slightly forward, curling his lip in derision even as he felt a bead of sweat roll down the back of his neck. "Don't insult me by calling me names. I ain't no cop."

Hulk studied him as if trying to decide whether to believe him. He subtly jerked his head. Axel and Blade slid the side door open behind him and hopped inside the van. Wolverine jumped into the passenger seat up front.

"Ian!" the voice called out again, closer.

Think fast. You can fix this. You have *to fix this.*

Butch looked past Ian's shoulder, then pocketed his gun. "That guy looks familiar. Who is he?"

Ian was seriously sweating now. Did Butch have a run-in with Adam in the past? Would he remember where he saw him? He went all in, and prayed his bluff would work. He jerked his thumb over his shoulder.

"That's the piece of crap who screwed my girlfriend. I'll get rid of him. Then you and I can finish business."

He whirled and strode toward Adam, half expecting to feel the burn of a bullet between his shoulders. He funneled all of his frustration and anger into an expression of pure malice as he glared at the man who was endangering everything. Of all the people to recognize him and interrupt his mission, why did it have to be Adam? He was two inches taller than Ian, if not more muscular. And, naturally, he was standing beside a cool blacked-out SUV that he must have parked when he saw Ian.

He didn't stop until he was right in Adam's face. "Punch me." His voice was pitched low so no one else would hear. "Hard."

"Punch you? Why would I punch—"

Ian slugged him in the jaw, spinning him around. He followed up with a solid left hook to the middle, making him double over.

Adam coughed, his eyes watering as he glared up at Ian. He slowly straightened and wiped a thin trickle of blood from the corner of his mouth. "You want to give me one good reason why I shouldn't beat the crap out of you for that?"

"Nope." Ian braced himself for what he knew was coming, and slowly drew back his fist again, giving Adam plenty of opportunity. The punch caught him in the shoulder like a battering ram, slamming him to the pavement. His head bounced against the concrete and his mouth filled with blood. Holy hell. He'd forgotten just how strong Adam was. The man was built like a bull.

Somewhere behind him laughter sounded. Some truckers watching the fun? Or Butch and his crew? An engine revved. The van. Ian's stomach sank. He'd lost his opportunity to rescue the girls, at least tonight. He shook his head, desperately trying to clear his double vision as he pushed himself to his feet. Maybe Butch would give him another chance. Ian had to convince him this fight was for real, and that Adam wasn't a cop. He had to keep this up until the van was gone. Even if it killed him.

He spit out a stream of blood and turned, then ducked just in time to avoid a fist to the face.

The white van pulled out of its spot, slowly passing them. Butch was definitely watching. Ian had to make this convincing.

He straightened, both fists in front of him as he tried to figure out which blurry image to hit. He made a half-hearted jab toward the middle one, then braced himself for the return punch. It was a one-two combo, making him double over from the first hit, then spin around with the second. He wobbled, the white of the van barely in his field of vision now. They were still watching. Was that a good thing? Or a bad thing? Were bullets about to fly or was Butch going to lie low and set up a new meeting later?

One more weak jab at Adam hit air as planned. Even knowing what was coming, he wasn't prepared for the violence of the return punch. It slammed into his ribs, knocking the wind out of him and sending him flying backward.

He managed to cover his head with his arm this time before he hit the concrete.

Fiery lava shot up his left arm and zinged through his shoulder. The only thing that kept him from shouting was a mouthful of blood. He spit again, then coughed and rolled onto his stomach, trying to push himself up on all fours. His left arm hung useless at his side. He swore. How was he supposed to go up against thugs like the Hulk with a bum shooting arm? Maybe he should have slugged Adam for real. He might have lost more by throwing this fight than he'd gained.

"Ian, good grief. Stay down. I'll call an ambulance."

"No." He coughed up more blood. "No ambulance." At least, that was what he tried to say. He was pretty sure it came out something like "nolnce."

The van sped off.

Thank God.

Adam crouched in front of him, a little unsteady himself, seeming to favor his left leg even though Ian didn't think he'd hit it. "Be still. Quit trying to stand." He pulled out his phone. "I'll call—"

Tires screeched. An engine roared.

"What the—" Adam jumped back to avoid being hit by Ian's black Dodge Charger.

Ah, hell.

"Hey, big bully. Back off. Now," Shannon called through the open window. "Ian, get in." The passenger door popped open beside him. "Stay back, jerk, or I'll put a hole in you."

Ian squinted toward the car. She was pointing his .357 Magnum at Adam. Things had just gone from bad to about ten levels worse than that. He wobbled to his feet just as Adam brought up his Glock.

"Drop it, lady," Adam ordered.

Ian staggered between them, using his body as a shield, hoping they both didn't start a shoot-out with him in the middle. He rarely wore a Kevlar vest while undercover, just in case a bad guy wanted to see proof that he wasn't wearing a wire. Now he was reconsidering the sanity of that decision.

"Ergmrph." He shook his head in defeat. Either his brain was scrambled or the cut in his mouth was garbling his words. Probably both.

"Ian, get out of the way." Adam jerked his gun down. Progress.

He forced his uncooperative legs to shuffle and fell back into the car.

Adam's gun came up.

Ian threw himself against Shannon, once more acting as her human shield.

Adam swore and yanked his gun down.

"Go." Ian's order came out a pained grunt, but must have gotten the message across.

The car took off, the momentum slamming the passenger door shut. Ian couldn't hold on and rolled back the other way, crunching his ruined arm between his body and the door before managing to twist around and fall back into the seat. His garbled curses were the last thing he heard before surrendering to the darkness.

when he saw Ian. He turned and motioned toward the doors. Two more men ran to ... doors. As vehicle sped up in reverse, the unnaturally ... Ian and ...

Chapter Three

Shannon slammed the brakes, bringing the Charger to a bouncing stop in front of the emergency room doors. Muffled cursing had her wincing and looking at Ian. His normally handsome, chiseled features were almost unrecognizable beneath his blood-matted black-and-blond hair. He was slumped in the passenger seat, cradling his left arm against his abdomen, his deep blue eyes glazed with pain.

"We're here." She grabbed the massive revolver from the console and hid it in her purse just as a man in green scrubs ran out the sliding doors, motioning for her to move.

"Lady, you can't park here. This is the ambulance entrance. We've got one on the way, five minutes out."

"I need help!" she yelled through the open passenger window. "This man, he's hurt. I...found him a couple of blocks away, lying in the street. I think he got mugged or something. His left arm may be broken."

Ian grunted, the corner of his swollen mouth lifting in a half grin as he nodded. He approved of her lies. No surprise there. She was good at lying, had been doing it most of her life just to survive.

The man in scrubs leaned in, his eyes going wide

when he saw Ian. He turned and motioned toward the doors to someone Shannon couldn't see. A moment later another man in scrubs ran outside, pushing a wheelchair at a run.

"Sir, I'm Nurse Jack. I'm going to help you. Can you tell me what happened?" The first man eased open the door and crouched inside, checking Ian's injuries.

For some reason, the nurse's name seemed to amuse Ian. He chuckled and mumbled something that sounded oddly like "Sparrow."

"What's his name?" Jack asked.

"I'm not sure. He mumbled *Ian*, I think."

Ian gave her a thumbs-up, acting loopy. He never acted loopy. Just what had that jerk at the truck stop done to him?

The two men struggled to lift Ian out of the car. But they managed to get him into the wheelchair without dumping him onto the concrete. The second one took off, pushing Ian toward the emergency room doors. Jack shut the car door and crouched by the window, motioning toward the parking lot to Shannon's left.

"Park over there and come inside. We've got policemen here 24/7. One of them will want to take your statement."

"Of course. Be right in. Thank you so much for your help."

He gave her a tight, suspicious smile. "We don't see enough Good Samaritans these days. That guy owes you. Thanks." He backed up to the curb.

Feeling like the fraud she was, she smiled back, then pulled Ian's car into the lot. With Nurse Jack watching, she parked in the first spot she came to, halfway down the row. She stalled for time by rolling up the windows one at a time. Then she grabbed her purse and cut the engine before slowly getting out of the car.

She could feel Jack watching her, so she kept up the charade. She smoothed her T-shirt over her jeans and strolled toward the emergency room.

Giving up his vigil, he jogged back to the hospital, convinced that his Good Samaritan was coming inside to talk to the police as instructed.

Like *that* would ever happen.

She ducked down the next row of cars, then took off running in the opposite direction. The next two hours were spent shuffling between fast-food restaurants and convenience stores, all within a few blocks of the hospital. Every time she stayed in one place long enough to start getting curious stares, she'd switch locations and start over.

Now, standing outside the ER once again, she debated the wisdom of going inside. Had she waited long enough to avoid the cops? Were they looking for her? What about Ian? Where was he? There was no way to know whether the doctors had already patched up his injuries. Emergency rooms were notorious for long waits. But he'd been in rough shape. Surely they would have taken care of him by now.

As she cautiously approached, she kept an eye out for Nurse Jack and the man who'd wheeled Ian into the emergency room. When she didn't see either one, she straightened her shoulders and marched inside. One of the things that Ian had taught her since moving into the other side of the duplex that she rented was to hide in plain sight. Most people wouldn't question a person's right to be somewhere if they acted with confidence, pretending they belonged. Proving the point, no one stopped her or questioned her as she moved through the maze of rooms, gleaning bits of information left for anyone to take if they paid attention.

Like the sign-in sheet at the triage desk when the nurse turned away to talk to someone.

And the whiteboard with patient numbers instead of names, but with medical descriptions beside them: *flu-like symptoms, fever, possible dislocated or fractured arm.*

That dislocation or fracture could be Ian. Nothing else on the board fit. It still shocked her that he'd lost the fight so easily. She'd seen him take on four guys a few days ago outside their duplex because he was incensed that they were selling weed to the neighborhood kids. Those guys had left bleeding and bruised with their drugs confiscated. Ian had come away relatively unscathed. So how had he been beaten up by one lone man?

True, the guy was brawny and a few inches taller than Ian. But his shoulders weren't as broad, his arms not as ripped. Normally Ian fought like a junkyard dog, scrappy and vicious, holding nothing back. Today he'd seemed sluggish. It didn't make sense.

After a few more minutes of snooping and some unauthorized trips into areas off-limits to patients, she had a room number. He'd been taken to the fifth floor half an hour ago. From what she could understand from the medical jargon she'd sneaked and read, he'd been lucky. His arm was deeply bruised and sprained, dislocated and rotated back into place, but not broken. He did have a minor concussion. No surprise there. And he also had bruised ribs. Again, he was lucky they weren't broken. The blood he'd been coughing up had come from a cut on the inside of his cheek. He'd be in a lot of pain for a few days. But at least he was going to be okay, or so she hoped. She wanted to see him for herself to be sure.

Ducking out of a restricted area into the main hallway, she swept her gaze back and forth, on the lookout for Nurse Jack or the cops he'd mentioned. The elevators were a little farther down. She just might make it. Then she'd find out if Ian was okay, and whether he'd been able to discover anything about Maria before that stupid bully had interfered.

She scanned the intersecting hallway just before the ladies' room and the bank of elevators, then froze. Three impressively muscled, tall, dark-haired men in business suits were striding down the hall toward her. The one in the middle was half-turned, talking to the man on his right. He had the slightest limp, barely noticeable, as if his left leg bothered him. She'd seen that limp before. And she'd seen that profile, at the truck stop.

He was the man who'd beaten Ian.

She put on a burst of speed and ducked into the ladies' room. The door had just swung shut when footsteps echoed outside. Had he seen her? Recognized her? She waited, pressing a hand to her chest as if she could force her pulse to stop racing so fast.

A toilet flushed in one of the stalls. She started primping in the mirror, finger-combing her black hair to make the blue tips lie flat against her shoulders.

An older lady in a yellow sunflower-print dress stepped to a sink two down from her, smiling politely even though her disapproving gaze shot to the tattoos on Shannon's arms.

She'd probably faint if she saw the ones on her back.

Shannon hid a smile and grabbed a paper towel, pretending to dry her hands as she listened for sounds from the hallway. The footsteps had stopped. The elevator dinged. She tensed, her hand dropping to her purse, where the .357 rested inside. As soon as the elevator dinged again, she peeked out the door. The men were gone. She rushed into the hallway to the elevators. Only one was moving, the digital numbers above it marking its ascent.

Two. Three.

Keep going. Keep going.

Four.

Don't stop, don't stop.

Five. The elevator stopped.

Her stomach sank. The man who'd attacked Ian and possibly wrecked their plans to finally rescue Maria had somehow figured out where he was.

And he'd brought reinforcements.

Chapter Four

Ian awkwardly shifted against the pillows in his hospital bed as he clutched the phone to his right ear. While he listened to his boss, he watched the door at the other end of the room. He'd managed to keep his true identity a secret from the doctors and nurses so far. He aimed to keep it that way, at least until he discovered whether his cover had been blown with Butch.

"Did you get all that, Ian?"

"Yeah. Got it. Assistant District Attorney Cameron Ellison is a wuss. He wants me to drop my investigation. Doesn't mean I will."

A heavy sigh sounded in his ear. "We can't run roughshod over the locals. We have to play nice in their sandbox. And he's not asking us to drop it, just put it on hold for a few days, let things cool off. There were complaints at the truck stop. Several people saw the fight and called it in. That kind of exposure doesn't help any of us."

Ian's hand tightened around the phone so hard his knuckles ached. "If those same people paid attention to the *real* trouble going on around them, maybe we wouldn't have this human trafficking epidemic."

"Ian—"

"Please tell me you don't really expect me to back off.

What do you think is going to happen to those girls if I do? I'm pretty sure I told you about ten of them were kids. We're talking thirteen, fourteen, *maybe*. And two of them, my God, Nash. They were children. Little kids. We can't sit on this. Don't ask me to do that. I won't. I *can't*."

Another sigh sounded through the phone. "What do you think you can do at this point? They saw you with Adam. They either suspect or know you're in law enforcement."

"Maybe, maybe not. They don't know for sure what Adam does. Butch just got the cop vibe from him is all. And they wouldn't expect a cop to pick a fight with another cop the way I did. There's plenty of doubt there. I can build on that."

"And how do you propose to do that?"

"I go back to work, back to the shop. Stick to my routine. If they still want a deal, Wolverine will contact me again."

"And if they think you tried to set them up, they may try to kill you."

"It wouldn't be the first time someone tried to finish me off, and I'm still here. Nash, come on. Let me do this. Give me one more chance to set the trap and catch these slimeballs. For the love of all that's holy, help me get those little kids back to their parents." The phone went silent. "Boss, you still there?"

"I'm here."

"What's it gonna be? Let some local prosecutor call the shots and sacrifice dozens of young victims? Or do I get to wrap this thing up and make a difference for once?"

"You've rescued hundreds of victims since becoming an agent. You're making a difference."

"Doesn't feel that way from where I'm sitting. I've spent months building my cover, getting that noxious Wolverine kid to trust me. We're almost at the end. You pull me out now and bring someone else in, it'll take them months, longer, to get back to this point. Maybe you end up with a prosecutable case. Maybe you don't. Either way, it doesn't help the victims we know are in or near Gatlinburg right this minute. Rescuing those in need comes before prosecution. That's how we've always done things. A victim-centered approach. Or did our charter change while I was unconscious?"

"You know dang well it didn't. Fine, fine. You win. Based on those photographs, we know there are approximately thirty victims in jeopardy—"

"Thirty-two. He mentioned two Latina women."

"All right. Thirty-two. You and I both know how fast this scum likes to move their inventory, especially around a hub like you've discovered out here. If you've still got this Butch guy interested, maybe he'll wait and give you one more chance. Forty-eight hours, Ian. That's all I can give you. After that, we do it ADA Ellison's way. Might as well try to put someone in prison after all these months even if we don't end up rescuing the victims."

He hated that his boss was right. If he didn't make a deal in the next day or two, the victims were likely beyond their reach, already sold to the highest bidder. Bringing down the trafficking ring would be the only way to prevent others from becoming future victims. But he wasn't giving up on the girls he'd seen in those pictures. *The children.* Not yet. Someone had to fight for them. It might as well be him.

"All right. Forty-eight hours. I still get Chris as my contact? Same signals, same setup? I don't have time to train someone else, establish new parameters and routines."

"Nothing's changed from my perspective. It's the scum you've been dealing with who may feel otherwise. If they even suspect who you really are—"

"They don't."

"Can you guarantee that?"

Ian's mouth tightened. What could he say? He had no way of knowing for sure what Butch suspected, or didn't suspect.

"I didn't think so," Nash said. "I'm adding a condition to your forty-eight hours. Every time you go out, you put on Kevlar."

"Boss—"

"Nonnegotiable. Either wear the vest, or I shut this operation down right now."

Ian swore. Kevlar added risk, especially with his contacts possibly spooked. But if something did happen, and he wasn't wearing his vest and somehow survived— Nash would can him in a second. Then what would Ian do? This wasn't just his career. It was his life. There wasn't anything else.

Shannon. There was still Shannon.

He shook his head. Stupid dreams. There was no possibility of a future between the two of them. She thought he was simply the mechanic who lived on the other side of her duplex. Once she found out he was in law enforcement, he'd become enemy number one. He'd never see her again.

Of all the people he'd duped in his career, Shannon was the one he truly regretted. She wasn't some criminal or thug. She was a genuinely good person, a survivor. She'd worked so hard trying to find her friend Maria, who was still trapped in the life that Shannon had escaped. That story had been shared with Ian over dinner and a few too many glasses of wine one night. It had also been the catalyst that had sent his investigation in an entirely new direction.

What Shannon told him about believing Maria might be in the area had eventually led him to Wolverine. She was a hero, and didn't even know it. She trusted him, thinking he wanted to help her find her friend, because of the attraction they shared and because he was a good person.

He hadn't faked the attraction.

But the guilt was eating him alive that he'd misled her about his motives, that everything else he'd told her was a lie. Almost. In order to gain her trust, he'd revealed his own extremely personal dark secret, a secret he'd never told anyone else. Which only went to show how obsessed he was with this case, or with Shannon. He'd always planned on taking that particular secret with him to the grave.

"Ian? You still there?"

He shook his head again, then winced when the movement jump-started the headache that had been threatening since the fight with Adam. Maybe he could bum an aspirin or something stronger off a nurse before escaping this place. "I'm here."

"What about the vest? Do we have a deal?"

He blinked against the bright fluorescent lights overhead and longed to rub his aching temples. But with his left hand in a sling and the phone in his right, all he could do was squeeze his eyes shut. "We have a deal. My vest is at the duplex. I'll put it on before I head to the shop in the morning."

"You'd better. If these guys decide they can't trust you, that vest is your only chance. First sign of trouble, use the nuclear option. I'll have the cavalry in place to come running. Understood?"

The nuclear option meant blowing his cover, sending the signal for agent in distress. It would activate every asset in the area to come help him. But it would ruin his chances of rescuing anyone. He had no intention of using it. Ever.

"Understood." Technically, he hadn't made a promise. "What about the ADA?"

"Leave him to me. I'll tell him you're lying low, letting things settle. Don't make me regret this, Ian. Be careful. See if you can figure out the location of the victims so we can set up a rescue operation. Then shut it down. Don't try to be a hero and get yourself killed. The paperwork would be a nightmare."

Ian laughed, then winced at the sharp jolt that shot through his cut cheek. His stomach clenched. The pain was making him nauseous.

"Ian?"

"Okay, okay. I'll do what I can to keep you from all that paperwork. You're going to pick up the hospital tab, right? My crappy car mechanic insurance won't cover an ER visit without a hefty deductible."

"I'll take care of it." The line clicked.

Chapter Five

Ian dumped the landline phone onto the side table and clutched his aching head. But he couldn't allow himself the luxury of sitting there until the pain receded. He needed to leave. Now.

He stood, then had to grab the bed railing to keep from falling. When the room stopped spinning, he hobbled to the bathroom and splashed water on his face. A few deep breaths seemed to help with the nausea. He cupped his hands beneath the faucet and drank some water. Then, seeing the blood smeared on his face and matting his hair, he did a quick wash in the sink. Finally, looking more presentable and feeling less shaky, he went on a hunt for his clothes.

A few minutes and several curses later, he was fully dressed, minus his favorite leather jacket. It had died a tragic death beneath the scissors of a nurse trying to work it off his injured arm. It would have come in handy right now to hide the splotches of blood on his shirt. But he figured that was to be expected in a hospital. People would just assume it was someone else's blood, that he'd helped a friend into the emergency room. He couldn't imagine anyone would try to stop him, as long as he made sure the nurse assigned to him didn't see him leaving the room.

He still felt naked without a gun. Shannon had his .357 Magnum and his car, which meant she presumably had his Glock .22 pistol, as well. Thankfully, his house key and wallet were in his jeans pocket, so he'd be able to hire a car to drive him home. And he wouldn't have to kick in the door when he got there. Bonus. That was one tiny bright spot in what had turned into a wasted day.

The second bright spot was that Shannon hadn't gotten hurt. When she'd pulled that gun on Adam, Ian had been terrified that she'd get killed. Hopefully, she'd gone home and was lying low. He didn't think Butch or the others had seen her rescuing him at the end of the fight. The van had been gone by then. But he wanted her away from any potential danger, just in case.

He never should have taken her to that truck stop with him, even if it meant rescheduling the meeting. He should have ignored her impassioned pleas that he not delay, that he go directly to the rendezvous point. He shouldn't have believed her promises that she'd stay in the car and wouldn't interfere.

Then again, she *had* stayed in the car.

He grinned at the memory of her daring to call Adam a bully. The woman was just as feisty as she was gorgeous. But knowing Adam, he probably had a BOLO out on her *and* Ian, just on principle. Every cop in Gatlinburg, Tennessee, had likely been alerted to be on the lookout for the two of them. Which meant if they saw her, especially driving the Charger Adam had seen, she'd be handcuffed and thrown in jail.

In the few months that Ian had known her, one thing was clear—she had a deep-seated fear of law enforcement. If she ended up under arrest, the second she made bail she'd run. He'd never see her again. That shouldn't matter. But it did.

He was halfway to the door when it started to open. He was mentally spinning a cover story to explain why he was dressed and walking when the nurse stepped inside. Except it wasn't a nurse. And it wasn't just one person. It was three.

Adam was flanked by Duncan and Colin. And they were looking at him as if they thought he was the slime stuck to the bottom of their shoes. Nothing had changed since the last time they'd all seen each other. When was that? Probably last Easter, a good seven months ago. Not nearly long enough.

"Where do you think you're going?" Adam stepped in front of him, blocking his way.

Ian braced his legs and fisted his right hand at his side, fully expecting all three of them to take a turn trying to wallop him. One-on-one, even though each of them was a tad bigger than him, he'd normally have at least a fifty-fifty chance. But he wasn't exactly at his best tonight. Still, he'd give it a good solid try if they pushed him. As ticked off as he was about this truly screwed-up day, it could give him the advantage.

"If you're here for round two, Adam, be warned that I'm not throwing the fight this time. You're the one who'll be bleeding on the floor when we're through."

"I knew it," Adam said. "You were pulling punches at the truck stop. I figured it was either that or you'd gone soft. Why did you pick the fight to begin with? And what in the world were you doing with those losers by that van?"

He shrugged, then pressed his hand against his protesting ribs. "Losers hang with losers, right?" The other two were intently watching him, but seemed content to let Adam do the talking for this little welcoming committee. "I'd love to reminisce about old times with you boys, but I have things that need doing."

He stepped around Adam. As one, Colin and Duncan moved to block him, spreading their legs and bracing themselves against whatever he might try.

He blew out a deep breath. "So that's how it's going to be, huh? You can't butt out and let it lie? Fine. There's still some fight left in me. But to be fair, let's do this one at a time." He motioned toward the sling on his left arm. "Just to even the odds."

"Knock off the sarcasm." Adam crossed his arms, his brow knitting into a frown.

"Who's being sarcastic? I can take you guys." He motioned toward Adam. "You first. Payback time."

He rolled his eyes, unimpressed. "What did the doctors say was wrong? Do you have broken ribs? A concussion? They don't typically admit someone for a broken arm."

"What do you care?"

Colin shoved him. "Knock it off, Ian. What's really going on? Adam told us about those pieces of scum that you were with at the truck stop. Associating with guys like that is low, even for you."

"Even for me? Gee, thanks, Colin. That makes me feel all warm and fuzzy inside. Can't wait to see what you write on my next Christmas card." He tried to shove him out of his way.

Colin shoved right back.

"Leave him alone," a feminine voice called out from behind the Colin-Duncan wall.

Ian groaned as Colin and Duncan turned around. Shannon stood just inside the door, holding his .357 Magnum revolver in both her hands.

In the blink of an eye, three pistols were pointing directly at her.

"Drop it," Adam ordered. "Now."

Her face turned chalk white. Her arms started to shake.

Ian moved between Colin and Shannon, once again playing human shield. He was really getting tired of that role. "Guys, dial it back. Shannon, give me the gun."

"But they were—"

"It's okay. Trust me. Please." He held out his hand.

She hesitated, her hands shaking dangerously, her finger on the trigger.

He purposely kept his voice gentle and calming as he spoke. "Shannon, darlin', I really need you to move your finger off the trigger and give me the gun. You think you can do that?"

Her blue-tipped black bangs had fallen into her eyes. She tossed her head, green eyes darting back and forth from the others to him. None of them had lowered their weapons. They'd simply shifted their stances so they could aim at her without him in the line of fire. They wouldn't shoot him. But they didn't know Shannon and weren't taking any chances with her.

"Shannon—"

"Okay, okay." She moved her finger off the trigger and turned the gun around.

He blew out a relieved breath as he took the gun. "Thank you. You did great." He smiled encouragingly and shoved the revolver into his jeans pocket.

The others lowered their weapons and slowly put

them away, as if they were worried that she might draw another gun.

Ian turned sideways so he could keep an eye on all of them. He smiled at Shannon again and motioned to the others. "Shannon Murphy, allow me to introduce you to the brute I allowed to beat the crap out of me at the truck stop. This is Adam McKenzie, a law enforcement ranger for the National Park Service."

Adam nodded, but maintained a tense watchful wariness.

Shannon's eyes widened, panic welling in them as soon as she'd heard the words *law enforcement*. He rushed through the rest of the introductions.

"The second one who looks like he could be Adam's twin, but isn't, is Special Agent Duncan McKenzie, also with NPS. Our last black-haired blue-eyed Irish lad is Deputy US Marshal Colin McKenzie."

She swallowed, her haunted eyes zeroing in on him. "Why are they here, Ian? And why do they look so much like *you*?"

The knowledge was in her eyes. But she obviously needed to hear him admit it before she'd accept what to her was likely an unforgivable deception. He thought about lying. But there'd been enough lies between them already. And he knew the others wouldn't go along with whatever story he wove, not without understanding *why*. All he could do was hope the fragile bond that he and Shannon had formed over the past few months survived the next few minutes.

"They're here because they're my brothers."

She swallowed again, twisting her hands together. "I'm guessing that Ian Savage isn't your real name. And you're not really a mechanic?"

He glanced at his brothers, who were watching the conversation with riveted interest, before he met her tortured gaze again.

"I *am* a mechanic. I can fix pretty much anything with an engine. But I only work at the shop as my cover while working a case. My real name is Ian *McKenzie*. I'm a special agent for Homeland Security, specializing in the fight against human trafficking."

A sob burst from her lips and she ran from the room.

Colin started after her, yanking open the door to give chase.

Ian grabbed his arm. "Let her go. She's terrified of anyone with a badge. For good reason."

Colin hesitated, then let the door close. "Special agent with Homeland Security, huh?" His voice was heavy with disbelief. "Since when?"

"Ian *Savage*?" Duncan cocked his head and grinned. "What a lame cover name." He winked, letting Ian know he was teasing.

Normally Ian didn't get Duncan's jokes or appreciate the lighthearted way he approached life. But at this moment, he was Ian's favorite brother.

"Let's hold the twenty questions until Ian's back in bed." Adam firmly grasped his shoulders and steered him farther into the room.

"I must have hit you harder than I thought," Ian mused. "You're limping."

"Old injury. You don't get any credit for that. Come on. You're about ready to fall over."

"I'm only going to lie down because there's no point in leaving now. You'll just follow me and badger me with questions."

Adam chuckled. "Right. It has nothing to do with

how wobbly you are or that you look like you're about to pass out."

Ian stopped beside the bed. "You forgot something else."

"What's that?"

"I'm also about to throw up."

Adam's eyes widened. He jumped back just as Ian lost the contents of his stomach on the floor.

Chapter Six

"*Four years*, Ian?" Adam's brows drew down in a thunderous frown as he dried his hands in the bathroom doorway. While he'd cleaned the floor moments earlier, and his shoes, the others had dragged extra chairs into the room. Now, as Adam took a seat, he and the others formed a ring around the bed, effectively boxing Ian in as if to keep him from trying to leave again.

"You must have gone to college after taking off and never told anyone about it. Then you joined Homeland Security shortly after you graduated."

"Your deductive reasoning and math skills are extraordinary. You're wasting your talents as a ranger."

Adam's eyes narrowed dangerously.

Colin swore. "Why all the subterfuge? We see you once, twice a year if that. And every time we ask about your life, you give a different story about your occupation. One time you were a bartender. Once you were a taxi driver in New York."

"Don't forget cowboy on a dude ranch in Montana," Duncan chimed in. "That was my favorite." He motioned toward Ian's neck and arms. "Those tats real?"

"Why all the lies?" Colin demanded.

"I didn't lie. I *was* all those things. And, yes, Duncan, the tattoos are real."

Duncan waved toward his hair. "The blond streaks are new. Can't say I care for them."

Ian shot him an aggravated look. "Can't say I care about your opinion."

Duncan grinned.

Colin frowned. "Those were never real jobs. They were cover for whatever you were doing for Homeland Security." He waved toward the other two. "It's not like we can't relate. We've all done undercover work. And we're brothers in blue in addition to blood. We would have kept your secrets, been there for you over the years instead of—"

"Instead of judging me and telling me what a screwup I was all the time?" Ian started to cross his arms, but the sling stopped him. "Thanks, but no thanks. I got enough of that from all of you—and Dad—while growing up."

Adam fisted his hand on top of the bed railing to Ian's right. "That's not fair. You *were* a screwup back in those days. You vandalized houses, stole cars, did drugs. All we ever did was try to help you."

"Uh, no. You beat the crap out of me and tattled to Mom and Dad. And for the record, I've never done drugs. Not even while undercover."

Adam rolled his eyes. "What are we? Ten? Let's talk about this like grown adults. Or if we can't do that, let's speak to each other as the professionals that we are. Ian, if you're in some kind of trouble, we can help."

Ian snorted. "Of course you'd think I was in trouble."

"Stop it." This time it was Duncan who spoke up, sounding serious for a change. "I don't think Adam was saying that on a personal level. He meant on whatever case you're working. You told that girl—"

"Shannon."

"Right. Shannon. You told her that you were working as a mechanic as your cover. That you specialize in fighting human trafficking. Is that why you're in town? You're after a trafficking ring? Where does Shannon Murphy fit into that? Who is she?"

Adam tapped the railing. "And what does it all have to do with Butch Gillespie? Has he risen from common pimp to running modern slavery rings?"

Ian straightened, then sucked in a breath and rubbed his aching ribs. "Gillespie? That's his last name? You know him?"

"When I was a Memphis cop, I worked on numerous task forces. That included vice, specifically prostitution. Gillespie was arrested during one of our raids. The net was wide, mostly circumstantial evidence. He was one of the fish who got away. Not enough to hold him beyond the first twenty-four hours. No one was willing to turn on him, make any deals. He walked. But there's no doubt in my mind that he was one of the ones behind the ring we broke up."

"When was that?" Ian asked.

Adam considered it a moment. "Two, maybe two and a half years ago."

"What did you find out about him? Did he run with anyone called Axel or Jagger?"

"Not that I remember. His right-hand guys went to prison. No way they're out already. Are Axel and Jagger the other two big guys who were leaning against that van when I saw you?"

Ian nodded. "My thug contact, the scrawny guy by

the front bumper, finally got me a face-to-face meeting after I'd been trying to talk deals for weeks using him as an intermediary. I'd hoped to make the bust tonight, rescue dozens of girls and bring down a major trafficking hub right here in Gatlinburg."

Adam held his hands out. "Sorry, man. I had no way of knowing you were working a case. I didn't even know you were in town. Maybe if you'd told us that you had—"

"Don't," Ian warned.

Adam let out a deep breath. "No judgment, all right? I'm just saying that had I known you were a special agent with Homeland Security, I wouldn't have interfered. As for Gillespie, if you want, I can call some of my guys in Memphis and have them email me what they've got on him."

Ian stared at him in surprise. "O...kay. Sure. I'd appreciate that."

"You don't have to act so shocked. We're brothers, in and out of uniform. I'm always here for you, Ian. We all are."

Duncan and Colin nodded as if on cue.

Ian was so used to being on the defensive around his family that he wasn't sure how to react to this new uneasy truce, of sorts. He finally nodded his thanks, hoping that was enough.

Duncan thumped the railing. "Homeland Security, huh? Impressive. Tell us about it."

It was surreal sitting in the hospital bed chatting with his brothers. That never happened. Since leaving home at eighteen, his return visits had been short and more for his mom than anyone else. He'd never once considered that the others might really care about him. Or did they?

After giving them a small glimpse into the kind of

work he did, he said, "Tell me the truth. If I wasn't in law enforcement, would you even be talking to me right now?"

Duncan considered the question, then rested his forearms on the railing. "Probably not. Your turn. If you weren't still woozy and thought you could get past the three of us, would you still be here?"

He reluctantly smiled. "Probably not."

Duncan grinned. "Back to your current case. You working alone?"

"Except for a liaison agent I meet at a pizza parlor every now and then so he can update my boss and provide resources, it's just me. I've spent months following dozens of tips and leads through three states. Everything pointed to Gatlinburg being a hub, a distribution point. We've made some minor busts along the way. But here in Tennessee, I'm hoping to bring it all to a head. I want Butch and his men in handcuffs. But mostly I want to rescue the girls he's currently holding. Unfortunately, I haven't figured out where he's keeping them or I'd have gotten them out by now."

"I'm so sorry," Adam repeated. "I had no idea about the damage I was doing when I confronted you in that parking lot."

"Do you realize that's the first time you've ever apologized to me?"

Adam snorted. "It's the first time you ever deserved it."

Ian's jaw tightened.

"That was a joke. Not a good one, but an attempt regardless." Adam smiled, but his look was wary. "I'm not Duncan. I don't have the silly gene."

"Hey, hey. Duncan's in the room here, guys," Duncan said.

Adam arched a brow. "Insulting you wouldn't be any fun if you weren't."

Duncan grinned. "There's hope for you yet, my serious brother."

Adam rolled his eyes. "What's your number, Ian? I'll text you once I hear back from Memphis PD about Gillespie." He pulled out his phone.

Ian hesitated.

Adam arched a brow. "What am I supposed to do? Shine the bat signal and hope you see it?"

The weight of all three brothers' stares focused on him. Did they think that this civil conversation meant all was forgiven? That they could suddenly be friends? When they thought he was Ian the rebel, Ian the delinquent, they wanted nothing to do with him. But now that they knew he'd followed the family tradition of going into law enforcement after all, they suddenly wanted to be cozy?

Screw that.

They might consider everything that had happened as water under the McKenzie family bridge, but he wasn't ready to throw out an olive branch. Especially since he hadn't taken this job to make their retired-judge father proud. He'd taken it *in spite* of his father, to right the terrible wrong that Mighty McKenzie had done so many years ago. Not that anything could ever atone for what he'd done.

For what Ian *hadn't* done, but *should* have done.

He rattled off a number and waited until Adam had saved it in his contacts. "That's my boss's line. His name is Barry Nash. You can text him about the case file on Gillespie. He'll see that I get the information."

Adam jerked his head up. "You gave me your boss's number?"

"It's the best I can do right now without risking blowing my cover. I don't have an electronic trail in my real name here in town. I'm Ian Savage. Period. Mostly I use burner phones."

Adam gave him a resigned look. "All right."

Surprised at how easily his oldest brother had given in, Ian thanked him. "I appreciate you accepting my decision."

"Oh, I'm not accepting it. I respect that you don't want us interfering in an investigation. But now that we've found you again, I have no intention of letting you disappear like you usually do. Things are different now, Ian." He held up his left hand. A gold band winked in the overhead lights.

"What the— You got hitched?"

"Last June. And both Colin and Duncan are engaged. They're tying the knots in a double ceremony this Christmas. Are you going to miss every important moment in our lives because of your silly grievances against Dad and your resentment at us for not hating him like you do? Or are you going to finally grow up and work through whatever made you leave all those years ago?"

"Get out."

Adam blinked. "Excuse me?"

"Get out. Forget about Gillespie. I'll get the information myself. Forget about me and my *silly grievances*. I never asked for this little reunion, and I have no intention of *growing up* anytime soon." He pushed the call button on the side of the bed.

Colin put his hand on Adam's shoulder. "Come on. He's not ready. We'll come back later."

"What exactly do you think Dad did?" Adam demanded.

"Nurse's station." A woman's voice crackled through the speaker built into the bed railing.

"I have some guests who've overstayed their welcome," Ian told her. "They don't seem inclined to leave on their own."

"Do you need me to call security, Mr. Savage?"

Ian arched a brow.

Adam swore. "This isn't over." He stood, jerked his suit jacket into place and strode to the door. Colin followed without a backward glance. Duncan gave Ian a sad smile and exited with them.

"Mr. Savage?" the nurse called out again.

"Never mind. They've left now. Thank you."

He wrestled down the bed railing that Adam had raised after Ian had nearly thrown up on him. He swung his legs over the side and used the bedside phone to call Shannon's cell. No answer. He left her a message, then called his own cell in case she'd answer that. She didn't. For a day that had started out so promising, it was turning out to be one of the worst ones ever. And he'd had more than his share of bad days in his twenty-seven years.

Less than five minutes later, he walked out the emergency room doors without anyone trying to stop him. Not wanting to risk his brothers seeing him if they were still hanging around the hospital, he'd phoned for a car for hire to pick him up a few blocks away.

He was halfway through the parking lot to the agreed pickup place when he spotted a familiar black Charger parked in one of the spots. *His* black Charger. He hurried toward it, half expecting to see Shannon waiting there. His shoulders slumped with disappointment when he saw it was empty. He'd stupidly hoped she might have come back to give him a chance to explain. Where was she? Had she hired someone to drive her home, as he'd planned for himself? Maybe she'd left a note inside the car.

He'd just unlocked the door when tires screeched behind him. He turned to see an all-too-familiar white panel van, idling behind the Charger.

Ah, hell.

He kept his expression bland and nodded at Butch, who was driving. "I was going to call you to reschedule our meeting since we were rudely interrupted."

"I'll just bet you were, *cop*."

The side door slid open to reveal Blade aiming a sawed-off shotgun at him. "Get in."

Chapter Seven

Shannon strode toward the emergency room exit. She'd debated taking Ian's car when she ran from his hospital room. After all, he'd lied to her all this time. He deserved to be stranded when they discharged him, forced to figure out his own way to get home. Maybe he could ask one of his brothers for help.

Brothers.

He'd told her he didn't have any family. He was an orphan, grew up in foster care. And those were just a few of his lies. Had anything he'd said been true? Had the make-out sessions on his couch been real? Or was that some kind of cover for a reason that she hadn't figured out yet?

She clenched her fists and moved back to allow a gurney to roll past. Just thinking about how badly she'd been duped, and used, had her lungs squeezing in her chest. Had he been laughing at her this whole time? Pretending to commiserate with her, pretending to be her friend? Why? Why had he done it?

She shook her head. Didn't matter. They were done. Over. All the silly fantasies she'd had that their fledgling relationship might turn into something deeper, that maybe she'd finally found someone who *got* her, who didn't judge her for her past, had died the moment he'd introduced himself as a cop.

Ian Savage, a cop. No, Ian *McKenzie*. Brother of three other cops. Or special agents. Or investigators. Or whatever they were. None of it computed. None of it mattered.

Not anymore.

He deserved to be stranded at the hospital. She didn't trust him now any more than she did the strangers in his room, those men who'd looked so much like him that her heart had broken the moment they'd turned around. She'd known, immediately upon seeing them shoulder to shoulder with Ian, that they were all brothers. She'd known Ian had lied to her about being an orphan. And then it had only gotten worse.

Still, she couldn't quite bring herself to steal his car when his arm was in a sling and he had a concussion. Stupid, yes. But there it was. She was a sucker and felt sorry for him even though he didn't deserve her sympathy. But just because he was a jerk didn't mean she had to stoop to his level. His phone and pistol were already hidden inside the car. All she had to do was leave the key under the mat and walk away.

She'd hire a car to pick her up at one of the fast-food restaurants close by. Hanging around the hospital any longer than she already had was too risky. She'd wasted half an hour hiding out, walking the halls, worried he or his brothers were after her. Now she had to get home and pack. It wouldn't take long. She never set roots down very deep. Most of her stuff she could put into one suitcase. The duplex she rented came mostly furnished. What few pieces of furniture she'd added weren't worth taking.

The emergency room doors slid open. She'd just

reached the end of the row where she'd left his car when she realized a white van was parked behind it. A familiar-looking man dressed in black straightened beside the Charger, slammed the passenger door and shoved something into his pocket. Then he ran to the van and hopped inside. It took off, tires squealing, and turned down another row as the side door slid shut.

But not before she saw Ian inside, with one of the thugs from the truck stop pointing a shotgun at him.

She took off running toward the Charger.

Risking her life to help him made no sense, except that in spite of the lies, he'd helped her a dozen times since they'd first met—from loaning her grocery money when unexpected expenses ate into her emergency fund to fixing her car for free. No matter how betrayed she felt, she couldn't do nothing and just let him be murdered. Even the idea of him being hurt squeezed her heart. She'd begun to fall for him, and it was going to be frustratingly hard undoing that mistake. Meanwhile, she had to help him, if she could just figure out how.

She watched the van make a right turn out of the parking lot as she grabbed the car key from her jeans pocket. *Hurry, hurry, hurry.*

She shoved the key in the door lock.

The van stopped at the light three blocks down.

A hand clamped down on her shoulder. She whirled, fist drawn back, ready to let it fly.

The man swore and grabbed both her arms before she could throw the punch. "Why are you trying to run me over, shoot me or hit me every time I see you?"

She blinked and looked up into the face of one of Ian's brothers. Adam, the one from the truck stop. Cop. He was a cop. She started to shake. *Ian, what about Ian?*

She looked over her shoulder. The white van was gone. Where was it? She scanned the road.

"It's Shannon Murphy, right? I'll let you go if you promise not to try to coldcock me again."

There. The van turned right at the next light. She jerked back toward Ian's brother. "Adam, right? You're the ranger, with the National Park Service?"

He frowned and let her go. "That's right." He glanced at the car, then at the key in her hand. "Can we talk? About my brother? I have a few questions, and when I saw you, I thought you might—"

"Not now. I'm in a hurry." She flung the door open.

He grabbed her arm again. "Listen, lady. I can arrest you right now for assault and half a dozen other charges for pulling a gun on me twice today. I just want to ask you a few questions."

She jerked back toward the road. The van was gone. They were getting away. And she didn't know where it was going. She had to do something. Fast. But this man was a cop, or a ranger, whatever. Could she trust him?

"Shannon?"

He was Ian's brother, and his life was on the line right now. She'd just have to hope that mattered to him. "The guys from the truck stop, they were here, just now."

His eyes widened. His left hand went to his hip like a reflex even though the gun she knew he had was covered by his suit jacket. He was left-handed, like Ian. The thought made her heart squeeze again.

"Did they hurt you? Are you okay?"

She blinked, surprised that he'd bother to ask. "I'm fine. But Ian isn't."

His gaze whipped back to hers. "What do you mean?"

"I saw him, inside the van. One of Butch's men was

pointing a shotgun at him as the door slid shut." She pointed down the street. "They turned right at the light. I don't know where they're taking him but—"

"Give me the key. I'll try to catch up to him. You can wait here and—"

She tossed him the key and then dove inside, rolling over the center console into the passenger seat.

He jumped into the driver's seat, glaring at her. But he didn't waste time arguing. His jaw was set in a grim line as he drove out of the parking lot, dodging other cars that honked their horns at them.

He raced down the street, skidding through an intersection against the light, barely squeaking past an oncoming car without getting hit. They were on a main road through town, but there was no sign of a white van.

"Look right. I'll look left," he said.

She craned her neck, searching every street they passed. Brake lights caught her eye on a side street. "There, there! They just turned left."

"Hold on."

She braced her arms against the dash as he did a one-eighty in the middle of the road. Other drivers squealed their brakes and honked again. He ignored them, slamming the accelerator, bumping over a curb before heading down the road she'd indicated.

Shannon swallowed hard and clicked the seat belt into place.

"Where did they turn? Where?" Adam demanded.

"Just up ahead, past that white house. There!"

He careened around the corner without even slowing down.

The white van was in front of them now, a good sixty or so yards ahead. But it was a narrow residential street with lots of parked cars. Adam couldn't let the Charger go full speed without risking hitting a car or running someone down if they happened to step into the road.

He tossed his phone in the console and told Shannon his passcode. "Hit the favorites button. My boss is the first number, Yeong Lee. Tell him I need backup, to get Gatlinburg PD to try to cut the van off ahead of us."

She grabbed the phone. The van turned again. "It just turned—"

"Right. Got it. Make the call."

Her skin itched and her fingers shook as she did as Adam had directed. Calling the police for help went against everything in her experience. She'd called them for help when she was much younger. Instead of believing her, instead of helping her, they'd slapped her in handcuffs and put her in jail. But she knew she was no match for the men in that van. Ian needed help, real help, not her.

She pitched the phone into the console. "He said he'd direct Gatlinburg PD to this area, and to call him back as soon as we have a location."

Several hair-raising turns later she straightened in her seat. The van made another right turn, so far ahead of them they could barely see it.

"We're losing them," Adam snarled. "These dang streets. Why do people park all over the road?" He dodged several cars, sped ahead, then had to bump up into a front yard to avoid an oncoming car. With so many parked cars it was like going down a one-way road, the wrong way.

They rounded a corner. There was no sign of the van. Adam cursed and slowed, looking down each side street. Shannon thought about the various turns the van had made. "Adam, speed up. Head to the third street on the right."

"You saw them?" He floored the gas and a few seconds later they raced around the corner onto the next street. "I don't see the van. You sure you saw them?"

She shook her head. "No. I didn't see them. But I know where they're going."

Chapter Eight

When the van finally pulled to a stop and the door slid open, Ian breathed a sigh of relief that he was still alive. That relief disappeared when he looked around and realized they were in his garage. That must have been why Jack insisted on taking his car keys at the hospital. He must have retrieved the garage remote control, planning to come here since Wolverine knew this was where mechanic Ian Savage lived. If Shannon was in her side of the duplex right now, then she was in a world of danger. If she came over, Butch's henchmen would eliminate her as a potential witness to whatever they had planned for Ian.

Please don't be home, Shannon. Please be safe somewhere else.

Butch appeared in front of the van's open sliding door, tossed the garage door opener and car key to the concrete floor and grinned. "Home sweet home, eh, *cop*?"

A spark of alarm shot through him, but he rolled his eyes. "I'm the furthest thing from a cop you can get. Are you thinking that Gatlinburg PD saw my black-and-blond hair and my tattoos and thought I'd fit right in?" He snorted. "Yep, that's it. They rushed right over to sign me up. Get real, man. What is this? A shakedown to see whether I'm legit?" He gave Jagger and Axel disgusted looks, trying not to sweat over them both aiming long guns at him from opposite sides of the van's interior. "My buyers aren't going to be happy with the delay because of your grandstanding."

Butch braced both hands on the open doorway. "I recognized that guy from the truck stop. He's a cop from Memphis. And you know what? You sure do look an awful lot like him."

"Really? That's why you're accusing me of being a pig? Because I look like another one? That's just messed up." He motioned toward the thug he'd likened to Captain Jack Sparrow. "This guy could be a stunt double for Johnny Depp. Why's he here with you instead of soaking in a pool in Hollywood with his brother Johnny?"

Butch frowned. "You said that cop slept with your girlfriend. You may not like each other, but he called you by name. And I happen to know he's one of them McKenzies, that family of law enforcement brothers. What's their dad's name? The Mighty McKenzie or something like that? He used to run this town, and his sons are all in law enforcement. Coincidentally, I heard one of them is named Ian. I figure you're either a cop or a special agent of some kind, *McKenzie*."

Ian bluffed like he'd never bluffed before, like his life depended on it—which it did.

"McKenzie?" He rolled his eyes again. "Dude, those guys are rich. Some wealthy grandpappy passed down a dozen companies to those spoiled jerks." He motioned to the garage. "You think even if I wanted to be a cop like those guys that I'd be living in this dump if I had millions in the bank? You've lost your ever-lovin' mind."

Butch narrowed his eyes suspiciously, but he looked

less certain than before. "If you ain't one of 'em, how do you know that Adam guy?"

Ian snorted. "He was at a party along with me and dozens of other people last summer. Other than being introduced when I came in, that was it. Except for the fact that I saw him making out with my girl in the kitchen. I was too ticked off to do anything that night. I left the party, and my girl. Next time I saw him was at the truck stop. Heck, you know more about him than I do. I didn't even remember his name. Probably the only reason he remembers mine is because my ex-girlfriend cries out my name every time he screws her."

Blade surprised him by laughing. He sobered when Butch shot him an aggravated look.

Butch gestured toward Ian. "That's why he knew your name? A party?"

"A party with dozens of other people. Hell, man. We were all there for the same reason—good food, free booze and hot chicks. You tellin' me you know everyone who shows up at parties? Get real."

Continuing his bluff, he shoved Butch out of his way and hopped down from the van. The garage walls seemed to bow in and out, making him dizzy. He covered it by leaning down and scooping up the garage door opener and car key. He immediately regretted the movement when his ribs sent a slice of burning pain lancing through him. He took shallow breaths and shoved the opener into his pocket, all the while trying not to wince or reveal how dizzy he was. Showing weakness around these types of men could be fatal. He casually leaned against the side of the van as if he had no worries in the world while he waited for the garage to stop spinning around him.

"You about done with the twenty questions?" he demanded. "Or are we done here?"

Butch exchanged a long look with his men, but didn't say anything.

Hoping he'd be able to walk without falling, Ian pushed away from the van. "Thanks for the ride home, boys. But unless you want to pick up where we left off and let me place an order, I'd just as soon you get your butts out of my garage. Heck, even if you do want to take an order, forget it. I'm too disgusted to even want to do business with you. I'll find a shipment somewhere else." He took a step toward the door to the house.

"Hold it. Let's not be too hasty here. Maybe I jumped to some conclusions and shouldn't have."

"You think?" Ian stalked to the door that led into the duplex, mainly because he desperately needed to hold on to the railing to keep from falling down.

"Ian, wait."

He let out an exaggerated sigh and turned, still clutching the railing. "Unless you're giving me back my .357 that your guys stole from me in the van, we've got nothing left to discuss."

"It's a nice gun. I'll have to think about that."

Ian turned around.

"Hold up."

He slowly faced Butch again, forced to let go of the railing. Thankfully, the dizziness was fading now. "What?"

Butch motioned to his men, and they drew their guns back inside the van. Ian was careful not to let his relief show on his face.

Butch stopped in front of him and held up the stack of pictures he'd had earlier. But before Ian could reach for them, Butch shoved them back into his jacket pocket. "I'm not saying I'm willing to trust you just yet. But I'm on the fence enough not to blow your head off."

"Is there a point to this?"

"The point is that I'm going to give it a few days, think on this. And if I decide you truly aren't messing with me, I'll be in touch."

Ian shook his head. "You want to deal with me, a few days won't cut it. My guy wants a shipment to take with him out of the country in the next twenty-four hours. I don't have two days. I'll have to get my girls somewhere else." He motioned toward the street out front. "Go on. Get out of my garage."

The two of them stood toe to toe, each one trying to read the other. Ian hoped he wasn't overplaying his hand. Reading people was his thing, and he sensed that Butch wanted to make a deal. Maybe he was having trouble moving inventory and didn't have enough buyers at the ready. Ian was walking a fine line so he wouldn't seem overeager. And yet he needed to keep this creep interested, or the poor women and girls he had would end up being sold to someone else, someone who wasn't interested in helping them, or saving them.

"Tell you what, Savage." He threw out a price. "You pay that, and I'll give you every girl I got. This town's getting way too hot, and I'm ready to move on. What do you say?"

Ian sighed as if bored, and took a chance, knowing it might be his last. "What about the two Latinas you mentioned at the truck stop? I've gone to way too much trouble not to get something for myself out of all this. That is, if they're as sexy as you claim."

"All my girls are top choice," Butch snarled as if insulted. "But these Spanish chicks are older, like I told you. That a problem?"

"Depends. You got pictures?"

Butch pulled out his cell phone. "Not printed up. They pretty much cater to me and the boys. I hadn't planned on letting them go. But a change might not be bad, something fresh." He grinned.

Ian kept his expression carefully blank as he fantasized about wrapping his fingers around Butch's throat and squeezing.

Butch turned the phone around. "What do you think? Pretty enough for you?"

Ian's breath caught. Finally, after all this time. There she was: Maria. Had to be. The lighting in the picture was terrible. All he could see of their features were dark eyes and dark hair. But there was no mistaking the pink butterfly tattoo on the right side of one of the women's necks, just as Shannon had described.

Ian shrugged, acting as nonchalant as he could manage. "They'll do. And the price is good. You've got a deal. I'll need some time to get the money from my buyer and arrange a truck for transport." *And get both Homeland Security agents and local law enforcement in place for a takedown.* "We can meet back at the truck stop at one in the morning. That work for you?"

Butch shook his head. "Too much heat there right now. Wolverine will be in touch with the details. Tomorrow."

That was cutting far too close to the forty-eight-hour window his boss, Nash, had given him before pulling the plug on the investigation. "I told you my buyer's in a hurry."

"Tomorrow or no deal. I'm not a hundred percent believing everything you've told me. I need to make sure you're on the up-and-up. Wolverine will contact you at your shop, like always. That's the deal."

Ian didn't have to fake his frown. He wasn't happy with the delay, especially with Butch wanting to check his cover. It was solid, had stood up under heavy scrutiny so far. But no one had ever made the connection between Ian Savage and Ian McKenzie before either. Had he changed his appearance enough to fool anyone who might remember him from his high school days? He'd kept his visits to Gatlinburg centered around his family's cabin, never venturing into town as Ian McKenzie. Had he made a mistake somewhere? Was there anyone who knew his real identity aside from his family and Shannon?

He shrugged nonchalantly. "Just keep in mind that my buyer is a powerful, unforgiving man. If he expects a delivery, and you don't show, I wouldn't want to be in your shoes."

Butch narrowed his eyes. "And if you're actually Ian McKenzie, I wouldn't want to be in your shoes either." He clicked his thumb and forefinger at Ian as if he was pulling a trigger. Then he laughed and headed for the van.

Ian shot him the bird and then unlocked the door to the house. He went inside, slamming it behind him. Resisting the urge to flip the dead bolt, which the others would hear and assume he was worried about them, he left the door unlocked. He reached above one of the kitchen cabinets and took down the loaded shotgun he kept concealed there. Then he stood off to the side, aiming it at the door.

Seconds ticked by. A full minute. The van's engine

started. A few seconds later, tires squealed as the van raced down the driveway. He yanked open the door, aiming his shotgun into the garage. Empty. No one was lying in wait. Butch and his thugs were gone.

He let out a deep breath before pressing the panel on the wall to close the garage door. This time, when he went inside the house, he flipped the dead bolt. He was reaching up to stow the shotgun when a shadow moved off to his right. He spun around.

"Whoa, whoa, it's me, Adam." A hand shoved his gun up toward the ceiling.

The lights flipped on. His brother stood a few feet away. Behind him, off to the side with her hand on the light switch, was Shannon.

Ian tucked the gun back above the cabinet. "What the hell, Adam? I could have killed you. And what are you doing here, Shannon?"

She stiffened. "We were saving you. Adam saw me in the parking lot at the hospital right after those guys abducted you. He drove me here so we could keep you from getting killed."

He speared his brother with a look of disgust. "You drove her here, knowing those guys were with me? You put her smack in the middle of danger."

"Kind of like you did at the truck stop?"

Ian took a menacing step toward his brother.

Adam raised his hands in surrender. "She was coming after you with or without me. I came along to keep her safe and help you. Instead of yelling at us, you should thank us. No telling what would have happened if she hadn't jumped in your car to rescue you. We scared those guys off."

Ian's eyes widened. "What do you mean you scared

them off?" He looked toward the front windows. Red and blue lights flashed against the blinds. "You called the cops?"

Adam put his hands on his hips. "Well, of course I called the police. I figure those thugs saw the lights coming up the street and that's why they left. If I hadn't called the cops, those jerks would have stormed your house and filled you with bullet holes by now. What's your problem? Do you have to turn everything into a fight?"

"I'm trying to maintain my cover, no thanks to you. I had those guys ninety-nine percent convinced there's no connection between you and me, even though they recognized you as a cop. If they saw you come inside—"

"They didn't. We parked on a side street and came in through Shannon's half of the duplex, the door in the hall closet you two use for going back and forth."

The door Ian had put in when they'd begun their odd working relationship. A door they'd used more and more often, far too regularly to justify it as just because of their mutual desire to find Maria. The look on Adam's face said he suspected as much.

Ian didn't care what he thought. What he cared about was that Shannon had been placed in danger, and whether his whole case was now ruined. He'd been so close. Would this destroy the deal he'd just made? He would have said as much, but the disappointment on Shannon's face had him biting back his harsh words.

"Look, I appreciate that you were trying to help. Both of you. I honestly do. But I was negotiating with Butch, setting up a—"

A loud knock sounded on the front door. "Gatlinburg Police."

"Great." Ian shook his head. "The only way I'm getting out of this with my cover intact is if they arrest me. For something." He gave his brother a baleful look. "I don't suppose you'd mind if I punch you when they bust down the door?"

Adam narrowed his eyes in warning.

"Yeah. Didn't think so."

"Police! Open up!" Loud knocks sounded on the door.

"Go on." Ian motioned toward the hall. "You two get back to the other side of the duplex. I'll think of something. And, Adam, don't go to the jail to bail me out. That would ruin everything. Can you just let my boss know what's going on? Please? He'll get me out without blowing my cover."

Adam gave him a curt nod, then urged Shannon to the hallway. They disappeared into the closet.

The police were kicking the front door now. It was a cheap door. No need for a battering ram. It wouldn't hold much longer. Ian turned, desperately looking for something that would get him locked up, hopefully without getting shot. Then he remembered the weed he'd taken from some punks a few days ago to keep them from selling it to neighborhood kids. He'd come into the garage and tossed it in a kitchen drawer, intending to get rid of it later and never had.

He yanked open a kitchen drawer, grabbed the baggie and tossed it onto the countertop in front of him just as the door crashed open and slammed against the wall.

"Freeze!" Two cops pointed their pistols at him.

He slowly raised his hands.

Chapter Nine

Shannon snapped the lid closed on her tattered suitcase. But instead of picking it up, she plopped down onto the bed beside it. The eggs and toast she'd eaten for breakfast sat like lead in her stomach. Worry and anger and despair were tearing her apart, physically and emotionally. Should she stay or should she go? The answer seemed to be eluding her.

She glanced around the room she'd slept in for the past six months. It wasn't much to look at, just big enough for the full-size bed. Her clothes were normally folded in cardboard boxes inside the closet. The rest of the rental was pretty much the same—a three-piece bathroom, galley-style kitchen with laminate counters, and a living room barely big enough for the worn love seat and a folding chair. The peeling fake-brass fixtures in the kitchen and the stained brown carpet had gone out of style decades ago. But the place still had more pluses than minuses.

Like the single-car garage with an automatic door opener that kept her from getting soaked in the rain or snow when she brought groceries home.

A charming foyer that boasted a surprisingly large coat closet.

A deep front porch with gleaming white railings and a swing. She sat out there most evenings, watching the neighborhood children play, wistfully wondering what it would have felt like to be so carefree when she was a little girl—instead of looking over her shoulder all the time, trying to stay out of the clutches of her mother's constant stream of "boyfriends."

In a word, the duplex was *home*. The first place that had ever felt that way. She'd started a life here, a real life, with a real job as a restaurant hostess at one of the resort hotels overlooking town. She'd even managed to tuck a little bit into savings. At twenty-one, she was finally her own person, making her own decisions, and looking forward to the future. Leaving this place would feel like she was going backward, starting over. Worst of all, it would mean not seeing Ian every day, maybe never seeing him again.

She dropped her head in her hands. It had taken months for him to work past her defenses. Months of gentle smiles, front porch hellos, the half-dozen times he'd insisted on fixing her pathetic car then refused to let her pay him. He'd earned her trust and had begun to wiggle his way into her heart.

After a few too many glasses of wine one evening, she'd confessed all the dirty secrets about her past. Instead of being disgusted, he'd been furious on her behalf. He held her through her tears, vowed to keep her safe and demanded nothing in return. *She* was the one who'd pushed for more, breaking down *his* defenses over time. Eventually, he too had confessed about the turmoil with his father, before his parents had been killed and he'd been put in foster care. It was his deepest secret.

Or so she'd thought.

It turned out he hadn't told her the most important secret of all—that he was a cop, and that his interest in helping her find her friend Maria was all about his job, not that he cared about Shannon and wanted to help her. Was anything they'd shared real?

Was what he'd told her about his father true or had he made that up too? If he'd grown up in foster care, how could his three brothers have been at the hospital today? None of it made sense. She didn't know what to believe. Or what to do. Because in spite of everything, she still cared about him.

"What's with the suitcase?"

She jerked her head up. Over six feet of mouthwatering male lounged in her doorway, looking so handsome it nearly shredded her heart. The cuts and bruises only made him look tougher, cooler. She hated the relief that flooded through her, the yearning that had her curling her fingers against the mattress to keep from jumping up and throwing herself into his arms. Ever since the police had hauled him away, she'd been terrified that she'd never see him again.

And equally terrified that she might.

"How did you get out of jail so fast?" Score one point for her. She'd managed to speak without bursting into tears.

His mouth curled in one of those sexy half smiles of his. "The old-fashioned way. I made bail."

She glanced at the clock on the wall. "A judge set bail at eight o'clock in the morning?"

"I might have had my boss pull a few strings behind the scenes." His smile faded. "You okay? My brother didn't harass you, did he?"

She shook her head. "No. He was…nice. For a cop."

She waved toward the sling on his left arm. "And for a guy who beat the crap out of his own brother."

He straightened and took two steps forward, which placed him squarely at the foot of her bed, forcing her to look up to meet his blue-eyed gaze. She used to think no one could possibly have eyes that particular gorgeous shade of blue, like a mountain lake after a summer shower. Until she'd met his brothers. She clutched the bedspread harder, this time to keep from slugging him for all the lies he'd told her.

"All my brothers and I have beaten the crap out of each other over the years. It's pretty normal, or so I hear. Too much testosterone, I guess. There's a lot more fighting than hugging in my family. But we don't mean anything by it. Usually."

She shook her head. "You have three brothers. And every one of them is a cop. What are the odds of that?"

"It's a family tradition. My dad's a retired federal judge. And very much alive, in spite of what I told you."

She stared at him in shock, more freaked out over his father's occupation than to learn that he wasn't really dead. "He's alive? And he was a federal judge?"

"He is. He was." He drew a deep breath, let it out. "My father was a force to be reckoned with, back in the day, for more reasons than you and I ever spoke about. Everyone looked up to him, happy to do his bidding. He had tentacles in every alphabet agency and attorney's office this side of the Mississippi. Governors, state legislators, attorneys on both sides of the aisle came to him for advice. They probably still do. They don't call him Mighty McKenzie for nothing."

She blinked. "Mighty McKenzie? Good grief. What did your mom think of all of that? Oh, wait. She's probably still alive too, right? The orphan, Ian Savage, seems to be overflowing in the family department these days."

He gave her a solemn look. "I thank God that, yes, my mom is still alive and doing well. I visit her once or twice a year. It's all I can stomach because it means seeing my dad too, and sometimes my brothers. She's a retired prosecutor."

"Well, of course she is." She rolled her eyes. "Is the family dog a K9 police officer too?"

He crouched in front of her, close, but not touching. The look of yearning and regret in his eyes nearly stole her breath. "I'm so sorry, Shannon. I never meant to hurt you."

She swallowed against the tightness in her throat. "But you did. Hurt me."

"I know."

"You lied to me. Not little lies either. Doozies."

His mouth quirked. "Doozies?"

"Don't make fun of me. I'm not in the mood."

He sobered. "Sorry. Again. Yes, I lied. Great big lies. Doozies."

He reached out as if to brush aside her bangs, but she jerked back before he could touch her. He sighed and dropped his hand.

"I never told you that I was with Homeland Security, that I was working undercover. I fed you the same backstory I'd told others, so I could maintain my cover. But everything else, what really matters, was true." His gaze searched hers. *"Everything."*

The kissing, the make-out sessions on her couch.

"What you told me about your father, about Willow, was that a lie too?"

He winced. "No. That was true, every word. I've

never talked to anyone about that time in my life. Except you."

He was being charming, and sweet, and making her want to believe him so badly that she ached. *Don't be a fool.* She couldn't allow herself to fall for his lies, not again.

"You said your father died. That you never knew your mother, that you were an only child."

"I did. That was part of my—"

"Cover. So that you could catch the bad guys."

He nodded, his still-sad eyes watching her intently. Did he think she could just work this out of her system? That he'd answer a few questions and they could go back to being...whatever they were?

"There's something that has me stumped," she said. "I can't figure out what you got out of pretending to be my friend, pretending to care."

He blew out a deep breath before straightening. He leaned back against the wall, his gaze never leaving hers. "I wasn't pretending. I am your friend. I do care."

She shook her head. "No. You aren't. You don't. I told you about my past, and you pretended that it mattered to you. You said you wanted to go after those traffickers, at the truck stop, so you could keep other girls from suffering what I went through. That was cruel, Ian. How could you use my pain like that? You had to be laughing inside the whole time at how gullible I was."

He was shaking his head before she finished. "I've *never* laughed at you, Shannon. You're a strong, independent woman. Most of all, you're a survivor. I admire you."

She stiffened. "Don't. Don't stand there trying to charm me and tell more lies—"

"No lies. No hidden agendas. Ask me anything. I promise you I'll tell the truth."

She blinked. "Anything? You'll answer any question?"

He nodded. "I owe you that."

She thought a moment, then asked, "Why did you befriend me?"

His eyes widened with surprise. "Have you looked in the mirror lately?"

She glanced at the cracked oval mirror hanging on the wall beside the door, thinking about what she saw every time she looked at her reflection. "I see an average-looking woman with hair that refuses to lie the way I want it to. I'm short, too skinny, flat-chested with almost no butt. I'm the exact opposite of what guys like you look for in a woman."

His dark brows arched. "Guys like me?"

She refused to flatter his ego by stating the obvious—that he was the definition of gorgeous. Tall, buff, with a smile that could melt butter. It had definitely melted her on more than one occasion. She crossed her arms and waited.

"Okay, truth. You're the perfect height for me to tuck you against my side. You're slim, not skinny. Most girls would kill for your flat tummy and those curvy hips. Your…ah, chest is perfectly proportioned for your frame. And the rest of you, well, in case you haven't noticed, you've revved my engine plenty of times. There's absolutely nothing lacking about you in the looks department. Guys like me—whatever that means—would line up just to get a woman like you to smile at them. Top that off with your brains and a great sense of humor, and you're basically irresistible."

All the warm squishy feelings flooding through her at his words died a quick death with his last statement. She crossed her arms. "Irresistible? Right. That's why you always came up with an excuse whenever we got hot and heavy. Instead of taking things to the logical next level—" she motioned toward the bed "—you always came up with a reason to leave. That's not what I'd call irresistible."

He pushed away from the wall and knelt in front of her again. Before she realized what he was going to do, he'd taken her hand in his. With his intent gaze locked on hers, he slowly drew her hand to his chest, then slid it down, down, down. She sucked in a breath when it dawned on her what he was doing, and that he was giving her the opportunity to stop him if she wanted to.

She couldn't have stopped him any more than she could have given up air.

With his hand on hers, he cupped himself through his jeans. The hard length of him warmed her fingers. She let out a shuddering breath.

"That's what you do to me, Shannon. Just thinking about touching you, kissing you, loving you, I get a hard-on. That's not something I can fake or lie about."

Her pulse was rushing in her ears. All this time, she'd craved touching him this way. But it wasn't right; nothing was right anymore. She drew a ragged breath and forced herself to tug her hand away.

He dropped his hand to his side. "It would have been wrong to make love to you while my fake identity stood between us. It was torture keeping my hands off you." He searched her gaze, then let out a deep sigh and stood again. "You can't forgive me, can you?"

"You never asked."

He hesitated, studying her. "Will you forgive me?"

Yes. No. She wanted to, so badly. But would she be letting him back in her heart to hurt her yet again? She drew another ragged breath, then shook her head. "I can't. Not yet."

"Not ever?"

"Maybe. I honestly don't know."

His jaw tightened. "I understand. It's probably for the best, anyway. Once this case is over, I'll go on to another one, in another town, maybe another state." He shrugged. "You've made a good life here. And one day you'll meet the perfect guy for you, one who's willing to give up his career and settle down. You deserve that. You deserve to be treated like a queen. You deserve to be happy." He stepped forward and pressed a kiss against her forehead, then moved to the doorway.

His words were still tightening like a band around her chest when he looked back. "I never got a chance to tell you last night. But Butch showed me more pictures in the garage. One of them was Maria."

She pressed a hand to her throat. "Are you sure?"

"As sure as I can be. Same build and general features you described. And a pink butterfly on the right side of her neck. Wolverine's supposed to contact me at the shop sometime today to agree on where to make the exchange. If everything goes as planned, your friend will be freed by this evening."

He started to leave, but she jumped up and grabbed his good arm, stopping him. "Wait. Your arm was nearly broken, your *gun* arm. And you've got a concussion. Doesn't Homeland Security have someone else who can take care of this?"

He shook his head. "It took me months to gain Wolverine's and Butch's trust. That trust is hanging by a thread. If I leave and someone new tries to get in on the action, that thread will snap. Butch and his guys will take their victims somewhere else, and I'll lose my chance to help those girls. Your friend Maria will disappear again. No telling how long it would take to find her, or if she'll even still be alive the next time we get a lead on her whereabouts. You know how violent and unpredictable the sex trade can be. I have to do this, try to rescue all of them, including Maria."

"No."

He frowned. "No? You don't want me to rescue your friend?"

"Of course I do. But it's too dangerous for you to do it alone. If Homeland Security won't help you, then I will." She held up her hands. "I still have the use of both my arms. And I didn't escape the sex trade through brains and tenacity alone. I can fire a gun as well as or better than you."

His eyes narrowed. "You've never mentioned that before."

She lifted her chin. "It didn't seem relevant."

He rubbed his hand on the back of his neck. "I wish we had more time to discuss this. But I have to get going or risk missing Wolverine's call at the shop. Don't worry about me, Shannon. I may be the only agent in plain sight, but I've got backup ready to go the moment I need them. I'm not in this alone. I'll be okay. And there's no way that I'm going to take you with me into danger again. Yesterday could have ended in disaster for you. I don't need, or want, your help." He left her sputtering as he disappeared down the hallway.

She ran after him. "Ian."

He ignored her as he opened the hall closet door where the panel between the two sides of the duplex was hidden. He slid it open and she grabbed his arm.

"Ian, wait."

He looked back at her, his expression hard. "You could have been killed yesterday, Shannon. Butch and his men know where I live. They could be watching this place even now. You should lie low. Stay inside. Don't go out on the porch. Keep the shades drawn. Until this is over, you stay on your side and I'll stay on mine. I don't want to see you anywhere near the shop. No arguments."

He stepped through the panel and slid it shut.

She stood there fuming for several moments. Then she shoved the panel, determined to finish their discussion. The panel didn't budge. She frowned and pressed it again. Then she remembered the locking mechanisms on both sides. Neither of them had ever locked each other out. Until now.

Chapter Ten

Chapter Ten

Ian slid his ID badge through the card reader hanging on the shop's wall to clock in.

"Seven o'clock was two hours ago, Savage."

He turned around to see Ralph Sanders, owner of Sanders Auto Repair, standing beside the 1969 red Mustang whose carburetor Ian was supposed to rebuild this morning.

"Sorry, boss. Had a little trouble last night."

His boss motioned toward Ian's face. "What's the other guy look like?"

"Unfortunately, a lot better than me." He'd left his sling in his Charger and downed several pain pills, determined to force his way through the pain since he'd need both hands to work on cars today. But there was nothing he could do to hide the cuts and bruises on his face. He nodded toward the Mustang. "I'll get right on that. Shouldn't take long to get it running like new."

"The owner's leaving town this morning. I didn't know if you'd show up or not, so I had Andy work on it."

Ian groaned. "You didn't."

"There wasn't anyone else available. I didn't have a choice." He checked the old-fashioned gold-toned watch on his wrist. "You've got forty-three minutes to figure out what our beginner mechanic screwed up and get that car purring like a kitten."

"Where's the kid now?"

"After he put the fire out, I assigned him to delivery duty for the day. He's on his way to pick up a set of tires for a customer."

"Fire?" Dread shot through him as he glanced at the classic sports car that would have been the envy of every boy with a pulse back in high school. Its current owner kept it in pristine condition, coddling it like a baby. "I don't see any burn marks. What's the damage?"

"Pop the hood. You'll see." He checked his watch. "Forty-two minutes and counting. Don't let me down, Savage. The owner's fanaticism about bringing that car in for the slightest little hiccup pays my light bill every month. I can't afford to lose his business." He strode toward the other side of the garage where another mechanic was replacing brake pads beneath a truck on a hydraulic lift.

When Ian raised the Mustang's hood, he immediately knew why his boss had sent his novice apprentice out on deliveries. If the kid had been standing here right now, Ian would have blistered his pride with a lecture that would have had his ears ringing the rest of the day. Not because of the damage to the car—a melted distributor cap and wires. Those were easily fixed. Ian wasn't even angry that the kid had installed the carburetor float upside down, which must have been what had caused gas to shoot up and coat the distributor cap. What had him fuming was the source of the spark that had started the fire—a charred half-smoked cigarette butt lying on top of the battery. The foolish kid was lucky he hadn't killed himself, or at the least ended up with debilitating burns. Ian's brother Colin had spent months in a burn center after saving some people from a burning building and was left with deep scars on his arms and chest. Ian wouldn't want anyone to suffer the way his brother had. He shook his head in disgust and got to work.

By the time the Mustang's owner arrived, the engine was purring like a kitten and all evidence of the fire had been removed. Sanders nodded his approval from across the bay. But it was clear as the day wore on that Ian still wasn't forgiven for being late and, in Sanders's mind, almost losing him a treasured repeat client. Every mind-numbingly dull and dirty job that came in was routed to Ian. He was so busy he could barely catch his breath, although he did stop several times to take more pain pills. It was that or admit defeat.

His left arm was throbbing when he noticed the sun was sinking on the horizon outside the open bay doors. It was quitting time. But he still hadn't heard from Wolverine. After washing the grime off his hands and clocking out, he knew why. Wolverine didn't *need* to call in order to reach Ian. He was already here, lounging in his bright yellow VW across the street in Sanders's overflow gravel lot.

Fast-food bags tossed onto the ground outside the car told the story. He'd been performing surveillance on Ian all day, and Ian had been too consumed pushing through the pain of his wrenched arm to even realize it. Having Butch's thug spying on him wasn't half as alarming as the fact that he hadn't noticed. That kind of mistake could get him killed.

He nodded goodbye to some of the guys from the shop, promised his boss he'd call the next time he was running late, then headed across the street. He idled his

Charger beside the VW and rolled down his driver's-side window.

"What's with the cloak-and-dagger spy routine, Wolverine? If you wanted to talk to me, all you have to do is step into the shop."

Wolverine grinned. "Cloak-and-dagger. I like that."

Ian arched a brow, his patience nonexistent after the pain-filled, aggravating day he'd had. What a waste. He had precious little time remaining to bring this case to a close or all of his months of undercover would be for nothing. "I'm tired and hungry and have to give my buyer an update. Do we have a deal or not?"

"Whoa. Chill, bro." He cocked his head as if studying Ian. "You seem really stressed out, man. When's the last time you and that hot chick next door hooked up?"

Cold fear shot through Ian. Had Butch seen Shannon? Did he recognize her from the truck stop and think she was a threat, that maybe she knew too much? He kept his expression bland and rolled his eyes.

"If you're talking about my duplex neighbor, the answer is never. I'm not her type."

Wolverine's brows shot up. "A handsome dude like you? You expect me to believe that?"

Ian gave him a droll look. "I don't have the right kind of plumbing for her, if you get my meaning."

Wolverine grinned again. "She likes chicks, huh? Dang. That makes *me* hot."

"I have better things to do than discuss your fetishes. And I'm not wasting another minute on you or your boss. We're done here." He shifted into Drive.

"Hold it, hold it." He held his hands up in a placating gesture. "Man, you really are uptight tonight, aren't you?"

"Wolverine—"

"Okay. All right. Butch told me if no red flags were raised today, and he didn't call with anything from his side, that the deal is on. Eleven o'clock at a warehouse outside of town." He gave Ian the address. "Bring a truck and the money. You get there one minute late, no deal. There will be guns trained on you the moment you enter the parking lot. Bring someone with you, try anything at all, you're a dead man. Understood?"

Wolverine's transition from his usual jovial, silly personality to a threatening, deadly serious persona had the hairs rising on the back of Ian's neck, and alarm bells going off in his head.

Suddenly Wolverine grinned. "Did I do that good? Butch told me to try to keep it serious for once." He laughed and popped a french fry into his mouth, then grimaced and spit it out. "Old and cold. Well, what's it gonna be? Deal or no deal?"

"I'll be there."

"Cool, dude. You see? All those months ago, I told you I'd get you an in. I came through, didn't I?"

Ian smiled. "You sure did."

"And we'll make more deals with other buyers, right? That's what you said you wanted when we started, an *in* so we could both make some cash." He held out his hand and made the universal sign of money by rubbing his fingers together.

"No kickback until I have the girls."

Wolverine shrugged. "That's fine. But you better slip me my finder's fee without alerting Butch tonight. He realizes I'm getting money from both sides, I'm toast." He gave a dramatic shiver, then laughed and drove away.

Ian's smile faded as he watched the taillights of the

garish yellow car fade into the distance, then turn down a side street. Something was off about his neighborhood human trafficking connection. Did Wolverine know something about tonight that Ian didn't? Was it a setup or was Butch really going to go through with the buy? Either way, Ian needed to be prepared. That meant getting a truck and backup, and making sure his fellow agents knew about the conditions that Butch had dictated, and the accompanying threats. They'd have to be very careful and precise, or someone might get killed.

He grabbed a pen and paper from his console and scribbled down some notes while he made the call to set everything in motion. "Tony's Pizza? I'd like to order a large pizza for curbside pickup. It's not on the menu, but one of the take-out guys—Chris—knows about it. I've gotten it there before. It's called the Homeland Special."

A few minutes later, Ian pulled into one of the curbside pickup spots on the side of the familiar redbrick building that boasted a neon sign on the roof in the shape of a slice of pizza.

It didn't take long for the take-out door to open and a young man in black jeans and a red T-shirt with the restaurant's logo on the front to come bopping out with a pizza box in his hands.

Ian rolled down his window. "Hey, Chris. How's business tonight?"

The young man's gaze locked on Ian with a seriousness that contrasted sharply with the polite smile he flashed. To anyone else in the parking lot, or watching from inside, he was simply a pizza boy. But Ian knew better.

"Hopping like always, Mr. Savage. Typical Friday night, barely enough time to catch my breath." He held up the box in his hands. "One large Homeland Special to go. Pepperoni, bacon, extra cheese, extra sauce, New York–style crust, well-done. That'll be—" he tilted the box to read the bottom of the ticket taped to the lid "—twenty-two fifty-seven."

Ian set the box on the seat beside him, then pulled out his wallet. He concealed a folded piece of paper inside a wad of bills and handed it out the window. "Keep the change."

Chris grinned and shoved the money along with the piece of paper into his pocket. "Thanks, Mr. Savage. Always a pleasure. Enjoy." With that, he hurried back inside.

Ian pulled out of the parking lot and headed for the duplex.

Chapter Eleven

A thumping sound had Shannon looking up from the Lisa Gardner thriller she was reading. The noise sounded again, and she realized it was coming from the hall closet. Ian. In a fit of anger, she'd locked her side of the panel too. And now he wanted to come in.

Someone with far more poise than her, someone more sophisticated, would have ignored his knock. Or at least made him wait, maybe even grovel a little bit. But Shannon was too pathetically relieved that he wanted to see her again that she ran to the closet and unlocked her side.

He slid open the door and they stood in the semidarkness looking at each other, with only the lights from their respective living rooms shining inside.

"Hey," he breathed.

She smiled. "Hey yourself." She moved closer, then jumped back when she hit something sharp.

He grinned and held up a pizza box. "Sorry. I think you ran into the corner. You okay?"

She rubbed her chest. "Slain by cardboard. I think I'll live. Is that a peace offering?"

"Pepperoni, bacon, extra sauce, extra cheese."

"You're not playing fair. That's my favorite."

His grin widened. "I know." He held it toward her,

his smile fading. "I didn't exactly leave on the best of terms earlier. I was a jerk, and I'm sorry. You're welcome to take this and enjoy it by yourself. I wouldn't blame you if you do."

"I'm not that petty. There's enough to share. Come on."

He followed her inside as she took the box to the bar that separated the kitchen from the living room. She used to have only one bar stool. But after he'd moved in next door, she'd hoped the gorgeous man would come over sometime, so she'd gotten another one. It was one of the best buying decisions she'd ever made. They'd shared many a pizza on this bar top while sitting on these bar stools.

She tossed some paper plates and napkins beside the box. "I see you aren't wearing your sling. Your arm can't be all better this fast."

"I can't do my job with the sling on. I'm taking pain pills when I need to." When she started to protest, he interrupted her. "I'm okay, Shannon. Honestly. But thanks for the concern."

She sighed and opened the refrigerator. "Want a beer? Wine?"

He shook his head. "Water's fine."

She hesitated. While Ian was never a heavy drinker, he rarely said no to a beer to go with his pizza. "Something going on tonight?" She handed him a water bottle and took the stool beside him.

As he set a piece on her plate, he arched a brow in question. "What do you mean?"

"No alcohol. Are you...are you still on the clock? As

in doing special-agent kind of stuff?" Her eyes widened. "Is it Maria and the others? You finally made a deal?"

She waited impatiently for him to chew and swallow the bite of pizza he'd taken.

"A deal is in the works," he admitted, sounding reluctant. "But I'm not going to discuss it. You know far too much about me as it is. It's not safe for you to know more."

"I'm not trying to get in the way or put myself in danger. But if you're going to rescue Maria and the others soon, I'd like to be there, to help with their transition."

"There will be counselors for them as soon as we get them out of danger."

She shook her head. "Take it from someone who knows. It would take months, maybe longer, for someone coming out of that life to learn to trust someone enough to talk about it. In the meantime, they'll be scared, confused. Having someone who's been through what they've been through could really help. Use me. Seriously. I want to do this. Can't I wait somewhere close by? Then as soon as you have the bad guys in cuffs, let me come out? I haven't seen Maria in so long. I need to see her, talk to her, tell her—"

He stood and tossed his half-eaten piece onto his plate. "Coming over was a mistake. As soon as I have something concrete on your friend, I'll let you know."

Regret had her chasing after him and jumping in front of the closet door. "Ian. Wait. I'm sorry. I don't want to fight again."

He braced his good arm on the door frame. "I can't discuss the case or any plans I'm making."

"I know. I understand, really. I'm disappointed, but I

get it." She gave him a friendly tap on the chest. "Come on. I was so upset this morning I called out at work. This is basically the first day I've had off in two weeks. Let's not ruin it by being angry with each other." She held out her hand toward his. "Eat some more pizza with me. Maybe watch a movie on TV. We'll pretend we're two normal people without any baggage or secret-agent jobs between us and just enjoy each other. Okay?"

He smiled and then kissed her on the forehead before taking her hand. "All right. Dinner and a movie. No work talk."

They both stuck to their agreement, and before long they were laughing and talking and then tucked in close beside each other on the couch with a blanket over the both of them as they watched one of her favorite movies—*Sabrina*. It was the original, the black-and-white one with Audrey Hepburn. It never failed to make her cry, both sad tears and happy ones when the girl got her guy at the end.

With all those feelings swirling around inside, when she looked up at the gorgeous man smiling at her, she couldn't resist pulling him down for a kiss. He accommodated her nicely, his lips moving expertly over hers, quickening her pulse and making her jealous at the same time. How many women did a guy have to kiss in his life to get this good at it? She immediately wanted to rip out their hair and thank them at the same time.

He pulled back and framed her face in his hands. "You really are beautiful, Shannon Murphy."

Her body went all soft and warm at his words. "So are you, Ian Savage." She blinked, some of the delicious feelings fading beneath the onslaught of reality. "I mean McKenzie. Special Agent McKenzie." She pushed out of his arms, suddenly feeling awkward with the man who'd been her best friend until yesterday.

"Is that really such a bad thing?" His voice sounded sad.

She shrugged. "It's going to take some getting used to. I'm still processing the fact that I'm sleeping with the enemy." Her face heated. "So to speak. I mean, it's not like we've ever…you know." She frowned. "Why is that again?"

His brows drew down. "Imagine if we had, and then you found out who I really am. You would have felt—"

"Violated."

He winced, then nodded. "Is that how you feel now?"

She wrapped her arms around her middle, unable to meet his gaze. "Don't be silly. Of course not. You're not like the cops in my old life, the ones on the take, who traded sex with my mom and others in exchange for not arresting them." She shivered at the memories. "Or ignored a little girl asking for help, telling them her mom's boyfriends were hurting her."

He gently tilted her chin up. "I'm so sorry that happened to you. But being a cop is like any other profession. There are good people and bad people. Thankfully, the training and oversight weed out most of the bad. I'm far from perfect, but I like to think I'm one of the good ones."

She knew he was right, that he was one of the good ones, even if she didn't believe that the rest of them were more good than bad. But just the reminder about who he was and that he'd fooled her for so long had anger simmering inside her again. "Maybe you should head back home now. It's getting late."

He glanced at the sleek black watch on his right wrist,

an anachronism since most men as young as him didn't wear a watch. She'd always wondered at that before. Now she realized it was probably because of his job. No doubt he needed to be aware of the time at a moment's notice, quicker than it took to take out his phone and check it, so he could coordinate missions with his fellow agents.

"It's later than I realized." He stood. "Thanks for sharing dinner and a movie with me. We'll talk more tomorrow. Okay?"

She nodded, but she didn't get up when he headed down the hall to the pass-through. Instead, she sat there a long time thinking about what she knew and didn't know about Ian McKenzie. Actually, all she knew about him as *McKenzie* was that he worked for Homeland Security. And that he had a family—a mom, dad and three brothers. That was pretty much it. Everything she knew, or thought she knew, was about Ian *Savage*.

Did she really know Ian at all?

As she put her treasured DVD of *Sabrina* away and straightened up the kitchen, memories of times she'd spent with him flashed through her mind. He'd always been patient, kind, protective. He'd shared his smiles and always made a point of bringing her favorite pizza when he brought her dinner. She'd really been falling for *that* Ian. The problem was that she didn't know which Ian was the real one.

As always when she was upset or mulling over a problem, she started cleaning. But her house was fairly clean to begin with. It was so tiny she had to keep it picked up or she'd kill herself tripping over things. It didn't take long before it was sparkling. Of course, that meant she was back to thinking about Ian again. And Maria. And how long it would be before Maria was free. And on and on and on. She finally realized she'd never be able to relax or sleep tonight. Too much had happened in the past few days. She needed that promised talk with Ian right now, not later.

She went to the hall closet to check if he was still home and slid the panel open. She'd stepped into his side of the closet and was about to open the door when she heard a man's voice.

And it wasn't Ian's.

She pressed her ear to the cheap hollow door that did little to dampen sound, then breathed a sigh of relief when she heard Ian's deep voice in answer to whatever the man had asked. When Ian responded, he called the man Chris. She'd never heard him mention anyone named Chris before. That wasn't the name of one of the mechanics from the shop. In fact, this was the first time that she'd known him to have anyone else in the duplex, besides her. But their voices weren't raised in anger, so the man must be a friend—not one of Butch's thugs or even one of Ian's brothers.

She was about to return to her place when she heard Ian mention *her* name. Unabashedly curious as to why he'd talk about her with someone she'd never met, she pressed her ear to the door again.

"—Wolverine seemed way too interested in her when we spoke earlier today," Ian said. "That's why I came straight here after passing you that note at the pizza place. I needed to see for myself that Shannon was okay, that no one had bothered her."

Shannon's heart sank. Had he come by only to check on her well-being? He'd gone there because he felt obligated, because it was his job to make sure no one was hurt while he was trying to wheel and deal with the dregs of society.

"Does he think she knows something? Or that she and you are an item and he wants to use her as leverage?"

"I don't see how. We're casual friends because we rent two sides of the same house. That's it. I guarantee that even if Wolverine has been watching this place, the most he would have seen is us talking on occasion or me working on her car."

His casual-friends comment had her heart twisting in her chest.

"But you still want me to keep an eye on the place?" the other man asked.

"Just for tonight, until the deal is done. I can't risk any civilians getting hurt. Once Butch and the others are in custody and we've rescued the victims, any potential for danger will be over. Okay, Chris, now it's your turn. Tell me what Nash has planned. We have to make sure no one is seen anywhere near the warehouse. Wolverine said Butch's men would kill anyone out there, that I'm to go alone."

"Nash brought ADA Ellison up to speed, and he's going to provide logistical support and—"

She blinked in shock as Ian and Chris discussed the details of the transaction, planned for this very night in just a few hours, at a warehouse outside of town. She recognized the location. It had been a trail-horse stable at one time, but the recent wildfires in the area had destroyed all of the fencing and the house. While the horses had been spared, the owner didn't have insurance. He'd had to sell them and the land.

It had been sad seeing a row of warehouses go up where the stable had once been. Even more shocking was that the warehouses were being used by Butch and his men. Was that where Maria and the others were being housed in between being forced to turn tricks or perform in porn movies that would be distributed across the dark web?

Ian's deep voice broke into her thoughts. "I've shown you where everything is. Any other questions?"

"Just one. Where do you keep the beer?"

Ian laughed. "None of that, Chris. Sober is your middle name while you're on guard duty. But I do have a couple of steaks you can pop in the broiler if you get hungry."

The sound of their footsteps retreating across the room into the kitchen had her tripping over her own feet in a hurry to get back to her side of the duplex. She slid down onto the couch and dropped her face into her hands. How could Ian have kissed her so sweetly earlier, and several other times, and then act like they were barely even friends? His voice had been so matter-of-fact, so…businesslike when he'd talked about her. Was she really just that, a job, a civilian to protect while he was forced to live here for his undercover work? What would happen when the case was over and he moved on to the next case? Would he just disappear one day? Would he even bother to say goodbye?

Good grief, how had she fallen so hard and so fast for him? She was acting like some lovestruck teenager instead of a grown woman who'd survived some of the worst abuse imaginable. She'd survived, escaped and begun a new life. She was stronger than this. So why did it hurt so much?

She sat there a long time, furiously trying to get back her equilibrium and her confidence. The metallic screech of Ian's garage door opening had her lifting her head. A moment later the throaty roar of his Charger started up. It slowly faded into the distance. He was off to the warehouse, to finally get Maria and the others. He didn't want her help. He didn't even want her, period. But she wasn't going to sit here feeling sorry for herself any longer.

Maria was what mattered.

All those young women were what mattered. She'd been in their place before, sold into modern-day slavery by her very own mother. And it had taken years to find her way back to freedom. It had been Maria who'd covered for her so Shannon could finally escape. When the hunt had died down, and Shannon was able to sneak back to try to help Maria get out too—she was gone, sold to yet another buyer.

Now, with Maria found once again and about to be freed, Shannon wasn't about to miss that moment and not be there for her friend. No matter what Ian wanted. Shannon wouldn't interfere. But she was determined to be ready once it was over, and help the woman who'd once helped her.

Still, she knew all about the dangers of this kind of world, the kind where slavery still existed and destroyed lives. A world with large amounts of money at stake. The men and women who ran it were rabid about defending their livelihood. Shannon needed to be prepared in case things went horribly wrong.

She headed into her bedroom and went to the far back corner. After sliding the TV tray that she used as a nightstand out of the way, she pried up a scuffed piece of the wood flooring to reveal a dark hole. Reaching inside, she drew out her savings, a roll of bills held together by a ponytail holder. She peeled off two bills and dropped them back into the hole as her emergency fund. The rest she shoved into her jeans pocket. Finally she'd be able to pay Maria back for the money she'd given Shannon all those years ago. It was money Maria was supposed to give her "owner" later that night, the haul from that day's tricks. And she'd likely paid the balance in flesh when she'd had nothing to turn over at the end of the evening. Now it was Shannon's turn to pay her back as best she could.

But that wasn't all that she kept in her little cubby-hole. Money wasn't the only thing her friend had given her so very long ago.

She reached down again and pulled out a pistol.

Chapter Twelve

Ian itched to get out of the eighteen-foot rental truck and go into the warehouse. But his boss was adamant that he wait in the parking lot for Butch and the others to show. Because of Ian's history with Butch taking him at gunpoint, and Butch's earlier suspicion that Ian's cover might not be real, Nash wasn't taking any chances. Which had Ian frustrated as hell. He didn't join Homeland Security to sit in the cab of a truck waiting for the bad guy to show. And waiting was all he'd been doing for the past hour.

He checked his watch yet again. Almost midnight. He scanned the empty parking lot and surrounding tree line for the hundredth time. Nothing. Not even headlights flashing in the distance, indicating a vehicle was coming up the mountain. He'd followed Wolverine's instructions, had gotten here a few minutes before eleven, mindful of the warning that if he was late the deal was off. He hadn't been late. His knocks on the door of the warehouse had gone unanswered before he'd returned to the truck to wait. So why hadn't Butch and his men shown up?

The radio in the truck squawked. "Heard anything from them?" Nash asked.

Determined not to risk even moving his lips in case Butch was out there watching, he tapped twice on the transmitter, indicating no.

"Ellison is pushing us to raid the warehouse. He claims probable cause, wants to go in."

Ian tightened his grip on the steering wheel. If this was a test to find out if Ian was a cop, if Butch was watching to make sure that Ian was alone, then raiding the warehouse now would ruin everything. He tapped twice on the transmitter again, hard.

A sigh sounded from his boss. "I don't know that I can put him off much longer. He's insistent. And he's got plenty of officers with him. He doesn't have to wait for us. If those women are inside the warehouse, or if your contact got scared and took off, I want Homeland Security to be the first on scene to get the credit. I think we should move in soon. Something has either spooked your guy or—"

Ian shoved the door open and hopped out of the truck, ignoring his boss's alarmed calls through the radio. He slammed the door shut and stalked toward the warehouse. If his contacts were here, maybe going inside would be the push they needed. If it had been up to him, he'd have gone inside long ago. And if Gatlinburg PD and his fellow agents were about to pour down the mountainside into the parking lot, this was his last chance to get in ahead of them and hopefully salvage the deal.

He crossed his fingers that his gut was wrong, that he hadn't been sitting in that truck for over an hour for nothing. That all of his months of hard work hadn't been thrown away because one of his brothers happened by the same truck stop as him. If the warehouse was empty, then Butch had decided not to make the deal. Which meant something had spooked him and he was likely on his way out of town already with his haul.

And Ian wouldn't be able to save Maria or the others.

He reached the door to the warehouse and cautiously turned the handle. It wasn't locked, yet another bad sign. If there was something inside worth protecting, the door would have been padlocked from the outside, maybe even barred from within with a guard inside.

He yanked out his pistol, then pulled open the door and ran inside, sweeping his gun back and forth. The lights had turned on automatically. They must have been on a motion sensor. And what they revealed made him sick to his stomach. The warehouse was empty.

Ian prayed his boss kept everyone outside until he had a chance to find out what was going on. They'd all concealed their vehicles at the bottom of the mountain and had hiked through the woods, in the cold, to get here. They'd been hiding for hours, well before the planned meeting time to ensure that Butch didn't see them. Hopefully all of that work wouldn't be thrown away because of some impatient ADA pushing everyone to run into the warehouse before Ian had a chance to see if there was anything left to salvage.

Even though the place seemed empty, there were some doors on the back and sides, going into other rooms. He made a complete circuit of the interior, keeping his gun out as he checked every potential hiding place. But every door he opened revealed the same thing—nothing—until he reached the very last door. He yanked it open, sweeping his pistol back and forth. There was no one there, not even a piece of furniture, like the other rooms he'd tried. But there was something, a bright yellow index card dead center in the middle of the floor.

He rushed forward and crouched to read the card. He scanned it, then jerked his head up toward the ceiling. The sounds of shouting and doors being thrown open had him grabbing his pistol and aiming it at the door.

It burst open and his boss stood in the opening, flanked by half a dozen agents in full body armor, pistols drawn.

"Hold your fire! He's one of us," Nash yelled, as the agents swarmed in beside him.

Ian swore and shoved his gun into his holster. The other agents rushed back out of the room, presumably to search the rest of the warehouse.

Ian swore again, shaking his head. "You couldn't give me even five minutes in here before bringing in the damn cavalry?"

Nash frowned as he holstered his gun. "You were supposed to wait in the truck, and you went in without backup. What did you expect me to do?" He thumped Ian's chest. "And you were supposed to wear your vest, McKenzie."

Ian pointed up at the ceiling and repeated the words written on the index card. "Smile for the camera."

Nash looked up, his face going pale as he noticed the red blinking light. He looked at Ian. "What's going on?"

Ian motioned toward the index card. "Butch was testing me, to make sure I'd follow orders and wouldn't bring anyone from law enforcement. The card has instructions to meet Wolverine tomorrow in the parking lot across from the garage where I work. He'll give me the true meeting time and place, but only if I passed tonight's test. And then it said to look up and smile for the camera." Ian shook his head. "It was a freaking test. And we just failed the hell out of it. No way will Wolverine meet me tomorrow. Six months wasted. All those girls, those little girls—" He fisted his hands and stalked out of the room.

He left the collection of the index card to his boss. Not that it would matter. It wasn't like any fingerprints or trace evidence would have been left on it to help them find Butch and his victims. He was too smart for that.

Ian wove his way through the cops and agents milling around the parking lot and was halfway to the truck when he noticed familiar dark hair with blue tips as a woman was led toward him by a Gatlinburg police officer.

Shannon. Her hands were cuffed behind her.

By the time he'd reached her and the officer who'd detained her, Nash and Assistant District Attorney Ellison had caught up to him.

"Let her go," Ian snarled. "She's a civilian and not associated with the traffickers."

The officer shook his head. "I've placed her under arrest. She was hiding in the bushes at the edge of the lot and was armed." He pointed to a pistol shoved into his utility belt.

Ian stared at Shannon in disbelief.

She stared defiantly back at him. "I wanted to be here for Maria, to help her. The gun was for my protection in case something bad happened." She looked around. "Where is she? Inside the warehouse?"

Ian turned to the police officer. "This is Shannon Murphy. I can vouch for her. She's not one of the ones we're after. You can release her into my custody."

The officer shook his head again. But Ellison stepped forward. "Do as he says. Special Agent McKenzie can take custody of the gun and this young woman. I'll update Chief Thomas."

Ian winced at the use of his real name. Not that it really mattered at this point. His cover was blown.

"Where's Maria?" Shannon demanded as the police officer unlocked her handcuffs.

"Later," Ian snapped.

Her eyes widened, but she didn't say anything else.

Ian checked the loading on her pistol, his jaw tightening when he saw the magazine was full, except for one round. The officer had either ejected the chambered round or she hadn't chambered one herself. Thank God for small favors. He ejected the magazine and slid it into his pocket, then shoved the now-empty pistol in his other pocket.

"What's the status here?" Ellison asked, glancing from Nash to Ian.

Since the officer was still standing there, Ian glanced at his uniform to get his name. "Officer Jennings, thank you for your help tonight. Would you mind placing Miss Murphy in the back of your squad car until I can retrieve my personal car hidden down the mountain?"

The lot was rapidly filling as officers were driving each other to bring their squad cars out of hiding.

Jennings looked to Ellison for permission.

Ellison nodded. "If Chief Thomas comes looking for you, I'll let him know you're guarding a civilian on behalf of Homeland Security. Go ahead."

"Thank you, sir. My car's not here yet, but I'll borrow someone else's. No problem."

"I don't want to sit in the back of a police car," Shannon insisted. "I want to know what happened. Where's Maria?"

Ian noticed the panic in her expression. At any other time, her deep-seated fear of the police would have had him making some kind of concession. But not tonight. Her actions could have gotten her killed. And he needed to know, for sure, that she was safe.

"Home or the police station?" he gritted out. "Those are your choices."

Hurt flashed in her eyes. But she quickly covered it with a nonchalant expression as if she couldn't care less about what was going on.

Jennings took Shannon's arm and led her toward a patrol car near the tree line.

Ian deliberately turned his back on them, too incensed to even look at Shannon. It had almost destroyed him seeing her there, knowing that she could have been killed. Twice now, because of him, she'd been placed in an untenably dangerous situation. He wasn't sure what he was going to do about her. But that decision would have to wait.

"Give me the sitrep," Ellison demanded. "Chief Thomas said the warehouse is empty."

Ian narrowed his eyes and stepped forward, ready to let Ellison have it for ruining months of undercover work.

Nash moved between them, his back to Ellison. "Take a walk, Special Agent."

Ian gritted his teeth. "He ruined—"

"Take a walk. Now. I'll handle this."

Ian strode to the truck. He had too much adrenaline and anger running through his system to sit in the cab. Instead, he paced back and forth, waiting for the political grandstanding between agencies to end. That didn't seem like it would happen anytime soon since the Gatlinburg PD police chief had just joined the ADA and Nash.

Finally, disgusted with the whole thing, he decided to head back into the warehouse to see if maybe he'd missed something the first time around. Obviously, Butch and his men had been here recently to have placed that index card inside. Maybe they'd left something else lying around that could give him a clue about their current whereabouts.

He went in and headed straight for the room with the index card. He wanted a picture of it, if it hadn't been taken into evidence yet. A Gatlinburg PD evidence tech was placing the card into a clear evidence bag when Ian got there.

"Can I see that a second?" Ian pulled out his cell phone. "I'm the one who discovered it. I'd like a picture. It could help me with the investigation instead of waiting for the card to be processed."

The tech hesitated.

"Just hold it up," Ian said. "I won't touch the bag. No evidence chain of custody wrinkles here, okay?"

The man held it up, not looking happy about it.

Ian snapped a picture. "Thanks. Appreciate it." He turned to leave.

"Hey," the tech called out. "Don't you want a picture of the writing on the other side too?"

Ian slowly turned around. "There's writing on the back?"

The tech flipped it over. "Looks like it's addressed to somebody."

Ian's entire body went cold when he saw what was written there. He snapped the picture and kept his ex-

· pression carefully blank. "Thanks. Does anyone else know about the writing on the back?"

He shrugged. "I doubt it. I'm pretty sure I was the first person to pick it up so it could be preserved for fingerprint analysis and testing of trace."

"No problem," Ian said, as if he was disappointed that the tech hadn't told anyone about it. "If you don't mind, I'll let the bosses know so they don't have to wait for processing. Is that okay?"

"Of course. It will save me the trouble of doing it. Thanks, Special Agent…um—"

"Savage." Ian nodded instead of offering to shake hands since the tech was still wearing gloves. The tech introduced himself, and Ian thanked him again for his assistance, then headed outside.

His boss was waiting for him when he reached the truck.

Nash frowned. "What were you doing inside?"

"Looking to see if anything useful was missed."

"Did you find anything?"

Ian shook his head. "Nope. What's our next step with the investigation?"

Nash snorted. "What investigation? It was all caught on camera. You were the inside guy to lure our traffickers into the open. That's all shot to heck now. We have nothing."

"We have suspects—Butch and his henchmen. We know they've been trafficking women. We just need proof."

"And how do you propose to get that now? It's over, Ian. I'm sorry, but that's the way it is. This one is a dead end. The bad guy is long gone—"

"We don't know that. Yes, my cover's blown. But

Butch could still be doing business here and looking for a new buyer. We can't give up. We need to keep digging, do some old-fashioned investigative work, maybe try to get another agent snooping around town undercover, posing as a buyer. We can't just wash our hands of this now. What will happen to those women? We have to keep working."

"*We* aren't doing anything on this. *I'll* evaluate what happened here tonight and figure out what, if anything, will be done. But I'm pulling most of the agents and sending them on other more promising cases. I'll keep a skeleton staff in town in case something else pops up. But if nothing does, we're out of here in the next few days."

"Nash, don't do this. Keep everyone on the case. We have to find where Butch is holding those women. Victims first, remember?"

Nash's face reddened. "I don't need you to keep reminding me about my job, Ian. This whole evening is a blight on both agencies. Ellison is all over me for not putting things on hold like we'd originally agreed. He insists that if we had, we could have had enough time to adequately plan the buy and nab these guys instead of the screwed-up situation at the last minute like we did today. And I can't even tell him he's wrong."

Ian started to argue, but Nash shook his head. "No. Not another word. Consider yourself on administrative leave for the next week. Make that two weeks. When you come back, I want your head on straight." He motioned toward the patrol car where Shannon was watching them through the back window. "And do something about Miss Murphy. I don't want her popping up in the middle of something if we do end up figuring out a way to salvage this mess."

Nash didn't give him a chance to argue further. He strode back to where the ADA and Chief Thomas were standing with some of the uniformed officers.

Ian stood there, mulling over what to do. He could try to argue with his boss again, but he didn't think it would do any good. And he wasn't sure he wanted to argue with him anyway, in light of what had been written on the back of the index card. He needed to think about his options and what to do next.

He glanced at the patrol car. Shannon looked away, refusing to meet his gaze. He let out a deep breath and pulled out his phone to bring up the picture of the card. He read the front, then flipped to the picture of the back. It contained six words.

For Homeland Security Agent Ian McKenzie.

Those six words, unbeknownst to the technician who'd collected the index card, canceled out everything written on the front. Those words meant that Butch had known that Ian was with Homeland Security, even before the swarm of cops and special agents descended on the warehouse. It was one thing for Butch to suspect he might be a cop. But Ian had made sure that only a few people had known that he was a special agent. That index card could only mean one thing.

Someone in law enforcement had tipped off Butch and his men, someone who knew that Ian worked for Homeland Security.

Chapter Thirteen

Ian pulled up his Charger in front of a small, remote mountainside hotel that looked down on the night lights of Gatlinburg.

In the passenger seat, Shannon stared mutinously ahead, arms crossed. "I've been safe at the duplex all these months that you've been living your double life. I still don't get why you suddenly think I'm in danger, especially since you said Butch and the others have most likely left town by now."

"Guys like him are unpredictable."

"Yeah, yeah, he's angry. Whatever."

He sighed. "Shannon, it's more serious than him simply being *angry*. He was expecting a big paycheck in exchange for off-loading what he calls inventory. Now he knows that Homeland Security and the local police are working together, looking for him. The heat is on, and he can't move easily with that many women in tow. It makes him vulnerable. He might even have to lie low here in town while he waits for things to cool down. That will cost him money. He'll blame me for that. He knows where I've been living. And Wolverine showed some interest in you the other day. He may decide to take revenge on me by hurting you."

"And that's why you had that other agent spying on me."

He dropped his hands to his lap. "Yes. As I already said, that's why Chris was there. Not that it did any good. You managed to slip right past him. Which is why I'm not taking you back there. Too many entrances and exits to watch. It's not safe."

"Right. Like you care." She shoved open the car door.

He reached across her and yanked the door shut. He was just inches from her face as she stared at him with her accusing green eyes.

"I do care, Shannon, or I wouldn't have put up with all of the cursing and hateful things you've been saying to me since I got you out of the patrol car."

She arched a brow. "You wouldn't have put up with it? What's that mean? You gonna hit me to prove how big and strong you are? *Cop?*"

He stared at her in shock. "You think I would hit you?"

"It wouldn't be the first time some guy I was hanging with beat the crap out of me."

"Then you've been hanging with the wrong men. I will never, ever hurt you. Never."

She stared at him, a disbelieving look on her face. "Right. You'll just take me prisoner instead. Isn't that called kidnapping or something? It's against the law. But I guess your fellow law enforcement buddies will cover for you. They always cover for each other, the brotherhood in blue."

"Good grief. You sure have a low opinion of me. Did I earn that tonight—because I wanted to protect you? Or have you felt that way a long time and have just done a really great job of hiding your true feelings?"

Her eyes widened. Then she quickly looked away, her mouth drawn into a tight line.

He let go of the door and sat back, but anchored her wrist with his hand before she could jump out of the car. "I didn't kidnap you. It's called protective custody. Whether you choose to believe it or not, there's a good possibility that your life is in danger. Until Butch and his men are caught, or I have definitive proof that they've left the area, you're staying with me. Unless you prefer a jail cell. Those are your choices."

"That's the second time you've threatened to lock me up tonight. You getting kinky on me, Ian McKenzie?" She wiggled her brows, but the flash of anger in her eyes told the real story.

He shoved out of the car. It was either that or yell at her. Of all the lines that he'd crossed in his youthful rebel days, or even deep undercover pretending to be a thug, yelling at a woman—or worse—was a line he refused to cross.

He grabbed the small duffel bag from the back seat that Special Agent Chris Parker had brought to him from the duplex. A policewoman had packed items for Shannon while Chris had packed for Ian.

He settled the bag's strap over his shoulder and headed to the passenger side. For someone who'd been so adamant about getting out of the car earlier, Shannon seemed in no hurry to emerge now. He opened the door and stood back. "You coming, or are we driving to Gatlinburg PD?"

"If you give me my gun back, I can protect myself at the duplex."

"Not happening."

She rolled her eyes and got out.

Once they were inside their hotel suite she flounced into the bedroom and slammed the door.

Ian's shoulders slumped. He set the duffel bag on the little café table, took out his toothbrush and toothpaste and headed to the kitchenette in the corner. After changing into some warm-up pants and a T-shirt, he set the duffel bag outside the bedroom door.

"Shannon?" He waited, then rapped on the door. "Shannon, I've set the bag outside the door in case you need anything—"

The door opened. She grabbed the bag, then slammed the door closed.

He stared at the closed door for several long moments. But there wasn't anything he could think of to say that would make her overlook his biggest sin—that he was in law enforcement.

After making sure the locks were secure on the back window and only door into the suite, he checked the entry closet, hoping to find an extra pillow and a blanket. The closet was empty. He looked back at the couch, which was about two feet too short for him, then at the closed bedroom door. Sighing, he padded to the couch, lay down and drew his knees up against his chest.

Chapter Fourteen

Sleep was elusive for Shannon. She dozed off and on, but a combination of things kept waking her up. Not the least of which was guilt. She'd been awful to Ian. Her frustration and worry over her friend Maria, and her resentment at being forced to do something she didn't want to do, had her reverting to the smart-ass tough-girl persona she'd adopted in order to survive on the streets. But no matter how mean she was, and how angry Ian became, he'd been true to his word.

He hadn't hurt her.

And even though his high-handed insistence on taking her into protective custody had her panicking at the thought of giving control over to a man—*any* man—he'd proved time and again that he was only trying to help.

She'd seen the flash of regret on his face each time he'd forced her to do something she didn't want to do. And now that some time had passed, the panic and anger had faded enough for her to realize the truth. Ian didn't want to control her or force his will on her. He didn't want to hurt her and make her feel uncomfortable. He wanted only one thing—for her to be safe. And what had she done in return? She hadn't thanked him. Instead, she'd made every minute of the car ride—from the warehouse to the meeting with Chris to get the duffel bag and then finally to the hotel—a living hell for him.

And he didn't deserve that.

She sat up in the bed and threw off the covers. She'd finally met the genuinely nice, smart, sexy, sweet and protective man that she'd prayed would come into her life one day. And she'd done everything she could to turn him against her.

She was such an idiot.

She shuffled into the bathroom and freshened up. When she checked the time on her phone, she saw it was almost three in the morning. There was a light shining beneath the bedroom door. Maybe Ian was having trouble sleeping too. She owed him a huge apology. Might as well take care of it right now.

She pulled open the bedroom door, then felt lower than the lowest pond scum. There was big, brawny Ian looking like a pretzel, his long legs practically touching his chin on the short couch. She hadn't given a single thought to whether the furniture would accommodate his size before taking the king bed for herself. And since she'd shut the door that accessed the bathroom, he'd either been forced to go to the lobby to use their facilities, or hold it. Good grief, she was such a jerk. If he ever spoke to her again, it would be a miracle.

She knelt beside the couch and gently shook him.

His eyes flew open and he grabbed her, yanking her to the floor, crushing her beneath him as he swept his pistol back and forth toward the room around them. "What is it?" he demanded. "What happened?"

"Ian, it's just me." Her voice came out a harsh croak. She cleared her throat. "There's no one else here."

He frowned and looked down at her. "You're okay?"

She pressed shaking hands against his chest, an unexpected rush of tears clogging her throat. After everything she'd done, he was shielding her with his body, thinking someone was there to hurt her. He was willing to give his life for hers. The enormity of that knowledge had the tears flowing down her cheeks.

He shoved his pistol back into the holster and pulled her up with him, his concerned gaze searching hers. "I'm so sorry. I didn't mean to frighten you."

"Frighten me?" She laughed and wiped her tears. "You scared me nearly to death. But that's not why I'm crying. You shielded me with your body, trying to protect me, even after how badly I treated you."

His brow furrowed. "Are you sure you're okay? Did you hit your head?"

She laughed again. "No. I mean yes, I'm okay. I didn't…" She shook her head. "I'm fine. But you're not." She swept her hand toward the couch. "You shouldn't have let me keep the bedroom. This couch is way too small for you. And I was too stubborn and selfish to even think about that when I had my temper tantrum and went into the bedroom."

She grabbed his hand. When he winced, she let go, realizing she'd grabbed his left hand. "Oh, gosh. I'm so sorry. I forgot about your arm. Have you taken anything for the pain?"

He frowned. "I'm fine, Shannon. And I'm okay sleeping on the couch. Although if you have an extra pillow, I wouldn't turn it down."

"A pillow. Of course." She grabbed his other hand this time and tugged him toward the bedroom.

"Shannon—"

She pulled him into the bedroom. "Here you go. Four pillows, two for each of us. Plenty of room."

He stopped beside the bed and tugged his hand free. "Are you sleepwalking or something?" He waved a hand in front of her face.

She rolled her eyes. "I don't sleepwalk."

He glanced around the room. "Drunk, then? Did you hit the minibar?"

She put her hands on her hips. "I'm not asleep and I'm not drunk. I'm trying to be nice here."

He rubbed the back of his neck. "Yeah, that's the part that has me confused. I thought you hated me."

She narrowed her eyes at him.

"There we go. That's more like it." He grabbed a couple of pillows. "I'll be leaving now."

She stepped in his path, blocking his way to the door. "Shannon?"

"Yes, Ian?"

"It's really late, or early by now. I could use a few more hours of sleep."

His eyes dipped down, then back up so fast she almost missed it. She was wearing a short nightshirt that barely fell below her hips. With no bra. And the bead of sweat trickling down the side of his neck told her he'd definitely noticed.

She took a step forward, her breasts pressing against his chest.

He swallowed, his gaze glued to hers. "Um, Shannon?"

"Yes, Ian?" She slid her arms up his biceps and locked her fingers behind his neck.

"I'm getting mixed signals here. Do you still, ah, hate me?"

She slowly shook her head. "I was mad, Ian. But I could never hate you. And I'm way past the mad stage. That's behind us now." She stroked the back of his neck.

He shuddered and briefly closed his eyes. "You know I'm still a cop, a special agent."

"That's your biggest flaw. I've decided to look past it." She stroked his neck again.

He stumbled, then swore and pulled her arms down from behind his neck. "I don't think this is a good idea. You're either overwrought or overtired or… Heck, I don't know. But you'll end up hating me later. Because that big flaw of mine is the core of who I am. Either you're okay with me being in law enforcement or you're not. Either you hate me or you don't. When you get it figured out, let me know. Until then, I think it's best that the door stays closed with you on one side and me on the other. It's safer. For both of us." He practically ran from the room, pulling the door shut behind him.

Chapter Fifteen

Ian shoved the last of their breakfast trash into the garbage can beneath the kitchenette sink. The restaurant down the street that delivered to the tourist-rentals and hotels up this mountain had brought a delicious assortment of pancakes, eggs, bacon, and even oatmeal and fruit. But it had proved to be a waste. Neither of them seemed to have an appetite. And Shannon couldn't seem to even look at him since coming out of the bedroom this morning.

After barely eating anything, she'd thanked him politely, then planted herself on the couch in front of the TV to watch the morning news. Her thanking him was the longest conversation they'd had since last night's confusing drama in the bedroom. If he'd thought for one second that she truly wanted him, he'd have been all over her. But he hadn't trusted her motives, not after everything that happened yesterday. Seeing how she was acting this morning, he wasn't sure if he'd been right last night, or whether he'd made the biggest mistake of his life.

"Shannon?"

"Mmm-hmm." She didn't look at him.

"I'm about to leave now. Like I said, I'm going to

follow up on a few things, see if anyone's making any headway trying to find out where Maria and the others might be."

He waited, then tried again. "If you're still upset about last night—"

"I'm fine."

He sighed. "I'll be back later today, definitely before dark. I've left cash on the counter so you can call that same restaurant that I called this morning to deliver any time you're hungry. Please don't use any of your credit cards or call anyone you know."

"You've said that three times now. I know the drill. And I know my choice is to stay here or go to jail. You can leave now. I'm not going anywhere."

He missed the easy friendship they'd shared for so long. Even the other night when he'd brought pizza by, and they'd watched that sappy love story, he'd rank that evening as one of the most enjoyable he'd ever had. He loved being with her, listening to her jokes, watching her face soften with emotion as she watched the actors on TV. How had they gone from that to this in such a short time?

"I said you could go now, Ian." She pushed the remote and changed the channel.

"You promise you won't go anywhere?"

"Cross my heart and hope to die," she said sarcastically.

"Then it should be okay to leave this with you." He set her pistol and the magazine on top of the counter.

She glanced over, then blinked. "You're giving me my gun back?"

"Is there a reason that I shouldn't? I can trust you. Right?"

She hesitated, then said, "Yes. Of course."

"There's no way for Butch or the others to know that you're here or even suspect it. But if a casual burglar were to decide to try to break in, or something like that, I want to know you'll be protected."

Her gaze finally lifted to his. "Thank you, Ian. I appreciate it."

He nodded. "I'll lock the door. But you'll need to throw the bar across it. Okay?"

"Okay." She smiled. "Be careful."

The smile surprised him, confused him. He didn't know what to make of it, so he just left.

Half an hour later he pulled up in front of the duplex. But instead of parking inside the garage, he left his Charger on the curb. Then he headed inside. Keeping all the lights off so no one could see him if they looked in from the street, he sat on the couch watching the car. Then he pulled out his cell phone and settled in to make some calls.

"Sanders Auto Repair. This is Ralph Sanders. Can I help you?"

"Boss, it's Ian."

"You'd better be on your way to the shop right now, Savage. Or you can kiss your job goodbye."

"Yeah, that's why I called. Partly, anyway." He explained who he really was and confessed that he'd been working there as a cover for the past six months. Convincing him would have been easier in person. But going to the shop today wasn't part of his plan.

"Well, I'll be a son of a… I can't believe it," Sanders finally said. "I mean, I do. But I gotta say, I'm mad as hell. Not that you were undercover all this time, but because I'm losing the best mechanic that I've ever had working for me. You sure you don't want to quit working for the Feds and come work for me full-time?"

Ian laughed. "The way things are going right now, I may need to take you up on that offer sometime. But not yet." Hopefully his boss at Homeland Security wouldn't fire him for working the case on his own when he was supposed to be on administrative leave. But he was playing with fire right now as far as his career was concerned.

"My door is always open, son. You did great work for me."

"Thank you, sir. I appreciate it. Since I've been gone, has anyone come around looking for me? They might not have come inside. They could be hanging around the place, maybe sitting in the lot across the street. One of them drives a white cargo van. Another drives a bright yellow Volkswagen, a fairly new Beetle. Seen anything like that parked outside the garage for no good reason?"

"Can't say that I've noticed. But we've been pretty slammed lately, and I've been pitching in working on the cars since my best worker ditched me."

Ian winced. "Sorry, sir."

"What makes you think I meant you?" Sanders laughed. "I'll check with the guys, keep an eye out. If I see this Bug hanging around, you want me to call you at this number?"

Ian was taking every precaution he could to ensure that nothing could be used to trace back to the hotel where he was keeping Shannon. That meant destroying his current burner phone as soon as today's work was done. Instead, he told Sanders that he'd call him back tomorrow to see if he'd found out anything that might help.

He called dozens of other contacts that he'd made in

the time that he'd been working this investigation, including confidential informants willingly working in the sex trade. They claimed to enjoy what they did for a living, and since no one was technically forcing them, there wasn't much Ian could do other than to provide them a list of agencies, shelters and churches that made it their work to help sex trade workers. In return, his CIs provided him with tips.

As he made his calls, he kept a close watch on his car parked out front. But no one had even slowed down as they passed the duplex. No garish yellow Beetle pulled up behind the Charger. And even though he spoke to dozens of people in places where he'd gone in the guise of Ian Savage, no one claimed to have heard of anyone looking for him or asking questions about him. No one fitting Butch's description, or any of his minions, popped up on the radar.

It had been a long shot, but he was still surprised that everything was so quiet. He'd assumed that Butch or one of his right-hand men, or Wolverine at least, would have been out scouring the city trying to find the man who'd double-crossed them. He couldn't see them letting a slight like that go without wanting retribution. Either no one was searching for him, or they were driving yet another vehicle that he didn't know about. Or they'd left town already. Since that would mean the victims with Butch were completely beyond his reach and unlikely to be rescued, Ian was praying that wasn't the case.

While he worked through his contacts, he created a list of places he planned to canvass himself, places where his contacts weren't as likely to carry phones around. But at the top of his list was to start right where he was, in his current neighborhood. He wanted to see whether his neighbors had noticed anything suspicious. But before he could do that, there was one more call he needed to make.

He'd been putting this one off because he didn't want to make this call. But allowing his personal preferences to get in the way of solving a case and rescuing human trafficking victims was unacceptable. It was time to step up and get this particular chore over with. He dialed a number that he'd never used, even though it had been given to him years ago.

The line clicked. "McKenzie."

"Adam, it's Ian."

Chapter Sixteen

Shannon smoothed her blouse over her jeans, hesitating at the door to the hotel suite. She was breaking a promise by leaving. But Ian had lied to her for so long, it hardly seemed fair that she should feel so guilty over one little lie. And yet she did. He'd wanted her to stay here for her own protection. But how could she do that when the friend who'd risked her own life for her, a friend Shannon had spent much of her adult life tracking down, could be here somewhere in Gatlinburg at this very moment, in need of rescuing?

A car horn honked outside. The taxi she'd called was getting impatient. She took one last look around, then headed out the door.

Uncomfortable with the idea of sitting beside a driver she didn't know, she sat in the back seat.

He glanced at her in the rearview mirror. "Where to, ma'am?"

She gave him the duplex's address and brutally shoved her feelings of guilt aside. She knew the risks, that Butch or one of his men could be watching the place. But if she was going to pass as a street person again to try to hunt down news about Maria, she needed the right clothes for it. Her meager savings couldn't cover luxuries like a new outfit. Especially since her call this morning to let her boss know she was going to miss another shift had been short and *not* sweet. He'd fired her.

When the taxi pulled up in front of her home, she counted out the exact amount and handed it to the driver. He didn't look happy to not be getting a tip. But she couldn't afford one, and she refused to use Ian's equally hard-earned money when she was going against his wishes.

The taxi's tires squealed as he took off, making her wince as she turned the key in the lock. After one last glance around to make sure that she didn't see anyone skulking in the bushes or parked on the street watching her, she headed inside.

IAN ADJUSTED the collar of his leather trench coat, since his favorite leather jacket had been destroyed, and headed inside the internet café. He immediately spotted his oldest brother. Adam was doing his best to blend in, having chosen a table in the back corner away from the busy counter. But McKenzies, because of their large build and height, were more likely to be noticed than not. Ian imagined the thousand-dollar suit that Adam was wearing, along with his coal-black hair and striking blue eyes, didn't help. But he seemed oblivious to all the women casting glances his way.

Adam motioned toward him. Ian returned the greeting and headed to his table. He couldn't help grinning when he noticed that he had the opposite effect on the women around them. His blond-streaked spiky black hair and dragon tattoos must not be to their taste.

"Something funny?" Adam asked, looking puzzled.

Ian shrugged. "Nothing I'm not used to. Thanks for meeting me here."

"Not a problem." He gestured toward Ian's face. "The bruises are fading fast. How's the arm?"

"Nothing a few pain pills don't knock out. You said you have information on Gillespie?"

The disappointment on Adam's face told Ian he'd messed up, again. His brother must have wanted more small talk, to catch up on a personal level before turning to business. Ian was too out of practice with polite conversation to realize it.

Ian cleared his throat. "How's, ah, your new bride? Jody, I think you said?"

Adam smiled sadly. "Thanks for the effort. But you're obviously in a hurry, so I'll get right to the point of our meeting." He pulled a manila folder out of the briefcase on the seat beside him and set it on the table in front of Ian. "You can take those with you. I just got the information together this morning and haven't had a chance to digitize it. It's a good thing you called."

"This stuff wasn't already in Memphis PD's computer databases?"

"I imagine it is. But my former partner grew up in the days of typewriters and legal pads. I doubt he even went online in the department's system to gather this information. He probably got it from the archive paper backups in the basement and made copies. At least he sent it overnight instead of your typical snail mail, or we still wouldn't have it." He pointed to one of the reports as Ian thumbed through the pages. "That's an overview of the investigation into the sex ring I told you about."

"What are all these? Surveillance photographs?" Ian began sifting through a stack of pictures.

"Most of them, yes. They were taken in the months and weeks before we did our sting. Others are mug shots of the guys we arrested." He pulled one of them from beneath a few others and set it on top. "That's your guy there, Gillespie."

Ian frowned and held up the picture. "How long ago was this?"

"A little over two years." He flipped the photo over and grinned. "Two years, three weeks and two days, to be exact." He tapped the handwriting on the back. "That's my old partner's work." He handed it back to Ian.

"He sure has bulked up since then. I almost don't recognize him."

"Yeah, well, as I'm sure you know in your line of work, these guys do everything they can to change their appearance when they start over somewhere else. They don't want anyone from their old life to spot them. Every indication is that he left Memphis shortly after that mug shot was taken and the charges against him didn't stick."

"When I was in the hospital, I remember you saying something about his right-hand men, that they went to prison. Were you able to verify that they're still locked up?"

Adam held his hand out for the pictures. "May I?"

Ian gave the stack to him and Adam fanned them out. He selected three and set them in front of Ian. "These are the main guys, the ones giving the orders. All three are serving time as we speak. But everyone in our task force believed Gillespie was the brains behind the operation. He had everyone too scared to turn on him and testify against him. It killed me that we had to let him walk."

"Okay, well, I'll look through all of this, study Gillespie's background. If I can figure out where he's been, maybe I can find out where he's going. Maybe some of these smaller fish caught in your net are out and working with him again. I can follow up that angle, as well."

"What about your fellow agents at Homeland Security? They helping you with this?"

Ian grimaced. "Not officially. I called a few I trust this morning to discuss the investigation."

"A few you trust? You don't trust everyone you work with?"

He wasn't quite ready to discuss all the particulars with his brother. This new truce, or whatever it was between them, wasn't something he was comfortable with just yet. So he didn't tell him about the index card and his suspicions about a mole.

"I wouldn't say that. But I'm on administrative leave right now. My cover was blown, so I'm officially off the investigation. Any snooping I do, if it's reported up to my boss, won't be good for my career. I'm being careful about whom I contact on the inside right now."

"I see."

The disappointment on Adam's face had Ian tensing. This was what he normally expected from his brothers rather than the friendly cooperation of a moment before. They expected him to fail, to screw up everything. So naturally Adam assumed the worst. Never mind that Ian had done everything right, everything by the book, and it was someone else who'd blown his cover.

He gathered up all the pictures and reports and slid them back into the folder. "Thanks, Adam. I really appreciate this." He pushed his chair back.

"Ian?"

He arched a brow in question.

"Christmas is in three weeks."

"Yeah. What about it?"

Adam frowned. "You missed Thanksgiving—"

"I usually miss Thanksgiving." He didn't want to feel like a hypocrite sitting around the table trying to come up with something to say when it was his turn to say why he was thankful. Not having to see his father every day didn't seem appropriate.

"You missed my wedding in June. I posted the information in the paper and sent an invitation to your PO box and—"

"I was undercover. It would have been too risky to be seen at an event like that, especially here in Gatlinburg. And, honestly, I haven't checked that PO box in ages. I have to admit that I didn't know about the wedding." He'd rented that box at his family's insistence years ago and put it on automatic renewal. But he rarely ever checked it.

Adam held up his hands in a placating gesture. "I get it. But you said your cover has been blown now, that you're off the case, at least officially. It sure would be great if you could be there for Duncan's and Colin's weddings at Christmas. The ceremony will be at one in the converted barn at the family cabin. It would mean a lot to Mom if you're there. It would mean a lot to all of us."

Ian snorted in disbelief.

"I'm serious, Ian. We want you there."

"Including Dad?"

Adam hesitated.

"That's what I thought." Ian stood and held up the manila folder. "I really appreciate this. It could be the break I need."

Adam stood, as well. "Enough to repay me by showing up at the weddings?"

It was Ian's turn to hesitate. He had planned on being there Christmas morning for his mother's sake. Easter and Christmas were her favorite holidays, and he always tried to be at one of them every year. But pretending he was part of a big happy family at something like a wedding left a sour taste in his mouth. Still, his brother had never asked him for anything before. That alone had him holding back a quick no. "What are their names? Colin's and Duncan's fiancées?"

"Duncan's marrying someone from Colorado, a former FBI agent, Remi Jordan."

"And Colin?"

"Peyton Sterling."

Ian stared at him in shock. "Her arsonist sibling nearly killed Colin. The fire—"

"I know. Some crazy stuff happened this year. I'd like to bring you up to speed, when you have time."

Ian couldn't seem to process what his brother had just said. How could Colin forgive and then propose to the woman who'd supposedly loved him, then abandoned him in a burn unit to support the man responsible for putting him there? That had to be a hell of a story.

"Ian? Will you do it? Will you come to the weddings?"

Ian shrugged, then winced and made a mental note to take another pain pill once he got to his car. "I'll think about it. No promises."

Adam nodded. "I can't ask for more than that, all things considered. Thanks, Ian."

The brother Ian was used to would have argued with him, maybe even berated him for being a rebel, the bad boy who continued to bring disgrace to the McKenzie name. Marriage must have mellowed him. Maybe Duncan and Colin would be easier to get along with too, after they got married. But that was probably too much to hope for.

Ian left without another word.

In his car in the lot behind the building, he swallowed some pain pills. Then he took out the contents of the folder again. A name had caught his attention on one of the reports. Sure enough, when he looked again, he saw it—Cameron Ellison. He'd been an assistant district attorney in Memphis before transferring to Gatlinburg. The DA who Ellison reported to worked out of Memphis, not Gatlinburg. It was an odd setup. And it was a change in location, not a change in jobs. So why was Ellison here? Was it temporary on some special assignment, and he just happened to also be given the role of liaison with Homeland Security for the current human trafficking investigation? Or was there a more sinister reason for his transfer? Ian couldn't help thinking about that yellow index card in the warehouse. Was Ellison the one who'd ratted him out to Gillespie?

It was definitely an angle he'd have to explore. He sorted through the pictures again, remembering one that had caught his eye in the café. It was a mug shot. The inmate had terrible taste in clothing. His black-and-yellow shirt made him look like a bumblebee. The information on the back of the picture said the perpetrator was a suspected low-level member of the organization. But there hadn't been enough evidence to hold him over for prosecution, just as there hadn't been for Gillespie. They'd both been released at the same time. The man's name was Andrew Branum.

But Ian knew him as Wolverine.

Now that he knew Wolverine's real name, maybe it was time to dig a little and find out what else he was hiding.

Ian pulled out his phone and made a call.

Chapter Seventeen

Having traveled from her hometown in Ohio to both Virginias, Kentucky and now Tennessee, Shannon had lived in so many small towns and big cities that she'd lost track of them all. But one thing was the same in every place she'd been—a part of town where extreme poverty, homelessness and people who wanted to make a profit no matter what the human cost came together to cause misery and destroy lives.

Shannon had been one of the victims of that world for over five years, since the age of fourteen. And even though she'd escaped "the life" a few years ago, it was depressingly easy to slip back into that role, as if she'd never managed to claw her way out of it. Except this time, she wasn't anyone else's property. And she wasn't defenseless.

She kept her right hand firmly on the bulge of the pistol in her purse as she navigated back alleys in a pair of red stilettos, a black leather miniskirt and an off-the-shoulder short crimson blouse that allowed the sunlight to sparkle off her belly ring. Her only concession to the chilly temperatures was the waist-length leopard-print jacket that she kept unbuttoned as any good street girl would. After all, you couldn't make a sale if you didn't advertise the goods.

Back on either River Road or Parkway, she'd have stuck out like a black bear in a herd of elk. But here on the outskirts, she blended right in. Which was exactly what she wanted.

Business was slow this early in the day. But there were still a few johns idling on the curbs, negotiating prices with achingly young women leaning into their windows, displaying their cleavage in the hopes of bumping up the prices. As Shannon approached, one of the women hopped into a car and was driven away. The bleakness in her eyes as she looked out the window tugged at Shannon's heart, and reminded her of herself not long ago, when she'd been forced into the same kind of life.

Tears burned the backs of her eyes as she stepped over a homeless man huddled beneath his cardboard house, covered in piles of dirty blankets. If she thought her jacket would come even close to fitting him, she'd have given it to him. As it was, she couldn't walk past him without stopping to stuff one of her few remaining twenty-dollar bills into his hand.

Hurrying past him before his fervent thank-yous made someone wonder if she had more cash on her, she turned down another side street. Perhaps sensing that she was the real deal, or at least had been at one time, the women on the curbs and sheltering in doorways weren't alarmed about her inquiries. They seemed to genuinely want to help her find her "big sister, Maria." It would have been much easier if she'd had a picture to show them. But with Maria's striking Spanish looks and the butterfly tattoo on her neck, it was easy to provide a useful description.

Several of the women claimed to have seen Maria. But every lead that Shannon followed took her to another woman or the occasional pimp out checking on his ladies. And none of them led to her friend.

After several hours of walking the streets, her feet were starting to ache and burn, which surprised her. She wore high heels every day as part of being a hostess at the hotel restaurant. But the stilettos stretched her arches and cramped her toes in a way her everyday heels didn't. If she couldn't find anyone with knowledge of Maria's whereabouts soon, she'd have to call it a day.

She glanced around before dipping her hand into her purse to check the time on her phone. It was even later than she'd realized. If she didn't get back to the hotel soon, Ian might very well make it back before her. That was a conversation she didn't want to have. It was time to give up, at least for now.

She turned the corner to make her way back toward the more respectable part of town, where she'd be more likely to find a taxi. She'd just passed a darkened doorway when movement out of the corner of her eye sent alarm skittering up her spine. She shoved her hand into her purse for her gun and tried to whirl around. The man behind her grabbed her wrist, his other arm going around her waist. She screamed as he yanked her back toward the darkened doorway.

He grabbed the gun out of her hand, then immediately let her go.

Shannon whipped around, ready to destroy his chances of fathering children with one swift kick of her stiletto. But the moment she turned, she froze. The man dressed in black looking down at her with fury in his deep blue eyes wasn't a stranger.

"I-Ian? What are you doing here?"

He ejected the magazine in her pistol and cleared the chamber before giving them both back to her. "I was speaking to confidential informants, searching for clues to help me rescue your friend and the women with her. But I had to stop all that when I heard about a woman with blue-tipped black hair making a stir. You about done here?"

His words were short and clipped, his anger so palpable it made goose bumps rise on her arms.

"Yes, actually. I was about to find a taxi."

His jaw tightened. "A taxi. That's how you got here?"

"Well, you didn't exactly leave me a car. What was I supposed to do?"

A muscle started to tick in the side of his cheek. "Keeping your word and staying at the hotel would have been good for a start." He flicked the collar of her leopard-print jacket. "I seem to remember something like that in your closet. You went to the duplex?"

"Well, I couldn't exactly blend in around here in my normal clothes. I had to get a different outfit. But I was careful. I had my gun."

His nostrils flared as if he was having trouble drawing enough oxygen. He motioned toward the next corner. "My car is that way." He didn't wait for Shannon. Instead, he stalked down the sidewalk away from her.

Stubbornness and pride wanted her to refuse his implied order that she follow him. But she wasn't going to waste her precious store of cash on another taxi just to make a point, and she was ready to return to the hotel anyway. She started after him, hurrying to catch up.

By the time she rounded the corner, she was limping. How had she survived so many years wearing these stupid shoes?

Ian, in spite of the anger darkening his expression, couldn't seem to ignore the gentlemanly manners that had always set him apart from other men she'd known. He stood with the passenger door open, waiting for her.

She got inside and soon they were whipping through back streets, making their way up the mountain toward the hotel. She kept expecting him to berate her, yell at her, something. Instead, he didn't say a word.

By the time they reached the hotel, she was so relieved to escape the tense atmosphere inside the car that she shoved out of her door before he'd even put the car in Park. Once she was in the main room, she drew a deep breath and turned around to explain. Ian strode right past her into the bedroom.

Was he going to lock her out? Make her take the couch in retaliation for last night? It was close to dinnertime, not quite bedtime. What was he doing? She stepped to the door, and was almost run down when he shoved past her with the duffel bag. He held the main door open and stared at the far wall, waiting.

"I guess we're switching hotels?" she said.

"Something like that."

"Why? I thought this place was supposed to be safe."

He finally looked at her. "Did the taxi that you took to the duplex pick you up here?"

She blinked as his words sank in. If someone had been watching the duplex as Ian suspected, and saw her arrive in the cab, they could have bribed the driver—the one she hadn't tipped—to tell them where he'd picked her up. All of Ian's careful measures, like driving in circles and constantly looking in his mirrors to ensure that no one followed them in his car, were for nothing. She'd just left a bread-crumb trail for Butch and the others to follow directly to the hotel, if they were truly looking for her and Ian.

She cleared her throat. "Ian, I'm sorry. I just wanted to look for Maria and—"

He motioned toward the open door.

She straightened her shoulders and marched outside.

After what seemed like an eternity because of how meticulous Ian was about making sure they weren't followed, Ian slowed on the winding mountain road and turned into a driveway. In front of them was an enormous two-story log cabin. It was the biggest cabin she'd ever seen. Mansion seemed like a more appropriate label for something that huge.

He pulled into the three-car garage and cut the engine. Once the door was closed, he got out and led her into the main house.

Her jaw dropped open when she saw the interior. Thick golden logs crisscrossed two stories above to support the wide-open space inside. A one-of-a-kind hand-hewn log railing formed an interior balcony that looked down over the massive great room. And at the far end, a wide staircase with more log railings and stone steps soared up to the balcony, leading to several doors off both ends of the house, presumably the bedrooms.

"This is incredible," she breathed. "Whoever owns it must be a bajillionaire. Whose place is it?"

"Mine."

Chapter Eighteen

Ian strode through the monstrosity of a cabin, giving Shannon the grand tour as she padded barefoot behind him, her stilettos discarded near the front door. At first, he was still so shaken and livid over her risking her life yet again that it didn't bother him one bit that she was silent as he showed her the downstairs. She simply nodded when he gave her the security alarm code, and later explained how to work the remote controls for the wall of electronics built into the stone ledges beside the two-story fireplace. But as the tour went on, and she still didn't say anything, his anger began to fade and concern took its place.

Beside the marble-topped kitchen island that overlooked the great room, he turned to face her. "I have people come up here once a week to clean and perform any required maintenance inside and out. But since I'm rarely ever here myself, there's nothing to eat. There are some bottles of water in the refrigerator, but that's pretty much it. What do you want for dinner? I can have something delivered."

She shook her head. "No, thank you. I'm not really hungry."

He studied her pale complexion, the shadows in her eyes. "Did you eat lunch?"

"I'm fine. Really. I just…"

"You just what?"

She shrugged. "I wonder why you think we'll be safe here. Can't Butch search the internet for your name and find this address?"

"No one is going to find us here. The deed isn't under my real name."

"Because of your job?"

"Because of my family. They don't know I have this place, and I'd prefer it stay that way."

Her eyes widened. Then she looked away. "I'm a little tired. If you don't mind, I'd like to lie down."

When she still wouldn't look at him, he sighed and turned around. "I'll show you the bedrooms. They're all upstairs." He grabbed the duffel bag that he'd left in the great room and led the way up the curved staircase to the second-floor balcony. At the top, he motioned to the right. "There are some guest rooms down there. More here in the middle. The master's at the other end."

"Does it matter which room I take?"

He shook his head. "They each have their own bathroom. Clean towels and sheets are in the linen closets."

She stepped into the guest room that was the closest to where they were standing. "This will be fine. Thank you." She moved past the king-size bed, lightly running her hands across the deep blue duvet before turning around.

Ian set the duffel bag on top of the mahogany dresser and took out the smaller bag inside that held his things, plus the manila folder that Adam had given him. He waved toward one of the doors. "The bathroom should have everything you need—shampoo, soap, hair dryer. But if you think of something else you want, let me know. I'll—"

"Call someone and have it delivered?"

He frowned at her strained tone, but nodded. "If you're worried that it's not safe to have someone deliver something, don't. Nothing's—"

"In your name. Got that." She wrapped her arms around her middle and glanced around the room.

Ian waited, but when she didn't say anything else, he turned to leave.

"I guess Homeland Security pays really well these days."

He stopped, then slowly turned around. "Is there something you want to ask me, Shannon?"

She pierced him with an accusing look and motioned to encompass the room. "Cops can't afford places like this. Please tell me you won the lottery."

He stiffened, his earlier anger surging through him again. But this time it wasn't because she could have gotten herself killed. "I don't play the lottery."

She stared at him, waiting. "Are you going to make me say it?"

"Yeah. I guess I am."

She sighed. "I thought you were one of the good ones, Ian. How can you afford a mansion? One you don't even live in?"

He breathed through the anger and the disappointment, not answering until he was sure he could speak without yelling. "Of all the people I've met in my life, only one made me feel accepted for who I am, inside. She didn't judge me, condemn me for the choices I'd made in my life. She judged me on my character, on how I acted, on how I treat other people. Until the past few days, and right now."

Her eyes widened.

"This stupid cabin was my first rebellious act after I came into my first million when I turned twenty-one—the day my father turned over my inheritance to me. He was certain I'd waste the money, so of course that was the first thing I did—built a house I hated from day one and have never lived in for more than a few days at a time. I realized the stupidity of building this place as soon as it was finished. I never told my family about it, because I didn't want to give them proof that they were right."

She started to say something, but he held up a hand to stop her. "The money came from my great-great-grandfather, passed down through the generations. He was a genius in the business world. By the time he passed away, he was a multimillionaire a dozen times over. And that's not even in today's money. He'd have been a billionaire if you account for inflation."

"Ian, I'm sorry. I shouldn't have—"

"No. You shouldn't have." He rubbed the back of his neck, then dropped his hand to his side. "I don't know why you keep comparing me to the scumbags of your past. Cop or not, I'd do anything it takes to protect you. I don't want to die for you, Shannon. But if someone points a gun at you, I'll be the first one to jump in front of it."

He stepped out the door, then looked back over his shoulder. "You've always worried that others would judge you because of your past. That they would think less of you for it. I've never done that. I see you for the victim you once were, the survivor you've become. And yet, the moment you find out that I'm in law enforcement, you judge me. You think the worst of me in spite of everything else you know about my character." He motioned to encompass the room as she'd done a few minutes earlier. "I have more money than my future grandchildren's children could ever spend, and yet I risk my life every day on the streets. I do it because I want to help people. I want to make a difference in this world. And you know what? I'm done apologizing for it."

He stalked out the door and didn't stop until he was downstairs in his office, on the opposite side of the house.

Chapter Nineteen

The smell of pizza wafted up from downstairs about an hour later. Shannon didn't bother going down to have some even though she knew Ian would have ordered enough to share. She didn't deserve anything from him, not after how she'd acted. Not that she was planning on going on a hunger strike. A girl had to eat. But she'd wait, give him time to go back to his office or wherever he'd gone earlier, so he didn't have to look at her across the table while he ate.

She'd been so horrible to him.

Everything he'd said was true. He'd never judged her on her past. Not once. He'd never raised his voice to her, even when he was furious as he'd been earlier this evening. And she had no doubt that he was telling her the truth now, about everything. She knew his character. He was right about that. She knew more about him than his own family in many ways, things he'd told her about his past, about why he didn't have a relationship with his father and barely spoke to his brothers. That if it wasn't for his mom, whom he loved dearly, he'd never go back home for his infrequent visits. And yet, when she'd been put to the test, instead of believing the best of him—as she should have—she'd proved she was no better than his judgmental father.

She really hated herself right now.

But if she could do it over, and she was honest with herself, she'd have done it the same way. She'd have asked the same questions, said the same things. Because even though she knew in her heart that he was the best person she'd ever met, probably ever would, the difficult lessons of her past continued to rear their ugly heads. The fear that something would happen, that if she and Ian were actually together as a couple one day, he'd destroy all her illusions. He'd hit her, hurt her, turn into the ugly, angry kind of person all of the men in her life had eventually become.

It wasn't fair, to either of them, that she had this irrational fear. But there it was. And she had no idea how she'd ever move past it. Maybe if Ian ever really took a bullet for her, that would destroy her unreasonable fears. And wasn't that a horrible thought? The awful scene between them tonight had been fate intervening. Fate was protecting Ian from the kind of life he might have if they were ever really together. Her mama and all her "daddies" had really messed her up. Ian deserved someone who wasn't damaged goods. He deserved someone supportive, someone who realized how wonderful he was and didn't look at him with doubt, and wonder when the fairy tale would fall apart.

Several hours had passed before she crept down the stairs to stop the growling in her stomach. The house, or at least this part of the massive structure, was dark, lit only by the moonlight in the floor-to-ceiling wall of glass that framed the fireplace.

Assuming Ian was asleep in the master bedroom upstairs, she was as quiet as she could be and didn't turn on any lights. She grabbed a bottle of water and two pieces of pizza from the refrigerator. Whoever had brought the pizza last night must have brought groceries too, because there was fresh milk, eggs and dozens of other items that hadn't been there earlier.

Not wanting to risk the ding of the microwave waking Ian, she sat at the island to eat her slices cold. When she took her first bite and realized the pizza was pepperoni, bacon, extra sauce and extra cheese, the tears started rolling down her face.

She dropped the pizza to the paper towel that she was using as a plate and covered her mouth to keep her sobs of anguish from being heard.

The lights flickered on overhead. Ian stood near the other end of the massive island, still wearing the jeans and navy-blue T-shirt he'd been wearing earlier. He must have been in his office this whole time. His brows furrowed with concern. "Are you okay?"

"Am I okay?" She laughed without humor and swiped at the tears on her face. "How awful do I have to be to you before you stop being so nice to me? I don't deserve your concern. You should hate me by now."

His expression turned sad as he shook his head. "It would be impossible for me to hate you, Shannon." He crossed to the countertop and grabbed a stack of napkins, then set them down in front of her. "Why are you crying? Is it Maria? I haven't given up trying to find her. I've been working on the investigation all evening. Not that I have much to show for it. But I'm doing everything I can. And my guys tell me they're still following up on leads, as well."

She dropped one of the napkins on top of her pizza,

her appetite gone. "Maria. Here I am feeling sorry for myself, not even thinking about my friend. And you've been up all night working to find her. How can you stand the sight of me?"

He moved to stand beside her bar stool, smiling down at her. "Oh, I don't know. From where I stand, you look pretty good."

"I'm serious, Ian."

"So am I." He leaned his hip against the island. "And I haven't been up all night. It's only a little past nine, Grandma."

His good-natured teasing had her smiling in spite of herself. "How do you do it?"

"Do what?"

"You can always make me smile, no matter how bleak things look. I don't deserve to have you for a friend, assuming we're still friends?" She couldn't help the desperately hopeful note in her voice.

He cupped her face and pressed a whisper-soft kiss against her lips, then stepped back. "Friends. Always. If you can forgive my rotten disposition earlier. I shouldn't have gone off on you like that."

"Stop it. Please. Just stop. I'm the one who should apologize—"

"Apology accepted, as long as you agree to eat more than a few bites. Here." He retrieved her pizza from beneath the napkin and put it on a plate. "I'll nuke it for you. Don't forget that I know your worst secrets, like that you hate cold pizza." He shoved it into the microwave.

"You definitely know my worst secrets."

He set the now-warm pizza slices in front of Shannon and took the bar stool beside her. "I think we're even on that score. No more secrets between us. No more lies.

Friends should be able to trust each other and count on each other. Deal?"

"I don't deserve you, Ian."

"We're even on that score too. I don't deserve you either. Do we have a deal?"

She smiled and held up her hand. "Pinkie swear."

He grinned and hooked his finger around hers. "Pinkie swear. And don't ever tell anyone else that I did that. They'll take my man card."

"I'll keep that information in my back pocket in case I ever need to force you to do my bidding."

He laughed, and just like that, it was as if all the hurt of the last few hours had never happened. But it had. And she knew that until she could learn to let go of her fears, if that was even possible, that there was no hope of a permanent future between them. Not the kind of future she'd dreamed about at least. Before finding out that he was a special agent for Homeland Security, she'd thought she'd found her perfect partner. She loved his tattoos. He loved hers. He found her belly ring sexy. And his blond-streaked black hair made her blue-tipped hair seem almost conventional.

"Note to self," he said. "Lose that joke. It fell flat."

She blinked. "Sorry. I was kind of lost in thought."

"Something more important than listening to my jokes?"

She smiled and grabbed for the first thing that came to mind. She certainly wasn't going to tell him that she was fantasizing about his tattoos and what might have been. "Earlier you said you hate this house. It's beautiful. And not pretentious like you might expect from something this big. It has a homey feel to it."

He looked around as if trying to see it through her

eyes. "I guess so. Saying I hate it might be an overstatement. I hate the idea of it, of my rebellious folly just to spite my father. It's a ridiculous waste of money, way too big for one person. And since I'm out of town or out of state most of the time, deep undercover a lot of times, I'm never here. I really should sell it."

"Hmm. Maybe. It would be perfect for a large family. I can see kids sitting around the stone hearth roasting marshmallows in the fireplace. Or catching lightning bugs outside."

"Shannon Rose Murphy, when did you become so conventional? The next thing I know, you'll be wanting a white picket fence and to join the PTA."

She shoved him good-naturedly. "Just because I'm not conventional doesn't mean I wouldn't like to have a family and a nice house someday—minus the picket fence, of course."

"Of course." He tilted his head, studying her. "I can see it. I bet you'd be a great mom. How many kids does future Shannon want?"

She blinked, surprised to feel tears starting in her eyes again.

His smile faded. "Shannon, what—"

She held her hands up to stop him. "It's stupid. I'm sorry. I just… The idea of really having kids is…" She drew a shaky breath. "I never knew who my dad was. He could have been any number of men in and out of my mother's life. And there wasn't a maternal bone in her body. All I was good for was cleaning our run-down apartment or, later, turning tricks to help put food on the table. I'm damaged goods all the way around. No one would want me to be the mother of their children. I'm sure I'd do something to screw them up for life, just like my mom did to me." She hopped off the bar stool. "I'll clean up my mess in here later. I just want to go to bed now. Good night, Ian."

She'd just reached the stairs when he stepped in front of her, blocking her way. He didn't say anything. Instead, he opened his arms. She sobbed and threw herself against him. Then he was lifting her and cradling her in his arms against his chest.

"Ian, stop. Your hurt arm," she protested between tears as he carried her up the stairs.

"You weigh less than a feather. Don't worry about my arm."

She laid her head against him, the feel of his chest beneath her cheek, his arms tight around her so wonderful she quit protesting. He kissed the top of her head and whispered soothing words as he took her into the guest bedroom. A quick dip and he'd raked the covers back. Then he settled her onto the sheets and tucked the covers up around her.

The loss of his touch had her crying again. Being held by him had felt so right, so perfect, as if that was where she belonged.

He gently swept her hair back from her face, his deep blue eyes filled with concern. And something else. His gaze heated as he stared down at her, his fingers growing still in her hair. His Adam's apple bobbed in his throat, and he straightened away from the bed. "I'd better go."

She grabbed his hand and threaded their fingers together. "You don't have to. You can stay. I *want* you to stay."

"I don't think that's a good idea." He tugged his hand free and strode toward the door.

"Ian, wait." She slid off the bed and stopped in front

of him by the balcony outside the guest room. "We've kissed too many times for you to tell me that you don't want me. And I seem to remember you proving to me not long ago that you wanted me very much." She pressed her hand against his chest, then slid it down.

He swore and grabbed her hand, then drew a ragged breath. "Wanting you isn't the problem. It's about doing what's right."

"We're two consenting adults. Unless you're saving yourself for marriage or something."

He laughed and pushed her hand away. "It's a little late for me to save myself."

"Well, we both know I never got the chance to save myself for marriage." She grimaced. "Is that it?" She swallowed and took a step back, pressing a hand to her throat. "Oh my gosh. That's it, isn't it? It's because of my past. You say you don't care, that you don't judge me. But when it comes to the idea of getting naked with me, you're disgusted, aren't you? Because of all those men—"

His eyes flashed with anger, but somehow, she knew the anger wasn't directed at her. He pulled her against him and cupped her face. "Don't ever think that. Nothing that happened to you is your fault. And none of it could make me think any less of you in any way. You're sexy and smart and funny and…" He shook his head. "It's not about your past. It's about who we are and what we want." He pressed his hand over his heart. "What drives me is my passion for law enforcement. But the very idea of that frightens you. I don't think we could ever move past that."

She frowned. "I'm not asking you to marry me,

Ian. I'm not talking about forever. I'm talking about one night."

His hands shook as he cupped her face again and searched her eyes. "Aren't you? I heard the catch in your voice when you talked about having a home, children. I've held myself back all the time we lived in the duplex because there were lies between us. It wouldn't have been right for me to sleep with you while I was hiding the fact that I was a cop—the one thing you hate most. And now that you know the truth, I'm still what you fear. Admit it. You can't trust me."

She started to deny it, but all the hurts and pain of her past made her hesitate. By the time she was able to gather her scattered thoughts again, he'd already dropped his hands. She hated herself in that moment.

He smiled sadly. "Even if we didn't have that between us," he continued, "you hunger for a stable home, for everything you were denied while growing up. I've had that—a mom who loved me, a dad I loved and who loved me back until we had our falling-out. My times with my brothers weren't all bad either. There were a lot of good times. But when I turned seventeen, everything changed. You know why."

"Willow."

He nodded. "Everything changed after that. I changed. I don't want the house and the picket fence and babies. I want freedom to move every few months, to start a new investigation. If I was married, I couldn't do that. I wouldn't do that. It wouldn't be right. I'd settle down, build a life. But I'd be miserable doing it. And that's not a recipe for a successful marriage. So, no, I won't make love to you, Shannon. Even though I want to, so much sometimes I feel like I'll die if I don't."

She fisted her hands and stared up at him. "I don't understand how everything you said means that we can't make love."

"Don't you?" He searched her gaze. "You still haven't figured it out?"

She shook her head. "No. You're completely confusing me."

He shut his eyes for a moment, then blew out a long, slow breath before looking at her again. "I'm in love with you, Shannon. Hopelessly, head over heels in love with you."

Her mouth dropped open in shock.

He laughed bitterly. "I've done a really good job of hiding that. But it's true. And if I take you to my bed, and then have to let you go, I don't know that I could survive. And since I know there's no way that I can make you happy, even if you could look past the fact that I'm a special agent, a future between us isn't even in the realm of possibilities. It's better that we stay friends. Very good friends. And after this case is resolved, you go your way and I go mine. You'll eventually find a man who can give you everything you want, someone who will treat you like a queen and give you babies and a home and who will be there every day. But I'm not that man." He kissed her on the top of her head, then slowly walked away.

Chapter Twenty

What did a girl wear when she was going to see the man who'd told her the night before that he was in love with her? Then promptly rejected her and walked away? Should she pay extra attention to her makeup and hair to tempt him to change his mind? Or should she do herself up to salvage her wounded ego? Whatever the real reason, she fussed over her makeup and hair far longer than usual. And now she stood contemplating which top to wear with her jeans. The red one or the blue one—the only two blouses she had that were clean.

Telling herself it didn't matter since Ian only wanted to be friends, she threw on the red top. Then she changed her mind because it clashed with the blue tips of her hair and put on the blue blouse. Then she cursed herself for caring what she looked like at all and threw the red one back on just to be ornery.

She flounced down the staircase, holding her head high and bracing herself for her first glimpse of Ian. The great room and kitchen were empty. She passed them and headed down the hallway that led to a maze of other rooms, including a game room and a home theater, as well as rooms whose purposes she couldn't quite discern. At the very end was Ian's office. But the door was closed. Afraid that he might be in the middle of working on the case, she went back to the kitchen.

Her stomach chose that moment to rumble, reminding her that she'd eaten only one of her pieces of pizza last night after going most of the day without eating. She felt as if her stomach was going to rub right through her spine if she didn't have something soon.

The groceries in the refrigerator were probably a chef's dream. She imagined someone who knew how to cook really well could whip up an amazing omelet or some other kind of eggs and bacon, and maybe French toast. Since her breakfast cooking skills consisted of knowing how to pour a bowl of cereal or make toast, she did both—first the toast, then the cereal. She knew that much at least. No one liked soggy cereal.

After placing her dirty dishes in one of two drawer-style dishwashers, she thumped her hands on top of the island, wondering what to do next. Had Ian already eaten? Should she bring him some toast and cereal in his office? Rather than guess, she decided to brave the lion's den and simply ask him. She headed down the hallway toward his office.

"Morning. Looking for me?"

She turned around. Ian was coming down the stairs, looking so good in his jeans and black collared shirt that she had to remind herself to breathe. She also had to remind herself that he didn't want her in his life, even though he supposedly loved her. If she went down that rabbit hole again of trying to understand his reasoning, she'd just get herself twisted into knots. Instead, she forced a smile and tried to pretend that everything was normal, that he'd never told her he loved her.

And that she hadn't sat up most of the night trying to figure out whether she loved him too.

Not that it mattered. Love wasn't something she'd ever had in her life, and had never expected to have. How was she supposed to even recognize it? And since he hadn't asked her if she loved him back, did it even matter?

"Did you eat?" he asked as he headed into the kitchen.

"Cereal and toast. Want me to fix you some?"

He wrinkled his nose. "Not my idea of a good way to start the morning, but thanks just the same. I'll whip up an omelet."

Her mouth watered.

He glanced at her as if he could read her mind. "I'll make two, just in case you saved any room."

"I should politely say no since I already ate. But an omelet sounds wonderful."

"Bacon, cheese, peppers and tomatoes okay?"

"Better than okay. Perfect."

He smiled, but she noticed it didn't quite reach his eyes. Regret sat like a cold knot in her stomach.

They ate in strained silence, with an occasional polite inquiry or answer. She'd never felt uncomfortable around him before, and she longed for the easy friendship they'd shared for so many months.

After helping him clean up, she stood on the opposite side of the marble island. "What's the plan today? Are you going into town again to talk to more confidential informants?"

"I don't think so. I put the word out yesterday with the ones I spoke to about letting others know what kind of information I was seeking. One of them will call me if something comes up." He rubbed the back of his neck.

"Honestly, I'm kind of at a loss, not knowing who to trust anymore."

"I don't understand. Did something else happen? Why don't you know who to trust?"

He studied her a long moment, then rounded the island. "Come to my office. I'll show you something."

She followed him down the long hall and stopped in surprise just inside what he'd referred to as his office. "This is a library, not an office."

He'd continued to the large desk sitting in the middle of the room and turned to look at her. Then he glanced around as if for the first time. "I suppose you could call it that. I hired someone to decorate this place. I don't really pay all that much attention to the details since I'm so rarely here."

She stopped beside one of the built-in bookshelves that lined every wall, for two full stories. A balcony that ran the perimeter of the room provided access to the higher shelves. Rolling ladders gave access to the lower ones. "I could read a book every day and never read all of these. This must be what heaven is like."

He shrugged and turned back to his desk.

Her delight in the space dampened with his lack of enthusiasm. She took a seat on the other side of his desk and waited to see what he wanted to show her.

He opened a laptop and typed for a moment, then turned it around, showing a picture of a yellow index card. "This was found in the warehouse where I was supposed to meet Butch and exchange money for Maria and the others."

"Okay." She crossed her arms on the desk so she could lean closer to read it. "Wait. I thought you said he didn't show, that your cover was blown. That card says to meet Wolverine in a parking lot for further instructions."

"It does. But it also says to smile for the camera. The warehouse was wired all over with cameras inside and out. And the original deal was no law enforcement or there was no deal. You were there. You saw what happened."

She nodded. "Within moments of you going inside the warehouse, cops and special agents poured out of the woods and went inside too. I thought that was planned, part of the sting to rescue the women."

"Yes, and to give them the benefit of the doubt, they did wait quite a while. Butch was a no-show. But I wanted to go inside and scope it out before they followed. Unfortunately, they didn't wait. And as a result, no deal. Butch disappeared."

"Did Wolverine show up the next day at the parking lot?"

He shook his head. "I was off the case officially then. But my contacts tell me that my boss staked out the lot all day, just in case Wolverine showed. He didn't."

She sat back. "Then he really is gone. The women have been taken somewhere else. I've lost my chance to rescue Maria."

"I'm not so sure. Homeland Security put a net around Gatlinburg before we even went to the warehouse. They've been working with the state, using agricultural inspections as a guise to search trucks traveling on the highways. Bus stations and airports are under heavy surveillance. There's no easy way for Butch to transport all those girls without coming under some kind of scrutiny. I imagine he's hunkered down somewhere, in a house, maybe a remote barn or something like that until the heat dies down."

The hope that had started to die inside her sputtered back to life. "That's good, if all those people are trying to find them. Someone will see something, notice something. There's still a chance. Right?"

"Yes and no. There are enough people involved so that Gatlinburg PD and Homeland Security have to make it look like they're working hard to prevent Butch from leaving with his victims. But I believe that someone on the inside, maybe even someone in the district attorney's office, is helping Butch, tipping him off so he can stay ahead of any searches. With them protecting him, it makes finding him nearly impossible."

He stared at her, his jaw tight. "In spite of me trying to convince you that most of us in law enforcement are the good guys, it appears that you may have been right to fear me and the people I work with." He punched a key on the laptop and another picture of a yellow index card appeared. "That's what was on the back of the index card in the warehouse."

For Homeland Security Agent Ian McKenzie.

She pressed a hand to her throat, immediately understanding. "Butch knew who you really were even before you went inside the warehouse, before the others showed up."

"He did. And only a handful of people knew my true identity. I've been deep undercover for a long time, putting everything into motion. The only way for him to have known I'm a special agent with Homeland Security is if one of the men I've trusted all this time betrayed me." He snapped the laptop shut and sat back.

"That's what I meant earlier when I said I wasn't sure who to trust."

She swallowed, hard, and asked the question that she had to ask. "I knew who you really were. At least, I did in the days before the warehouse meeting. Am I on your list of suspects?"

He frowned, then blinked as if the idea had never occurred to him. He immediately shook his head. "Of course not. Even if you weren't vested in wanting your friend Maria rescued, you're not the kind of person who would do that."

She gave him a relieved smile. "I'm glad you know that I would never do something like that." She frowned. "Wait. If you found that index card in the warehouse, then whoever betrayed you knows that you know, right?"

"Not yet, or at least I don't think so. I was the only one there with the crime scene tech when he picked up the index card and turned it over. I haven't told anyone about what was on the back because I've been trying to dig into who's working the case to figure out who'd have a motive to help Butch. It's not like a murder scene where we're trying to get DNA or anything like that. Processing the index card isn't uppermost on anyone's priorities. It was dusted for fingerprints and came away clean. As far as I know, it's now sitting in an evidence locker. Eventually, someone will see it, I'm sure. But there's really no reason at present. The focus right now is on locating Butch and his victims."

"How short is your list of suspects?"

He held up his fingers and used them to list the people most likely involved. "My boss at Homeland Security, the Gatlinburg police chief, an assistant district attorney who's been our liaison all along in this investigation, the special agent who's been my liaison with my boss while undercover—"

"Chris Parker? The guy you asked to watch me at the duplex?"

He nodded and lowered his hands. "And you, of course. But I would never consider you as a suspect. Of the four I mentioned, Chris is the least likely. I called in an anonymous tip about him possibly accepting bribes, which initiated an immediate internal review of his finances. He's been put on paid leave while the investigation continues. But my boss mentioned it offhandedly in a status call yesterday when I asked him how the search for Butch was going. From what Nash says, Chris's bank records look squeaky clean, so they realize the tip is likely wrong."

"And he's a friend of yours?"

He winced. "Yeah, I know. Heck of a way to treat a friend. But lives are on the line here. I'll tell him later why I did it. The most it does is inconvenience him and give him a paid vacation for a while. I'm sure he'll understand."

"I appreciate you letting me in on these details about the investigation. But I'm puzzled about why you did it."

"No more secrets or lies. That was my vow to you yesterday. And I know how much Maria means to you. I wanted to lay it all out there so you'd know what's being done to find her."

"You're a good man, Ian."

His mouth tilted in an almost-smile. "For a cop, right?"

"You're a good man, period. Proof that there are good cops out there. I'm just sorry it took me so long to realize it."

His gaze captured hers for a long moment, as if he was searching for something. Then he picked up the manila folder sitting on one side of his desk and set it in the middle. "I need to get back to studying the case file, diving into the backgrounds on my pool of suspects and seeing if there's anything I can do to steer the investigation based on my findings." He waved toward the bookshelves. "You're welcome to look around, find something to occupy your time while you have to stay here. I know you love to read."

She glanced longingly at the bookshelves, but shook her head. "Maybe later. Ian, how long do you think Butch will keep the women in hiding before he gives up?"

"Gives up? I don't see him ever turning himself in."

"That's not what I mean." She splayed her hands on top of the desk and drew a shaky breath before voicing her deepest fear. "If he feels the net around the city is too tight and he won't be able to escape with the women, do you think he'd try to escape on his own? Would he leave the women behind somewhere, locked up so they can't get away and tell anyone about him? Could they even now be without food, water, left on their own to…" She choked on the last word, but from the grave look in his gaze, she knew she didn't have to say it. And her questions didn't seem to surprise him either.

"You've already thought about that possibility, haven't you?"

He gave her a crisp nod. "It's my deepest fear, that we'll find them after it's too late to save them. Which is why I need to get back to work."

She put her hand on top of his, stopping him from opening the folder. "You need a sounding board, don't you? Someone other than me. Someone who's smart *and* has a background in law enforcement. Someone who knows the system and has established contacts over several decades. Someone who isn't currently connected with the police, Homeland Security or the district attorney's office, but yet knows the inner workings—I would imagine—of all three groups."

His jaw tightened, and he tugged his hand from beneath hers. "Don't, Shannon. Don't ask me to do that. You know I can't. You know why."

She gave him a sad smile. "Yes, I know why. Maybe it's time he knows why too. And maybe you can give him this chance to atone for what he did, and in the process save the lives of thirty women. Ian, the time has finally come. You need to go see your father."

He shoved back from his desk and left the room, firmly shutting the door behind him.

Shannon's shoulders slumped. In the span of just a few days, she'd managed to destroy her most treasured friendship. And now she'd made the man who'd professed to love her become the man who hated her. He'd trusted her enough to tell her about what happened all those years ago. He'd trusted her enough to tell her how he felt about her. And he'd trusted her enough to share details about the case, even though she knew it was against the rules of his job. And what had she done? She'd turned on him. Or at least that was how he must feel. And now he'd literally walked out of her life. There was no coming back from this. She'd well and truly lost him.

The door opened behind her. She turned in her chair to see Ian standing there in his black leather coat, carrying her jacket across his arm.

She stood and slowly crossed the room. "This is it, then, I guess. You're turning me over to someone else to guard me until the danger has passed?"

"No. We're going to see the Mighty McKenzie."

Chapter Twenty-One

When Ian pulled into the long row of paved parking spots in front of his parents' two-story cabin that rivaled his monstrosity in size, he didn't recognize any of the vehicles parked out front. But the green-and-white SUV with a National Park Service shield on the door was a big clue.

"Ian?" Shannon asked beside him. "Is something wrong?"

He arched a brow.

Her face flushed. "I mean, besides the fact that we're even here—which I sincerely appreciate. I know how hard it was to—"

He covered her hand with his. "It's okay, Shannon. I can never stay angry at you for long, and I'm way past that. It's just that asking my father for help in any way is a bitter pill to swallow." He motioned toward the other vehicles. "Especially since he took my phone call as an opportunity to stage a mini family reunion, or maybe an intervention. My brothers are here."

"Oh." She gave him an apologetic look. "I'm really, *really* sorry."

"If the Mighty McKenzie patriarch can help us rescue some victims of human trafficking, it will all be worth it." At least, that was what he kept telling himself.

One of the thick wooden double front doors opened and his mother stood there, smiling and waving. He could see the sparkle of tears on her cheeks. "Ah, hell. She's crying."

Shannon followed his gaze. "Your mom?"

"Margaret McKenzie, in the flesh." He squeezed her hand again. "Prepare yourself. She's a hugger."

The look of panic that swept over her face had him regretting his warning. "It's okay. If you want, I can be the bad guy and tell her to leave you alone, not to touch you. I'm pretty used to the bad-guy role in my family. I don't mind."

"No, no." She wiped her hands on her jeans and smiled through the windshield at his mother, who looked about ready to jump out of her skin waiting for them. "It's just…weird. I don't think my mother ever hugged me."

Ian was so stunned that he didn't get out of the Charger fast enough to open Shannon's door. Like the amazing woman she was, she marched right up to his mom and let herself be wrapped in what was likely a bone-crushing grip. His mom was almost as tall as him, and not exactly on the small side.

"Mom, let her go. I don't think she can breathe," he teased as he reached them.

"Oh, goodness. I'm so sorry." She smiled through her tears at Shannon. "It's just that Ian has never brought anyone home to meet us before." His mother held both of Shannon's hands in hers. "It *is* Shannon, right? I think that's what William said."

"Yes, ma'am."

Shannon seemed about ready to hyperventilate as she looked at Ian. He was about to correct his mother's assumption that they were a couple, but she didn't give him a chance. It was his turn for a bone-crushing hug.

A few moments later, a cough sounded behind her and she let him go, wiping her eyes. "It's been so long. I wish you'd visit more often."

"Let them in, Margaret. It's downright cold outside."

Ian stiffened at the sound of his father's voice. It was Shannon's turn to comfort him. She slid her hand in his and squeezed, then continued to hold his hand, which gave him the perfect excuse not to shake his father's hand as they moved into the foyer. Instead, he nodded.

His father nodded just as stiffly, then smiled warmly at Shannon. "Miss Murphy. I'm Ian's father, William. The woman who was crying all over you is his mom, Margaret. Welcome to our home."

"Um, thank you, sir. We, ah, appreciate your help, especially on such short notice."

Ian knew how intimidating his parents could be. Given Shannon's past and how uncomfortable she had to be meeting a former judge and prosecutor, he couldn't be prouder of her. He squeezed her hand again and smiled when she looked at him. She offered him a tentative smile in return.

His father's smile faded as he turned to Ian. "You indicated in our phone call that you're in a hurry, that the reason for this meeting is of an urgent nature. We can talk in my office." He smiled at Shannon again. "Miss Murphy, would you like to join us or would you prefer to stay out here with Margaret? I'm sure she'd love another opinion on the decorations she's planning for our sons' upcoming weddings here on the property."

Ian's mom surprised him by shaking her head. "I can tell that Shannon wants to be a part of your discussion."

Shannon looked grateful when she met his mom's gaze. "Yes, ma'am. I'd like that very much."

Margaret smiled. "No problem, dear. You go on ahead with the men. Normally I'd insist on being a part of the discussion too. But I really am behind on helping make some decisions on the upcoming weddings. I'll get back to it." She headed toward the kitchen.

His father hesitated. "Might as well be comfortable. We'll meet in the great room instead of the office."

As if on cue, or as if they'd been listening, which was what Ian assumed, his brothers emerged from the hallway that led to the office. Shannon seemed to sink against his side as he reintroduced his brothers to her. He knew she was remembering their first meeting in the hospital, when they'd all pointed guns at her. To be fair, she'd aimed a gun at them too.

Ian chose a love seat to the left of the fireplace for him and Shannon. Once everyone was settled, he dove right in and brought them up to speed on what was happening with the human trafficking investigation and the dilemma he found himself in.

"I don't know who to trust. Someone on the inside had to have blown my cover. I can't think of any other way for them to have found out." To his family's credit, not one of them looked at Shannon with any suspicion or questioned whether she could be the mole.

Ian continued. "I can't even tell my boss about what was written on the other side of that index card without knowing whether he's the one who betrayed me. I'm at an impasse, and time is running out for the victims."

Adam sat forward. "Your boss put you on administrative leave. I'm putting my money on him being the mole."

"That's my thought too," Ian agreed. "He's never done anything before to make me suspect that I couldn't trust him. And I can't think of any reason for him to have suddenly turned to the dark side. But if he is sabotaging the search, then it's my duty to prove it so I can ensure that we have the best chance at actually finding and saving these young women." He grimaced. "And kids. From the pictures I saw, two of them are little more than children."

His father rested his forearms on his knees, looking deep in thought. "Either the chief of police is rotten, the special agent in charge at Homeland Security is rotten, or it's the assistant district attorney. Have I got that right? No one else knew about your cover?"

"I did," Shannon admitted. "Not all along, just recently. But I knew before the botched deal at the warehouse."

His father smiled kindly. "I appreciate that, Miss Murphy. But Ian is here with you, which means he trusts you one hundred percent. That's good enough for me."

She exchanged a surprised glance with Ian.

He gave his father a curt nod. "Thank you, sir." He cleared his throat. "There's one other person who knew—Special Agent Chris Parker. He's been my liaison in the field the whole time I've been here. Chris and I have been in the trenches together many times, and I don't feel that he could be involved. However, to be certain, I sent an anonymous tip to internal investigations that he was accepting bribes. They suspended him pending an investigation."

Duncan let out a bark of laughter. "I'll bet he loved and appreciated that."

"I'll make it up to him sometime. The investigation is ongoing. But they dove in fast, and everything is checking out. He's not our guy. That kind of strategy, an anonymous tip, won't fly for someone more senior like my boss. They'd investigate, but they'd be a lot more careful and would take their time. He wouldn't be suspended until they found credible evidence."

"You don't need to get him suspended," his dad offered. "You need to trick him, and the others. Keep it simple. The goal isn't to gather evidence for prosecution at this point. You need to identify the mole, remove him from the investigation so you can get the ball rolling and make sure every effort is truly being made to find the women. And those poor kids." He shook his head. "You won't need anything elaborate. Just fast."

"What do you suggest?" Ian asked.

"Pick three different locations for a sting operation. You can put out the word to each of your suspects that one of Butch's men contacted you and is willing to trade information and testify against everyone else involved if he can cut a deal. I'm assuming this Butch guy has enough men in his chain of command that it will fly."

Duncan nodded. "I like that. It's simple, like Dad said. And it lets you find out right away which one is your mole."

Shannon glanced around, then looked at Ian. "Everyone else looks like they understand. But I'm lost. How exactly will you find out who blew your cover?"

"My father is suggesting that I feed the same fake information to the police chief, my boss and the ADA and let them know that I'm meeting Butch's guy who's squealing on him. I tell them each a different location, but the same time. I'd have to get each of them to agree not to come there, that it has to be just me and the informant or they'll bolt. I can use the disastrous warehouse debacle as justification for going it alone. Whichever one of them shows up is the mole."

Shannon's eyes widened with alarm. "But won't the mole show up planning to try to kill you and the informant?"

"Yes, but I wouldn't give him that opportunity. I'd pick locations with limited access, then spy on all the approaches using long-range binoculars. It won't matter if he tries to ambush me. I won't be in a position for him to get me. The goal is just to find out who shows up. Low risk, high reward." He nodded. "It could work." He stood, and this time he offered his father his hand. "Thank you, sir. Sometimes an obvious answer is hard to see when you're deep inside of the problem you're trying to solve. I appreciate your perspective."

Everyone stood.

His father smiled as he shook Ian's hand. "Happy to help, son."

"You can't be in three places at once," Adam said. "And you're still pursuing the investigation on the side, isn't that right?"

Ian shrugged. "I've got a few contacts I can tap, see if they'll help." He put his hand on Shannon's back to lead her out.

"You already have three people right here who can help." This time it was Duncan who spoke.

Ian stared at him in surprise. "Are you volunteering?"

His three brothers exchanged looks, then nodded in unison.

"We all are," Colin said.

"Why?" Ian asked. "Why would you offer to do that?"

Adam stepped forward and put his hand on Ian's good shoulder, probably remembering that his left one was still sore. "We're family. That's what family does. We have each other's backs. Let us do this for you."

Ian studied each of them, automatically suspicious of their motives. "What do you get in return? What do you want?"

Shannon gasped beside him. "Ian, I think they really do want to help."

Colin grinned. "He's right, lass. There's a catch."

"I knew it," Ian grumbled.

Duncan and Adam frowned as if they had no idea what their brother was talking about.

"Just a minute." Colin jogged to a decorative table against the far wall that was stacked with envelopes. He brought one back and handed it to Ian. "Your official wedding invitation. Agree to be there, and we'll help you find your mole. Using us will be way faster than you having to find three other people in a short time frame like this."

Ian reluctantly took the envelope. "This is blackmail. I'm pretty sure you're committing a felony right now."

Colin's grin widened. "Peyton will be thrilled to see you there."

Duncan smiled. "Remi has been dying of curiosity to meet you. She'll be happy to see you there too. Thanks, Ian."

He gave them a curt nod, still not comfortable with the way they were all getting along these days. Maybe he should start a fistfight just to get his world back on its normal axis.

An hour later they'd planned out the locations, time, and Ian had finished contacting the ADA, police chief and his boss to set everything up. He rose again to leave. But when he held out his hand to Shannon, she shook her head and settled back against the love seat.

"I'm not going anywhere," she insisted, crossing her arms.

Ian sat back down and leaned in close so he could whisper. "Are you okay? What's wrong?"

She gave him an irritated look and made no attempt to whisper her reply. "Your brothers don't have to leave right away since the meeting time everyone agreed to is several hours from now. Which means we all have time to address the elephant in the room. Ian, I think it's high time that you told your father why you ran off when you were eighteen. It's time for you to tell him why you've resented him all these years. You need to tell him about Willow."

Ian's entire body flushed hot and cold as he stared at the one person he'd trusted, ever, with his secret. And now she was throwing it out in front of his family like a bone to a dog.

"Why are you doing this to me?" he whispered harshly.

"Willow?" his father asked behind him. "Is she talking about Willow Rivera?"

Ian ignored him and continued to look at Shannon. "Why?"

"Because I know what it's like to harbor resentments inside you. You nurture your wounds and feed them until they fester like poison. You have to get them out in order to heal. You have to forgive in order to move on and find peace."

"What do you know about getting out the poison and moving on?" he bit out.

She stiffened but didn't look away. "I forgive you for lying to me."

He stared at her in shock. "You forgive me?"

"Who's Willow Rivera?" Colin asked.

"Beats me," Adam replied.

Shannon took Ian's hands in hers, her eyes brimming with tears. "I do. I forgive you. And I trust you, with all my heart. I really do. And that's what I want for you. I want you to get the poison out and begin to heal."

"Ian?" His father sounded shaken. "Please, son. What's this about?"

Uncaring of his audience, Ian cupped Shannon's beloved face in his hands and kissed her. When he pulled back, she shuddered and gave him a fierce hug. He held her a long moment, then kissed her again before sitting back beside her with his arm around her shoulders. But this time he wasn't trying to give her strength. He was drawing his strength from her.

His brothers and father stared at him, a host of confused expressions on their faces as they each sat back down and waited.

Ian announced to the room at large, "Willow Rivera was an eighteen-year-old woman I met when I was fifteen. Father found out about her and thought she was a bad influence on me. He ordered me not to see her anymore. I tried to explain to him about our relationship and what was really going on. I tried many times. But he refused to listen."

His father's face reddened. "There was nothing to explain. She had a criminal record, for prostitution. What has this got to do with anything?"

"You refused to listen," Ian repeated. "Willow needed help, not condemnation. She wasn't a prostitute by choice. She was a victim. Her stepfather was pimping her out, beating her, withholding food. He forced her to walk the streets. I was her friend. I was trying to help her. But when she needed me the most, you essentially kidnapped me and took me up to a cabin hundreds of miles away for a two-week father-son fishing trip. You tricked me into going with you. Had I known we'd be gone that long, I would have refused to go."

His father frowned. "I was trying to get my son away from a bad influence."

Ian gritted his teeth. "When we finally came back," Ian said, "Willow was gone."

"Thank God," his father said.

Ian stared at him incredulously. "God had nothing to do with her fate. You can chalk that up to the Mighty McKenzie. She was desperate, with nowhere to turn. Her one friend in the whole world—" he thumped his chest "—me, I wasn't there for her. She ran away to escape her abusive stepfather and got taken in by what we now call a human trafficker. He killed her, Dad. You failed her. We both failed her. And she paid for our sins with her life."

His father's face turned ghost-white. "That's why you hate me? You blame me for her death?"

Ian closed his eyes for a long moment, then slowly shook his head and met his father's tortured gaze. "I don't hate you. I thought I did, for a very long time. But I hated myself even more, for not standing up to you, for being too afraid to outshout Mighty McKenzie and make him listen. Every time I tried to tell you the truth about her, you shut me down. I should have fought harder, made you listen. After her death, I was so disgusted and ashamed that I became the juvenile delinquent you believed me to be. And from then on out, everything I did was to spite you. If I was doing too well in school, I'd purposely not turn in an assignment or flunk a test. You wanted me to go to college, so I ran off the day I turned eighteen, determined that you would never see me make anything of my life. I wanted you to feel like a failure because I'd failed already, in the worst possible way, and blamed you."

His father's eyes were bright with unshed tears. He cleared his throat. "But you're with Homeland Security. I don't—"

"Understand how they'd take a total screwup?" Ian glanced at his brothers, who were riveted on the conversation but, surprisingly, weren't jumping in to tell him what an idiot he was. Beside him, Shannon had tucked herself against him and had her hand on his back, as if to give him strength. The anger that had been flowing through him as he recounted his disastrous youth seemed to drain away. "I went to college on a full scholarship. I just never told you about it. I got a degree in criminal justice and worked briefly as a sheriff's office intern before joining Homeland Security. I became what you wanted me to be. But I never told you, because I didn't want you to have that satisfaction. And I've spent my entire life blaming you every time something went wrong, when all along—" he blew out a deep breath "—it was my failings that haunted me."

His father tentatively put his hand on Ian's shoulder and stared deep into his eyes. "I was so worried about you, thinking that woman—"

"Willow."

He swallowed. "Willow. I thought I was protecting my son. I cut off every conversation where you tried to bring her up, because I was so upset that I'd failed you in the first place by not realizing you were associating with someone whom I thought to be a bad influence, until it was nearly too late. I thought I was doing the right thing." He shook his head. "I was wrong. I'm so sorry, son. So deeply sorry that I hurt you, and that Willow paid the price for my stubbornness."

"I'm sorry too." This time it was Adam who spoke. "I was your big brother. When you started to rebel and get in trouble, I should have sat you down and talked it out, found out what was really going on. Instead, I let my anger drive my actions. I should have been there for you, but I wasn't. I'm sorry, Ian."

Duncan cleared his throat, looking decidedly uncomfortable. "We were all too quick to judge you. We were your worst tormentors as teenagers. We should have had your back. Instead, we just got mad because it seemed like you were getting all of the attention, bringing the family down, making Mom and Dad look bad to their friends. We should have known there was a reason you were acting out. But none of us took the time to ask you. I wish I could have a do-over, Ian. But hopefully we can move forward and have a new start. That's the best I can offer. But it's a sincere offer. I want you in my life, in our lives."

His father, who still had his hand on Ian's shoulder, nodded in agreement, as did Adam.

Colin slapped his hands on top of his thighs and looked around at all of them. "I agree that Adam and Duncan were total jerks growing up. It's about time they apologized for it."

Adam and Duncan both shoved him off the couch onto the floor.

"Hey, hey, quit picking on the favorite son here." Colin grinned, then pointed at Ian. "Made you smile."

Ian shook his head, surprised to realize that he was indeed smiling at his brothers' antics.

His father's hand tightened on his shoulder. "I love you, son. More than you'll ever know. I hope you'll give me the opportunity to prove it, and be a part of our lives going forward. I don't deserve it. But I'm asking you to give me a chance." He stood and held out his hand.

Ian hesitated. He'd never expected this moment to come in his life. His father had been the villain of his story for so long. Even as an adult when he'd finally realized he'd overblown his father's culpability, that he was using him as a crutch, blaming everything wrong in his life on his relationship with his father, he'd never once envisioned a moment where they'd be able to set the hurts of the past aside. And if it wasn't for Shannon, he'd never have known how badly he wanted to do that.

He stood and shook his father's hand.

His mother came into the room, wiping her hands on her apron and smiling. "I've got fresh-baked chocolate-chip cookies and some…" She blinked and stared at Ian and his dad, who still hadn't let go of Ian's hand. "Ian? William?" She couldn't seem to formulate anything beyond that.

Colin jumped up from the floor and shoved Adam and Duncan before hurrying out of their reach to stand beside his mother. "Cookies sound great, Ma. I'm starving." He put his arm around her shoulders and pulled her with him toward the kitchen.

Adam and Duncan got up, shaking their heads.

"You're always starving," Adam accused.

Shannon smiled up at Ian from the couch.

His father let his hand go and motioned toward the kitchen. "Your mother still makes the best chocolate-chip cookies in Tennessee. And she won't let you leave without trying them. You might as well give in." He winked at Shannon, then followed the others out of the room.

Ian pulled Shannon to her feet and wrapped his arms around her, holding her tight. "I was furious with you for starting all of that. Now I realize you're wise beyond your years. I feel like a weight has lifted off my shoulders. Maybe not quite all the way yet, but mostly."

"It will take more than one conversation and a handshake to heal your soul, Ian. It took me years to forgive my mom for what she did to me. But when I did, I realized forgiveness is something you do for yourself, not for others. It's important to forgive in order to move on. I'm so glad you're beginning to feel that same joy."

He stared at her in wonder. "About what I said, at the cabin. I'm not so sure that I—"

"Ian, Shannon." Colin stood on the other side of the room. "You coming or what? Adam's scarfing down all the cookies. We'll have to roll him out the door later."

"I heard that," Adam yelled from the kitchen.

Colin grinned and winked before disappearing again.

Ian took Shannon's hand. "Come on. It looks like the rule is that when you more or less reconcile with your family, you have to eat chocolate-chip cookies."

"I can think of worse things."

They headed into the kitchen.

A short time later, Ian led Shannon outside to his car. He held the passenger door open for her, then pulled her in for a kiss. When he finally came up for air, she pressed a shaking hand against his chest.

"Wow," she breathed. "Whatever I did to deserve that, let me know so I can do it again."

He grinned, feeling lighter than he had in a long time. But as they headed back down the mountain, the reality of what still remained to be done and the life-and-death stakes pressed in on him. "After I drop you off at my cabin, I'm going to check in on my confidential informants and look around town to see if there have been any sightings of Butch or the others. Eventually I'll head to the duplex and get us both some fresh clothes. Even with my brothers' help, I don't know how many more days this thing will drag on."

"I'm sure I can amuse myself with that wall of electronics at your cabin, or that library. It makes me drool just thinking about all of those books. Although if you don't mind grabbing the book I was reading at my house, that would be great. I'd like to finish it."

"The Lisa Gardner thriller?"

She blinked. "You remember which book I was reading? I'm impressed."

"Yeah, well. I'm a special agent, you know. I notice things like that."

She rolled her eyes.

He grinned.

When he pulled into the driveway, he started to get out, but she put her hand on his. "You've given me your alarm code, a door key and the phone number for your current burner phone. I think I can handle walking myself to the front door. Go on. You have a lot to do. I'll be fine."

He cupped her face and kissed her, but forced himself not to deepen the kiss, or he'd be there all day. He wanted her so much. And there were things he needed to tell her, things that had surprised him, things he'd never expected until he'd sat in the kitchen with his family today and looked around and, for the first time, felt like maybe he just might belong. But those things, those epiphanies about himself—about the future he now realized he wanted—would have to wait.

After watching to make sure that she got in okay, he took off down the winding mountain road toward Gatlinburg.

Chapter Twenty-Two

Shannon had just finished straightening up the kitchen after lunch when the doorbell rang. She froze, not sure what to do. No one knew that Ian McKenzie lived here, not even his family.

If he'd ordered a package to be delivered, he'd have told her. She was sure of it.

Her gun was upstairs, in the bedside table. Should she get it? Or just ignore whoever was at the door and hope they'd go away?

The doorbell rang again. She jogged to the stairs to get her gun. Then she'd call Ian and—

"Shannon?" a woman's muffled voice called through the front door.

She froze, her hand tightening on the railing. This wasn't possible. It had to be a trick. That voice couldn't be who it sounded like.

A frantic knock echoed in the foyer. "Shannon, it's Maria. Please. I came to warn you. They're on their way here."

The palpable fear in the woman's voice along with her words sent a chill snaking up Shannon's spine.

"Please, hurry. Shannon?" The doorbell rang several

more times. "Hurry! If they see me standing out here, warning you, they'll kill me. Let me in."

Shannon ran to the front door and looked through the peephole. A sob caught in her throat when she saw that her ears weren't playing tricks on her. Maria stood there in a tattered blue dress and bare feet, dark curly hair matted and whipping around her face in the frigid wintry air. She didn't have a coat. Her entire body shook, either from the cold or fear, probably both. Her dark brown eyes looked hollow and bleak. Tears streamed down her face.

Behind her in the driveway was a bright yellow Camaro with the driver's door standing open. It was parked sideways as if Maria had turned a half circle for a quick getaway. With the house's elevated position in front of the steep driveway, Shannon could clearly see that no one else was in the car. She looked left and right. The road that wound around the mountain out front was clear.

"Shannon, please—"

"Maria," she called through the door, desperately wanting to open it. But none of this made sense. "What's going on? How did you know I was here?"

"I heard them talking about you, the men holding me. One of them said they found out your boyfriend was a special agent, and discovered where his parents lived. They hid in the woods by the parents' cabin. You were there with the agent earlier today, right?"

Shannon pressed a hand to her throat. "How did you know that?"

"I told you. I heard them. They put a GPS tracker on your boyfriend's car and got this address. They're planning an ambush. Let me in before they get here or we're both dead. Please!"

An ambush? Oh, no. She had to warn Ian.

"Come on," Maria pleaded, looking over her shoulder. She banged on the door again.

Shannon threw it open and wrapped her arms around her friend. Maria clung to her, tears wetting Shannon's blouse.

"I can't believe you're actually here," Shannon said. "I'd almost given up hope of finding you. Don't worry. I'll call Ian and he'll—" Behind her a rapid beep started in the hall.

Maria shoved out of her arms. "I think that's your alarm. It's about to go off."

"Oh. Hang on." She ran to the keypad and entered the code, disabling the security system.

"I'm so sorry, Shannon. He was going to kill my baby. I didn't have a choice."

Shannon turned, her mouth dropping open in shock. Maria was now clutching an infant against her chest, wrapped in a yellow blanket.

Beside her was the tall, lanky man who must have handed her the child. Shannon recognized him as one of the men she'd seen at the truck stop when Ian had told her to wait in the car.

Ian had called him Wolverine.

Greasy hair hung to his shoulders. A triumphant grin curved his lips as he aimed a pistol at her.

She slowly raised her hands. "What do you want?"

He cocked his head, as if contemplating her question. "What do I want? Hmm. I want a lot of things. I want to make a living without interference from do-gooders. I want the money I would have made from this latest shipment. But mostly, I want to kill a very special agent, the one who ruined everything and brought the heat down on our operation. And after I saw that tender kiss he gave you outside his family's cabin, I decided a bullet was too good for him. It will be much more enjoyable to make him suffer, by making you suffer." He narrowed his eyes and stepped closer. "Then I'll kill you both." He slammed the side of the pistol against her head.

Chapter Twenty-Three

With still no sightings of Butch or his minions, Ian finally headed to the duplex. Once he had another duffel loaded with shoes and clothes for both him and Shannon, he started for the garage. He'd only made it to the couch before his phone rang. It was Adam. He plopped the duffel onto the couch beside him and sat to take the call.

"The ADA was a no-show," Adam announced. "Which is good to know. Cameron Ellison always seemed like a stand-up guy to me. I'd worked with him in Memphis before both of us moved back here. I'm glad I didn't completely misjudge him."

"You know Ellison personally? From your Memphis days?"

"Personally might be stretching it. But professionally, yeah. He always seemed fair, and had a great prosecution record. Looks like you can mark him off the list of potential suspects for blowing your cover."

"That's good to know. Thanks. Really appreciate your help."

A few minutes later, Duncan checked in, followed by Colin. They both said pretty much the same thing as Adam. Neither the police chief nor Ian's boss at Homeland Security took the bait. After thanking them, Ian called his boss to tell him everything that he'd been doing. He told him about Wolverine being Andrew Branum, about his lack of success in any of his informants seeing or hearing any word on the street about any of the traffickers they were trying to find. Lastly, he told him about the evidence on the back of the index card. He had to hold the phone away from his ear while his boss yelled obscenities at him for even suspecting he could be a mole. It took several minutes to calm him down.

"Have you made any progress in the investigation?" Ian asked.

"Not much better than you. I've got the full cooperation of Gatlinburg PD as well as our guys, resources coming at me left and right. But we still don't have a lead on where the women are being held."

"Maybe knowing Wolverine's real name will help shake something loose on your end. I had someone look him up but he didn't find any assets here in town. And I haven't figured out the real names of the other two thugs that work for Gillespie. So, basically, I've got nothing."

"I'll get some of my guys to dig deep into this Andrew Branum. Maybe he's hidden assets under some shell companies. Everything else has been a bust so far. The BOLO on his yellow Beetle hasn't yielded any sightings. If he's still in town, he's driving something else now."

"About my administrative leave—"

"Ah, hell. Consider it over. It's not like you really took a break anyway. Might as well be official so you can commandeer any resources you need in a pinch. But once this thing is over, you're taking some time off. A lot of it. That's an order."

Ian grinned as he ended the call and slid the phone

into the pocket of his leather coat. He reached for the duffel, then paused. If the ADA, police chief and his boss weren't moles, then how had Butch and his men found out that he worked for Homeland Security? He couldn't think of anyone else who knew his secret, aside from Shannon, Chris and, of course, his brothers. None of those were viable possibilities. Who, then?

No one. There just wasn't anyone else.

Then how?

He sat on the couch, thinking it through, looking at every angle. He thought back to all the times when he'd even discussed the fact that his real name was Ian McKenzie, and that he was a special agent with Homeland Security. And he realized there just weren't that many times he'd said those two things out loud. Even in his dealings with his liaison, Chris, everything was in code. When they spoke, they made cryptic references to what they were doing, or put things in writing—which was rare—and then destroyed those messages immediately. Heck, the only place he'd ever spoken to Chris openly about their mission was when he'd brought him to the duplex to guard Shannon.

He straightened. It was also at the duplex where he'd spoken to her about being a special agent. He'd been in her bedroom and apologized for all the lies. And he'd been in jail all night right before that. If Wolverine saw him being arrested, which he'd assumed he would since the van had left right before the police arrived, then he would have known his side of the duplex would be empty.

His blood ran cold. He jumped up and started tossing the place, looking under lamps, taking apart the smoke detectors in the ceiling, unscrewing light switches. Then he stood at the kitchen counter looking down at the re-sults of his search—six electronic listening devices, three from Shannon's side of the duplex and three from his. Knowing that the traffickers had been in Shannon's home had him sick to his stomach. Thank God she hadn't been hurt.

He stared at the transmitters. They were still on and sending data. Which meant that everything he'd just said to his boss had been heard by whoever was on the other end of the bugs.

He swore.

If his boss was right, and Wolverine did have as-sets in town hidden under a maze of shell companies, it wasn't likely that he'd be sitting around waiting for them if they showed up to seize those assets. Wolver-ine was in the wind now, on the run. So how were they going to find him?

Ian pondered that question as he smashed the devices. Then he grabbed the duffel and headed into the garage. He was about to get in his car when another thought occurred to him. If Butch's men had bugged the duplex after becoming suspicious that Ian was a cop, could they have done something else? Like put a tracker on his car?

He didn't see how. Since that night at the hospital, he'd kept his car in the garage specifically because of the fear that someone might put a tracker on it. He'd parked it on the street out front only once, hoping to draw Butch's men out. But he'd watched it the whole time. No one had come near it.

Plus, every time he'd come back to the duplex or driven around town, he'd taken the long way back to his cabin outside of Gatlinburg for the specific purpose of making sure that no one could follow him. In fact, the only time the Charger had been out of his sight was when he'd gone to the café to talk to Adam. But, as always, he'd kept an eye on his mirrors and drove a circuitous route to ensure that no one followed him to the café. There was no reason to think that anyone would have randomly seen his car parked behind the building and decided to put a tracker on it.

He shook his head. He was getting paranoid. He tossed the duffel into the back seat and slid behind the wheel when it occurred to him that there *was* one place he'd gone where he hadn't parked in a garage. A place where he'd been for several hours without being in view of his car.

His parents' cabin.

No one could have followed him there without him knowing. But Butch and his men knew his real identity. A short internet search would lead them to the Mighty McKenzie, and his parents' cabin. They could have hidden in the woods, waiting to see whether he'd show up at the house. But when they saw the National Park Service SUV parked out front, they decided it was too risky to shoot him there. Instead, they could hide a GPS device on his car while he was inside, and attack him later when he wasn't with other law enforcement officers.

He shoved the door open and made a quick check of the car's underbelly. A few minutes later, he stared in growing dread at the magnetic tracking device that he'd found in the rear wheel well. They'd known every place he'd gone since leaving his parents' home. Which meant they knew where his cabin was located, and where he'd left Shannon, alone.

Oh, dear God. Please, no.

He grabbed his phone in a panic and pressed the button for his home number.

No one answered.

SHANNON WOKE TO the rancid smell of unwashed bodies and urine, and to the worst headache she'd ever had. She groaned and reached for her head.

"Don't," a familiar-sounding voice told her as fingers slid up Shannon's arm and gently eased her hand back down. "Don't move or even try to talk. And please don't touch your head. I just got it to stop bleeding. I don't want you bumping it and starting it up again."

"Maria?" Her voice sounded as groggy as she felt. "Is that you?" She blinked, but she couldn't see anything. It was pitch-dark. She blinked again, panic rising inside her. "I can't see."

"Shh, it's okay. None of us can. The cops are searching for them, so no lights. Nothing that might give away our location. It sucks, but it is what it is. There's a portable toilet in the corner. And some bottles of water and a small stash of food. You need to pee? I can help you to the toilet."

She started to shake her head, then realized Maria couldn't see her. "No. Where are we? What happened? You had a baby in your arms. And then that awful man—"

"Wolverine. That's what the little twerp likes to call himself. And it fits, in spite of how scrawny he looks. He's like a rabid animal and he'll turn on you in a second, tear you to pieces. Shannon, sweetie, I'm so sorry for betraying you. I didn't have a choice. He had my baby. He was going to kill her. He forced me to go up there and draw you out of the house. I didn't want—"

"Stop. I understand. I'm just glad that you're okay. But how did he know to use you to draw me out?"

"I've talked about you often enough that he knew we were friends. Once he figured out that you had a connection to that special agent—"

"Ian."

"Right. Once he heard that, he came up with a plan to use me as bait. I'm really sorry."

"It's all right. We're both alive. And so is your baby. That's what matters. But we need to get out of here if we're going to stay alive. We need to—"

A loud metallic screech was followed by a blast of sunlight. She raised her hand to shade her eyes, blinking to try to focus with the sudden change in light.

"No, leave us alone," Maria yelled. She cowered over a small yellow blanket, shielding her child with her body. And for the first time, Shannon realized where they were. And that she wasn't alone. There were dozens of women—most of them painfully young—huddled around each other like cattle in a barn.

A shadow fell over her. She looked up at a man, his features obscured because the sun was behind him. But she'd know that silhouette anywhere. He was the man who'd hit her back at Ian's house—Wolverine.

Two more men stood off to his right, one to his left. She recognized all of them from the truck stop meeting. Ian had been trying to locate Maria while rescuing human trafficking victims in his constant bid to atone for what had happened to Willow. Or at least that was what Shannon had thought. Now she knew he was also doing it as part of his job. Most likely the women he'd been trying to save were the same ones stuffed into this tight space with her right now.

Wolverine motioned toward the men on his right. "Hulk, Blade, put the fear of God into our girls. I don't want anyone making any noise and giving us away."

Our girls? Why was he talking like the boss, instead of one of the lackeys?

The red-haired man gave Wolverine an aggravated look. "You know I hate that nickname."

"Yeah, well. I like it. Go on."

Wolverine turned to the man on his left. "Grab her."

Shannon jerked back but he lifted her off the floor, pinning her arms to her sides. She drew breath to scream, but Wolverine slapped a piece of duct tape over her mouth.

Chapter Twenty-Four

Ian paced back and forth in front of the fireplace in his cabin, trying to blot out the sounds of the police and special agents on the phone, rattling papers and milling around in what had become their impromptu headquarters for the search for Shannon. He kept replaying the events of the past few days over and over in his mind. But he was coming up empty. He'd followed every possible lead to find Maria and the others. And now the traffickers had Shannon too. And much to Ian's surprise, he now knew that it was Wolverine who was their leader, not Butch. There was no question about that. Wolverine had jammed a knife into the log wall outside the front door, impaling a bright yellow index card that read, YOUR GIRLFRIEND DIES TONIGHT.

And just in case Ian hadn't finally connected the dots of yet another yellow index card to Wolverine's love of yellow clothes and cars, Wolverine had done him the favor of actually signing his name.

Ian reached the end of the room and turned around again. Nash rushed in from the kitchen area, where he'd been speaking to a group of agents studying the maps spread out on top of the island.

"What?" Ian demanded. "You've got something?"

Nash held his hands out. "We haven't found her yet. But I was right about the Andrew Branum name leading us through shell companies. He has a home in the Smokies just west of Gatlinburg. And he didn't get a chance to strip the place before we found it. The home is a treasure trove. Pictures, journals, cash." He handed his phone to Ian. "Recognize any of those guys? The team at the house took pictures of photographs inside Branum's home office. They seem to match your descriptions of the thugs that hang with him."

Ian swiped through the pictures. "Hulk, Blade, Jack. That's them." He handed the phone back.

"In addition to Butch Gillespie—your Hulk fellow—we've got the other two guys' real names now. Our buddies at the FBI ran their pictures from the Branum house search through their facial recognition database and got hits. We're following up on last-known addresses and getting warrants to search their properties. But Branum is the only local. The other guys are from out of state."

Ian grimaced. "Which means they're dead ends as far as leading to somewhere around here and finding Shannon."

"Maybe, maybe not. We've got their pictures now, and we're circulating them all over the place. Someone has to have seen them." He put his hand on Ian's shoulder. "I'll let you know when I've got something more." He motioned toward one of the groups of agents, and they headed down the hallway toward Ian's office.

"Nice place."

Ian turned to see Adam striding in from the foyer. Behind him were Duncan and Colin.

Stunned to see them, Ian asked, "What are you doing here?"

"Alerts about Shannon's abduction have been sent to everyone in law enforcement in a hundred-mile radius. A few quick calls and we heard the task force is forming right here, in my brother's cabin, which I didn't know about."

Ian rubbed the back of his neck, not sure what to say. "I don't... I should have—"

"I was teasing," Adam said. "I'm just not that good at it. Seriously, we're here to help. What's been done so far? What's the status of the search?"

Colin and Duncan flanked him, both nodding to indicate their willingness to help in the hunt for Shannon.

Ian brought them up to speed. "We've got people everywhere looking. Except for going door-to-door to every single cabin in the Smoky Mountains, I'm at a loss." He fisted his hands at his sides. "I've never felt so helpless in my life."

"What about the truck stop?" Adam asked. "Hiding Shannon and the other women in the back of one of those semis would be the perfect setup. Easily mobile, if it wasn't for all the roadblocks and traffic stops that are being done. He could have the women sitting there waiting until the cops give up. Then he just drives away."

"It's been searched already."

Colin and Duncan exchanged a surprised glance. Duncan said, "There must be two hundred semis parked there on any given day. Shannon's only been missing for a few hours."

"It was searched a few days ago while trying to find the thirty women that we believed Butch Gillespie was keeping prisoner. Of course, now it seems that Branum, Wolverine, is our main guy. Anyway, it wouldn't make sense for him to risk going in there for one person. He'd take Shannon wherever he's keeping the others, to con-solidate resources."

"Every truck was searched?" Colin asked. "How did your boss get warrants to search every single truck?"

Ian frowned and glanced down the hall where Nash had disappeared. "I didn't ask him for the details. I was supposed to be on administrative leave at the time. I just assumed... Ah, hell." He strode down the hallway with his brothers following behind.

Nash was talking to some other agents working at Ian's desk. Without preamble, Ian interrupted him. "When you had the truck stop searched, did our guys go inside every truck?"

"I can answer that," one of the other agents said. "I was in charge of the search. Of the two hundred ten vehicles there at the time, the owners of one hundred seventy-two of them agreed to a search, which we did."

"And the remaining thirty-eight?" Ian demanded. "What about those?"

"Some left without being searched." He held his hands up. "We couldn't legally stop them on private property without a warrant, and we don't have proba-ble cause to get warrants without some kind of evidence specific to each truck. But our nets around the city have been effective. Each semi is forced to stop at an agricul-tural inspection station out on the highway. We're using the regulations in place to force searches. It's been one hundred percent effective."

"Except that you haven't found the missing women yet," Adam added.

The agent's face flushed. "Not yet."

"How many of the original thirty-eight are still at the truck stop?" Ian asked. "Any of them?"

The agent swallowed and pulled out his phone. He thumbed through a series of texts, then said, "Ten. There are ten rigs we haven't searched that are still there."

Nash joined the conversation. "What are the odds of getting warrants to search them?"

"Pretty much zero, sir. No one has reported seeing anything unusual, nothing we can use to get a judge to sign a warrant."

"What about *smelling* something unusual?" Adam pulled out his phone. "You cram a bunch of people in a small, tight container like that, even during the winter it's going to stink. A cornucopia for air-scent tracking canines. If one of them alerts on a container, you've got your probable cause. No warrant needed."

He stepped away from them to speak on the phone for a moment. When he returned, he said, "I've got one of the National Park Service's search-and-rescue teams on their way to the truck stop right now. ETA is only five minutes. The dog handler lives down the road from the truck stop."

Nash motioned toward the agent who'd been in charge of the original search. "Get our guys in the area to head over to the truck stop. Have them meet the SAR team and show them which rigs to check out."

"On it." He punched some numbers on his phone.

Ian moved to stand beside his brothers, so tense he felt like he'd explode any second. About ten minutes later, Nash's phone rang. He answered, then set the phone on the desk. "You're on speaker, Special Agent Bledzinski. Give us the status."

"Yes, sir. The dog's here now. An agent is with the handler, directing him to the trucks."

The room went quiet, everyone listening as the agent continued to broadcast the status of the search.

"What's taking so long?" Nash demanded. "We're only talking ten trucks."

"Yes, sir, but it's a huge area to cover. The ones we need to search are spread out all over the place."

"Is there a yellow one?" Ian asked. "I remember a yellow rig at the back-left corner when I met Wolverine and his men there. He's got a weird fascination with the color yellow."

Nash nodded. "Did you hear that, Bledzinski?"

"Yes, sir. That rig is on our list. We'll head there right now."

Ian's stomach flipped. Adam put a hand on his shoulder while Colin and Duncan flanked him on the other side, all of them waiting.

An excited bark sounded through the phone.

"He's alerted on the trailer, sir!" Bledzinski yelled.

Ian waited, barely breathing as he listened intently.

"No driver. The back is padlocked. They're cutting it now."

Ian closed his eyes. Adam's hand tightened on his shoulder.

Chaos erupted through the phone. Some screams, shouts.

"Bledzinski," Nash demanded. "Sitrep. What's going on? Bledzinski?"

"Just a moment, sir." There was more noise in the background, then the sound of static before Bledzinski's voice sounded through the speaker again. "We've got them, sir. Thirty-one souls. And they're all alive."

A chorus of yells sounded behind them where other

agents and police had come into the office to listen to the search in progress.

Adam grinned at Ian. "Thirty-one. You said there were thirty, plus Shannon makes thirty-one."

Ian forced a smile, but until he knew for sure that she'd been found, he wasn't ready to celebrate. He crossed to the desk. His boss was on the side of the room now, speaking to some of the policemen. His phone was still sitting on the desk. Ian picked it up and spoke into it. "Special Agent Bledzinski, can you confirm that one of the women is Shannon Murphy?"

"Of course. Hold on, sir." He could be heard in the background yelling over the noise, asking if one of the women was named Shannon Murphy.

It was an agonizing few minutes before he finally came back on the line. "Negative, sir. According to a woman here with a baby, Shannon was here. But she was taken away before we arrived."

Ian squeezed his eyes shut. Thirty-one, the thirty women in the photographs, plus a baby. Not Shannon.

"How long?" he asked, his voice hoarse. "How long ago was she taken away?"

"Approximately fifteen minutes, sir."

The room went silent again. Ian wanted to shout and storm and rage. Fifteen minutes. They'd missed her by fifteen minutes. But venting his anguish wouldn't help her. And every moment he stood here doing nothing was a minute more that she was in Wolverine's clutches.

He grabbed the phone and began barking orders as he ran toward the kitchen. "See if the witness saw the vehicle that took Shannon. Check the surveillance video. Find out which way it turned once it left the truck stop.

Put out a BOLO and get officers out on I-40. I need a description of that car, Bledzinski."

"Yes, sir. Working on it."

Ian stopped in front of the kitchen island and shoved his way in between some of the agents to look at the large map spread out on top.

"Hey, wait a minute, here," the agent complained.

"Back off." Colin moved into the room, followed by Adam and Duncan. "Give him space."

"Do it." Nash ran in, slightly out of breath. He wedged his way in beside Ian. "We'll talk about chain of command later, McKenzie. But I've got your car description." He plopped a piece of paper onto the map. "It's a Hummer H2. Yellow."

"Of course it is," Ian muttered. "Which way did it go out of the truck stop?"

"East on I-40."

Ian grabbed one of the pens on the island. "Assuming he'll go the speed limit to avoid attracting attention, there's only so far he could have gone. Roadblocks can be set up within ten minutes. Accounting for speed and distance…" He mentally made the calculations, then drew a large circle that encompassed the truck stop and a large radius around it. "We'll need roadblocks here, here, here and here. And a lot of resources out searching." He glanced up. "Assuming you approve, of course. Boss?"

Nash rolled his eyes and grabbed his phone. "I'll take care of it."

Ian tossed the pen on the island and motioned his brothers to follow him into the great room. "The state troopers will be looking for him on the interstate. That's covered. Which means he'll exit soon, if not already, and end up on one of the roads I marked on the map.

That's a lot of miles in between, from the truck stop to where they'll set up the barriers. And there's a lot of forest and rough terrain surrounding that area. With that Hummer, he could go off-road. I want to get out there and be a part of the search, try to figure out where he may have left the pavement. We'll need every man or woman we can get."

"Four main roads," Adam said. "Looks like we're splitting up again."

They agreed which roads they'd cover. Ian looked at each of his brothers in turn, then cleared his throat. "She means the world to me. I appreciate this, more than you know."

"Then we'd better find her," Adam said.

They took off running for the door.

Chapter Twenty-Five

Ian passed half a dozen Gatlinburg police cars on his way down the road that he'd chosen to search. He was relieved that so many of them were out looking for Shannon. But like him, they must not have found any evidence of the Hummer having come this way, or he'd have received a call.

He'd stopped at probably fifteen houses along the way doing knock and talks, seeing whether anyone had noticed the flashy yellow vehicle. But no one had. As he slowed to turn around at the roadblock to search this side road yet again, his phone buzzed in his pocket. He pulled to the shoulder and checked the screen. But he didn't recognize the number. "Special Agent McKenzie."

"This is Special Agent Bledzinski. Nash gave me your number."

"Did someone find her?"

"Uh, no, sir. Not that I know of. I'm still here at the truck stop, interviewing potential witnesses while the techs comb the inside of the truck and—"

"Is this going somewhere, Bledzinski? I'm trying to find a missing woman."

"Sorry, sir. Yes, it's just, well, I got a call from one of the women we rescued, the one with the infant. You remember, she was the one who saw Miss Murphy. Well, an agent at the hospital patched her in on a conference line with me so we could talk and—"

"Bledzinski. Spit it out."

"Right. She said the suspect known as Wolverine said something odd to Miss Murphy. It was something along the lines of 'Smile. You're going to be on camera.' Does that mean anything to you?"

"You bet it does." He ended the call, flashed his badge and drove around the roadblock. At the next turnoff, he punched the number for Adam and sped down the two-lane road.

Adam answered on the first ring. "Ian, have you found her?"

"No, but I think I know where she is. Remember I told you about that warehouse outside of town, the one where I was supposed to do the exchange to free the women? There were cameras all over the place. And the yellow index card read, 'Smile for the camera.' The woman who saw Shannon taken at the truck stop said the man who took her said, 'Smile. You're going to be on camera.' I think he's taken her there so he can—" he cleared his tight throat "—so he can film whatever he's going to do to her. He probably plans on sending it to me later, to make me suffer, after he makes his escape."

Adam swore. "Is Nash on the way with some agents?"

Ian made a sharp left onto another side road and slammed the accelerator again. The Charger's powerful engine whined as the car started up the mountain. "I haven't told Nash or the others yet. This may be my only chance to save her. I'm worried some yahoo will go in hot with lights and sirens, speed up the access road and be seen by Wolverine's cameras. This has to be done right, or she doesn't stand a chance. I want the element of surprise on my side. But I can't do this alone. I need someone I can trust."

"You can trust me, Ian. You can trust Colin and Duncan too. You know that, right?"

He turned another curve, then began to slow. "I do. I'm trusting all of you with Shannon's life. And mine. I need you to be my backup."

"Give me the address. I'll contact the others."

He gave him the address. He pulled his Charger to the side of the road and popped open the glove box. Being deep undercover rubbing elbows with bad guys had its perks, like owning a picklock set and knowing how to use it. He shoved the kit into his pocket and headed into the woods.

"I'm ten minutes from there," Adam said. "I just texted Duncan and Colin. They're even closer. We'll all rendezvous on the access road. I assume there's some tree cover close by so we can hoof it from there without being seen."

"There is. The best approach is behind the structure, the southwest corner." He hopped over a small ditch and jogged up the other side, then took off running again. "I don't remember any cameras back there since the lot doesn't run behind the building. That's where I'll come in, and where you guys can come in once you get there."

He crouched and carefully parted some bushes. Sure enough, a yellow Hummer sat boldly in the parking lot, right in front of the warehouse. He crept backward, then took off through the trees again, giving the parking lot and its cameras a wide berth.

"Ian, give me a call when you get there so we can coordinate our entry."

"I'm already here. Wolverine's Hummer is here too. I can't wait for backup." He ended the call and turned off the phone in case his brother called back. He didn't want the sound to give away his position. Then he leaped over the last ditch and ran to the back door of the building, picklock set in hand.

SHANNON STIFFENED AS Wolverine traced the knife across her throat, then used it to flick the ends of her hair.

"Blue tips." He snickered. "I suppose you consider yourself a rebel. A badass."

She strained against the zip ties that bound her to the folding chair in the middle of the room. "Cut me loose and find out. Just you and me. One-on-one."

He grinned and continued to circle the chair, running his knife across her hair, her shoulders, her legs, before stopping in front of her. "One-on-one time is what we're having right now. Aren't you enjoying it?" He leaned in closer. "I know your boyfriend will." He laughed and pointed toward the camera on the ceiling above her. "I want him to agonize over every…little… slice." He flicked the knife across her bare knees to emphasize each word, drawing more blood as he added to the dozens of cuts he'd already made.

Shannon sucked in a breath at the burning pain, biting her lip to keep from screaming. She knew that was what he wanted. And she wasn't about to give in. He wanted to send the video to Ian, her final moments. She prayed he'd never see it. But just in case he did, she wanted to make sure it was quick. She'd been baiting Wolverine since he'd enclosed her in this room and sent his men off to guard the warehouse. But no matter what she said, she couldn't seem to rattle him and make him just kill her and end his sick game.

His phone buzzed in his pocket. He frowned and pulled it out, studied the screen. Then he made a call. "Jack, Hulk, one of the sensors picked up something in the woods. Form a welcoming committee outside in the tree line. Blade, back hallway, southwest corridor. Keep an eye out. I think McKenzie might already be in the building. Remember, hurt him. But don't kill him."

Shannon made a choking sound in her throat.

He smiled, enjoying her fear. "Looks like I underestimated your boyfriend." He shoved the phone in his pocket. "He doesn't stand a chance against Blade." He grinned. "I really do love that name."

"Leave Ian alone," she gritted out between clenched teeth.

"Now, now. Don't look so worried. Blade knows that I want your lover to see the video before he dies. He'll just soften him up, get him ready. But he won't kill him. I get to do that. After he sees the video." He cocked his head. "Or should we do a live show for him? Draw him out in the open to make Blade's job easier? Then he can watch in real time as I carve you up." He drew back the knife and plunged it into her thigh.

A BLOOD-CURDLING SCREAM echoed in the warehouse. *Shannon.* The picklock kit fell from Ian's hands to the floor. The metal wands pinged across the concrete. He took off running through the maze of dark hallways toward the main part of the warehouse.

A light shone through a rectangular window in a door at the end of a hall. Ian ran to it. He could see the open part of the warehouse on the other side, all lit up, empty.

And the only other rooms where Shannon could be were on the opposite side. Grasping his pistol in his left hand, he threw back the door and charged through the opening.

A flash of movement to his left had him whirling around. Something hard and solid came crashing down on his arm, sending his pistol clattering across the concrete floor and knocking Ian to the ground. He rolled over to face the threat. Blade. He glared down at Ian, a two-foot length of iron pipe in his right hand. He tapped it against his open palm and slowly approached.

Ian jerked his head back, searching for the pistol. Six feet away.

Blade roared and brought the pipe down in a lethal arc toward Ian's head.

Ian slammed his shoe against the other man's knee and dove to the side. Blade screamed with pain and rage as he crashed to the floor, but he still managed to swing the pipe toward Ian. He jerked out of the way, the whistle of the pipe just inches from his ear. It banged against the floor, showering both men in stinging flecks of chipped concrete.

Blade staggered to his feet and raised the pipe again.

On the other side of the warehouse, a pale face peered out through another glass cutout in one of the doors. Wolverine.

Blade roared.

Ian dove for his gun. The pipe slammed against his side. White-hot pain incinerated the breath in his lungs. Black spots swam before his eyes. His fingers cramped around the gun but he held on, fighting through the blinding pain to flop onto his back. He blinked furiously, trying to focus. Blade towered over him, lifting the pipe above his head. Ian twisted the pistol up toward him and squeezed the trigger. *Bam! Bam! Bam!*

The pipe dropped from Blade's hand. He stared in disbelief at Ian. Then his eyes rolled back in his head and he crumpled to the floor.

Ian struggled to draw air into his lungs as he fought through the haze of pain in his ribs. He looked across the warehouse toward the door. Wolverine jerked back from the glass.

A gunshot echoed outside. Two more followed in quick succession.

Another scream filled the warehouse.

Ian staggered to his feet and then took off in a pained crouch toward the door where he'd seen Wolverine.

"CHANGE OF PLANS," Wolverine snarled to Shannon. "Your boyfriend is here. You die *now*." He raised the knife above his head.

Ian was here? Shannon no longer wanted to die. She wanted, needed, to live, to keep this creep occupied to give Ian a better chance at survival.

The knife came down in a deadly arc.

She threw all her weight to the side, turning the chair over and crashing to the floor, the metal frame banging against the concrete.

Wolverine fell to the floor beside her, swearing as the knife clattered across the room and bounced against the far wall. Blood smeared his wrist where the knife had cut him as he fell. He glared at her, his face contorted with rage. "You'll pay for that."

A loud thump sounded against the door. "Shannon!" The doorknob rattled, but it was locked from the inside.

Shannon twisted around to see Ian banging his fist on

the glass. "Ian!" She furiously strained against the plastic straps tying her to the chair. She had to let him inside or she'd die in here. She didn't want his last glimpse of her to be Wolverine stabbing her to death.

Wolverine swore and shoved to his feet. He ran across the room where the knife lay on the floor. Shannon rocked her body, scooting the chair toward the door as she struggled to pull her arms free.

"Cover your eyes!" Ian yelled.

She turned her head away from the door and squeezed her eyes shut.

Something slammed against the glass. It shattered, raining down onto the floor like pennies hitting a metal roof.

Wolverine twisted around on his knees, knife in hand.

Shannon looked back over her shoulder.

A shadow loomed behind Ian.

"Look out!" Shannon warned.

He jerked away from the small opening in the top of the door where the glass window had been. She couldn't see him. The sounds of grunting and bodies slamming against the door told of the violent struggle on the other side. She desperately shimmied and scooted, moving closer to the door.

Another shot echoed outside. Seconds later loud banging sounded from somewhere in the warehouse. Someone else was here. *Please let it be the police.* Her silent plea startled her, and she would have laughed if she weren't so terrified. Who would have thought she'd ever hope for the police to come help her?

Wolverine shouted his frustration and scrambled to his feet, holding the knife out in front of him.

Another loud thump sounded from outside. The door rattled in its frame.

Wolverine let out a terrifying war cry and ran toward Shannon.

The door burst open and slammed against the wall, an iron bar bouncing across the floor. Ian stumbled inside, a pistol clutched in his hand. He swung it toward Wolverine.

Bam!

Wolverine's body jerked, then fell to the floor, his knife skittering over to land right in front of Shannon. His body went limp and his eyes closed. Blood began to seep out from underneath him.

"Shannon, oh my God. Shannon. How badly are you hurt?" Ian dropped to his knees beside her, setting down his pistol so he could run his hands frantically across the cuts on her arms and legs, smearing the blood as he tried to see how bad her injuries were.

"I'm okay." She grimaced when his hand touched the deep stab wound on her thigh.

Ian swore and took off his leather coat, wincing and moving awkwardly.

"You're hurt," she said. "Did you get shot?"

"I got hit by a truck."

"Oh, no, Ian!"

"Kidding. It just felt that way." He gently wrapped the coat around her thigh and tried to tie the sleeves together.

She gasped at the white-hot pain that shot through her leg.

He shot her a sympathetic look. "Sorry. Trying to stop the bleeding, but this stupid leather is too bulky." He looked around, then unbuckled his belt and wrapped it

around her thigh, looping the ends together before stopping. "This is going to hurt. Bad. But it has to be done."

"I know. It's okay. Do it." She turned her face away,
bracing herself. He jerked the belt tight. Blazing hot
pain radiated up her body. She gulped in deep breaths,
trying not to cry. But she couldn't help the whimper
that escaped.

"All done," he told her, his voice hoarse. "Let me get
those zip ties." He grabbed the knife and moved behind her.

The sounds of footsteps had both of them looking
through the open doorway. Ian's brothers were running
through the warehouse toward them.

Ian snorted. "The cavalry's here. A little late, but they
still get points. I think they ran into Jack outside. He
must have been tougher than he looked." He cut through
the ties on Shannon's legs and moved to her hands.

She smiled up at him. A whisper of noise from the
other side of the room had her jerking her head to the
side.

Wolverine was staring at her, a mad light in his eyes
as he brought up a pistol she hadn't even realized he had.

Ian dove over Shannon's body, throwing the knife
like a javelin toward Wolverine.

Bam! Bam!

Wolverine dropped the gun and clawed at the hilt
protruding from his neck.

Ian's brothers raced into the room, pistols out as they
scanned for danger.

"Ian?" Shannon nudged him with her good leg. "Ian?"
He lay on top of her, unmoving. "Ian!"

Adam ran to Wolverine's body and kicked his gun out
of reach, then dropped to his knees to check his pulse.

Colin and Duncan raced to Ian and rolled him over.

Shannon gasped in horror at the bullet hole in his shirt. "Ian, damn you! When you said you'd jump in front of a bullet for me, I never actually wanted you to do it."

He groaned. His eyes fluttered open.

Hot tears ran down Shannon's face. "Oh my gosh, oh my gosh. Ian?"

"Ouuucch." He grimaced. "I don't know what hurts worse. Where Wolverine shot me or where Blade slammed an iron pipe against my ribs."

The two brothers exchanged a glance. Then Colin pulled out a pocketknife and moved behind Shannon.

"Ian's been shot?" Adam rushed over to them, his phone to his ear. "I've got an ambulance and police on the way. Wolverine won't be hurting anyone else. He's gone." He got down on his knees beside his brother.

Shannon willed Ian to look at her, but he stared straight up at the ceiling. "Ian, talk to me. Say something."

"What's that crackling sound every time I breathe?"

"I think it's your ribs." Duncan grasped Ian's shirt and ripped it open. "God bless whoever invented bullet-resistant vests."

The plastic ties around Shannon's wrists fell away, and Colin moved to check on Ian. Shannon reached for him, but Duncan stopped her and gently pushed her down on her back. "Sorry, lass. You're bleeding from a couple dozen different places. We need to get the bleeding under control."

"How bad are her wounds?" Ian's voice sounded oddly weak.

"Bad enough. How far out is that ambulance, Adam?"

Shannon blinked up at Duncan. He was pressing against her wounds, but she couldn't feel anything. Except...cold, so very, very cold.

"ETA ten minutes." Adam leaned over Shannon, his brow furrowed with concern. "Don't worry. The ambulance will be here soon."

"Guys," Colin called out, sounding worried. "I don't think all the blood on the floor is from Shannon."

Adam leaned over Ian, running his hands up and down his shirt. He froze, then met Colin's gaze. "One of the bullets missed the vest. It went in through the arm opening."

"Ian?" Shannon called out, except it sounded fuzzy to her ears. "Ian?"

Adam swore. "We're losing both of them. Duncan, keep pressure on her wounds. Colin, call 911 again. Tell them we need a medevac chopper out here."

While Adam stripped off his coat and then balled up his shirt to stanch the bleeding, Shannon stretched her fingers toward Ian. She entwined them with his and squeezed.

He didn't squeeze back.

Chapter Twenty-Six

Shannon leaned back on her crutches beside one of the massive outdoor heaters, doing her best to blend into the background of the massive tent. The McKenzies were across the way in a receiving line, shaking hands with the last of their wedding guests as they said their good-byes. Ian glanced at her, looking more handsome than ever in his black tuxedo, even sitting in a wheelchair.

She'd teased him about dyeing his hair back to its natural black color, telling him he might have to turn over his rebel card. He'd insisted that he'd only done it so that he'd match the tuxedo better. Just like she'd chosen to wear a blue dress to match the blue tips of her hair. If she didn't know better, she'd think he was developing a sense of humor, much like his brother Duncan.

Since the shooting a little over two weeks ago, Ian had definitely been smiling more than she was used to seeing. He seemed happier, less tense. And she didn't think that it was because the case he'd been working on was wrapped up. It was all about being reunited with his family, especially his father. They had a long way to go to heal years of hurts between them. But they were well on their way.

He winked and turned back to shake the hand of some

senator or representative, or maybe it was a judge. She'd lost track of all the dignitaries who had attended the double-wedding ceremony of Colin to Peyton and Duncan to Remi. The Christmas weddings had been amazing, taking place in the building a few feet away from the tent. The family called it a barn, even though it had never been used to house any animals.

The barn's interior was rustic, but homey, filled to bursting with strands of white party lights and red poinsettias to go along with the holiday-themed occasion. Everything had been perfect, especially Ian's family. They'd been so kind and welcoming, as if she was one of them.

She and Ian had both been staying at his parents' cabin, although in separate bedrooms, while they recovered from their injuries. A home-care nurse stopped by daily to check on both of them, but mainly she was there for Ian. Wolverine's bullet had tumbled around inside his chest and done enormous damage. And Blade had shattered two of Ian's ribs. It would take a long time for him to heal.

Shannon's injuries had been far less severe. The blood loss had nearly killed her, and she'd needed surgery to repair the lacerated muscles in her thigh. But all of her other cuts had been paltry compared to what Ian had suffered. Tomorrow morning, she was returning to the duplex.

Ian had insisted she could stay with him at his parents' home as long as she wanted. She'd given him some lame excuse about being homesick. In reality her savings were pretty much wiped out, and she desperately needed to get another job. She couldn't afford to stay here any longer, even though she would have loved to continue to be by Ian's side. Thankfully, a victim's fund had covered her medical bills or she would have had those hanging over her head too.

Now that the guests were gone, the McKenzies surprised Shannon by returning to the barn instead of going up to the family's cabin.

Ian maneuvered his motorized wheelchair until he was directly in front of Shannon.

"Hey, pretty lady," he teased. "Did you have fun tonight?"

"You know I did, handsome man. I only hyperventilated twice, when the police chief shook my hand and when your boss stopped to chat with me."

"You'll get over your law enforcement phobia yet."

She smiled. "Some of them aren't that bad." She leaned down and pressed a soft kiss against his cheek.

He grinned. "Whatever I did to deserve that, tell me so I can do it again."

"Your boss said you'd donated the use of your cabin as a temporary halfway house for the human trafficking victims. You're an amazing man, Ian McKenzie."

He shrugged, looking uncomfortable with her praise. "Yeah, well. It sits there empty most of the time. Might as well serve some kind of purpose. Besides, once I met your Maria, and found out she was actually Willow Rivera, I had to do something to help her get a new start in life. I'd already failed her all those years ago. I'm just glad her stepfather lied and she was still alive. Had I known, I would have—"

"You would have joined Homeland Security and dedicated your life to helping others? I think you can let go of all that guilt, Ian. You did everything that can be done and more. You've done far more to help other people than most ever dream of doing. Maria—Willow—is happy and healthy. And now she can look forward to giving her baby girl the life she never had for herself. You did that, Ian. You and you alone."

He stared at her intently, but didn't say anything.

Beginning to feel uncomfortable, she forced a laugh and waved toward the barn. "I assumed your family would head up to the house. Why did they go back inside the barn?"

"Pictures. Mom wanted to snap some of her own on her phone so she can post them on social media without having to wait for the professional photos. You'll join us, won't you?"

"Of course. I'd love to." She reached for his hand, but instead of turning the wheelchair and heading up the path, he jerked her forward and caught her in his lap, knocking her crutches to the ground. "Ian, what are you doing? I could hurt your ribs and—"

"My ribs are wrapped so tight I can barely breathe. Trust me. There's no way you could hurt them."

He pushed the button on his wheelchair and carried her forward until they were in front of the barn's massive entrance, which was standing wide open. His family was smiling and laughing inside at the other end as his mother snapped pictures.

Shannon smiled and looked up at Ian. "I love your family. I'm going to miss them terribly."

He gently cupped her face. "They love you too. So do I."

She blinked against the rush of tears that burned the backs of her eyes. "Don't."

He frowned. "Don't tell you I love you?"

She twisted her hands in her lap. "It's cruel. As soon

as you're healed, you'll go back to work and disappear deep undercover on another case. I'll probably never see you again."

He gently tilted her chin up so she would look at him. "Explain to me how it's cruel that I tell you I'm in love with you."

A single tear slipped down her cheek. "You know why," she whispered.

He smiled tenderly. "I think so. But I need you to tell me, to be sure."

She shoved his hand away and stared down at her lap again. "Because I'm in love with you too." She drew a ragged breath. "There. I said it. Okay? We love each other and it doesn't matter."

"Then I wasted a lot of money on this for nothing."

She jerked her head up, then froze. He was holding a gorgeous pear-shaped diamond solitaire ring on a band of white gold. And the diamond wasn't like any other diamond she'd ever seen. She drew a sharp breath and pressed her hand against her throat. "It's…blue."

He laughed, his eyes sparkling. "To match your hair." He gently brushed the tears from her cheeks. "I thought I knew what I wanted, and then I met you and realized I'd been fooling myself all these years. I've been running away from the very things that matter most—family, belonging and, most important, love. I love you, Shannon. You gave me back my family. You gave me acceptance, hope and love before I even knew that's what I needed. *You're* what I need. And it took almost losing you for me to understand that. Marry me, Shannon. Marry me and make me the happiest man in the world. And I swear that I'll do everything I can to make you happy too."

She drew another ragged breath and shook her head. "I can't."

His smile faded, and he slowly lowered his hands to his lap. "Why? We love each other."

"Because I don't want you to hate me years down the road when you look back and realize you gave up the career that you'd worked so hard for, because of me. You're an amazing special agent. You love the work you do. I couldn't bear it if I took that away from you."

He cupped her face again, the ring sparkling where he'd shoved it on the end of his thumb. "What I want is you, and everything that comes with that. A home, whatever kind of house or cabin you want. And babies. I want babies with your gorgeous green eyes and jet-black hair. The blue tips can wait until their teenage years."

She drew a ragged breath again. "You're being cruel again."

"No, I'm putting all my cards on the table. I'm going all in to get what I want. Because we both want the same things. We want a life we can be proud of, a life we can build with each other. And I want to get to know my family again. That means being here, not running off for months and years. I don't have to be a special agent working undercover to help others. All I have to do is open my checkbook. Think about it, Shannon. If you can't marry me for love, marry me for money. You can help me use it to build real halfway houses and help victims of human trafficking and other horrors far more than I could as a special agent."

She stared at him in shock, too afraid to hope. "You really want to do all that?"

He nodded. "I do."

"Then the answer is no. I can't marry you for your

money." This time she cupped his face in her hands. "But I will marry you for love." She leaned forward and kissed him.

He growled deep in his throat and deepened the kiss, threading his fingers through her hair and showing her just how much he loved her and wanted her.

"Um, excuse me. Does this mean she said yes?" Adam called out.

Shannon broke the kiss, her face flushing with heat when she saw that all of Ian's family was watching them from inside.

Ian held up the ring. "Well?"

She grinned and held up her hand. He slid the ring on her finger and kissed her again.

His family cheered and clapped.

"Hurry up," his father called out. "The governor only swore me in as a temporary judge until midnight. If I'm officiating, we have to do this in the next few minutes."

Ian drew back, laughing.

Shannon stared at his family, who'd all suddenly lined up at the front as if they were a wedding party. And his father was standing behind the podium with a Bible on top, just like he'd done hours earlier when he'd officiated at his other sons' weddings.

"A surprise wedding, Ian? You planned this?"

"Let's just say I was really, really hoping. I didn't want you to leave tomorrow and go back to the duplex. What do you say?" He searched her gaze. "I was banking on your love of the unconventional. But if you prefer to wait and get a white wedding dress and—"

She pressed her fingers against his mouth. "No. This is perfect, better than anything I could ever hope for. I love you, Ian. More than you could possibly imagine. I love you, and I want to marry you right this minute."

"That's good," his father called out. "Because that's about all we have left. Hurry!"

Ian pressed the button on his wheelchair and zipped up the aisle. Shannon laughed as she held on to the arms of the chair to keep from falling against his chest and hurting him.

"I do," he said, as soon as they were in front of his father.

Laughing, Shannon said, "I do too."

His father blinked and looked around, then shrugged. "Then I guess I pronounce you husband and wife. Go on. Kiss or whatever." He rolled his eyes and closed the Bible.

Ian's family cheered and surrounded them as he planted a laughing, sloppy kiss against her lips.

* * * * *

SOUTH DAKOTA SHOWDOWN

NICOLE HELM

outh Dakota,
the inspiration I needed.

Chapter One

Bonesteel, South Dakota, wasn't even a dot on most maps, which was precisely why Jamison Wyatt enjoyed being its attached officer. Though he was officially a deputy with the Valiant County Sheriff's Department, as attached officer his patrol focused on Bonesteel and its small number of residents.

One of six brothers, he wasn't the only Wyatt who acted as an officer of the law—but he was the only man who'd signed up for the job of protecting Bonesteel.

He'd grown up in the dangerous, unforgiving world of a biker gang run by his father. The Sons of the Badlands were a cutthroat group who'd been wreaking havoc on the small communities of South Dakota—just like this one—for decades.

Luckily, Jamison had spent the first five years of his life on his grandmother's ranch before his mother had fully given in to Ace Wyatt and moved them into the fold of the nomadic biker gang.

Through tenacity and grit, Jamison had held on to a belief in right and wrong that his grandmother had instilled in him in those early years. When his mother had given birth to son after son on the inside of the Sons, Jamison had known he would get them out—and he had, one by one—and escaped to their grandmother's ranch situated at the very edge of Valiant County.

It was Jamison's rough childhood in the gang and the immense responsibility he'd placed on himself to get his brothers away from it that had shaped him into a man who took everything perhaps a shade too seriously. Or so his brothers said.

Jamison had no regrets on that score. Seriousness kept people safe. He was old enough now to enjoy the relative quiet of patrolling a small town like Bonesteel. He had no desire to see lawbreaking. He'd seen enough. But he had a deep, abiding desire to make sure everything was *right*.

So, it was odd to be faced with a clear B and E at just a quarter past nine at night on the nearly deserted streets. Maybe if it had been the general store or gas station, he might've understood. But the figure was trying to break into his small office attached to city hall.

It was bold and ridiculous enough to be moderately amusing. Probably a drunk, he thought. Maybe the… woman—yes, it appeared to be a woman—was drunk and looking to sleep it off.

When he did get calls, they were often alcohol related and mostly harmless, as this appeared to be.

Since Jamison was finishing up his normal last patrol for the night, he was on foot. He walked slowly over, keeping his steps light and his body in the shadows. The streets were quiet, having long since been rolled up for the night.

Still, the woman worked on his doorknob. If she was drunk, she was awfully steady. Either way, she didn't look to pose much of a threat.

He stepped out of the shadow. "Typically people who break and enter are better at picking a lock."

The woman stopped what she was doing—but she

hadn't jumped or shrieked or even stumbled. She just stilled. Closer now, he could see long dark hair pulled back into a braid, and an oddly familiar beat-up leather jacket that would hardly ward off the chill of a spring night in South Dakota.

Slowly, the woman stood to her full height, back to him. He rested his hand on the butt of his gun, ready for anything, even though he didn't feel particularly threatened by the tall, slender brunette.

The set of her shoulders reminded him of…something he couldn't put his finger on.

Until she turned, slowly, to face him.

He supposed it would have been a shock if he *hadn't* known the perpetrator, but this wasn't a local. It was someone he hadn't laid eyes on in fifteen years. "Liza."

She let out the breath she'd been holding and stepped forward as if it had been days since they'd last seen each other, instead of years. "Thank God, Jamison. You don't know how long I've been trying to find you."

He took her in. Fifteen years should have done more to change her, but she looked so much the same. Tall, scrappy, with dark, expressive eyes that had always gotten her into trouble with her father. And his own…

Then there was her mouth, which was full and could make a grizzled sailor blush with the creative swearing it could utter.

Once upon a time anyway. This was fifteen years later. Maybe it wasn't half his life, but it was pretty darn close. Liza might want to act like they were old pals, but he wasn't young and easily fooled anymore.

"I need you to come with me," she said, stepping forward, placing her hand on his arm as if they were *more than* old pals as they once had been.

He laughed, not missing how bitter it sounded, and

how it made her wince. Undeterred, she scanned the dark around them, fidgety and afraid. When her brown gaze met his, it was with *fear*.

"Do you really think I'd be here if I weren't desperate?" she asked in a tremulous whisper.

For a second, a terrible split second, he believed in that fear and was ready to jump in to help. Then he remembered who he was dealing with. "Desperate? Or working for my father?"

She released his arm as if it was a snake that had bitten her. She even managed to look hurt. Quite the touch.

He'd saved her once. Secreted her out of the eagle eye of her father, who was always in league with his own.

After managing to get his brothers out and to Grandma Pauline, it had taken some time to get himself out. In part because he wanted his father to know—to really know, once he was gone, that it was he who had gotten the others out.

He'd been eighteen to her sixteen. They'd been friends, though he'd known she was ready and willing to be more. It had felt wrong, like taking advantage. Still, he hadn't been able to leave her behind. Not with her father being as bad as his own. Not with all those feelings buried deep inside.

So, it had taken longer to plan, to work out the route and figure out a time when they'd both be out of the careful watch of their fathers' men.

He'd done it, too. Grandma hadn't been able to take her in, not with all those wild boys she was raising. But Duke Knight, Grandma's neighbor, had. He and his wife had only been able to have one child of their own despite wanting more, so they'd fostered girls over the years, even adopted some.

They would have adopted Liza. If she'd stayed.

But she'd run off, back to the biker gang, and to everything his father ruled with an iron fist and, sometimes Jamison was quite convinced, pure evil.

Even now he couldn't regret it. Maybe Liza had chosen to go back, but he'd given her the chance. Her choosing to throw it away was her deal. Not his.

"I'm not working for your father," she finally said, vibrating with a loosely controlled anger. The same kind of fury he'd once felt himself.

He'd stopped letting the world make him angry. It had been a hard lesson, but an accomplishment he took great pride in. Or so he had thought, at least before she'd shown up. Instead he could feel that old anger like a geyser getting ready to burst inside him.

But he would control it. He'd built a career and a life on maintaining steady emotions. On being detached enough to get the job done, and engaged enough to care to.

"You'll have to excuse me if I don't take anything a biker gang member says at face value," he managed to utter without too much bitterness tingeing his words. "Not when so many things you said to me once upon a time were lies." Okay, *that* sounded a little bitter.

She shook her head, but she didn't deny it. "You don't understand."

"No, I don't. And I don't want to. Go home, Liza. Back to the life you chose."

"You have no idea what I chose." She cut him off and grabbed his arm again, but this time hard. "Or why I chose it," she added, looking up at him with an emotion he didn't understand. "More important, it doesn't matter. Do you remember Carlee Bright?"

Jamison didn't like to remember anything about his life in that place. His father's camps, or the times they'd take over an entire town and drive people out. Because inflicting pain was Ace Wyatt's currency, and he was a very rich man.

But Jamison remembered the name. "Wasn't she Cody's age?" His youngest brother was nine years his junior, but it felt more like a century considering it was *those* nine years.

"Yes. My dad knocked her up a few years ago."

"Sounds about right, but I don't see why that concerns me. Or you, for that matter."

"Carlee is dead."

"I'm sorry to hear that. If you're looking for police help—"

"Police help? *Police help?* God, Jamison, you never change. A woman is dead, her daughter witnessed it and—"

"How am I supposed to think this isn't a matter for law enforcement?" he interrupted, frustration getting the better of him.

"What are the police going to do about a woman in that gang who is dead? Nothing. You and I both know it."

He didn't respond. He knew the case likely wouldn't have gotten the same kind of attention as another. Certainly not as much as someone who appeared on the grid with no gang association. But it wouldn't be ignored.

Liza would never believe that.

"Is there a body?"

"No. There's a terrified little girl. My half sister. She told me something, Jamison, and now she's disappeared, too. I need help, and I'm not going to get it from the inside."

"But you think you'll get it from me?"

She studied his face for the longest time before she finally smiled, if sadly. "Yeah, I do."

SOMEHOW JAMISON WYATT was almost exactly how Liza remembered. Age had weathered him some, but since he'd always been good-looking, it settled well on him. Lines in the right places, a wariness that made her nerves hum like she was thirteen years old again, watching him as he kept his brothers safe.

That feeling was *just* the same, which was how she knew, no matter how he blustered or accused her of being associated with his father, he'd help. He'd have to help.

Jamison was the one and only reason she believed in goodness. In the midst of all the bad of their childhoods, when they'd grown up as the direct progeny of some of the worst men in that group, Jamison had still somehow found integrity and honor. By finding it, he'd given it to his brothers and her.

Without him, she never would have seen what the real world looked like outside the Sons of the Badlands. She would have never had hope or love. She never would have known homes could be real and safe, and that stealing and lying and always, *always* watching your back was not the only way to live.

The last fifteen years back in the Sons had tried to beat that knowledge out of her, but she'd done what Jamison had always done. She'd gone back to protect her own. She'd failed with her sister, but for four years now she'd been determined to find a way to get her half sister out. Just like Jamison had saved his brothers, Liza was going to save Gigi.

Until she did, until Gigi was safe, she'd stay in the Sons. If she didn't ever get out, she'd always have the satisfaction that she'd worked to help a few other people leave a life that sucked all the good and decent out of them.

She had to find some hope for Gigi and keep it alive.

She looked up at the man who still had a good six inches on her, no matter how tall she was for a woman. She didn't have time for the arguments she'd practiced on her way over, not for reasoning, either. She squeezed his arm. "They're going to kill Gigi if I can't find her. If I can't… She's just an innocent bystander."

His jaw worked, his eyes squinting as if trying to hold on to indifference—a familiar move. Years ago she'd run her palm along the hard, chiseled edge of that jaw. She'd been so in awe of him. Too much hero worship and not enough sense.

She couldn't afford to make those mistakes when a little girl depended on her. She had to be strong on her own—to add her strength with his if she ever hoped to save Gigi. She had to believe that if she had a Wyatt brother on her side, she could do this. Rescue Gigi. It was too late for Carlee, but Gigi was still alive.

I hope.

The wave of dizziness that had been plaguing her today came back in full force. She really needed to eat, to get to a place where she could sleep and take care of herself.

"I can take you to the sheriff's department," Jamison said, his voice hard and infused with that cop smugness he'd just been starting to perfect when she'd had to leave the warmth of the Knights' house. "We can take your statement and—"

"I need *you*, Jamison. You know the Sons and you know the law. If you're too busy guarding all this—" she waved a hand to take in the darkened small town, where, at worst, he was taking care of petty crimes "—I'd take the help of one of your brothers. Dev or the twins. They'd know enough. But I need someone who knows Ace and the Sons—enough to be afraid, and how to beat them in spite of that fear."

Though she didn't ask herself why she'd come to him first, when she knew that of all the Wyatt brothers with their various law enforcement jobs, Jamison would be the least likely to forgo protocol.

Except he was the one she needed. If there was an Achilles' heel hidden inside the hard, upstanding man in front of her, it was the desire to save people.

He was silent for far too long. When he spoke, the pain of his words sliced her in two.

"If I could beat Ace, I would have done it already," he said quietly into the dark. A painful rasp made those words *hurt*.

She winced again. She'd known this would be thorny, but she'd also known Jamison was truly her only hope. Any other member of the Sons—man or woman—would be too afraid or too uninterested to help. Even a few sympathetic parties could be a liability in the end.

"When was the last time you tried?" she whispered, the hushed words too loud out here in a town that looked most especially lonely at night. Was Jamison just as lonely?

It was his turn to wince, or maybe take the blow she'd just landed.

He opened his mouth, either to answer or tell her to go, when something exploded, loud and close and painful.

For a second, Liza didn't recognize the sound as that of a gunshot. So much so she was almost surprised when Jamison crashed into her, pushing her underneath him and on to the hardscrabble gravel. His body covered her, warm and heavy.

After a moment—or was it a few moments?—he rolled her on to her back. His hands were on her, she thought, but she couldn't quite feel them. She could see his lips moving, but his voice was garbled.

It was the concern in his dark eyes that worried her. But she was floating away on a cloud of shock she didn't understand. Then radiating pain took her completely under.

Chapter Two

Jamison got Liza in his car, quick as he could. Much as he wanted to chase after the gunman, ascertaining Liza's injuries was first priority. Getting her out of here and to help was second.

Finding the Sons and hurting them would have to come later—for now. Because he had no doubt who'd shot at her.

He laid her out in the back seat of his patrol car. There wasn't enough room, and all his equipment made it all too difficult, but he searched her body for signs of a wound.

He didn't realize he was whispering prayers that she would be all right until he found the injury. Something about his frenzied words and the gash on her leg all coming to a head to remind him to pull himself together.

Taking her to the hospital wasn't the best option with the shooter still out there. A paramedic would insist on a trip to the hospital. So, that was a no go, too.

But his brother was a trained paramedic along with his duties as sheriff's deputy—out here it could be a life-line. Jamison himself knew a few first aid basics—like bandaging the leg wound, which he did with quick efficiency—but he didn't have the course training and licenses his brother had.

Brady would be able to figure out her loss of consciousness without insisting she be taken to the hospital. Because from what Jamison could tell, the spot on her leg was the only place she'd been hurt, and it wasn't enough for her to pass out for this long.

Debating again, he reached for the radio, then bypassed the idea. Even though it went against his instincts, his ingrained desire to be by the book—to prove he was nothing like Ace Wyatt. He decided this was bigger than the rules.

Just this once.

He picked up his cell and dialed Brady.

"Location?" he barked when Brady answered.

Brady didn't pause or ask why. He simply answered, "Sector A."

Northeast. Good. They could meet in the middle and figure this out. "Meet me on 302nd Avenue in Fuller Junction."

"That's out of my sector, J."

"I'm well aware of where it is. You're off the clock in fifteen."

There was a quiet moment as Jamison shut the doors and climbed into the driver's seat.

"Must be some emergency. Heading that way."

"Same. You'll beat me, but I won't be far behind. Anyone at Grandma's?"

"Just Dev."

"It'll do. Give her a call and tell her we're coming, and to have the first aid kit ready. Yours, too."

Even though Jamison could feel Brady's questions piling up into the silence between them, Brady didn't voice them.

They both hung up and drove toward the meeting point. Jamison had to pay attention to the road in the inky black. He didn't hear a peep from Liza in the back. Just slow, steady breathing. *Thank God.*

That was something at least.

She'd been shot. It wasn't that he didn't believe her story about Carlee Bright. The Sons of the Badlands weren't exactly known for their kind treatment of women. Jamison himself had always wondered about his mother's "drug overdose" when Cody had been a baby. But he hadn't been much more than a child himself. Certainly not adult enough to challenge it.

Sometimes he wondered if that would have mattered.

Carlee Bright wasn't his mother, and the supposed disappearance of Liza's half sister could all be…made-up. Getting shot hardly proved her story. If anything, it proved her connection. She knew too much to be an innocent bystander.

Still, Jamison sped through the dark, not seeing another soul on the streets. He turned onto 302nd, slowed on the gravel road until he spotted Brady's cruiser. Jamison pulled to a stop behind him.

Jamison got out and opened the back seat door. Without a word, Brady immediately examined Liza. If he recognized her, which surely he did, he didn't mention it.

"She didn't fall or hit her head?"

"Not that I saw."

Brady nodded toward the driver's seat. "She could have just passed out from shock. Let's get her to the ranch. I need more space and more light."

But they both knew a woman who'd grown up in a biker gang wasn't exactly gun-shy. She'd seen way worse than this kind of wound.

"You sure you want to take her to Grandma's? Hospital would be…safer," Brady said carefully.

Too carefully. As if he thought Jamison was still hung

up on a woman he hadn't seen in fifteen years and had gotten over years ago. *Years* and years ago. This was about the Sons, and it was about keeping someone safe. He'd dedicated his life to keeping strangers safe. Why wouldn't he keep Liza safe, too? It was just…his job. "I'll meet you at the ranch."

Brady nodded and strode back to his car.

They drove, and occasionally Liza would come to, move around a bit, ask where she was. Jamison tried to keep her talking, but she faded in and out. It worried him, even as the fact she kept waking up eased some of his fears.

Finally, he turned off onto the unmarked gravel road that would twist through the rolling hills of the South Dakota ranch and farmland. Then, behind the hills, home.

There was a light on outside the old farmhouse—there always ways. Pauline Reaves was used to visitors at all times of night. She kept her doors open, her windows homey and a variety of weapons within easy reach should any of the *bad* element ever show up at her door.

It was home, even if he'd spent most of his adolescence in various Sons of the Badlands camps. This house with its piecemeal layout, thanks to being over a century old and needing all sorts of additions and modern conveniences, was his heart and soul.

By the time he reached the end of the gravel road and pushed the car into Park, Grandma Pauline was at the door. Jamison opened the back door of his cruiser and Liza blinked at him.

"Come on now."

She closed her eyes and took a deep breath before pushing herself out of the back seat. She was on her feet a second before she swayed, so Jamison scooped her up

into his arms and started marching toward the house—
Brady closing the door for him and following.

Dev's two ranch dogs pranced at their feet but had
been trained not to bark at a Wyatt or a Knight. They
whimpered excitedly instead, obviously hoping to be
petted.

Brady obliged since Jamison had his hands full.

"I can walk," Liza said, attempting outrage, though
it was weak at best.

"No, you can't."

She was too light by half, and her clothes fairly hung
off her—except for that too-thin leather coat he did indeed remember from fifteen plus years ago.

He strode through the front door and Grandma didn't
blink an eye as her eldest grandson carried in a bleeding,
unsteady ex-girlfriend, followed by another grandson.

Both in uniform.

Brady closed the door, the dogs knowing better than
to enter here, where they'd have to trot through Grandma's kitchen. Grandma Pauline did not allow such things.

"Kitchen," she instructed. "Best light."

As if they didn't already know. It might not be so com-
monplace these days, but once upon a time the Wyatt
brothers had gotten into their share of scrapes and had
been patched up in Grandma's kitchen.

Dev was already there, with one of Grandma's "medical" sheets laid out over the kitchen table.

He raised an eyebrow at Liza but otherwise didn't
say anything. Not all that uncommon for Dev. But even
though he didn't speak, his disapproval came off him
in waves.

Jamison sat Liza down on the table. "Believe me
now?" she asked archly, before wincing as she moved
the leg that had been shot.

Jamison chose to follow Dev's example and kept silent.

"Let's have a look," Brady offered, approaching the table. He pulled back the bandage and examined the wound under better light. Grandma set a washcloth and small basin of water next to him—the first aid kit already opened and laid out.

Brady ripped the hole in her jeans so he had a large enough space to work. He cleaned out the wound, Grandma handing Liza an over-the-counter painkiller and a glass of water when she hissed out a breath.

"Have any idea why you might have passed out?" Brady asked, his voice calm and pleasant. "Recent head wound? Any other injuries?"

Liza shook her head.

"Pregnant?"

"No," she said flatly, and her gaze stayed resolutely on where Brady worked on her thigh.

"When was the last time you ate, girl?" Grandma demanded.

Liza ran a shaky hand through her hair as Brady rebandaged the wound. "I don't…"

"Girl needs a meal," Grandma said firmly, already moving for the refrigerator.

"Broth, Grandma," Brady ordered.

At Grandma's harrumph, Jamison knew Liza wouldn't just be getting broth.

The woman in question looked around the kitchen from her seat atop the table and tried to smile, but it frayed. "Didn't expect half the Wyatt crew at my beck and call."

"Don't get shot, then," Dev replied sharply.

"I'm no doctor," Brady said, interrupting the back-and-forth, though his comment made both Jamison and Dev shift because Brady certainly would have made a good physician. But an elderly woman raising six boys in the middle of nowhere, South Dakota, didn't have the kind of resources to make that happen.

So, Brady had become a paramedic and a cop, and he was excellent at both, but the two older brothers often wondered what if…?

"My guess would be the loss of consciousness came from a combination of a lack of food and shock. There aren't any other symptoms that point to anything more going on. Get enough food in her, keep the bandage clean, she should be fine."

"*She* is sitting right here."

"That she is," Brady replied with a patient smile. "You're going to want to take it easy. *And* you're going to want to tell us why someone's shooting at you."

She leveled Jamison with a haughty look. "I guess your brother can explain it."

Jamison held her stare. "Liza thinks her father murdered Carlee Bright, and that her half sister, who witnessed it, has been kidnapped and is in mortal danger. Like Liza herself apparently is."

THE WAY JAMISON so neutrally delivered the details of her situation made her shiver. She instantly had a blanket draped over her shoulders, thanks to Brady.

Silence descended over the kitchen, except for the sounds of Pauline puttering at the stove.

"How do you know Carlee is dead?" Jamison asked.

"Now you're interested?" she retorted. She felt shaky and off-kilter and her leg throbbed where the bullet had—thank God—just grazed her.

"I wouldn't go so far as to say interested. Obviously you're mixed up with something involving the Sons," he said, gesturing toward her torn jeans and the bandage.

"I certainly wouldn't be surprised if your father killed Carlee. I'm having a harder time imagining he'd harm his own daughter. If only because you're still alive. He's had ample time and reason to kill you."

She glanced at the three Wyatt brothers standing next to each other. Each with arms crossed over broad chests. They had the physical look of their father—big men, hard men. Dark hair and eyes that ranged from brown to green. Their jaws were chiseled, their mouths all in firm disapproval.

All had aged, Dev most especially. He didn't just look weathered, he looked…beaten. She knew any questions about his limp would be met with stony silence.

Just like she knew the Wyatt boys had souls, thanks to the woman bustling around her now. Ace had no soul, Liza knew. His sons had been born or become good men in spite of it.

"Gigi is four years old," Liza said, trying very hard to find the balance between overwrought and detached. If she was too emotional, they would dismiss her. If she wasn't emotional enough, they'd think she was some kind of plant sent by Ace. "She *saw* my father kill Carlee."

"Why would the Sons of the Badlands be scared about what a four-year-old girl says?" Jamison returned. "Surely there are enough kids running around those camps who've seen as much. And they have no recourse. There's no one to tell who would do anything about it."

"She told me, Jamison," Liza said, trying to eradicate the lump in her throat. "She told me. The next day she was gone. I… Someone's been following me ever since. They know I know and now someone's shot me. After I approached you."

"Aren't you one of them?" Dev returned, as hard if not harder than Jamison.

One of them. Years ago Pauline would have demanded an apology out of Dev, defended Liza to anyone that her ties to the Sons of the Badlands were severed.

But that was just another thing she'd lost when she'd gone back to them—Pauline's trust. There was no point being sad about it. She was here for Gigi, not herself.

"Regardless, if they really thought you knew something you'd already be dead," Jamison said, his voice flat and his eyes hard.

He was right, which scared her more than anything, but it also crystallized something about Jamison for her. If he didn't want to help her, she wouldn't be here. He would have taken her to the hospital. Not home.

He might put on the gruff, aloof cop act, but he'd brought her *home*. To his grandma's. Because even if she'd only had four years over at the Knights' ranch, Grandma Pauline had been hers, just like Duke and Eva Knight had been something like parents.

But she hadn't been able to stay with them. When Jamison had convinced her to escape the Sons with him, when he'd given her this home and *family*, she'd thought she could do it. She'd been sure she could accept her sister was a lost cause.

The more she'd been given at the Knights', the guiltier she'd felt that her sister was still in that awful place. The more she'd seen Jamison's brothers thrive—because he'd saved them before he'd saved himself—the harder it had been to live with herself.

She'd had to leave the Knights and go back to the Sons, to try to save Marci. In the end, it *had* been a lost cause. Marci didn't want to leave, didn't want to see the good in the world.

But Gigi was only four. She had a chance at a real life.

A safe, good life. So, Liza had given up on one sister and focused on another.

Now she had no one and nothing—here, where she'd once been loved. But that didn't mean she couldn't use what she knew to get Jamison's help.

"I just need to find Gigi, and I can't do it on my own. You know I can't ask for help in that place."

"And you know I can't help you *in* that place."

She closed her eyes against that simple truth. She just kept hoping… No. She didn't have time to hope. Gigi's life was at stake.

"One of you will help me," she said. "You know too much what it's like to be a kid in that place. You know what it's like to watch horrors, to lose your mother and only have an awful, scary father left. One of you has to help me. You know it."

No one said anything for the longest time. Pauline handed her a warm mug of broth and a plate with a sandwich on it.

Liza looked at the elderly woman handing her food and wanted to break down and cry, offer apologies and beg for forgiveness.

But fifteen years was too long, and she had bigger issues at hand.

Eventually Brady turned to face Jamison.

"You're still on duty," he said, keeping his voice low as if she wouldn't be able to hear it.

Jamison's jaw tensed.

"I'll take your car back. Take your place till shift change. If something goes down, it'll be both our butts in a sling, but I'll do it."

Jamison only nodded. Brady gave her one last enigmatic look, kissed his grandmother on the cheek, then left the kitchen.

Still, Jamison didn't say anything. No one offered to help. They maintained their silence and Liza tried to ignore panic. She had to eat, that much was for sure. Too many days trying to keep out of reach of the Sons, while also trying to find Gigi, had left her with almost no supplies and far, far too long between meals.

But it was hard to eat when your stomach was twisted in awful knots. When every move felt like one that might end Gigi's life, or her own.

She swallowed some broth, doing everything she could not to cry.

"You boys go make up two rooms," Pauline ordered.

Dev and Jamison looked like they wanted to argue, but Liza knew they wouldn't. Not with Grandma Pauline.

They turned and left the kitchen, leaving Liza alone with her food and the woman she'd looked up to as a teenager.

"You eat that all up before I let you out of my sight, you hear?"

Liza nodded, her vision wavering. This time not from exhaustion or losing consciousness, she didn't think, but because her eyes were full of tears.

"None of that now, girl. You've got a life to save. How are you going to do it?"

"I don't know," Liza whispered. "If Jamison won't help me, I don't know what I'll do." She wouldn't have said that aloud to anyone else, but she knew Pauline would keep her shameful weakness a secret.

In her no-fuss way Pauline used a dish towel to wipe the tears off Liza's cheeks. She picked up the sandwich herself and held it out to Liza until she accepted it and took a bite.

"Jamison will help you. Stomp around a bit and put on the manly act, but he'll help. Won't be able to stop himself." Pauline studied her. "But you can't let that stubborn pride of yours get in the way, girl. And he can't let his."

All Liza could think was: *good luck with that*.

Chapter Three

"I don't like it." Dev leaned more to the right than the left, because his left leg was bad. A gift from Ace when Dev had been a young cop determined to take their father down.

Each of the Wyatt boys had learned, in their own way, that you didn't take the Sons down without getting hurt.

None of them had let their past experiences sway them completely, but each of their obsessions had been stilted by Dev's near-death encounter ten years ago. Jamison had found it necessary to give up on revenge in the face of his brother almost dying.

Jamison sighed. "What *do* you like, Dev?"

He didn't answer that question. "She can't be here."

"And yet, here she is." Jamison hadn't thought it through, bringing her here, but there was no other option. He knew what it meant for himself, for his brothers. It was getting pulled back in when they'd all silently agreed to stay out.

No matter all those old feelings and promises, this felt something like inevitable.

They'd escaped the Sons of the Badlands, but their father still existed, still ran a group full of criminals, no matter how many of his biological sons had gone into law enforcement.

"You're not just bringing trouble home, you're bring-ing it to the Knights' doorstep, as well."

That poked at Jamison, but he had to believe he could handle it. "She seems fine. We'll get out of here in the morning."

"We?"

Jamison stood from where he'd made up the bed for Liza—perfectly because he knew Grandma would still box his ears if he didn't do the chore correctly.

"Do you remember what it was like to be four years old in that place?"

Dev was quiet for a moment, then shrugged and didn't meet Jamison's gaze. "I didn't know any better."

"You know you did. And if that little girl saw some-thing—"

"And if that not-so-little girl is BS-ing you, then what? You wind up dead?"

"I can see through Liza's BS." God, he hoped he was older and wiser than he'd been at twenty-two.

Dev laughed coldly. "Since when? You thought you two were going to get married and be the example for any kid stuck in that hellhole. A fairy tale told to dirty faces so they could believe they'd escape someday. Then she ditched you. For them."

It stung, because the truth could, but Jamison was too old to get riled up about his brother's barbs.

"I've got too many what-ifs, brother. I can't take on another. I'll be careful, but I've got to help her find this little girl."

Which was enough of an emotional truth for Dev not to say another word. They moved to the room across the hall, which had been the room Jamison and Dev had shared years and years ago. Now, Dev slept downstairs in the mudroom converted to bedroom.

Taking the stairs every day was too hard on his leg. Especially in the morning, when it was stiff from sleep.

"You'll have to be careful. You can't trust her. No matter what memories she stirs up."

"I don't trust her," Jamison said, maybe a pinch too loudly. Because his instincts when it came to Liza were a mess, that was for sure. But he knew it. If you could identify a problem, you could address it. So, there'd be no trust. He'd follow his own instincts and beliefs and—

"Good to know."

They both looked up to find Liza in the doorway. Jamison didn't feel particularly guilty—it was something he would have said to her face. But something about how pale she was and the sleeve of saltines in her hand poked at him.

He stood stiffly. "Your room is across the hall."

She glanced behind her, then smirked. "Lucky me."

She walked over to her room, favoring the leg that hadn't been shot.

"Watch yourself, J. She is nothing but trouble. I can guarantee it." Then Dev did his own limping out of the room.

Jamison let himself breathe in and then out a few calming times. Liza was no doubt trouble, always had been, but that didn't mean he could ignore a four-year-old stuck in a bad situation.

She was hardly the only little girl in a bad situation associated with the Sons, or the world at large, for that matter. As a cop Jamison had come to accept that he *couldn't* help everyone, but that he should certainly try to help whoever he could.

He opened the dresser drawers in his old room until he found what he wanted. He walked across the hall, knocked perfunctorily before opening the door.

She swore at him, then stood there glaring.

She'd taken off the ripped jeans, which had messed with the bandage. Now she stood only in a long-sleeved T-shirt and her underwear. Her legs were as long and mesmerizing as he remembered, and he stared a beat too long.

But that didn't mean he didn't know how to recover. He gestured at the bandage. "Need help?"

"Yeah. Why don't you put your hands on me while I'm half-naked?"

He raised his gaze to meet hers. "Worried you can't control yourself around me, darling?"

She scoffed, but the corner of her mouth kicked up with *some* humor. "Fine. Help."

He placed the map on the bed and then crouched down by her leg, refitting the bandage and smoothing the tape over. It required touching warm skin and a copious amount of control not to remember all the times he'd touched her for completely romantic reasons.

They'd been different people way back then—smooth skin or not.

He stood and didn't dare look at her face. "Let's talk logistics."

"God, that's so hot," she said dryly.

He sent her a look, saw her pulling her jeans back on and shook his head. "Wait."

She frowned, good leg in one leg of the jeans. "Huh?"

He strode out of the room again, went rummaging through his old drawers, found an old pair of gym shorts and returned to her room. "Here." He tossed them at her.

She caught them and studied them, then shrugged and dropped the jeans. She slipped the shorts on, tying the drawstring tight. They landed below her knees, although she was a tall woman herself. But it was hardly a good idea to be wearing shorts on a cold early-spring night in a rickety old farmhouse.

"Now, it's not near warm enough up here for that, so why don't you crawl under the covers?"

"You're really going to have to stop coming on to me, Jamison."

"Ha ha. Get in bed."

She fluttered her eyelashes at him as she slid under the covers, trying—and failing—to cover up the wince of pain as she presumably laid her weight a little too hard on her wound.

He picked up the map he'd brought in and smoothed it out over her lap. "Where?"

Her hesitation spoke volumes and reminded him of all the ways she'd once fooled him.

And never would again.

"You and your cop buddies can't go in there guns blazing. Gigi won't be the only one hurt."

"Do you see a slew of my 'cop buddies' crowding in here, Liza? Or is it just you and me?"

"It's complicated. Surely you understand that."

"Either you can tell me where the main camp is and I see what I can do to help Gigi, or you sleep off your gunshot wound and fend for yourself tomorrow in the morning."

She looked up at him, her dark eyes too direct and assessing. As if she still knew him, understood him. "You'd love to believe you're that tough, wouldn't you?"

"Try me."

LIZA LOOKED AT the paper map—of all things—of South Dakota spread out on her lap. She knew exactly what he wanted to know, and that she had all the information he desired. Except she didn't hesitate for the reasons he thought.

Jamison saw dealings with the Sons as black-and-white. He believed you were with them or against them—he'd had too many years winning against them as an officer of the law. He was a man after all, and it was so easy to see the world as with you or against you when you held the power.

But Liza had lost in that world, and losers had a much more complicated view of things.

She was worried about Gigi, about how to get to her. She was worried about *anyone* who risked their life to help her—because lives *were* on the line.

But specifically she worried about involving Jamison.

She knew Ace Wyatt would someday decide to exact revenge against his sons. He had plans, but he was a patient man. He'd go after them when they least expected it, when Ace most needed it. She knew Ace was always looking for that perfect moment to make it poetic justice or divine revenge or whatever went on in his head.

She didn't want to send Jamison riding into Sons territory knowing it could be the shot that started a war.

You know he's your only chance or you wouldn't have come here. Besides, you think Ace Wyatt doesn't know exactly where you are?

She looked up at Jamison—now in immediate danger because of her. She'd been shot. Of course Ace, or even her own father, had sent someone to do that. If either had pulled the trigger, she knew damn well she'd be dead.

The shot was meant to be a warning. Furthermore, whoever had shot her would have followed her. Jamison was involved now, whether he chose to be or not.

Guilt swamped her. She looked down at the map, surprised to find tears clouding her vision. She didn't think she had tears left anymore. "I'm sorry," she whispered.

"There are a lot of things you could be sorry for, Liza. I'm afraid you'll have to be more specific."

She would never be sorry for leaving the Knights to go back to the Sons all those years ago, but she didn't think telling him that in the moment would do any good for either of them. "I'm sorry for this, because they'll know you're involved, even if you decide not to be. Whatever happens, this will be the start of something. I didn't think that through."

He held her gaze for a long time. "Every beginning has an end, Liza." He pointed at the map. "Now. Where?"

Knowing it couldn't possibly end well, but that it was Gigi's only chance to survive, Liza pointed. "Here. They've taken over Flynn."

Jamison's expression hardened. "Flynn."

"You know it?"

"That's where dear old Dad was born, where his parents abandoned him. Where he took us out and taught us to be men. I don't think that's a coincidence he's settled down there right now, Liza. Whatever war you're worried about starting—Ace already beat you to it."

Chapter Four

Jamison didn't sleep much. Brady had finished off his shift without anything cropping up, and Jamison had done the unthinkable and called in to his superior officer, requesting to use all of his vacation time.

He'd built up quite a lot. There'd been questions, hemming and hawing, but in the end, Sheriff Sneef couldn't deny Jamison deserved a "vacation."

Yeah, some vacation.

Grandma came into the kitchen through the back porch. He heard the squeak of the door, the whimper of the dogs left outside, then the stomp of her boots against the rug before she bustled into the kitchen, a basket with a few eggs cradled inside on her arm.

"You're up, then."

There was just a *hint* of disapproval in her tone, but it was hard to wake up early enough to suit Grandma.

No doubt Dev was already out with the cows, grumbling over the fact his ranch hand was Sarah Pleasant, one of the Knights' foster girls. Not a girl anymore, and splitting her time helping her guardian on his ranch and wounded Dev on his.

Because life at the ranch went on no matter what was going on with Ace and the Sons. Whether you'd lost your wife to cancer like Duke had, or you'd lost full function of your body after a run-in with Ace like Dev had.

"We'll be out of your hair soon. I'd like Liza to get a good breakfast in first."

Grandma simply made a noise of assent as she pulled out a pan. She went about breakfast preparations as if everything was fine.

Jamison wished he believed that could be true. Bringing Liza here last night had brought Grandma into the thick of things. It wasn't the first time, and probably wouldn't be the last, but it was hard not to feel guilty about it.

She'd never asked for this. It was hardly her fault her only child had been taken in by the likes of Ace Wyatt. Certainly not her lot in life to take care of their six rowdy, traumatized boys.

But she'd done it. Now she was creeping up on eighty, and he could see the weight of the Wyatt world on her shoulders. It was a burden she'd taken on, and she'd done it without a complaint.

"You'll need to be on watch," he said as blandly as he could manage. Because any true expression of worry would be offensive to her, any command would make her bristle and sure to do the opposite.

"I'm always on watch." She turned from the stove and studied him in that way of hers. "Don't doubt yourself. Not on this."

It was no surprise Grandma Pauline could see right through him, but that didn't ease his concern. "It's complicated."

"The right thing usually is, Jamison," she said, turning back to her meal preparation.

Jamison had been attempting to do the right thing

his whole life. Getting there—like Grandma said—was rarely simple.

Liza walked into the kitchen. She looked like she'd had a rough night. Grandma immediately handed her a glass of water and some over-the-counter pills for pain.

"Thanks, Pauline."

"Sit. Breakfast will be just a bit."

Liza slid into the chair farthest from him. Which would have been great if they weren't about to embark on a dangerous mission together. Truth be told, he'd rather leave her behind, especially with her injuries.

But she knew what they were looking for better than he did.

Dev's warning sat in his gut. He couldn't ignore the possibility Liza had been sent. That this was an elaborate scheme to get him on his father's territory.

Jamison might have washed his hands of the Sons years ago, but he'd always known his father wasn't the kind of man to let that stand. Maybe Jamison had gotten a little complacent when his father hadn't instigated any attacks since Dev's run-in ten years ago. Maybe Jamison had begun to hope escape was really enough.

But that didn't mean he was surprised at being drawn back in.

Whatever parts of the truth Liza was telling him, Jamison did believe a little girl was in danger. Which meant he needed Liza if he was going to be able to find Gigi. Liza knew a lot more than she was telling him, he was sure, and she had far more insider knowledge of the Sons' recent movements than he did.

They'd have to work together.

"I'm surprised there aren't reinforcements," Liza offered into the quiet kitchen.

"Brady, Tucker and Gage all have jobs, Liza. Ones they can't leave at a whim."

"So, I *did* come to the right brother."

"I had vacation time to take, so I took it. You're welcome, by the way."

"What about Cody? You didn't include him in your laundry list of important men with important things to do."

Jamison's entire adult life was dealing with people who questioned and sometimes even challenged his authority—starting with being saddled with five brothers who had smart mouths and no compunction trying to get under his skin. He should be quite adept at handling Liza's little barbs.

Or so he told himself.

"Cody isn't any of your concern."

"Don't tell me one of the Wyatt brothers isn't quite so chummy with the rest. What? The baby Wyatt run away?"

"That'll be enough," Grandma said in that quiet way of hers that was scarier than when she was threatening a man with a wooden spoon to the head.

She slid a plate in front of Liza, then Jamison. Both were loaded with bacon and eggs and biscuits. Age had slowed her down some, but it hadn't stopped her from doing a darn thing.

"Jamison, I've packed up quite a few provisions. Obviously, you'll want to take your camping supplies just in case. Still, I'll put together some linens."

"I can—"

It only took a very carefully raised eyebrow for Jamison to swallow the rest of his words. Heaven forbid he try to patronize his grandmother with assistance.

She didn't want to be treated like an "old lady." It was

hard to learn the balance between truly helping her and jabbing at her pride.

"I see things haven't changed around here," Liza said once Grandma had left the kitchen.

Jamison wished that were true. But things had changed. Dev's injuries. Cody's evasiveness about his job that kept him far away from the ranch. The middle lot hadn't changed much and all worked for Valiant County. Gage enjoyed pretending he was a happy-go-lucky sheriff's deputy, his twin, Brady, taking on a more serious outlook with the same job, while Tucker's detachment to the detective bureau kept him busy and satisfied—supposedly.

But Jamison wondered if they'd just gotten better at hiding their scars as adults.

A concern and a worry for another day. He ate the breakfast Grandma had set in front of him. Liza did as well, without any more commentary. Thank God.

She scraped her plate clean, which comforted Jamison some. He took their plates to the sink once they were both done and didn't miss the way she watched him. She was here because she thought he was the only one who could help her—not because she necessarily *wanted* his help.

Wasn't that always the way with her?

As long as he remembered that, as long as he didn't get sucked into old memories, this would be fine.

He took Liza outside to help pack up the truck. Grandma's truck was a nondescript Ford that would suit him well. Brady and Gage would get Jamison's truck out to the ranch for Grandma to use later today.

"This is a lot," Liza said, sounding something between wary and exhausted as he crammed another cooler into the bed along with all his camping supplies. She crouched nearby, petting the dogs.

"We don't know what we'll need or for how long, and I don't want you passing out on me again."

She didn't smirk or even make a snotty comeback like he'd hoped—no, not hoped—expected. There could be nothing to do with hope when it came to Liza.

She stood and hugged herself instead, looking out at the endless rolling landscape of the ranch. "They're going to know we're coming."

There was a rawness to that statement he simply couldn't let affect him. "I know it's been a while, but surely you know me better than to think I don't understand that."

"You can't underestimate them."

Jamison looked over at Dev limping from the barn, and the small figure that was Sarah. Dev started walking toward them, and Sarah toward the house. The dogs raced to Dev. It made a nice picture, all in all, but his brother's limp stuck in his craw.

No, he'd never underestimate his father or the Sons again.

LIZA DIDN'T MISS the look Jamison gave his brother. She was definitely missing pieces of that story. Part of her wanted to ask, wanted to dig. The Wyatt brothers and their grandmother still felt like family even if she'd cut them off fifteen years ago.

Worse, so much worse than that feeling was the fact beyond Dev were rolling fields. Behind those hills was the Knight place.

Was Duke still running his cattle, laughing uproariously at himself and his over-the-top stories? Were her foster sisters from those beautiful few years she'd spent under their roof still there? Or had they built beautiful lives of their own?

Did they all hate her?

"I'd say you could stop by, but I don't want to drag Duke and the girls into this."

Liza swallowed, looking away from Sarah's far-off form and the only true home she'd ever had. "No, I don't, either." She didn't want to ask which girls. Leaving meant she'd learned that no information was better than some and knowing she couldn't be part of it.

"Sarah and Rachel still live on the ranch. Cecilia lives on the reservation—she's tribal police now. Felicity's a park ranger over at Badlands."

She didn't want to ask, but he'd started it. "What about Nina?"

Jamison shrugged. "She left."

"Left… How?"

"Do you really want to know, Liza? Because, by my count, the past fifteen years were yours for the knowing."

It hurt because it was true, and because it was true she didn't know what to say. But Dev approached, looking stormy and grumpy—which was different from the eager, determined teenager she remembered.

Maybe some things *had* changed.

"Heading out?"

"Looks like. Grandma was getting together a few more things. I'll be in touch."

Dev nodded, then turned his attention to her. Disapproval was etched into every line on his face, and none of it was softened by the beard that hid most of his mouth. "Watch your back, brother," he said, though he said the words while looking at her.

She didn't bother to plead her case to Dev, or to Jamison, for that matter. She'd broken their trust, knowing full well how slow trust was gained when it came to the Wyatts. Whatever they wanted to lay at her feet was fine, as long as they found Gigi.

Pauline came out with another load of who knew what. Liza felt like they were packing for a covered wagon trip across the prairie. She'd gotten by on next to nothing the past few days. Of course she'd ended up shot and unconscious.

Jamison said his goodbyes, giving strict instructions to be contacted if anything fishy happened at the ranch. Then they were loaded up in Pauline's truck and driving away the ranch.

Liza watched the gorgeous scenery go by. Spring was trying to get ahold of the land. There were touches of green peeking through just about every rolling brown hill. The scarce few bare trees they drove by were softening with buds.

Jamison drove west, which was right where the Sons were camped for the time being. It put Liza on considerable edge. Maybe he was just going to deliver her back to the Sons and be done with her.

But no. Jamison wouldn't willingly go into Sons territory. Certainly not for her. "Where exactly are we going?" she asked when she couldn't stand another minute of silence.

"Not directly to Flynn if that's what you're worried about."

She wasn't sure what she was worried about. Everything, maybe. She'd come to Jamison because he was the only one who could help, but that didn't mean she wouldn't doubt his methods. He was a *cop* now. He wouldn't be breaking any laws to bring her sister to safety.

It was about two hours between Flynn and Pauline's ranch, and they'd already been going for over an hour.

Jamison said they weren't going directly to Flynn, but it sure felt like they were.

Liza pressed her forehead against the passenger window. Out of the corner of her eyes she saw a flash and she looked in the rearview mirror. Her entire body went cold. "Right about now I'm worried about the tail we've got," she said, her throat tight with fear.

Jamison grinned, just like he'd done when they were younger. Irritatingly, her stomach did the same stupid swoop it had always done back then, too.

"I'm not," he offered, then without any warning punched the gas and sped off the road.

Chapter Five

Jamison wouldn't admit to anyone there was an excitement in all this that he'd missed. A thrill he'd thought he'd left behind when he'd become a cop.

But taking the truck over the edge of the road, slamming down the gas pedal a little too hard as they sped over the hills, turning too tight around rock formations, it filled him with a dark satisfaction he hadn't allowed himself to feel in a long time.

He slid a quick glance at Liza. Her expression vacillated between worry as she looked behind them, and that wicked smile he remembered. She'd always been fueled by danger—even more than him.

But this wasn't the old days, a fact he had a bad feeling he was going to have to remind himself of over and over.

There wasn't much cover, even as they got closer to the landscape that dipped and cratered with soaring stone ridges. The closer they got, the more impossible it would become to drive quickly or evade their pursuer.

"All right. Hold on."

He did a tight 180. Liza screeched—out of fear or delight it was hard to tell—but the truck held and Jamison sped directly toward their tail. He passed them, a pinch too close, their door mirrors crashing into each other and splintering off.

Jamison swore. "Grandma's going to kill me for that," he muttered, speeding back to the highway, gaining enough distance from their tail to get back on the road and make it to the turnoff he wanted without being seen.

Liza kept watching out the back window as Jamison maneuvered down a gravel side road that would take him where he wanted to go.

"It's not going to be that easy."

"No. I'd wager that's only the beginning. But the one thing we've got going for us is they're not going to kill us."

"How do you know that?"

"Because if anyone in that group is going to kill us, it's going to be our fathers. That's one thing they're not going to send their goons to do. Or we'd have been dead a long time ago."

"Isn't that even the tiniest bit depressing to you?"

"If a man like my father wants to kill me, I figure I've made a pretty good life for myself."

"Policing some Podunk town in the middle of no-where."

The insult didn't bother him. He wouldn't let it. He hadn't built his adult life to impress his ex-girlfriend who'd betrayed him once upon a time. So, he replied to her bland statement lightly, confidently, "Keeping the people of a small, tight-knit community safe from the likes of my father. It works for me."

"Some of us choose to protect the people inside from the likes of your father."

"Is that what you thought you were doing when you left, Liza? Protecting the people who willingly follow our fathers around—and willingly hurt and kill people in their paths?"

"Children don't have a choice, Jamison. You should know that better than anyone else."

He didn't have a response for that. He couldn't—*wouldn't*—believe she'd gone back to the Sons all those years ago to protect children when she'd still practically been a child. Or that she wouldn't have tried to explain that to him instead of disappearing in the middle of the night, making them all fear the worst.

He opened his mouth to say *that*, to ask her if she had any idea what she'd put all of them through those first few days. How worried sick the Knights and their girls had been, how he and his brothers had mounted a search-and-attack plan.

Until Grandma had stated the obvious. Clearly, Liza had left of her own accord.

Ancient history. Let it go.

He took the next turn a little too quickly considering he was almost certain they'd lost the tail. He followed this dirt road, backtracking toward Bonesteel, then taking a few paved roads back to the highway farther west.

"They'll still know where we're going," Liza said, not bothering to hide her disgust.

"But they won't know how. Or when. Do you think Gigi is in Flynn?"

"I'm not sure. I couldn't find her, but that doesn't mean anything. Dad was around the whole time, so she's either in Flynn, or someone's taken her away and is waiting for Dad."

"The second is more likely if you couldn't find her." Which made things more difficult, but not impossible.

She closed her eyes as if that truth hurt. "Yeah."

"So, where are the Sons holding ancillary camps right now?"

"I don't know, Jamison. I was hardly top of the food chain."

"You couldn't have been that low if you were there."

She shook her head. "You never, ever once understood that it's different for women in there. When you're property to be traded around, no one needs revenge on you. Being there is revenge enough."

Maybe there was a truth to that, but it didn't negate his truth, either. "The Sons don't let anything live that doesn't have use to them."

"And yet here you are, alive and well. What use do you serve, Jamison?"

It was pointless to try to get through to her. And she was wrong. He'd understood he had a different place in the Sons than she did when they were still stuck there. Why did she think he'd risked his life to get her out?

But with or without her cooperation he could make some educated guesses. Luckily, he knew the area around Flynn well. When he'd been growing up, the Sons had had two main camps—one directly in the Badlands, though outside the park, and another closer to Bonesteel. Flynn had been the middle ground, and Dad's special place. He'd called it sentimental, but Jamison had known better than that.

Flynn was where Ace Wyatt had taken his sons when he wanted to hurt them. Warp them and mold them into the kind of man Ace was.

The fact Ace had never been able to do it was probably his biggest and only regret. Which was why Jamison had known, no matter how he'd hoped otherwise, that he walked through this life with a target on his chest.

Dad wouldn't die until he exacted revenge on his sons

for refusing to be broken. Ace had built his gang and his power on his control, though. He didn't need death and revenge immediately. He wanted it to hurt. He wanted it to *mean* something.

Letting his children build lives, only to take them away, was exactly the kind of thing Ace got off on.

Jamison glanced at Liza. There was true fear there—for Gigi. But this could still be a trap. For all he knew, his father or hers could have demanded his head for Gigi's. He wouldn't put it past any of them, and he could hardly blame Liza for using him to save her sister.

"You know, if they sent you here under the guise of some kind of trade, it's not going to end well."

She laughed. Bitterly. "I know you don't know me at all, and, sure, I'd love to trade your life for my sister's, but they didn't ask. Even if they had, I'd know better than to make a deal with the devil. The devil always wins, and I will not let Gigi lose."

She was vehement and angry, and he wished that didn't make him believe her. He wished it could remind him to harden himself against her. But when it came to Liza, wishes had never come true.

"If we save her—get her out and safe, truly safe, you won't be able to go back. Not ever."

She turned her head to meet his gaze. Her dark eyes were wet but filled with fierce determination. "I know."

There was more he could say, but he figured they should get where they were going first. And he should get the emotions complicating this rescue mission under control.

LIZA DIDN'T TRY to keep track of the circuitous path Jamison was driving. They were getting closer to Flynn, and she was getting closer to falling apart altogether.

She should have asked one of his brothers. Or kept on trying to find Gigi herself. She never should have involved Jamison, thinking old hurts had been eradicated.

Because they weren't gone, only buried, and every disdainful look or overly obvious statement from him dug deeper to the heart of all that old pain.

But she'd suffer through it for Gigi. She hadn't been able to save Marci from the Sons. Liza didn't know how to live having failed both her sisters. One failure was hard enough.

If she could save Gigi, get her away from the Sons, well, yeah, she wouldn't be able to go back. But going back to the Sons had only ever been to save her sisters.

Just like, once upon a time, Jamison had saved his brothers.

She could have told him. If she explained to him why she left, he would have insisted she should have told him, and *he* would have taken care of the problem.

Maybe he would have, but she'd known how hard it had been. She'd watched him put all five of his brothers before him. She'd watched him put *her* before him. To have asked him to do that again for something that was her responsibility had felt wrong.

She'd wanted to live up to the unreachable example he'd set. Instead, no matter how Liza had fought for her, Marci had thrown her life into the Sons. Liza hadn't given up on Marci, which was why she'd stayed so long, until Marci had only laughed when her boyfriend had threatened to murder Liza in her sleep if she came near them again.

By then, Carlee had been pregnant, and Liza had spent the last four years trying to talk some sense into the girl. Get them all out—she knew what it was like to be separated from your mother and she didn't want to do it to

Gigi. Carlee had wavered back and forth, giving in just enough for Liza to keep hoping she could save them all.

Now Carlee was dead, Gigi was missing and the truth was Liza wasn't good enough for this. She needed the only man she knew who was.

"We'll camp here."

She sat up a little straighter, peering out the window. They'd gotten closer to the Badlands. The rock formations that made the area famous surrounded them. Craggy valleys and the eruption of rock stretched for miles, making it difficult to hide from all directions, but Liza had no doubt Jamison knew what he was doing.

"Camp?" It was still early enough spring that nights would be frigid.

"Did you think we were heading for a resort?"

She snorted. "Yeah. That's what I was expecting."

"Camper shell is set up on the bed. We'll be fine."

"Tight quarters."

"Safer that way. We'll eat a little something now. Then figure out our best bet for hideaways around Flynn."

"It's been three days since I've seen her. They could have taken her anywhere."

"Could have, but we know how they operate. Somewhere close."

"Jamison…" She didn't want to tell him. Didn't want to shift the focus away from finding Gigi, but if the whispers she heard were true, Gigi could be far, far away. "There's something more."

"Isn't there always," he muttered, pushing out of the truck.

Liza didn't know if his disgust was aimed at her or at the Sons in general, but she got out of the truck herself and crossed over to his side of the vehicle, where he was pulling out the food provisions.

"There've been rumors. Whispers. Nothing concrete and I haven't seen evidence, but if it's true…" Liza could hardly speak it. She so desperately didn't want it to be true.

Jamison put the cooler on the ground and stared expectantly at her, folding his arms over his chest when she still didn't talk. He gave her what she was sure was a very effective cop look. But she was too heartsick over Gigi to be intimidated by it.

"Trafficking," she managed to say through a too-tight throat.

"Drugs are hardly new to the Sons' operations."

"Human, Jamison. Human trafficking. Sex trafficking." She desperately tried to keep the tremor out of her voice and failed. "Gigi's such an innocent."

The impenetrable cop mask gave way to full-on horror. "She's four, you said."

"I don't know much about it, but I assume it doesn't matter how old you are. Long as a person is female and vulnerable. Hell, maybe only vulnerable. You're a cop. Surely you've seen the worst humans can do to children."

He turned away from her at that, focusing on the food.

"The point of me telling you that is if she got pulled into something…different, they're not going to follow the old rules."

He put together a sandwich and handed it to her. It took her a minute to get ahold of herself enough to take it. Despite it being her favorite—ham and Swiss, heavy on the cheese, light on the meat—she didn't have an appetite for it.

If nothing else, she could find some tiny satisfaction over the fact that he remembered what she liked to eat. That he didn't only remember the ways she'd betrayed him.

"The Sons do things a certain way," he said, making his own sandwich. "Even if it's new, the ways will be old. They evolve, but they don't change. We just have to figure out where they'd be able to hide human cargo instead of drugs. I think we can."

"You're awfully confident."

"You came to me for a reason, Liza. I have to believe it's because you thought I could do this."

Since she didn't trust her voice, she nodded.

"Then I'll do it."

Chapter Six

Jamison was pretty sure they hadn't been tailed, and they had a few hours before anyone in the Sons figured out their location. The tails would have tried to follow or figure out where he'd gone before contacting their superiors—probably not his father or Liza's. These geniuses were too low in the pecking order. So, the chain of communication would take time.

Once they sent more men—better trackers—it'd still take a good hour. Too many places to look—and he was still a distance from Flynn, which was naturally where the men would start their search.

But even knowing he had a few hours of safety, he wasn't about to sleep on the same little air mattress in the camper shell of Grandma's truck with his ex.

He had supreme willpower, but he also knew better than to test it with Liza.

Instead, he took the first shift, sleeping when he knew there would be the least chance of being caught. Though he told her to wake him up in two hours, he also set the timer on his phone because he didn't quite trust her.

He shouldn't trust her at all—with anything. This human trafficking thing could be a crock for all he knew.

But why would it be? Jamison certainly couldn't put it past the old man. Even though Liza might have lied to him once upon a time, he had a hard time believing even now that she was the kind of woman who could lie about her sister being in trouble like that.

Which probably made him an *excellent* mark.

He sighed. He could sleep with the best of them in the worst situations, but not with all this doubt and uncertainty.

Still, he wanted Liza to think he'd slept. That way she'd be more likely to sleep herself.

If this wasn't a giant con.

He pulled his phone out of his pocket. No service here, which he'd known going in. Still, he typed in a text to Cody and Brady about the potential of the Sons being involved in human trafficking. If he got into a place with service, the text would go through. Hopefully.

He put the phone back in his pocket and then pulled out the map of South Dakota. It was worn in the creases, and no doubt there were more high-tech ways to keep his records, but Jamison preferred what he could see spread out before him.

This wasn't the same map he'd shown Liza last night, which was up in the front of the truck. This was his personal map, and how he'd been keeping tabs on the Sons for most of his life. Even before he'd escaped and become an officer of the law.

He'd marked everything he'd known while he'd been in. Anyplace they hid people or drugs. Their entire array of camps over the years. Crimes. Disappearances. Deaths.

A story of all the things he hadn't been able to prevent. After Dev's near-death run-in with the Sons, Ace in particular, Jamison had given up on taking them down and had instead focused on keeping what he could and whom he could safe.

All along he'd marked this map every time he heard

something, hadn't he? So, it hadn't been giving up, no matter what he told himself. Maybe he'd just been waiting for the right opportunity.

He let out a slow breath. If he was only putting himself in danger, it wouldn't worry him. But it wasn't just him. Liza was here, too.

Jamison shoved that thought away. She was in danger because she wanted to be. He couldn't let that weigh on his conscience. Besides, she'd be in a heck of a lot more hot water if he *wasn't* here.

He studied the map. Flynn was a speck. Mostly a ghost town when Jamison had been growing up, and he imagined it still was. With the addition of the Sons camp.

They wouldn't keep Gigi there, and if Liza's trafficking story was right on, they'd be very careful.

What little Jamison knew about human trafficking wasn't pretty. He had a feeling Cody would know more. Maybe he should drive until they got service, get in touch with his brother.

But that would draw attention and he wanted to lie as low as he could. Whenever Dad's men arrived, and they would arrive, it would give Jamison an indication of what they were trying to hide.

There weren't many of Jamison's marks around Flynn on the map. Flynn was sacred ground to Dad. Where he'd been born. Where his parents had left him to die. Where he, in his mind, rose from the ashes as a poor castoff to the deadliest man in South Dakota.

Flynn was Dad's mecca. If he was having the whole gang camp there in his sacred spot, something was escalating. Was it the human trafficking?

If so, the hiding area would be somewhere close, but not too close. If Jamison had to guess, it would be somewhere in the buttes and gullies. Caves, maybe. Isolated, surely. Would they bring potential buyers there, or ship the cargo off?

If they were shipping, they'd go west into Wyoming. Best chance of being undetected while moving groups of people.

There were too many possibilities after that. Denver... farther west. Jamison folded Wyoming and Colorado out of view. Focus on one thing at a time. Narrow down the options to locate where they were potentially holding Gigi.

It would be somewhere west of Flynn, but not into the national park. Too easy and possible to be accidentally stumbled upon.

Jamison planned on canvassing from the national park line out toward Flynn. He tried not to think of the huge, nearly impossible task of finding people who didn't want to be found in the great, empty landscape beyond the national park.

When he got into cell range he'd call Felicity, see if she'd heard of any strange goings-on around the park. One of the Knight girls who was now a park ranger, Felicity was too dang nice to hold a grudge against Liza. She'd probably jump right in to help.

But that would only be when and if they got into cell service range. For now... Well, he'd stop pretending he was sleeping. Liza could get a few hours and he could make all sorts of contingency plans as he waited and watched for his father's men to hunt them down.

And lead them exactly where he wanted to go.

He opened the camper shell and slid out, already scanning his surroundings.

Liza nearly jerked where she was standing, something gold and familiar in her hand. She fisted her fingers over it, then stood there, still as a statue.

"Thought you were going to sleep longer," she offered when he did nothing more than crouch at the shell's opening.

He barely heard her over the awful pounding of his heart.

"What's that?" he demanded, even though he knew exactly what it was. Even though the last thing he wanted was confirmation. Not with the past whipping around them in the wind.

She looked down at her fisted hand, then met his gaze with defiance and sadness in her own. He'd been so convinced that if he got her out of the Sons he could get rid of that misery. But he'd been eighteen and foolish.

"You know what it is," she said, and he shouldn't have been able to hear her with the way the Dakota winds were swirling with their usual violence.

But he did.

"Why do you still have it?" Which was another question he didn't actually want an answer to. But somehow the questions kept falling out of his mouth, like his brain wasn't in charge—something instinctual was.

"You told me it was good luck," she said, opening her fingers and letting the chain dangle from them. The heart locket twirled in the wind. "Figured I'd need some of that in my life—now more than ever."

Too many questions piled up in his brain. Most of all: Was the same picture still inside that stupid locket?

It didn't matter. None of the questions about the past mattered. So, he'd focus on the surroundings, on the next move. He'd concentrate on anything except the way she looked down at the locket in her fist like it held all the answers to her broken dreams.

Walking among the ghosts between them was emotional suicide. It complicated everything and, most of all, it did not matter.

But his heart couldn't seem to let it go the way his brain urged him to. "Why did you leave?"

LIZA DIDN'T MOVE. She was afraid that if she did, she'd move toward him instead of far, far away.

"I thought you had it all figured out," she said, not daring to look at him. He'd see all the pain that was surely radiating from her like the dust the wind picked up and swirled between them.

He turned away with no small amount of disgust. She still knew him well enough to know the loathing was aimed inward. He didn't want to ask her questions like that. He wanted to be above the past.

But he wasn't. Something stirred inside her that would be close to deadly here in this moment, but she'd never been very adept at knowing what was good for her.

It was so hard to watch him be the man she'd always known he'd grow into. Hard to feel all those same emotions she thought time had eradicated. Could he love a woman he hadn't seen for fifteen years? *Someone whom he hated*, she thought.

He couldn't.

Maybe the locket was good luck, though, even with all these conflicting emotions, because Jamison's gaze went to the horizon, hard and cold. It was different than even back in Bonesteel before she'd been shot. There had been a heat to his disdain then.

This was pure, deadly cold.

Which stirred something inside her, too. That old need to soothe him, to give him the warmth everything about the Sons had dimmed into that coldness.

"Get in the truck," he ordered.

She didn't argue, didn't try to see what he saw, because there was no doubt in her mind the Sons had found them.

She got in the truck.

Back then, she'd fought Jamison tooth and nail more often than not, but these days she was grateful to have someone take the lead. She was tired of trying to stay one step ahead of the Sons and failing.

Jamison slid into the driver's seat, opening a map on his lap. He took a pencil from the middle console and marked a few things.

"What are you doing?" she asked, hoping the question didn't sound like an accusation. But men were after them and he was taking notes?

"We've got three cars—I'm guessing two men apiece. They're all coming from the west. So, we'll head there. Grab that pack there in the back."

He kept looking at the map while she struggled to pull the giant, heavy backpack into the front seat.

He made a few more notes on his map, and then carefully folded it and shoved it into his pocket. He took the bag from her, nodding into the back again. "Grab the smaller one. We're going on a hike. Your leg up for it?"

Even if it wasn't, she would have nodded. She wasn't about to be the person holding Jamison back. Not when she was the reason he was here in the first place.

She snatched the pack and followed his lead getting back out of the truck. She didn't see anything on the horizon to the west, except maybe some upturned dust. Still, she trusted Jamison's instincts.

They shouldered their individual packs. Without any verbal instruction, Liza knew to fall in step behind Jamison. Her leg hurt, but it was a low-level, throbbing ache she'd get used to.

And if she didn't, she'd just think of Gigi in danger and suck it up.

He led her down into a valley, over the crumbling rock that made up the strange formations that drew sightseers every year. They weren't as big or uninterrupted here as they were in the national park. Here there were still gaps of flat land with early green grass growing.

She tried not to make a sound when she stumbled and hit her leg the wrong way. Jamison didn't look back at her, his attention focused on what she assumed was the path in his mind.

"Why are we leaving the truck behind?" Liza asked as she skidded on a rock and just barely stopped herself from stumbling over a dangerous edge.

"We're going to hike around, let them think we abandoned the vehicle. They'll start looking for us on foot, and they'll probably start from the truck and move toward the target. If we circle up and around, we can get back to the truck in a few hours. From the direction they came, I've got a few ideas about where a trafficking hideout might be."

"What if they guard the truck? Or torch it?"

She could tell he hadn't thought of that, because his forward motion paused almost imperceptibly. "They won't torch it. Their prime objective is to find us, and likely bring us in front of our fathers. The truck is inconsequential."

Liza didn't bother to argue as she looked back at the truck, a sitting duck for the destruction the Sons liked to inflict on anything in their path.

Jamison no doubt had it right that if they were caught they'd be brought in front of their fathers and the "council." Judgment would be meted out, and Liza shuddered to think what awful things might be waiting for her and Jamison.

But she didn't think his assessment of what could happen with the truck was right—at all.

Chapter Seven

They hiked for a good hour. He had the route fixed in his mind, but still, he used his compass to make sure they weren't getting turned around in the rock formations that could start to look all the same if one didn't know how to navigate them.

The sun slowly started its descent, and Jamison began to lead them back to the truck. He was pretty sure he'd timed it right, but he still kept the pace slow and steady—Liza behind him rather than next to him—as they got closer and closer to where he'd left the truck.

He wanted to be back there by the time the sun went down. It would get exponentially colder as the day wore on, and while he'd packed Liza some warmer gear, he doubted she needed a long hike in the cold with her current injuries.

She'd held up like a champ and he opened his mouth to tell her so but closed it instead. She didn't need his encouragement. She was trying to save her sister. Not earn brownie points with him.

He wasn't her protector anymore, even if she'd come and asked him for a hand. Help wasn't the same as saving someone. He didn't need to rescue her. Just like all of these feelings wrapping around him would go away. It was memory, not reality.

They meant nothing to each other. Nothing at all.

He'd get it through his thick skull eventually.

There was a tinge to the air as they approached the truck, and a low-level dread crept across his skin. The acrid smell of fire and chemicals became more and more potent the closer they got to the vehicle.

Still, he wouldn't let himself believe the worst. What possible reason would they have had to burn the truck? It would draw notice—and the one thing the Sons had always shied away from was too much attention from the law.

But as he closed in on the clearing, he could see the dark smoke. They stepped level with the truck and all Jamison could do was stop and stare.

They'd torched it, just as Liza had worried about. It smoked, the blackened wreckage of his grandmother's truck a grotesque twisted skeletal remain on the dusty landscape. An incongruous image against the riotous sunset.

Jamison tried not to let it get to him, but it was living proof he'd gone soft. He'd been sure they wouldn't bother, so certain he knew what they were planning and how to defeat them. His stomach twisted and pitched at all the ways he'd been wrong—and all he might still miscalculate before this fool's mission was over.

"Grandma Pauline is going to kick your butt," Liza said with some amusement. The sunset was a splash of brilliant colors behind her. A sure sign a storm would roll in halfway through the night.

All they had were the packs on their back.

Kick his butt? Grandma was going to skin him. *If* they made it out of this alive. For the first time he fully understood why Liza had been so scared, why she'd come to him as a last resort. Lives were on the line—in a way they hadn't been as much when they'd been kids—or at least in a way he hadn't fully grasped when he'd been a teenager full of self-righteous outrage.

Worst of all, Liza didn't seem any kind of surprised. She'd warned him, hadn't she? He could only stare at the wreckage and wonder...

He'd saved his five brothers, and Liza for as long as she'd let that last. The Wyatt boys had built lives of their own, and while they hadn't brought down the Sons, they'd survived them. Escaped them. It was supposed to be enough. After Dev's close call, Jamison had told himself it was.

It burned like acid in his gut that he'd done exactly what Liza had told him not to do: underestimate the Sons. All because once upon a time he'd considered escape a win.

It had taken all of his thirty-seven years, but he finally accepted wholly and fully that escape and survival weren't a win. Not fully. Not yet.

"They're not the Sons you used to know, Jamison," Liza said softly. As if she was comforting him instead of saying "I told you so."

He'd kept tabs, though. He'd watched. How could he not have seen they were different now? Bolder. Surer. Far more dangerous.

"You have to know what unchecked power does to men," Liza continued, as if every emotion and thought was broadcast across his face. Which it might be. Which was as unacceptable as this miscalculation.

"It grows and grows until there is nothing left. No one challenges them. Everyone fears them. Even the bigger agencies haven't bothered trying to infiltrate in years. The Sons have everything they ever wanted, but they will always want more. So, they will destroy and destroy and destroy. Because nothing can stop them."

She'd started out unmoved. Resigned, almost, but as she spoke the emotion crept into her voice and vibrated there. And deep inside him.

"They were bad enough then," he said, still not able to wrap his mind around her words. How could they be stronger, more feared? How was it possible? Right was supposed to win—he'd won all those years ago.

Except right hadn't won. It had just escaped.

"They're worse now," Liza said with a conviction he no longer questioned.

Facts were facts, and the fact was that the Sons he'd known wouldn't have bothered. They wouldn't have wanted to draw attention with a burned-out truck in the middle of nowhere.

If what Liza said was true, and they'd grown and the powers that be had stopped their periodic attempts to infiltrate and disband…

He blew out a breath, letting concern out with it. Because he needed a new plan, and emotion wouldn't get him anywhere. Not guilt or failure or weakness.

He glanced at Liza, who was watching the smoke as if it were just an average sight. Care wouldn't get him anywhere, either, but it sat there in his gut like an old illness he hadn't fully cured.

But remembering that time, and the boy he'd been, Jamison realized he needed to access that person again. Find his youthful certainty. His adolescent arrogance. He had to be ready to risk anything again.

The goal wouldn't be *escape* this time. There would be an end.

He'd been resigned to the fact that getting involved

might bring him into contact with his father again, *might* be the tipping point for his father's eventual revenge.

But now he understood there was no *might* about it. It was time to end what he'd let fester and grow and rot the landscape he loved so much.

He stared at the truck and gave up everything he'd chosen to bury in the past fifteen years. He let it go on the wind. Maybe he'd subconsciously known this was coming, because there was only a little pain, quickly smothered by the cold certainty that had made up his teenage years.

"Unchecked power gets checked eventually, Liza. No one gets to rule forever."

"And when would that eventually come to pass?" she asked, as if she didn't see the change in him. As if she couldn't feel the change in the air.

He looked back at her then, met her furious and frightened, dark gaze, orange and red blazing behind her like the apocalypse was already coming for them.

It was. It was time.

They'd find Gigi.

Then he'd go after the Sons.

"It gets checked now."

THE LOOK ON Jamison's face made her shiver for more than one reason. It reminded her of the boy she'd known.

And loved.

Which was a terrible thing to be thrust into—those old feelings, made more potent by the fact they *weren't* teenagers anymore. This wasn't about *freedom* anymore.

It was about her sister's life, and maybe theirs.

The tremor was fear, but it was also something deeper, something more elemental. A sensation she would not under any circumstances let herself acknowledge.

She sincerely hoped.

"What are we going to do?" she asked, her voice barely more than a whisper.

He frowned, considered the landscape, then pinned her with another too-potent stare. "What do you think we should do?"

"What?"

"You were right about the truck. You..." He shook his head almost imperceptibly. "I thought I'd been keeping tabs, but clearly not well enough. You know them, have a better understanding of their moves than I do."

"I'm not *one* of them, Jamison. When will you—"

"I didn't say you were. I said you know them. We need to use that understanding, because I can't anticipate their moves anymore."

"I don't—"

"You'll stop that now."

She was too shocked by the snap in his tone to give him a piece of her mind.

"You know. You've been living inside the Sons for fifteen years. You don't have to pretend I know more than you. I'm not going to punish you for it."

"That isn't what I—"

He merely raised an eyebrow and she trailed off. He was right, partially. She was too used to the habit of pretending she didn't know anything—to save her skin. She was used to using all her skills and knowledge on the sly.

She wasn't used to...a partner. She didn't want one. "I'm tired, Jamison," she said, trying to keep her voice from breaking. "I've been fighting this battle for too long. You know what that feels like."

"Yeah. And I know you can't quit until Gigi is safe. But you have me, Liza. I'm not asking you to do this on your own. I'm asking you to use your brain."

"You always did it on your own."

"No, I didn't. My brothers and you were all old enough to hold your own when I helped you escape. Gigi is four. Besides, you said it yourself. They're more dangerous now. So, we need to work together. If you were alone—what would you do next?"

Liza scrubbed her hands over her face. Her leg ached, and so did her head. Her eyes were gritty from the dust in the wind and she desperately wanted to go to sleep.

But if she was alone, she'd press on. To somewhere she thought Gigi might be. "I'd just keep looking. They won't have given up on trying to find us. Burning the truck was a message. But you were right earlier—it isn't our fathers out searching for us, so they're not going to kill us. But they want to find us—bringing us to our fathers? Jackpot."

"Why didn't your father do anything to you when you went back?"

Liza didn't react to that question. It was one of the ones she'd been ready for. Still, the glib lie or clever redirect didn't flow off her tongue like she'd practiced.

"Just another thing I'm underestimating, isn't it?"

His voice was far too soft, far too much like the boy she remembered. "Women don't mean as much there. You know that." She kept her back to him and closed her eyes against how pathetic that lie sounded.

"Loyalty matters. Above all else."

"Yeah, well. I survived, didn't I? The task at hand is getting to Gigi. They'll know that she's what I'm after. If they're smart, they'll just lie in wait."

"If?"

"It's not that they're not smart, but they're cocky. Some can be impatient with Ace's orders, trying to move up the chain. I've noticed..." She trailed off but Jamison only waited. It was hard to break the habit of keeping her thoughts, her theories to herself. But he was right. They had to do this together—not him or her, but them. "Ace's best men? I haven't seen them around much. It's just a hunch, but I thought maybe they were put in charge of the trafficking. Which would leave his next tier with the job of finding us. They're not the top tier for a reason, though."

"More brawn than brains?"

She nodded. Some things he still understood.

"Hence the torched truck. All right. So, we'll keep heading toward Flynn. Do you think they'll come back?"

Liza looked around. Daylight was fading. In the east, darkness was beginning to twinkle with the first hint of stars. She could feel the temperature dropping already and the wind gave no sign of letting up.

"Not tonight. They'll spend the night closer to the other men. They'll check in with either our fathers or whoever their direct orders are coming from. They'll revise their plan and move out at daybreak."

"And whoever is in charge of the trafficking will likely be getting ready to mobilize. They won't wait."

"I don't know if it's true," Liza said, and this time not because she was afraid of voicing her opinion. But because she desperately didn't want it to be true. She had to believe it was *possible* she was overreacting.

But when she met Jamison's gaze it was too…kind. And laced with pity. She turned away. "We need to move through the night, get a head start on them if we can."

"Agreed." He moved over to her, but she didn't dare look up. She felt him unzip her pack and then slide it off her shoulders. When she finally worked up the nerve to look at him, he was holding out a sweatshirt. "Put this on, then the coat. Lose the leather."

She wanted to argue, but she had *some* common sense. The sweatshirt and the coat he held in his hand would keep her far warmer than her thin coat ever would. Still, the old leather coat was something of a talisman. It had survived and so had she.

He sighed, and as if reading her mind, shook out the sweatshirt, then did the honors himself. He pulled the sweatshirt over her head—and over the jacket. Then he held out the coat.

Swallowing against the lump in her throat, she slid one arm in, and then the other. Before she could move to zip it up herself, he did it.

Too close. Too Jamison. She wanted to lean forward because she knew, no matter how many reservations he still had about her, no matter how much bitterness he still held on to over the way she'd left, he'd hold her and tell her it would be okay.

Which would break her completely. So, she stood statue-still as he zipped up the coat.

"I've done this before," he said, that quiet sureness she remembered about him threading through those words. Making her waver against the determination not to lean into him. "I can do it again."

She let that break the spell. She'd once thought him infallible magic, but she didn't believe anyone was that anymore. "Don't make promises you don't know you can keep, Jamison. You'll only beat yourself up about it later."

"I'll beat myself up about it either way," he muttered, releasing the zipper. "If you need a break, a rest, a snack, speak up. Best we keep our strength up."

He hefted the pack onto her back again, then pulled two headlamps out of his. He handed her one. "Put it on your head, but leave the light off and stay close to me for as much of the hike as you can." He pulled the small light onto his head, illuminating the space between them.

Then he handed her a gun.

Chapter Eight

Once Jamison made a decision, he didn't waver. Usually. But handing a woman he didn't fully trust a loaded gun while ordering her to hike behind him left him vulnerable.

Hell, if he was going to go now, it might as well be at Liza's hand behind his back. Symbolic, and surely the rightful end to his own stupidity.

But as they set off, his own loaded gun strapped to his side, Liza didn't make any moves to turn the weapon on him. She kept her headlamp on her head, but the light off. Which meant she walked close enough to him that his light guided them both.

He couldn't watch her for signs of her limp worsening or her expression for signs of fatigue, but after at least a good hour of harrowing hiking in the dark, he decided to take it upon himself to say they needed a break.

He handed her a bottle of water and a protein bar and considered himself something of a saint for not lecturing her when she grimaced at it and stuck it in her coat pocket rather than eat it.

"We should change your bandage."

She shook her head. "Not yet. We need to be closer. Besides, it feels fine."

He doubted it very much, but studying her in the eerie

glow of his lamplight didn't show any undue signs of pain or worry. It would take up too much valuable time to argue with her, so he nodded, took another swig of water and then packed it all away.

They started out again. He kept on the lookout for signs of human and animal life. Bobcats were a concern, as was stumbling upon a sleeping anything. Then there were the rattlers—dangerous this time of year if only because disturbing rock as they hiked might accidentally unearth a den.

The last thing either of them needed was a run-in with the kind of wildlife that could injure them. Especially in the dark, without cell service and with a biker gang looking for them.

So, Jamison kept a slow, careful pace—refusing to let the irritation or impatience gain purchase. Maybe they were racing against the clock, but he doubted the Sons were racing against the same one. And if they were, he'd have to deal with that, but not at the expense of making a mistake here and now.

For now, slow and steady was the best they could do, and he could not let the driving need to get closer, faster, push him into doing something dumb.

He kept watch of the time, making sure they stopped and had a snack or drink each hour. Each time, he checked her over.

On the third stop, knowing they were getting closer to Flynn and they'd have to be even more careful so as not to stumble across members of the Sons, he looked her over with a critical eye.

She appeared tired, but he was sure he did, too. She'd stopped walking, so he couldn't assess her limp, but as he looked down at where the wound was, he swore. There was blood seeping into the pants Grandma had given her this morning—which meant she had probably broken a stitch and was bleeding through her bandage. "We need to change the dressing on your leg."

"We don't have time."

"I'll be quick."

"Trying to get me naked again. It's tiresome."

"As tiresome as that joke." He dropped his pack, pulled out the first aid kit. "You must have busted a stitch. You need a tighter bandage. If that doesn't stop bleeding…"

"Yeah, yeah, yeah," she muttered. She pushed the pants down past the bandage that was completely soaked with blood.

"This isn't good."

"It could be a heck of a lot worse."

True enough, and they didn't have time to argue over it. He removed the bloody gauze and packed it up in one of the zipper bags he'd brought. He did his best to disinfect in the cold, dusty wind and the dim light of his headlamp.

She shivered in the cold, and he worked as fast and efficiently as he could. It looked like only one stitch had broken, so he did his best to tighten the bandage over it. She needed to be in a hospital. If this got worse, she'd be more liability than help.

He opened his mouth to say just that, but then thought better of it. Liza was the one dealing with the pain. She wanted to save her sister. She knew what she was doing. It wasn't his job to police her.

It never had been, and he frowned at the thought he might have done it anyway. Had he been the reason she left? He'd been too heavy-handed in trying to keep her safe and she'd escaped to the only place she'd known to go?

Senseless questions. Useless thoughts. It did not matter, and he had to stop letting his mind go to the past.

But as he stood after patching her up and putting away the first aid kit, he had to accept that whether or not he wanted to deal with the past, it was here. Always in the air between them, an electricity that seemed to charge off each other. It was the past, it was attraction and it was as potent as it had been back then.

There was too much still *here*—maybe it was the unfinished ending they'd had or maybe it was something deeper—but it seemed to thicken and get harder to fight against.

They stood too close, looked at each other too long, and no matter that he knew his brain was cautioning him to move, to focus, to *stop*, he hovered exactly where he was. Too close to her. Too tempted to…

"You'd only hate yourself as much as you hate me," Liza whispered, breaking that moment. Thank God.

He would hate himself, she had that right, but something about the pitch-black night made it easier to access the full, awful truth, instead of burying it down deep. "Being hurt and hate aren't the same thing, Liza. Don't conflate that. They do. I won't."

He stepped back, letting her fix her pants over the bandage herself.

"It must be nice to have just left the Sons, cut out all that horror and be perfect and happy now," she said, her voice harsh and full of emotion here in the dark. "It must be so nice to have left it all behind."

"You could have," he reminded her, though it didn't come out harsh. He was starting to feel a tiredness creep in, which drained him of the energy to maintain a facade of strength. It left only the truth.

"No, I couldn't."

"If you say so."

"Marci was still in there."

He didn't want to get into the whys of her leaving. Or perhaps more honestly, he desperately wanted to get into it and knew it wouldn't satisfy either of them. "Your sister didn't want to be saved. It's why we left her in the first place. You said you were fine with it. I don't know why the four years you were out would have changed that."

"That's it for you? You don't try to save someone you love just because they don't want to be saved?"

He noted she didn't address all the holes he'd just punched in her argument, but he didn't need to keep falling into potholes of the past. He needed to complete this mission and move on before that temptation took him someplace he didn't want to be. "Not if you plan on saving yourself."

"You couldn't understand. You didn't have to leave anyone behind."

It was painful that she could think that. That anything he'd done then or now had been *easy*. That there was anything *nice* about knowing your father was a monster and if you weren't careful that perversion might bloom inside you, too.

So, instead of responding, he walked on.

HER LEG HURT so much she wanted to cry. Her heart hurt just as much. At too many things. Not just the way he'd gently rebandaged her wound, or the way he'd looked at her afterward—like no time had passed at all. But at what he'd said, at the way he'd dismissed Marci, and at the shock of hurt on his face when she'd said he'd left nothing behind.

Then he'd blanked it all away and started walking again.

Remorse pulsed inside her like a heartbeat. Regret

twined around her lungs, making it hard to breathe without crying.

But she forged ahead because Gigi was what was important, not her screwed-up past or any lingering feelings she had for Jamison Wyatt.

Being hurt and hate aren't the same thing, Liza. Don't conflate that.

Those words would haunt her until the day she died. Because all she'd ever known growing up was hate and hurt. She hadn't seen a sparkle of goodness anywhere except in the Wyatt boys, and then out there in the world Jamison had given her.

Maybe there were more reasons she hadn't been able to stay out there than just Marci. Maybe all that goodness of Grandma Pauline and the Knights had been too much to bear. Too good to accept when all she'd ever known was bad.

What a horribly depressing thought. But she had to cut herself *some* slack. She'd been twenty. Maybe things would have been different if she'd been younger, or older.

But things couldn't be different, because she'd made her choices. Just like Marci had made hers. Carlee hers.

But Gigi didn't have choices.

So, Liza kept moving, ignoring the pain in her leg. But she couldn't quite ignore the pain in her heart, too. "Did you ever want to go back?"

If he was surprised by the question, he didn't act it. "I don't know."

She'd expected an emphatic no, or a certainty at the very least, not *I don't know.* That was enough to throw her already unbalanced world even more off-kilter. Jamison *always* knew.

"What do you mean you don't know?" she demanded.

"It's too complicated," he replied, moving forward at a quicker pace that had her scurrying to catch up with him.

"That's not an answer, Jamison."

He sighed heavily. "The answer lies somewhere in the middle. It was home, much as I hated it. He's my father, much as I hate him. I didn't want to *go back*, but there were days I didn't…*not* want to go back."

She shook her head, as if she could negate what was clearly an honest answer. She knew that churn too well, wanting both things in the same breath. Never being quite right.

And she'd never been able to express that to anyone, but Jamison had distilled it into a few words. Ones that would probably only ever make sense to them.

Now was hardly the time to wade into it, but if not now—when? When would she ever be able to talk about this with someone? Jamison was the only one who understood both sides of the life. "If it was complicated to stay away, don't you think it was complicated to go back?"

Jamison was quiet for a while, but eventually he responded, though he sidestepped the question. "Conflicted or not. I didn't go back. That's the difference."

"I *had* to go back."

"If that's what you need to tell yourself, Liza, go ahead. You don't need me to absolve you of your choices. If you needed that, you wouldn't have left."

She stopped walking at that, because it was true. She didn't need his approval or his forgiveness. If she'd asked herself a day ago, she would have said she didn't want it.

But here in the middle of the howling, frigid dark, her leg pulsing with pain and her heart aching, she realized that was what she'd been craving since she'd sneaked out of the Knights' house all those years ago.

His approval. His forgiveness.

She was too old for both. Too old for this.

"As far as I'm concerned, it doesn't matter," Jamison said, still moving, far enough away she had to flip on her own lamp to catch up without tripping. "We're here for one thing and one thing only."

"Gigi."

Which meant she had to give all that acceptance and forgiveness to herself, rather than waiting for Jamison to give it to her.

She blew out a breath. It was a shaking realization, and yet it took no weight off her shoulders. Not until Gigi was safe. Once Gigi was safe, Liza could build her own life.

Her *own* life. Anywhere and anyhow she pleased. Regardless of Jamison or the Sons.

She breathed again, letting her heart beat in time with the pulse of her wounds. She'd use all that *hurt* to drive her through the fear. Straight into a future no one but her got to dictate.

She caught up to Jamison, flicking off her light once she was close enough to walk in the beam of his. They walked in silence, which Liza figured was for the best.

No more talking. No more trying to get him to believe or see something in her. It didn't matter. She just had to *remember* that. Remember *those* words of not needing his absolution over the words of hurt and hate.

They didn't hate each other. They didn't have to forgive each other.

They just had to forgive themselves. She wondered if he ever had, and doubted it very, very much.

Jamison stopped abruptly, quickly turning off his headlamp. Liza sucked in a breath and held it. Far off in the distance, something flickered. Firelight, if she had to guess.

Chapter Nine

"That'll be a camp of some kind. All of them?" Jamison glanced back at Liza because he was determined to rely on her information as much as his own instincts.

She had an odd expression on her face. The fear and uncertainty were gone. Even the snarky, careless mask she'd worn at first was missing.

She looked fierce. Determined. He glanced at her leg—as far as he could tell, the bandage was holding and no new blood was leaking out.

"Probably all of the ones looking for us. Most of them at the very least," she said with complete certainty.

"You stay here and—"

"No. Never separate," Liza said emphatically, which might have swayed him if those words and the way she said them didn't remind him of his father.

"That's a Sons rule."

"It's a smart one," she said, not wavering. "If we're going to outwit them, we need to play by their rules."

"Never."

"Jamison, I won't let your pride or honor or baggage or whatever you want to call it get in the way here. You said you were ready to check their power and face them and your father. You know you can't do it as a cop. You have to do it as Jamison Wyatt."

I'd rather die. He didn't say it out loud because he knew how words like *die* could become a little too real when dealing with the Sons. "I won't be Ace, Liza. I can't be."

"I'm not saying you have to be, Jamison. But we have to fight with some of the ruthlessness they do or we'll never survive."

Ruthlessness. He hated that word. As a cop he'd had to harden himself to things. Injustices he'd dreamed of solving. As he'd told Liza, some people didn't want to be saved—and you couldn't survive yourself if you were always trying to save them anyway. But ruthlessness was more than that. It was a loss of humanity—a blackness on your soul.

He'd watched that blackness swallow his father more and more with every year. Because unlike most of his brothers, he could still remember flashes of a man who wasn't *all* bad. At one point, there'd been *some* compassion in Ace Wyatt.

Jamison had never known what exactly eradicated it bit by bit, but he knew it was a slippery slope. The more hurt you inflicted, the less goodness you had inside you—and it didn't always matter if the people you were hurting deserved it.

Slippery slope or not, there was a little four-year-old girl in far more danger than he'd ever been. So, Liza had one thing right. He couldn't play by the cop rules he was used to. He couldn't toe the line of the law like he wanted to.

Ruthless, no, he couldn't promise that. But he'd come here for a reason, and she was right enough that if he was going to check the power of his Sons, and face his father once and for all, he had to be willing to cross some lines he'd promised himself he wouldn't.

But not all of them.

"I can't promise to be ruthless, Liza. I've made too many promises to myself about not becoming Ace. But for a little girl caught up in something that isn't right or fair, I'll do whatever it takes."

She let out a breath, but before she could talk anymore, he forged forward.

"We need to know how many men they have. I think it'd be better, safer and smarter if only one of us got close enough to count. I think since I'm the one without a gunshot wound, it would make the most sense if it was me."

"And if they find you, take you to your father, where does that leave me?"

"The more we know—"

"No. That's the cop talking. We don't need to know what they're doing. We need to know what *we're* doing. We're after Gigi, not them. So, we avoid. What if we hiked around them, keep heading toward Flynn? Surely wherever they're holding Gigi is somewhere between them and Flynn."

"Beyond Flynn. West. It makes it easier to either transport or have a meeting place without bringing outsiders into town," Jamison muttered, vaguely irritated her plan was better.

"So, we hike beyond. Avoid as much detection as possible."

She had a point. He doubted Dad's scouts expected them to hike through the night. If they could get past this group before the sun rose, then they'd only have to worry about camp lookouts, presumably.

If they could get around Flynn before sunrise? Their chances were even better.

"Get out that map of yours. The one with the marks," she ordered.

He shifted his pack and pulled the map out of his pocket. "No headlamps. Hold this while I get my penlight out."

He handed her the map, shrugged off his pack and sifted around until his fingers brushed the slim plastic of his small, precise flashlight.

"Hold out the map," he instructed.

She did, and he studied it with the light, but as they stood there in silence, he stiffened.

A rustle. It could be animal—most likely was, but the hairs on the back of Jamison's neck stood on end. He met Liza's shadowy gaze in the dim penlight. She opened her mouth, but he quickly reached forward and placed his palm over it.

He switched off the light in his other hand and shoved it into his pocket. He needed Liza to fold the map and put it away without him actually saying the words. With his free hand, he reached out until he found one of her hands still gripping the map.

She nodded imperceptibly against the hand on her mouth, so he let his arm drop. Then he took both her hands and pulled them together—trying to get it across that he wanted her to fold up the map. It took a few seconds, but then she finally seemed to get the message.

He turned toward the noise, shielding her body with his. The folding of the map made the hint of a *swish* against the quiet, pulsing dark, but just like the rustle he'd heard—someone could mistake it for animal or the wind.

His hand itched to reach for his gun, but a shot would echo through the canyons and quiet night and give them away. He could fight off one or two, but he doubted they'd survive a whole group of the Sons descending on them.

There was nothing around him but a thick blackness his eyes hadn't adjusted to after looking at the map with

the penlight. He listened through the off-and-on wind
for a sound that might give him an idea of which direction the prowler was coming from. Luckily, Liza was
behind him, pressed to a rock, so they couldn't be surrounded on all sides.

Unless someone came over the top of the rock outcropping.

He heard a *swish*—a knife being unsheathed, if he
had to guess. Jamison had his own knife, but he kept it
in his boot. The blade was short as well, and wouldn't be
useful if he had to use it to defend himself in the dark.

Liza's hand pressed into the small of his back, and
the other one curled around his right arm and pulled it
back. She unclenched his fist and pressed something to
his palm.

The handle of a knife. He couldn't see it, but based on
the weight it had a longer blade than the one in his boot.
He couldn't lunge blindly—it was too risky. He needed
to see his target and act with as little noise as possible.

The Sons usually did this kind of thing with radios or
walkies. If there was a man out there, he'd turned his off.
Which gave Jamison some hope they could neutralize
this threat without detection—at least for a little while.

But he needed light. And a whole hell of a lot of luck.

So, Liza's knife in hand and ready to move, he
switched on his headlamp and saw just what he'd hoped
he wouldn't. A man not ten feet away from them—luckily blinded by the sudden light.

Jamison lunged, hoping the element of surprise did
everything he'd need it to, to keep himself and Liza safe.

LIZA SWALLOWED THE scream that welled up inside her at
the last minute. Noise would likely mean capture.

Jamison's headlamp flew off his head as he jumped

for the man who'd been lurking around them. The light bounced against the rock below, creating enough of a beam that Liza could make out two figures grappling in the dark.

But not who was who. Too many times, the light flashed against something bright and silver. If Liza wasn't mistaken, both men had knives as they rolled and grunted.

She couldn't try to shoot—and not just because she might hit Jamison. Noise was the enemy here. They could fight off one man—

Wait. Sons never sent just one man. Liza switched on her own lamp. She looked around, but there was no one besides Jamison and the other man grunting and fighting.

She was standing next to an outcropping of rock and some pebbles tumbled down. She looked up just in time to dart out of the way as a man jumped down. She whirled to face him, half wishing she hadn't given Jamison her knife since a gun would draw too much attention.

Since she recognized the man as one of her father's lackeys, she sneered at him. "Hello, Claybourne."

"Hello, dead meat." He held a gun, but she had one thing going for her. Her father wouldn't allow his men to use it on her.

No, if she was going to be killed, it would be by her father's hand. So, she smiled. "In your dreams, sweetheart."

"You think who your daddy is protects you. There are lines even you can't cross, little girl."

She kept her smile firmly in place even as dread pooled in her gut. She didn't believe every idle threat one of her father's personal men threw her way, but there was enough going on for her to wonder.

They had to know she was after Gigi, and if Gigi was part of the alleged human trafficking ring, would that mean anyone had leave to kill her? Was the trafficking a big enough deal that her father wouldn't care if some-one besides him killed her?

It didn't matter. Not yet. Because she'd yet to interfere with anything, and no one knew she'd heard the traffick-ing rumors except Jamison. Jamison, who she didn't dare look at—because if he was winning against the other guy, it was best not to draw Claybourne's attention to it.

Instead, she focused on the man her father consid-ered his best tracker, but not one of his smartest men. "And just what line am I crossing right now?" she asked with a saccharine sweetness that would make anyone's teeth hurt.

"I'd say involving the Wyatts was the first one."

"You can't kill me for that one, Claybourne. I know it and you know it."

He smiled in the beam of her headlamp. "There's a lot of room between where we are right now, and you being a dead body at my feet, isn't there?"

The sounds of the fight had stopped, and Liza knew she had to keep talking, had to keep Claybourne's at-tention on her. If Jamison had won, he could surprise-attack Claybourne. If the other guy had won, well, Liza was screwed either way. She couldn't fight off two men *and* cart a hurt Jamison off somewhere safe.

God, he had to be safe.

"Don't get yourself too excited. I'll go with you will-ingly."

Claybourne snorted. "Sure you will." He pointed the gun at her leg. "Didn't take too good care of that, did you?"

"So, you were the bad shot back in Bonesteel."

He sneered at the insult. "I shot and hit exactly where I intended."

And so will I.

Peripherally, she saw Jamison edge just barely into the beam of light. He was a few feet behind Claybourne and completely out of sight as long as Claybourne kept his gaze on her.

Jamison edged in and out of the light and she noted his mouth was bloody and he looked angrier than a taunted mountain lion. She didn't see the other man, but she didn't dare take her main gaze away from Claybourne.

If they acted together, they could maybe bring down Claybourne without making too much noise. He wouldn't want to shoot and hurt them—though he might shoot just to make enough noise to be detected.

Liza moved her gaze to the gun he held, then back to Jamison standing in the very corner of where her beam of light reached. She ignored the sharp stab of pain at the stamp of injuries already blooming across his face.

She moved her gaze to the gun and back to Jamison again, hoping he understood her signal. And Claybourne didn't.

"What? You think you can fight me for it, little girl?" Claybourne laughed and both she and Jamison took that as the signal to move. Liza kicked out for the gun and Jamison wrapped something around Claybourne's face.

The gun clattered to the ground and whatever piece of cloth Jamison had on Claybourne muffled his screams.

Liza lunged for the gun, fumbling with it a little bit as she picked it up. She scanned the area, saw the other man tied up with rope Jamison must have gotten out of his pack. He was gagged and completely still. Dead or not, Liza wasn't sure, but it didn't matter.

"Light, Liza," Jamison ordered through clenched teeth.

Liza immediately whipped her head back so the headlamp shone over Jamison and a struggling Claybourne.

His fighting back was growing weaker as Jamison's arm held around his neck and choked him.

"I could shoot him," Liza said, noting the way blood was dripping from Jamison's mouth and his temple.

"And we'd have how many men on our tail immediately?" Jamison returned, his breathing labored as he wrestled Claybourne to the ground. "They'll be on us soon enough. You should have some rope in your pack. Get it out."

Liza did as she was told, and only when she handed it to Jamison did he release his grip from Claybourne's neck. The man gasped and wriggled, but Jamison kept him in place and quickly hogtied him just as he had the other man.

Jamison got to his feet, ripped a strip off his already torn sweatshirt and used it to create a gag.

"You're hurt," Liza said lamely as he turned to her.

"We'll deal with that later," he returned, striding quickly to where his pack was lying half-strewed-out by the other man. Quickly and carelessly he shoved the spilled contents back into his pack and shouldered it—as if he wasn't bleeding all over. He nodded toward where Claybourne had jumped from. "We move. Now."

She gave one last look at the men lying and groaning on the rocky ground—then over to where the firelight flickered. She could see shadows, but nothing concrete. Still, when these two didn't return or respond to the walkie within a certain period of time they'd come looking.

And they'd know just what happened.

So, she moved, just as Jamison instructed.

Chapter Ten

"You're still bleeding, Jamison."

He was, and his face hurt like hell, thanks to that pissant minion and his penchant for grabbing rocks and smashing them into Jamison's face. But there was only so much nightfall left.

"It'll keep."

"Yes, I hear that's what all doctors say about head injuries. They'll 'keep,' especially if you're hiking through the dark without any light or bandages."

"What do you suggest, Liza? Sit around and rest while you bandage me up as the Sons realize we took out two of their scouts?" He eyed the eastern horizon. There was a faint glow there. Dawn. He sighed. They didn't have much time. "We need to find a cave."

"A cave?"

Since he knew very well Liza was, or had been, somewhat claustrophobic and no fan of wildlife, he knew why she was questioning him. But that didn't change their reality. "They're going to be looking for us come daylight."

"Caves are full of bats and mountain lions and bears and *snakes*." She made a disgusted noise. "I am not finding a cave."

"Well, I am," he replied, the pulsing pain in his face

making him far too irritable to be kind, and threatening to make him far too irritable to think calmly and rationally.

"This wasn't the plan," Liza muttered, trudging behind him. She'd fallen more than once as they'd attempted to hike in the dark without their lamps. Everything was working against them—but he reminded himself they hadn't been captured by the Sons' scouts, so it wasn't the worst that could happen.

"No. It wasn't the plan. But plans change."

"You're alarmingly calm about all this. They could be following us. You're hurt. I'm hurt. They know for a fact we're out here and probably where we're going. And you're just… *Plans change*."

"What would you prefer? Some yelling? A rending of garments? A tantrum?"

"Actually I would *love* to see a Jamison Wyatt mantrum. Would make my entire life, I'm almost sure."

"Ha ha." He stumbled a bit on a dip in the ground, swore. He'd just about kill for a break. A nap. And yes, to clean up his bloody and hopefully not broken face. "If either of us are going to get any rest, we need a cave."

"So, we're going to crawl into a cave, risk mountain lion attack, and what?"

"Take turns sleeping during the day when it's harder to avoid people seeing us. Eat. Clean me up. Look at the map. Let them scour the whole damn place for us. They aren't going to find us. If we find a deep enough cave. Then we move again at night. Even if they figure out what we're doing, it won't be until it's too late to find us today." He hoped.

"I hate that that's a good idea," she muttered. "How are we going to find a cave without our lights?"

"If we're in the area I think we're in, we just have to keep moving due west."

"You know where we are?"

"Hopefully." He didn't know if being familiar with this area was lucky or a terrible omen of things to come, but these canyons and caves outside Flynn had been his childhood playground—and hell—all wrapped up into one.

Dad had considered the age of seven to be a great turning point for a boy, and each passing year more of one. Every summer he'd be left for as many days as years he had been on this earth to toughen him up. Learn to be a man.

The first summer had been sheer terror and torture, but he'd lasted seven days and earned his father's praise. There had been something *magical* in watching Ace Wyatt find pride in him.

Five years later, when his father had done the same thing to Dev, everything had changed for Jamison.

He'd known then and there he had to get them out. He'd spent the rest of his childhood doing just that—and surviving every one of his father's punishments or beatings when one of his brothers disappeared.

Ace had never given Jamison enough credit to think he orchestrated the escapes, but he'd blamed Jamison's lack of courage, strength and attention to detail for them happening. Jamison had always gotten a perverse thrill out of the fact that it was Ace's lack of attention to detail when it came to his sons that had made each escape possible.

By the time Jamison had gotten Dev out—the last one—the beating from his father had almost killed him. He knew his father had considered it in that moment.

Jamison had been resigned to that. He'd saved his brothers, and he could die knowing he'd done all he could. He'd felt a little bad about his friend Liza, but such was life.

Instead, Ace had pulled back. There'd been something terrible in his gaze in that moment, but he hadn't explained it. He'd only smiled and left Jamison alone in that cave to deal with his injuries and find his way back to camp.

Here he was, nearly twenty years later, in slightly better shape—and a man with a gun—looking for that same cave. It all felt a little too circular, but it was the only thing to do.

So, he kept moving to where he thought the caves from his youth should be. Walking and ignoring all the pain in his body until he saw the first signs of large rock faces they could climb in order to find the caves.

"We'll try to go by penlight first. I'm going to look for the cave. You're going to watch and listen for anyone else."

He worked in silence, trusting Liza to keep an eye and ear out for anything that might be a danger to them. It took time, but Liza kept close. A few times she placed a hand on his shoulder and they both paused, listening to the whistling wind as daylight flirted with the horizon.

Finally, he found one of the caves he'd had in mind. He no longer needed the penlight in the hazy dawn. He nodded toward the opening, watching Liza's face recoil.

But her body didn't.

"What if something's inside?"

Jamison picked up a few rocks from the ground and threw them as far into the cave as he could, even though it made the pain in his arm sing.

He listened intently for the sounds of life but didn't hear any. With a shrug, he climbed for the opening. When he reached it, he flipped on his headlamp, which he'd retrieved back when they'd fought off the scouts. Then he unholstered his gun and pulled it into his hand. He used the other hand to give him balance as he began to move inside.

He used the beam of his lamp to sweep the area, looking for any sign of a serious threat—bones or scat. A few bats fluttered by his head, deeper into the cave, but there was no sign of a big predator that might attack.

"I don't want to do this. I don't want to do this," Liza chanted, over and over, the farther they crept into the cave. But that was the thing about Liza. She might chant that for the next twenty-four hours straight, but here she was. Doing it anyway.

"Jamison. They could surround us. They could… There are *so* many possibilities."

"There are, but I have a bit of an ace in the hole, so to speak." Satisfied they'd moved deep enough into the cave, he eased himself to the rocky ground, grateful for the rest even if it was cold and damp. He pulled the item he'd lifted off the man he'd fought.

"You have their *walkie*!" She reached out to grab it, but he kept it out of reach.

"Palmed it off the guy I fought. We should be able to hear everything they're doing out there."

"And you're just telling me this *now*? Why haven't we been listening to it this whole time?" She hadn't sat, was stooped over, but still managed to look imperious and demanding, with her hands on her hips in this dim little cave.

"We couldn't use it until we were for sure out of hearing range," he said, rubbing at the ache in his chest that swept over him. An ache that had nothing to do with his injuries and everything to do with her.

Because fifteen years could sweep between them, but it didn't seem to change *this*. A wave of affection, mixed with desire and something like awe. He could be mad at her, he could think she'd betrayed him—chosen the Sons over him—but she was still here and standing. Anyone who survived that long in the Sons and still wanted to do something good and right had to be nearly superhuman.

Thoughts like that would get him into trouble—betrayed again, dead possibly—and yet he was getting worse and worse at fighting them away.

"We might be out of walkie range," she said, frowning at the device.

"We might be, but I doubt the Sons use these if they don't have good range." He switched it on. "Here goes nothing."

LIZA HELD HER BREATH. There was nothing but the low hum of static. She closed her eyes. Worthless.

But when she opened her eyes, her beam of light shone on Jamison's battered face. More to worry about in the here and now.

She dropped her pack and rummaged through it. She pulled out a windbreaker, hoping it was waterproof, and kneeled on it. Then she got out any first aid supplies she could find, along with a bottle of water.

"Drink that. Don't waste it on me."

"Don't be stupid." It was true they didn't know how long they'd be out here, and water would become a commodity they simply couldn't take for granted. But neither could infection—and his face was dirty and cut to pieces.

She found a cotton T-shirt in his pack and ripped it in half before wetting one half to use as a washcloth to clean his face.

He scowled at her and he didn't look the same as he had fifteen years ago. He was harder, and not as lean as he'd been at twenty-two. Time and age had packed muscles on. The sun had dug faint lines around his eyes and mouth—just a hint of age.

She supposed she had a few lines of her own that hadn't been there when she'd been twenty. She wasn't as lean, either—but instead of firm muscle, there were spots of softness to her.

Of course, going hungry more often than not hadn't exactly packed on the pounds Carlee had always been so worried about.

Carlee. Just thinking about her hurt. Reminded Liza of the last time she'd seen Gigi.

Mommy's gone. The bad men hurt her. She couldn't see. Her eyes were open, but she couldn't see.

Liza blew out a breath and stared at the man before her. He eyed her warily, but there was something more than caution in that gaze. She was reminded of that moment when she'd told him he'd only hate himself.

Because he might still feel the echoes of those old... emotions between them, but he wasn't about to wade down that same path. Save her. Love her. Promise to protect her always.

No, she'd blown that chance to pieces.

She swallowed at *everything* that whirled around inside her and leaned forward and began to wash the dirt off his face, trying to be gentle with his injuries. He didn't hiss out in pain, but she could feel the tension in his body as he fought off those responses to pain.

Without fully realizing it, she murmured encouraging words as she used the disinfectant in the kit, then bandaged up what cuts she could, touching his rough skin, the bristle of his whiskers, the bridge of his sharp nose she'd always thought was *noble*.

When had she ever been foolish enough to think about the shape of someone's nose and ascribe it to nobility?

She finished, still studying him. His complexion had grayed, but his eyes were alert and not so wary anymore. No, heat all but cracked from them. An awareness. Because they'd been skin to skin and were too close, breathing too much of the same air.

Time couldn't erase what their bodies had once found in each other.

She tried to remind herself he would have loved other women over the course of fifteen years. Probably forgotten what it was like to press his lips to hers. To fill her with that ridiculous desperation only teenagers ever truly felt. Because even in the harsh world they'd grown up in, they'd still just been teenagers. Hormones and recklessness and a belief—if not in their own immortality—in their ability to outwit and survive anything thrown at them.

Because for a few short, sweet years they had survived all this. Escaped and had their whole lives of freedom ahead of them.

She was older now, had seen too much, lost too much, to have that simple, joyous belief anymore.

It settled in her, a heavy weight. The loss, not just of him but of that feeling, and all she could do was lean forward and press her forehead to his shoulder.

When his arm came around her, a silent, strong comfort, she gave in to the sobs she'd been fighting for weeks.

"Sleep," he whispered, pulling her head down, until she was somehow cradled in his lap, curled up in a ball. He stroked her hair as her sobs subsided. Dried her cheeks. Exhaustion cloaked her like a blanket and she fell into a deep sleep.

Where she dreamed of the dead.

Chapter Eleven

Jamison hadn't meant to fall asleep, but he could hardly beat himself up over it. They'd hiked all night and exhaustion could only be fought for so long.

He opened his eyes, frowning at the fact Liza wasn't still curled up against him and sleeping as though she felt completely safe with him.

Something inside him had cracked open into a million pieces or *something*, and when he'd fallen into a sleep he'd tried to fight off, he'd dreamed of something he couldn't ever remember dreaming about or even feeling.

True peace.

Which was crazy. As long as the Sons existed, and his father was alive, there was no peace to be found. Jamison was practical enough not to believe in perfect worlds where he defeated both.

But maybe he could defeat one and slow down the other—at best.

He looked up to find Liza on the other side of the narrow cave not a few feet from him, watching him. All traces of vulnerability were gone and she chewed on a protein bar.

It irritated him that she'd woken up first and moved off him without him waking up. He should be more in tune with his surroundings. But he couldn't lean into that anger because they had more important things to deal with.

He watched her as she grabbed another bar and tossed it at him. He caught it but didn't stop staring.

She was the key to something. Something inside him. Something he'd been waiting for...all these years.

He didn't believe in fate or true love or any of the things either could *mean*, but here he was.

"You okay, champ?"

Nope. "Anything on the two-way?"

"Not that I've heard, but I haven't been awake much longer than you."

That was some comfort. Perhaps he'd woken because she'd gotten up and off him, and it had just taken a few minutes to jolt into clarity. Jamison looked at his watch. It was still before noon—so he'd slept about five hours. It could be they'd hiked far enough to be out of range. It could be that the search party—if they'd figured out their scouts had been taken out—had gone the wrong direction.

"Probably a good sign," he decided, trying to be hopeful though it wasn't his natural inclination.

"Unless they noted the missing walkie and changed the frequency," Liza pointed out.

"Lucky for us, we can test out that theory." He held out a hand, waiting for her to toss the handheld at him, but she didn't.

"You talk in your sleep," she said instead, dark eyes watching him with something he wasn't sure he'd be able to name if he lived to be a very old man.

Since he vaguely remembered his dreams, all about her, he stiffened, but he wouldn't let himself shift and give in to how exposed he felt. "Do I?" he replied blandly. "Anything interesting?"

"I guess it depends on who you were muttering about."

"I wouldn't know. I don't remember my dreams."

She made a considering sound but didn't comment further. He unwrapped the protein bar and took an unsatisfactory bite. "Change the channels. Give each one about ten minutes and see if we pick up on anything."

He reached for his pack, wincing at the way his body had stiffened over the course of their nap. Everything ached or was too stiff. Was he thirty-seven or ninety-seven? He stretched a bit, pulling his bottle of water out and taking a drink. Then he tried to roll the kinks out of his neck as he went to his pocket for the map.

But it wasn't there. There was a moment of blind panic before he remembered Liza had it. Trying to hide the galloping of his heartbeat, he took a slow, deliberate breath and kept his gaze on the protein bar until he calmed that unnecessary jolt.

"Map?" he finally asked casually, if he did say so himself.

She pulled the square of paper from her pocket. "This isn't going to hold up through much more of this." Instead of handing it to him like he would have preferred, she unfolded it on her own lap. "What is all this, by the way? Because these marks are something more than just what's been going on the past few days."

He shrugged. "Just a map."

"No. It's a map with a code. Spill it, Jamison."

"Why?"

She looked up from the map, met his gaze. "Because we're in this together."

She didn't say *always*, but it seemed to hang in the air between them. Whatever they were, whoever they were, *always* seemed just about right.

Maybe that was why the hurt from her disappearing all

those years ago had never healed, just left a jagged edge he'd never been able to set aside for any other woman.

Liza was his always, whether she was with him or not. Whether he wanted her to be or not.

Too vulnerable a thought and he'd rather discuss what they needed to focus on. "I've kept track over the years. Even after we—I got out, if I heard of something related to the Sons, I marked it. Dead bodies are an X. The hashtags represent petty crime. Camps are squares. Unexplained disappearances I thought might relate back to the Sons are circles—in the margins if there were no known last whereabouts."

She blinked and looked back down at the map. "You kept *track*? All these years you kept track and never..."

He knew what she meant to say before she trailed off. Knew because he was always wondering what more he could have done. But having her say it burned. "Never what?" he demanded.

"Did anything." She shook her head, raising her gaze from the map to him. "You knew all this was going on and you never did anything." She looked at him as if he'd morphed before her very eyes into a villain.

Her words weren't true, but that look hurt. Injured enough that he wouldn't defend himself. Why bother? She wanted to believe he was the ultimate bad guy— what did it matter?

He really didn't want it to matter. There was no point in trying to explain *anything* to her. But his mouth always had a mind of its own around her.

"Brady, Gage and Tucker work for the Valiant County Sheriff's Department, just like me. I have contacts in county departments across South Dakota. I put pressure where I could on those cases. So did they. We've done what we can."

But he was just one man—not a gang or a federal agency. There was only so much he could do within the confines of the law. It had never felt like a failure—even when the law handcuffed him—until Liza had looked at him with that hurt and horrified expression.

"Hand me the map," he said roughly.

She shook her head and grabbed her pack, rifling through it until she pulled out a pen. She made a few of her own marks, then tossed the map at him.

He scanned the map, noticed her big black X about fifteen miles north of Flynn.

"You know that's where Carlee was murdered?"

"No, not for sure. My father has some kind of house in that area—I don't have an exact location but it's somewhere there. You know how he always liked to keep a separate place. A step above. Keep his family out of reach so he could be their only tormentor. I don't know where else he would have killed Carlee that Gigi would have been able to witness it."

He nodded, a new idea occurring to him. He'd figured west made the most sense in terms of transportation, but if Liza's father was the point man on the trafficking...

"What's around the cabin? Give me details."

Liza shook her head. "I don't know."

Irritated that even now she'd keep things from him, he didn't bother to hide the sharpness in his tone. "Liza."

"Trust me. I wasn't allowed within miles. Gigi told me a few things, but nothing that will help us find it. They may have let me back in the Sons, but I wasn't trusted. Not in all those years. I'm the Mariah of this generation, just hoping my turn to die wasn't until after I'd helped my sisters."

Mariah. He remembered a woman in her forties. Tough and always mouthing off and getting knocked around when she did it to the wrong person. It never stopped her, and for the longest time Jamison and Liza had wondered why she got to live. No one else showed disrespect like that and got to stay—and keep breathing.

She'd even helped Jamison once, when he'd been getting Tucker out. He'd been about to get caught, and she'd created a diversion.

A year later, she'd been used—very much against her will—as a suicide bomber that had allowed the Sons to interfere with a prisoner transport and get one of their men back from the feds.

Because the true danger of the Sons, at least under his father's leadership, was that they were patient. They were smart. They didn't expend anyone until their usefulness had been completely wrung out.

Jamison supposed that was part of the reason for his own freedom the past fifteen years. Dad was waiting for the time he'd be most useful, and he could wait a very, very long time.

Maybe this was what they should have done, all along. Force Ace's hand. Take the power back. Be the ones to move, just like they'd been when Jamison had gotten them all out.

Regardless, here he was. "What if it's here? At your father's place or close—close enough Carlee caught wind. The Sons don't kill without planning, but if Gigi witnessed Carlee's death or just her *being* dead, it wasn't planned—or not very well. I never saw my mother. She was there one day. Gone the next."

Something like sympathy softened Liza's expression, so he pushed on because he didn't want any of her sympathy.

"Your father did always like his place on the hill, like you said, but fifteen miles? That's an awful lot for the

second in command. Ace wouldn't be good with that unless there was a reason."

"That's... Yeah, that could be."

"It would also explain why we're not getting any hits
on the two-way. We've gone west. If they're protecting your father or the trafficking, they might have gone
north."

She nodded, let out a little huff, not in relief but maybe
determination. She met his gaze. "So, I guess we're
headed north."

THEY LET THE afternoon wear on while they waited in the
cave. They took turns switching the dials on the two-
way, listening for clues or hints, but every channel was
low-level static.

As sunset crept closer, they began to prepare to leave.
Jamison thought that no walkie activity meant they'd be
safe to start before dark fully descended, and Liza was
glad to get *some* daylight hiking in before the stumbling,
panic-inducing night trek.

Now they had a clear target. She couldn't entertain
thoughts that Jamison might be off base. He had to be
right, and they had to be heading for Gigi.

She tried not to think about how it led straight to her
father.

They packed up the gear in silence. Jamison shoved
some trail mix at her, and his bottle of water. Since she
didn't want to break the silence and argue, she ate and
drank as much as her churning stomach could handle.

She insisted on checking his face and bandages, re-
applying a few. Of course, that only meant he insisted
on changing her bandage, which meant mostly remov-
ing her pants.

She was getting a little tired of feeling his hands on

her skin while he changed her bandage with absolutely no hint that it might affect him in any way.

She could be anyone. A stranger. One of his brothers. He'd bandage them all with the same gentle detachment. Actually, he'd be rougher with his brothers, because he cared about them. He'd be angry they'd been hurt.

She was as good as a stranger.

More than that she was an idiot for letting her mind go in these pointless circles when her sister was in grave danger. But Jamison had found a lead—a good one, if her instincts were on track like his.

She hissed a little when he used a disinfectant wipe against her wound, but he was quick with it and was almost immediately spreading the soft, cool bandage over the stitches.

His hands were rough—likely from work he did at the ranch to help out Dev and Grandma Pauline. He might live in Bonesteel, a good forty-five minutes away from the ranch, but Jamison would lend whatever help he could.

Help. It was his core. He'd kept track of things the Sons had done, and as much as she'd felt a moment of betrayal, it hadn't lasted. He'd used his law enforcement influence to try to right crimes committed by the Sons.

He hadn't explained what the check marks on the map had meant, but she knew. Those were cases where he'd actually been instrumental in getting an arrest made. She didn't recognize all of them, but Lyle Pearce had been arrested and convicted of murder three years ago—much to her father and Ace Wyatt's fury—which was most definitely Jamison's X and check mark just west of Bonesteel.

He hadn't forgotten, hadn't let it all go like he pretended. She had to wonder if Ace knew that—and was keeping the same kind of tabs for every time his son interfered.

She swallowed at the fear. It was one thing when she'd known she was the Mariah—that she could at any point be used for the Sons' ends and die—but it was another to think of just how much hatred Ace might have built up against his eldest son. More than she'd anticipated.

Which made this all the more dangerous for Jamison. Her heart and gut twisted and she wanted to say something as he finished with the bandage, but she couldn't.

He was still crouched at her feet, spreading the new bandage over her leg, his calloused fingers grazing across the skin just outside the bandage's reach.

His gaze lifted, heated. As he stood, he kept her gaze—and lifted her pants, the very tips of his fingers brushing along her skin as he did so. She held her breath, his heated gaze melting everything inside her, including the fear.

Because Jamison had always been her safe place—and she'd always wanted safe as much as her body had wanted his.

Now was not the time to give in, but she was drowning in all that sparked between them and deep inside her. He reached his full height, inches above her own, and she leaned toward him even as her brain told her it was a mistake.

She got up on her tiptoes and pressed her body against his. It matched, just the same as it always had. They matched, heart, soul, body. She gave herself time to watch him, to wait for some inkling he felt it, too.

He showed no signs of reaction. He held himself still, and his eyes remained cool. Which made something inside her crack in half—perhaps her sanity—because in the next moment she pressed her mouth to his, his lack of response be damned.

He didn't balk like she'd expected. He didn't push

her away. He let her kiss him. And somehow, second by second, inch by inch, he sank into the kiss. Softening, reacting, taking. It was such a surprise she threw herself into it wholly.

The kiss ignited—not like in the old days, with sparks of desperation and joy. This was different—deeper and more complex. Not just spark, but full-on explosion from the inside out. It was joy and need but also betrayal and confusion. It was hope and it was cynicism. It was everything they were and had been in their fifteen years apart.

But at its core the kiss was *them*—whatever had brought them together as friends when they'd been kids, whatever had bloomed between them as they'd learned what the opposite sex had to offer. It was their hearts, entwined still, after all these years—because for whatever reason, they were made for each other and could never bend or twist to be someone else's.

He was the only man she'd ever wanted, the only man she'd ever willingly touched intimately, and there was some *relief* that fifteen years hadn't changed that.

But the reprieve swirled with the sadness of reality. This world of theirs dulled the edges of euphoria. Yet she was still breathless, boneless maybe, throwing herself and her heart into this whirlwind of a kiss.

He wrapped his arms around her, strong and certain. He kissed her with *intention*, not just desperation. As if there was some way they could erase all those old hurts and start something new and purposeful.

But too few moments later, he pushed her away. Slowly and carefully, but a clear push nonetheless.

Silence and heat swirled around them in the low light of the cave. Her body pulsed with an electricity she'd nearly forgotten existed, because no one but Jamison had ever made her feel outside herself—just sensation and heart with no concern for the physical here and now.

It hardly mattered. It was a pointless kiss and he'd pushed her away, no matter what she felt.

It had been a waste of time at best, though it lingered inside her. She meant to give him a sassy smile and an offhand remark, but she was too steeped in feeling to manage it. "I just had to know if it was all still there," she whispered. The truth—in all its pointless glory.

His gaze was enigmatic and impossible to read—or maybe she didn't want to read it. Maybe she didn't want to know what he was feeling. His words certainly didn't give much away.

"I guess it is."

But it *was* an admission. Not exactly a timely one. "Not really the time to figure that out."

He kept watching her and giving her no clue as to how he felt. "Not especially."

"We should go." She made a move for the outside world, but Jamison's hand was still on her arm, and it held firm.

She thought he might kiss her again—hoped, maybe. But he only watched, searched. There was something very nearly vulnerable in his eyes, so she stood still before it and let him find what he sought.

"Was it me?" he asked, his voice a harsh rasp. "I was too…overbearing. A different version of them. You had to run away from—"

She didn't need an explanation to know he was talking about her leaving, to be horrified he'd blame himself. "Oh, Jamison. God. *No*. No, I wanted to *be* you. Save my sisters like you'd saved your brothers. I wanted to prove I was as good as you." It hit her then what she'd never fully allowed herself to admit. "I never could."

He flinched, as though the words were a slap. Then he let her go. "I guess it doesn't matter."

She'd thought that. That he'd never understand. That fifteen years was too long, but here in this moment she wondered.

Unfortunately, now was most definitely not the time to figure it out. "We should go," she repeated. If they didn't, what other emotional pain would they bring up to compete with the physical pain of their injuries?

"I'll exit first, search a little, then you. We've got a long walk."

Yes, they had a long, *long* way to go.

Chapter Twelve

It was another beautiful sunset streaking across the sky as they marched silently toward their target. Jamison could remember nights when they'd still been with the Sons, when he and Liza would hike some hill or rock outcropping, depending on where their camp had been, and watch the sunset.

She used to say sunsets held such promise—for a new day. He'd always responded that, technically, that happened with sunrises.

Every time she'd grin at him and say, *Yeah, but who wants to get up that early?*

He'd refused to touch her when they'd been in the Sons. It would have been a violation of what he was trying to do, the man he wanted to be. The first time she'd kissed him, he'd lectured her on proper behavior even as his heart had beaten so hard against his chest he thought it'd break through.

He could still remember the careless smirk she'd flashed him in the moonlight. How he'd wanted to wallow in it, and in her. How close he'd been to breaking his own vow to himself over a little kiss and a careless smile.

Hell. Now was not the time to wander down memory lane—especially the happier side to it.

If he was where he thought they were, and they didn't

run into any problems, and he didn't get turned around and lost, Jamison thought they could be close to Liza's father's place by dawn.

So, they walked. They didn't talk much. Every once in a while they'd take a rest, a few sips of water and have a snack. They'd go through the channels on the two-way and listen for anything.

Then they'd be back on their feet before too long, using headlamps to see in the inky dark. The lights made Jamison nervous, as did the fact they'd decided to keep the two-way on low despite the fact the sound might tip off someone searching for them.

They were risks they'd have to take to mitigate the risks of getting lost or more hurt in the dark.

When Jamison thought they were getting close, he had Liza shut off the handheld and her lamp. They walked just by his light for a while. The landscape had morphed. They were still hiking through rocky outcroppings, but now many of the rocks were surrounded by forest.

The trees were good cover for the light, and a good place to rest as dawn began to threaten.

Liza yawned, and he fought off one of his own.

"We should take a break."

Liza all but collapsed on a patch of grass, heaving out a sigh of relief. "Thank God."

"Not much of one. I think we're close. What do you think?"

She looked around the dark, shadowy woods. "I don't know. I really don't."

Jamison took a seat next to her and pulled out his map and penlight. He switched off his headlamp. He studied the map in the small circle of light, the geological features mixed with his own markings, which, amid the trail of crime, included landmarks that only meant anything to Jamison himself.

He pointed to the X she'd made that signified Carlee, then drew his finger a short distance south. "I think we're about here. Do you have any idea how big the place is?"

"I asked Gigi what it looked like. What she described sounded like a cabin—a decent one. She mentioned a fireplace and Carlee cooking before it happened. Baking brownies. Sounded like they had modern conveniences. When I asked her about outside, Gigi said she had a playground—swings, a slide."

"So, a nice place, likely. Bigger rather than smaller."

"Maybe, but Gigi didn't mention anything about anyone else. Just her and Carlee and my father. If they were trafficking under her nose, she would have mentioned other people."

"It could be more like a compound, and Gigi and Carlee were supposed to stay in the house. I have to believe if your father did something that drastic with a witness who wouldn't know to be quiet, Carlee had to be close. Maybe something not in the house, but near it."

"She mentioned horses," Liza said, almost to herself. "I'd forgotten that because it wasn't when we were talking about Carlee. It was before. Gigi said she missed her horse. At first I thought she was talking about a stuffed animal or something."

"Stables. Horses. That's not like the Sons." They were mobile, nomads. But things had changed. Liza had told him that and he needed to stop being surprised by it.

"No, it isn't. Your father could move anything he has in the snap of a finger, but it seems like my father was settling in for good."

"How did you get to Gigi after Carlee was dead?"

"I didn't know Carlee was dead yet. No one did—at

least no one had told me. I think I would have heard, though. I think if anyone else knew, they would have made sure to tell me—not out of loyalty, mind you, but because it would have been a way to make me feel bad."

At Jamison's outraged look, she shrugged. "I'm the Mariah, remember? Take shots at me as long as they don't interfere with my potential use. It would have been a shot. So, I think they were keeping it quiet."

"So, how did Gigi tell you?"

"Dad and Carlee and Gigi would come into the main camp about once a week. I tried to keep tabs on Gigi— be where she was when she was in camp. Talk to Carlee, plant the seeds of escape. The day Gigi told me, Dad had come in to meet with your father like he normally did, but Carlee wasn't with him. He gave Gigi to a couple of the teenage girls to watch after her while he conducted business. It was a nice day, so they were letting her throw rocks in the pond. The girls watching her were too busy on their phones to notice or care that I was talking to her. I thought. Maybe they told Dad after, I don't know. But I didn't expect Gigi to tell me all that, either."

"How many days between Gigi telling you and you coming to me in Bonesteel?"

"Three. I thought I was being sneaky. I followed them—not back to wherever Dad is living because he has too many guards, but I went as far down that path as I thought was safe. Then every time they came back into camp that way, I'd follow and try to find a time to get Gigi alone."

"How many times did you succeed?"

"Once after the first time. I didn't want to upset her or draw attention, so it was hard. The day I came to Bonesteel… Gigi wasn't there. Dad came to town without her. I don't know if he'd heard what we were talking about last time, but I knew if I stayed we'd both be hurt. I knew I needed help. So, that's when I came to you."

That shouldn't fill him with warmth, satisfy some rough edges inside him. But it did, as pathetic as that made him.

"Sleep. I'll keep watch." They didn't have much time before daylight would make things more dangerous, but she needed to rest.

She eyed him in the dark. "Are you sure?"

"Yeah."

When she tried to position herself against a tree, he rolled his eyes. "Come here," he said, the words coming out more as a sharp order than he'd intended. He took her arm and pulled until she was close enough to use him as a pillow.

She looked up at him for a fathomless second, all those old pulls urging him forward, the memory of the kiss in the cave urging him forward.

But Liza only sighed and leaned her head onto his shoulder, using him as the pillow he was meant to be.

He used the map and the penlight to keep him awake. One arm around a sleeping Liza meant he spread the map out on the ground at his other side, and used his hand to hold the penlight.

He studied and searched and considered different routes. As light began to dawn, he turned off the pen-light and pulled out the two-way handheld and turned the volume low and to its original channel.

Liza slept soundly. He watched, a little too long, as the brightening golden light haloed her features. He'd convinced himself all of what he felt in this moment had been gone. He'd been so sure he'd erased her from his mind and his heart after fifteen years.

But in some ways it felt like no time had passed. Here she was, right where she belonged. With him.

He scrubbed his free hand over his face and stopped on a dime when he caught sight of movement in the trees.

Someone, or *someones*, was out there. He could make out one figure—who didn't seem worried about hiding his presence.

Something about the way the figure moved was... familiar. Jamison held very still, watching the stranger, though he itched to look at Liza to make sure she was still asleep.

He slowly, slowly moved his hand toward his weapon. The figure in the distance did the same.

Liza shifted and Jamison immediately whispered a command to be silent. She stilled in his lap as his hand curled over the butt of his gun.

The figure moved a little closer, still too far away. But their gazes met and held, Jamison was sure of that.

"Cody?" He hadn't realized he'd muttered it out loud until Liza responded.

"Your brother?" Liza whispered.

"I don't..." But those were his brother's eyes, his brother's moves. The man simply stood there, off in the distance, but why would Jamison think it was Cody if it wasn't? Maybe he only saw his youngest brother at Christmas, and the occasional Easter Sunday, but that was Cody.

"Don't move," Jamison instructed Liza, slowly sliding out from under her.

He ignored her whispered arguments and moved toward the man. The man was armed, but not aiming a weapon in Jamison's direction.

Because it was his brother. As Jamison approached, Cody held his finger to his lips, nodded to the walkie on his hip. One that looked suspiciously like the one Jamison had in his pack. But it couldn't be possible Cody was *with* the Sons. He'd probably come across it just as Jamison had come across his.

But his brother didn't look harmed in any way, or even tired like he'd been hiking around all night.

Still, when Cody took Jamison's hand and lifted it, Jamison didn't fight him off or even get in a stance that might make him ready for attack.

This was his brother. His *baby* brother. Jamison had gotten Cody out of the Sons when Cody had been just shy of seven—before Cody had had to go through the seven-nights-alone "man" ritual. Jamison considered it his greatest success. Cody had lived with Grandma Pauline for the longest period of time. He'd gone to college. Jamison hadn't been able to save him from all memory of being in the Sons, but a lot of the worst parts.

Cody couldn't be with the Sons. Jamison wouldn't believe it.

He realized, belatedly, Cody was tapping his finger against Jamison's palm. It took Jamison a few times to realize Cody was using Morse code.

Go.

Jamison opened his mouth to respond, but Cody shook his head and brought his finger to his lips again.

So, Jamison tapped out his response on his brother's palm, perhaps more firmly than necessary.

No.

You have to.

No.

Not safe.

No.

Can't protect you.

Don't need to.

Cody made a sound of frustration and then looked around the woods.

Don't ruin this. Then his brother dropped Jamison's hand and melted into the woods.

Jamison wasn't sure how long he stood there after Cody had disappeared. It felt like a dream, or like he'd been visited by a ghost. The incident certainly gave him far more questions than it could ever answer.

Ruin *what*, most of all.

Eventually he turned, listening intently for the sounds of anyone else. But there was only him and Liza in the forest.

"What on earth was that?" she demanded when he returned.

Jamison stared out into the empty woods. "I wish I knew."

As JAMISON RELATED his exchange with Cody, Liza tried to choke down another disgusting protein bar. Fainting here like she had back in Bonesteel was a death sentence for both of them, but, boy, did she wish she had anything else to eat.

"He had a walkie, just like the one we have?" she asked, swallowing down a gummy bite.

"He had a walkie. If it was like the one we have, it would have been going off. He had it on."

"Ours hasn't been going off," Liza pointed out. She didn't want to say it, but that was a sympathy she didn't have room for right now. "You have to admit, it looks like he's with the Sons."

"Did you hear any whispers about that?" Jamison demanded.

"No, but—"

"Then he's not," he returned firmly and with completely certainty. "That news would spread like wildfire. If you didn't know—it's not possible."

She *almost* felt sorry for him, but she had to say it. "Unless it's Ace's secret."

Jamison shook his head and closed his backpack with more force than necessary. "There'd be no reason for Ace to keep Cody a secret. He'd crow from dusk till dawn about getting one of us back."

"Unless there's absolutely a reason for him to keep it a secret—one of Ace's many reasons and plans."

"Cody warned me off, Liza. The Sons don't do that."

She wanted to let it go, but they were walking straight into the lion's den here. She couldn't ignore what was possible. "Sure, mostly. But it would make sense if Cody had a soft spot for you. He might be with the Sons and still not want to tangle with anything that involved hurting *you*."

"It's not possible."

"Because you don't want it to be or because it's really not?"

He whipped his gaze to hers, furious. She might have been afraid of that fury, or even offended by it, but she understood that Cody joining the Sons would be worse than *anything* for Jamison. Worse than her leaving all those years ago. Worse than the Sons hurting Jamison himself.

One of his brothers—his youngest brother, whom he'd saved at the youngest age. It'd kill Jamison to consider Cody might have gone back.

But it was *possible*, and kill him or not, she had to be rational enough to accept that possibility. "Whatever he is, he's not going to hurt you. So he says, but that doesn't mean he won't tip some people off to our whereabouts." *Especially mine.*

"I will not, under any circumstances, consider my

brother is part of the Sons," he said, his voice not just cold but frigid and fierce. Icicles piercing their target. "Now. We move toward where we think your father's place might be."

She wouldn't get through to him about Cody when he was that angry, so she focused on her other concerns. "In broad daylight?"

"Did you have a better idea, Liza? I don't see any caves or good enough cover. Please, tell me, what *should* we do?"

"Well, you could stop taking your irritation out on me. It's not my fault your brother might have gone into the Sons."

Whatever storms ignited inside him, he kept a calm lid on them. But she could see all that *pain* brewing. "So, it's my fault, then."

Which was not stated as a question—which irritated *her*. "Do you ever listen to anyone besides yourself? Are you so self-absorbed you think you're the cause of everything?"

He started striding toward some point only he knew. "No," he said firmly, but it was hardly with the same vehemence he'd turned on her.

Liza sighed and trudged after him, but she couldn't let it go—much as she wished she could. "Oh, just us, then? You're responsible for us because we're so weak and stupid and—"

He whirled on her, and that calm lid was bubbling over into fury. "I *saved* you. Both of you. So, explain to me, if you both went back, what went wrong?"

He just about broke her heart. Because no, it wasn't fury bubbling over, it was fear. It was worry and guilt. She knew they didn't have time for the healing of old wounds, but she couldn't let that one bleed out while they walked. So, she took his face in her hands, resting her palms against his cheeks. "Not you, honey. What went wrong was never you."

"So, what was it?" He lifted his hands to her wrists as if he was going to pull her hands away, but in the end he just rested them there. She thought he meant the question to be rhetorical, but it hung there.

"We don't all know how to be good," she said, wishing she knew how to explain all the things he couldn't understand. Because he *was* good. It was some inherent thing inside him. "We don't all know how to want what's good—or keep it. It isn't in us like it's in you. Not all of us. That's not your failing, Jamison."

His eyebrows drew together, that edgy fury softening. "I don't think you can call it your own, either. Not how we grew up."

It wasn't the time to smile, but her lips curved anyway. "Oh, Jamison. How did you turn out so good? I'll never know. You don't need to absolve me. I know what I am."

"Do you?"

For a second, that simple question made her wonder. But no. She knew. "I wanted to be you, but I couldn't save Marci. Now I'll never save Carlee. Gigi is my last hope to do any kind of good for my sisters."

"You never had to be me. You said it yourself. It's different for men and women in there. It's different for the sons of Ace Wyatt than the daughter of Tony Dean. Always has been and always will be. Whatever you couldn't do isn't a failure."

No, there was no time to heal old wounds, but that soothed some. Even as she tried to fight the warm wave of relief away. She didn't need him to tell her what it was or how it was different. He did not and could not change the failure she'd had with Marci and Carlee.

But her heart felt less bruised no matter what her brain tried to tell it.

"Do you ever say that to yourself, Jamison? Or is everything your failure?"

"We should walk," he said, his voice still rough.

Liza nodded, though for another few seconds they stood there in the still woods, her hands on his face and his hands on her wrists.

A good man. Hard to let go. Older and wiser, it was harder to think she had to be noble and let him be that good man without her.

Now was not the time. He dropped his hands and she dropped hers, and then they set out for another hike. She tried not to think about her throbbing feet, her aching wound or that look on Jamison's face that caused a deep pain at the center of her chest.

After walking awhile, the sun climbing higher in the sky and making Liza more and more nervous they'd be seen and caught, Jamison held up his arm and stopped.

Slowly, he pulled his gun out of his holster and then nodded at her to get out the gun he'd given her. She did so, trying to be as quiet as possible as she shifted the contents of her pack.

When Jamison stepped forward, it was into a clearing. She realized he hadn't seen a direct threat, but they were treading on dangerous ground.

A small rustic-looking cabin sat in the middle of a small clearing in a thicket of a variety of trees. Leaves were lumped in random piles, likely dropped off by the wind. The windows were dark with grime where they weren't shattered by unknown forces. It looked deserted, old and not well kept.

But looks could be deceiving.

It wasn't her father's place that Gigi had described,

and if it was held by the Sons, no doubt she and Jamison would already be dead or threatened.

She followed Jamison, gun in hand, watching the woods and the black windows as they moved around the clearing in a broad circle, then a smaller one.

She wasn't the best shot, especially when she was nervous, but she knew how to work a gun, and hopefully that amounted to something. Well, hopefully she didn't have to shoot at all.

The outside looked deserted—for a rather long time. There weren't footprints or signs anything had been disturbed. There was no sight or sound of anyone. When they completed another, even smaller circle, Jamison nodded at the door. "Let's see what we've got."

Liza nodded. They moved, close enough to be one. Jamison reached out and turned the knob. It squeaked and groaned, but it turned and the door pushed open.

Jamison led with the gun, slowly pushing the door more and more open until sunlight spilled into the dim, dusty interior.

She followed Jamison close all the way through the cabin, searching the meager cabinets and closets and nooks and crannies. Some furniture that looked abandoned, but mostly just dust and grime, and a few signs of animal life.

"Someone's been here recently, but they didn't want anyone to know it," Jamison said, slowly lowering his gun.

Liza did the same with her gun, but frowned at the surroundings. It didn't look like anyone had been here in decades to her. "How can you tell?"

"The windows aren't as dusty as the counters. Someone's opened them and then brushed off their prints or tracks in the dust. That chair there—you can see the track in the dust where it's been moved."

"Could be animals."

"It's not. But whoever was here isn't anymore. Which is good news for us."

"How? If someone's been here, they could come back."

"They could, but they didn't leave anything behind, so I think we're safe there. We can rest here while we wait for nightfall."

"And what happens at nightfall?"

"We try to find your father's place. Ideally we do and can case it and formulate a plan of rescue."

"Just the two of us?"

"You know, it could be Cody was here trying to do the same thing we are."

Liza figured it was better to agree with him than keep mounting arguments. She wasn't so sure about Cody Wyatt, but Jamison probably knew his brother better than she did. "It could be."

"I know you don't believe me."

"I don't have to, Jamison. Just like I don't need you to believe me that I think he's with the Sons. We can think different things and still do everything we've got to do."

He scrubbed a hand over his face, then winced at the pain it must have caused his injuries from his previous scuffle. "Yeah." He blew out a breath, looking around the cabin. "We should rest."

Liza looked dubiously at the musty old mattress in the corner. It was better than a cave, she supposed. She inched onto it, wrinkling her nose. Definitely smelly and dusty.

"Here," Jamison muttered. He shrugged off his pack and then pulled out a pouch. He untied it and slowly unraveled what became a blanket.

"Well, aren't you handy."

"Something like that." He spread out the blanket, waited for her to sit down and then took a seat next to her.

She looked at him. The weight of the world on his shoulders, as it always was. The battle light that never tired no matter how much his body did. Cuts and bruises across his face that he acted as if didn't even exist, though they had to hurt. Constantly.

She reached out and brushed her fingers across his unmarred temple, like she used to do when she was swamped with love for a boy who was way too good for her. Way too good for the world he'd been stuck in. Slowly, he turned his head and met her gaze.

There were some things just as dangerous as the Sons, and the way he looked at her in this moment was definitely one of them.

Chapter Thirteen

He was tired, and he should sleep. Or eat. Or hydrate. He should do a long list of things that did not include sitting here wishing Liza would put her hands on more than just his battered face.

Her fingertips were solace against all the throbbing and burning. She was all he wanted, and he was tired enough of all *this* around them to think… It wouldn't be so wrong. It wouldn't compromise anything. Even knowing she thought his brother could have gone back. Even though *she'd* gone back.

Get up. Focus on the task at hand.

But he realized here, in this shimmering heat between him and Liza, that all the ways he'd been good and upstanding and dedicated to his job and the law the past fifteen years were only because she hadn't been there.

If she had been, everything would have come second to her. It always did. He leaned closer, keeping his arms at his sides even as her fingers slid through his hair.

"What are we doing here?" she asked, a whisper. Her eyes were shiny, and she shook her head almost imperceptibly.

But she didn't move away. She didn't look away.

He knew what she was asking, but he didn't want to answer that question. "Waiting for the sun to set."

She tried to smile. "Well, if we're just waiting." She slid onto his lap, an easy, fluid movement that reminded him of a past that had been easier, oddly. He'd felt more in danger, more desperate back then, but it had been... youth. He'd thought he could fight for right and always win, but the past fifteen years had taught him otherwise at every turn.

Right didn't always win. Good didn't always come out on top. Yet he'd never been able to give up the hope that it would, that it could.

And here she was—his good, his hope. He gave himself leave to slide his hands down her back. Fifteen years since he'd touched her like this, but there was no difference in this moment.

"Do you remember our first time?" she asked, her hands cupping his jaw gently so as to not put too much pressure on his bruises, her mouth brushing just below his ear.

It was a visceral memory. An awful lot like this— his grandmother's barn instead of an abandoned shack, safety instead of danger, but Liza making all the moves and him accepting them, even as his rational mind told him not to. Too many things piling against him—knowing it wasn't the right time, that it wasn't right, and giving in anyway.

Because Liza was always *right*.

"Yeah, I remember."

"You wanted to wait. You always wanted to wait." She looked at him, so close they were nose to nose and he could count every faint freckle that dusted across her nose. He could catalog the way her face had changed and hadn't. But he only drowned in the dark brown of her eyes.

"What were you waiting for, Jamison?"

"I'm not sure I remember," he lied easily. Because lying to her about how he felt had always been the only thing that kept him on that path to good and right he'd always been striving for.

She didn't even pretend to consider his lie. "Of course you do. You remember everything."

His mouth quirked in spite of himself. He wasn't so sure he remembered everything, but he remembered enough. Things he didn't want to remember or rehash. So, he let his hands span her hips, pull her closer and more flush against him, where he ached for her.

Always her.

"I remember you."

She let out a shaky breath, searching his gaze for something. Something he didn't want to give, but she'd always found anyway—always would.

Always pulsed between them.

"What was it?" she asked, her voice still just a whisper, even if there was more urgency behind it. "Because I never understood. Maybe I was afraid to. I want to understand now. I know you wanted me, I know you *loved* me, but you were always pushing me away. You didn't want to."

"No, I didn't want to." He could remember his own pious duty so well, and it hurt. It hurt because he didn't have it in him anymore. He was going to give in to this, and her, when he never would have before. Too old for pious duty, he supposed, or maybe just too cognizant of how little joy there was to be found when she wasn't with him.

"So, what was it, Jamison?"

She was sitting on his lap, the softest part of her nestled against the hardest part of him. Her hands held his face with a gentleness he'd never known in his life, and doubted she'd known in hers. His brother was out there. Her sister was missing. People were dead.

And they were rehashing old history while they waited for the sun to fall.

Somehow it seemed like all that fate he didn't believe in. Like they'd come to the moment made for rehashing. Rediscovering. Here, before they faced potential death and failure. Here, before the true war started—because this would be a war. With the Sons. With his father and hers.

So, he told her a truth he'd sworn he'd never tell her. "I wanted to do it right."

Her eyebrows drew together. "Right?"

"Get married. Be normal, upstanding people. You were too young for all that. So, I tried to wait until you weren't."

She sighed as if she was in some kind of pain. Then she kissed him, slow and sweet, which was new enough. "I was never too young. And we're too old for all that now," she whispered against his mouth.

"Are we?"

Her body froze—except for her eyes—which whipped to his.

No matter how much of the past was here between them, he wasn't the same man he'd been. Because he hadn't been a *man*. Not really. He'd been filled with a youthful sense of right and wrong. An idea he could be *noble* and good. That life was black-and-white, and he would always follow the white.

But life was gray, pretty much always, for good men. Only men with empty souls could follow extremes to the ends of the earth.

So, this wouldn't be Liza pushing through his defenses. It wouldn't be her convincing him.

No, it would be him choosing. Finally, fully accepting the gray areas life threw at him. Because loving her had always been a little bit good *and* bad—as had she been herself. And was. And always would be.

Always. Always.

Slowly, watching her the whole time, he lifted her shirt up and over her head, revealing skin the sun almost never touched. Pale, pale white. A contrast to all that dark hair that swirled around her.

She'd always been a contrast. Dark and light. Right and wrong. Hope and fear. Instead of choosing one and fearing the other. He chose both, would love both.

The gold locket he'd given her once upon a time hung from a chain. And while his brain told him not to, his heart was leading. When it came to her, it always had.

He reached out and flipped the locket open.

It had been a group shot, he remembered. Grandma had taken it with her old Polaroid camera—all the Wyatt boys, all the Knight girls in front of the barn. She'd taken a few because Brady kept accidentally blinking at the wrong moment.

Jamison had taken one of those and cut just him and Liza out, tucked it into the locket.

He opened the flimsy fake gold. Inside was the picture he'd cut out himself, put in there himself. A romantic gesture because he'd been trying to prove to her that life outside the Sons could be something *right*. Normal.

It shouldn't be that it still mattered, that somehow even knowing all he knew he wanted to find a way to give her that. It shouldn't be that fifteen years felt like nothing since the moment he'd caught her trying to break into his office.

But it was.

He moved her onto her back, underneath him. He

touched her, a choice—not only giving in. He kissed her—mouth, neck, shoulder. He touched her, gently and reverently. She pulled off his shirt, touching him until his skin felt like it was too tight, and only she could take away all the pressure building inside him.

Because only she could.

He slid off her pants, careful of her leg injury. She tugged at his, until they were both naked for each other. Joined. Like they'd always been meant to be.

The ache was unbearable and he wanted to live in it forever as she arched against him, as she whispered his name, begging for that unnamed release.

Then slow and sweet was gone. That old desperation conjured by talk of the past…by talk of a future.

Knowing history couldn't be erased, and the future wasn't a given, they gave themselves to each other. Falling over a blissful edge wrapped up together, just like then. Just like now.

"LIZA."

Liza didn't want to leave this warm bubble of sleep, no matter how incessant Jamison's voice was. She wasn't sleeping on the floor, and she wasn't cold. It was nice here, and she burrowed deeper into the soft blanket under her cheek.

"Liza."

But she was colder than she had been, because Jamison's body was no longer next to her. She blinked her eyes open. There was still a hint of sun shining through the window, so they couldn't have slept more than an hour or two.

She glared at him. Then remembered the whole point of her life was saving her sister, not sleeping.

Certainly not having sex with her ex-boyfriend from fifteen years ago.

But looking at that serious expression, the mussed hair and bruised face, she thought *ex-boyfriend* was hardly the right word. He was the love of her life. Then. Now. Always.

She'd said they were too old for things like marriage and being normal and doing it right, and he'd said "Are we?" like they had some kind of future spreading out before them.

It would be suicide to believe there was, but she could see it too clearly, feel it too clearly to resist.

If she survived this, maybe they could find each other again. Maybe.

But just like always, they had to survive first.

"I found something," he said, his voice devoid of all emotion. His eyes, though... She could see he felt everything she did right there in his eyes.

But he'd found something. "What kind of something?" she asked in a sigh.

"Get dressed."

She grumbled through it, finding her clothes had been laid out neatly beside her. She almost asked him where he came from—but she knew his kindness was simply a mix of two things. One, the fact that he'd spent his first five years living with Grandma Pauline and his mother, before his mother had been fully converted to the Sons' way of life and Ace had decided he didn't want any good influence on his children. Two, something innate inside him.

Dressed, she pushed herself off the bed. "It's still light out."

"Not for long, but that's not why I woke you up." He nodded toward the hall and led her back to the bathroom.

"I got up to use the bathroom and I saw this weird

light. Green. Coming from a crack in the wall. I guess it
was too light to notice it earlier."

"Let me guess. Nuclear waste."

But he didn't even try to crack a smile at her joke.
He squatted down next to a place where he'd apparently
pulled off a piece of the wall. Inside the dark hole was
something completely incongruous to this whole place.
Some kind of…computer.

"What does it mean?" she asked. There were boxes and
flashing circles on the screen. The green light Jamison
must have seen was from the power light on the side of
the laptop.

"Well, whoever was here before us left this behind.
It means we're not safe here. That's for darn sure, but…
It's explosives, Liza. Whatever this is, it's controlling
explosives."

"What?" she all but screeched, trying to figure out
why on earth he was being so calm about being blown up.

"I don't understand it all—don't know enough about
it. But it's marking down time before explosives go off."

"Here?"

"No. No, I think…" He shook his head. "I don't know
enough about it, but it might be your father's place. This
is something like a blueprint," he said, pointing to the
screen. "There's a house—decent sized. A horse stable here. A shed of some kind over here." He traced the
squares and rectangles on the screen. "And each of these
blinking dots is a point where explosives will go off. Is
my guess anyway."

She grabbed his arm, suddenly icy cold. "But Gigi
is there."

"We don't know that for sure," he said, so measured
and so *cop* she wanted to scream.

"But she could be, Jamison. She *could* be there, and

someone's going to blow it up." She squeezed the arm she was holding. "Cody. Cody wasn't that far away. He's the only one we saw, and if this is blowing up the Sons, this has to be Cody's. They're not blowing up themselves."

"I wouldn't put it past them, but…" He sighed. "Cody seems likely."

"Get him to stop it. Jamison—you have to get him to stop it."

"How? I don't know where he went. He told me to stay away."

Liza whirled out of the bathroom. She didn't have time to argue with him. She didn't have time for anything.

"We have to split up. I've got try to find the house and rescue Gigi. You find Cody." She grabbed her boots, and he grabbed her wrist, stopping her forward movement.

"We don't split up. *You* said that."

She didn't want to; that was the worst part. "We do when a little girl's life is at stake," she returned, jerking her arm out of his grasp. "There's not enough time to do both together. Someone needs to stop Cody, and someone needs to get Gigi. Now."

"We don't know where that house is. We don't know where Cody is. We don't, in fact, know where Gigi is."

"But we know they're not here."

He raked a hand through his hair. "I'm not suggesting we stay here and do nothing. I'm suggesting we *think*."

"Think about what? There is no time to think. You have to go where we were and try to find Cody. I have to go toward where we think my father's place might be and get Gigi. We don't have time for anything else." She sat on the bed and quickly tied her boots.

"Are you going to fight off your father and any other Sons by yourself with one gun? And let's say you could—when you get Gigi, what are you going to do with her? You can't just go in there and *die*. That doesn't serve anyone."

She stood and looked him square in the eye. "I couldn't live with myself, if Gigi dies and I didn't even try to get to her in time. Jamison, look at me." She wasted precious seconds waiting until he did. "If it were one of your brothers when they were four and helpless, or even one of the Knight girls, what would you do? Put yourself in my shoes."

"I'm already in your shoes. You think Gigi being hurt would mean nothing to me?"

The fact that she knew it would mean nearly as much to him as it did to her, even though he'd never met Gigi, only made her heart hurt more. But she'd wasted too much time. She hadn't started on this journey to find Jamison again. Anything they'd shared in this cabin was only…a weakness. One she couldn't keep letting change her. "We don't have time. We do not have time. I have to go and so do you." She grabbed the gun, then swung her pack onto her back. She opened her mouth to tell him to move, but he spoke first.

"I love you—"

She should have known he'd fight dirty. But she wouldn't fall for it, even as her heart swelled and her eyes pricked with tears. "Jamison, don't try to use—"

"I have always loved you. I will always love you." He was calm. Dead serious.

And it couldn't—*didn't*—matter.

"All the love in the world doesn't matter if she dies and I didn't try to get to her. I'll die with her, one way or another."

"If you die, so does she. I want you to remember that. I had to. More than once did I have to remind myself that nothing good happened for my brothers if I was dead in a ditch. Find the house. Find Gigi. Do what you have to do to get her to safety—but you can't be reckless doing what you have to do. You can't risk yourself, because that only risks her. Do you understand me?"

She didn't, for a few seconds, because he was… He was letting her go. Not that she would have let him stop her, but she thought he'd try. She'd thought he'd…

It didn't matter. Because he was letting her go without further argument or impediment. She moved onto her toes and pressed her mouth to his—hard and fast.

Then she gave him what he'd given her. "I love you. I have always loved you. I will always love you—whatever happens."

"As soon as I get Cody to stop this, I'll be there. If you get her out—we'll meet back here. Understood?"

She nodded. He grabbed his own pack and handed her the walkie from it. "You keep this on. If they're in there, one of the channels should pick it up if they're sending messages outside."

"But you—"

"I won't be next to the house they're in. Presumably." He zipped up his pack and shouldered the larger burden. He reattached his holstered weapon around his waist.

She didn't want to take this next leg alone. She'd gotten so used to being alone she would have considered herself immune to feeling this again, to needing someone again.

Here it was, though, an ache of longing. She wanted someone's hand to hold. Someone to patch up her wounds and vice versa. She wanted his quiet strength and surety leading her into saving her sister.

Didn't she already know she couldn't do this alone? She'd failed Marci and Carlee and—

"Liza."

She looked up at him, panic an icy cold bucket of reality on all those plans she'd been brimming to fulfill.

"We're still together in this. We're just working on two different ends of the same rope. We meet in the middle."

"I—"

"We'll meet in the middle. Now, here." He pulled his map, the marked one he'd spent *years* on, out of his pocket and handed it to her. "This might help. There are extra batteries for the headlamp in the bottom of your pack if you start to lose power. Okay?"

She stared at the map, then him. He was giving her a pep talk. Encouraging her. When she knew very well he did not want her to do it. When, if this was fifteen years ago, he already would have locked her in the cabin so he could do it all himself.

I wanted to do it right.

Letting her go, trusting her to get to Gigi like she trusted him to get to Cody and stop the explosives.

On a deep breath, she nodded. "We meet in the middle."

Then she walked out into the darkness, ready to do whatever it took to get Gigi to that middle.

Chapter Fourteen

With every step he took, Jamison cursed himself for letting Liza go alone. He should have gone with her. They could have liberated Gigi together and let every other part of the Sons compound burn.

But there were too many what-ifs. What if the explosives went off sooner rather than later? What if more than just Gigi was at stake when it came to innocent bystanders? There wasn't time. No matter how he tried to convince himself those were the reasons he'd let her go, it wasn't anything rational or reasonable.

He'd seen that look on Liza's face as she'd hesitated back there in the cabin. The way she'd been determined, and then doubt had crept in and left her frozen. She'd needed someone to trust her, to tell her she could do it.

Maybe she'd always needed that from him and he'd never seen it. Maybe that was what a lot of people in his life needed from him—not someone to sweep in and fix and save everything, but someone to say they could handle it on their own.

There was no use going through the past, no use thinking about all the ways he might have stifled his brothers, but he could fix his present.

Liza was a strong and capable woman, and she needed a win. She needed a few people to believe she could accomplish that win. Gigi needed to be alive. Jamison had to believe Liza when she said she couldn't survive losing another person, and he had to do everything in his power to help.

Which meant he had to stop the explosives. As quickly as possible, and at whatever cost. He had no experience with computers *or* explosives, so poking around on the computer was only a dangerous possibility.

He had to find Cody because Cody knew *all* about computers. Cody had gotten a degree in computer science—the only one of them to make it to college—not that they'd given him much of a choice. Once teachers had started commenting on Cody's intelligence in middle school, Jamison and his brothers had done everything in their power to learn about how to get their baby brother into college.

Cody had protested at first, made noise about the police academy, but eventually he'd given in to the pressure and gone off to South Dakota State. It wasn't Harvard, but it was something.

And Cody had used those opportunities. He'd done internships within the CIA. He'd finished his degree with honors. For the past few years he'd spoken of an on-again, off-again freelance computer job that kept him in Wyoming. He only came home around Christmas and never gave much by way of details.

If they weren't Cody's explosives, Cody would at least have a better idea of what was going on. Jamison had to believe Cody was involved with whatever was happening. There was no other explanation for him roaming around the Black Hills, carrying what appeared to be a Sons walkie and communicating in Morse code, all very far from where he was supposed to be.

Jamison reached the spot where he'd originally run

into Cody. He worried less about his headlamp now, because while the threat of being caught still existed, it was a risk he'd have to take if he was going to find Cody.

Jamison stopped and looked around. He'd been thinking about Liza and his brother, but he hadn't been thinking strategically. Cody had been striding away from the clearing—opposite to the cabin. Jamison thought about the map, about where they thought Liza's father's cabin was.

Immediately, he turned west. If his instincts were right, and he had the map clear in his head, Cody had been going in the direction of Tony Dean's place. Maybe to lay the explosives? Or something else to do with them?

There was only one way to find out.

Jamison didn't take the same path Liza had taken. They'd have better luck finding the place if they weren't approaching it from the same angle. So, he thought about the direction he'd seen Cody go.

Every so many steps he made an adjustment to the map in his head. Turning, thinking, analyzing.

He heard a crack. The whisper of movement. Slowly, cautiously, he moved one hand to his gun and the other hand to the switch of his headlamp. Another whisper, this time on the opposite side of him.

He switched off the light, plunging him and whoever—or whatever—else into darkness, and took a leap away from the spot he'd been standing in.

But that crashed him into something—and since he hadn't been standing that close to any trees, it had to be a person.

So, Jamison fought. Trying to wrestle the other person underneath him. The other man pushed but didn't hit, then whispered viciously.

"Stop trying to hit me, you moron," Cody's voice hissed.

Jamison stilled, then untangled himself from his brother and got to his feet. "You didn't think to say, 'Hey, Jamison, I'm lurking around the woods you're hiking through.' Who's the moron? Thinking I won't fight?"

"Shut up for a second, and don't turn on that idiotic light," Cody growled.

Jamison listened, though he didn't particularly want to take orders from his baby brother. After a few seconds, Cody made an irritated noise. "What are you doing?"

"Are we speaking now? Or did you want to hold hands and tap each other more?"

"Now's not the time for your sad attempts at humor. You can't go that direction, Jamison. Go back the way you came. Stop trying to do…whatever it is you're trying to do."

"I can't do that."

"This isn't a joke, and it's no place for—no offense—a sleepy small town's sheriff's deputy. I don't know what you think you're up to with Liza Dean of all people, but I don't have time. You have to vacate the premises. Both of you."

"If I could do that, Cody, I would have done it the first time you asked. I'm not here as a sheriff, and Liza isn't here as… Never mind. Listen to me. Are you the one with the explosives?"

Cody shoved him. Hard. Jamison scowled, though it was lost in the dark.

"Are you trying to get us all killed?" Cody hissed.

"I don't think you understand. If this is you, you can't do it. You can't… There are innocent lives at stake."

"There are Sons' lives at stake," Cody said with a cold fierceness that had Jamison feeling a chill go right through him. "I don't care much about those," Cody added.

"What about the kids?"

"Kids? There aren't kids there. Do you think I don't know what I'm doing? That I'm some rogue idiot trying to blow someone up for fun? For revenge. I have been canvassing this area and that house. I... I can't get into this with you. I know you fancy yourself savior supreme along with big brother, but this is bigger than you, Jamison. Get Liza and go and leave me to it."

"What about Carlee Bright?"

This time Cody didn't shove him. He grabbed him by the shirtfront. "You have no idea—no idea—what you are getting involved in."

And because his brother seemed genuinely—*scared* wasn't the right word—affected, concerned, sharp and poised, like a blade, Jamison didn't fight him off. He let Cody have his grip as he spoke calmly and quietly.

"No. I don't. But I know that Liza's sister saw Carlee murdered, and then Gigi disappeared after telling Liza. I know Tony killed Carlee—or at least was there when it happened. I know, having done no canvassing and spending no time here, that Gigi is four years old and in exactly the kind of danger we can imagine."

"Tony comes and goes. Three of his henchmen. A few women are in there always, but no kids."

"Did you check the shack? The stables?"

"I've been watching. There isn't—"

"What have you been watching, Cody? Not everything. Not every inch. You've been watching Tony and his men, but have you been paying attention?"

"You don't know what you're getting yourself mixed up in, Jamison. Go home. Go back to Bonesteel. Let me take care of this."

"I can't."

"Right. You can't. You can't listen to me, and you can't trust me. But you trust Liza. Who went back."

"I trust Liza, who's trying to save someone she loves. I know something about that. You have to stop the explosives, Cody. You *have to*. Until we know for sure."

"It's not my call, Jamison."

Jamison put his hand over Cody's, still twisted in his shirt. Not to pull it off, but to get through to his brother. "Make it your call. Now."

Cody's grip stayed tight on Jamison's shirt. "You don't get to boss me around anymore, big brother."

But someone apparently did. "What on earth are you involved in?"

"Bigger things than saving one little girl."

"There's no bigger thing than trying to save the kids caught in that place. If it was as easy as blowing up all the bad men, we could have done that twenty years ago. It isn't so easy, Cody. I know you know that. Somewhere deep down you have to know that."

Cody released Jamison's shirt, giving him another slight shove as he did. Then he swore, viciously, in the dark.

Jamison waited, though every second that ticked by tested his patience and his worry over Liza. Cody was doing something, tapping at what sounded like computer keys, but there was no light, no sign of what he was doing.

After a few minutes he took Jamison's hand and pressed a small rectangle into it.

"You're going to go to the compound." Cody swore at himself as if he already regretted giving that order. "You're going to search the stables—there is nothing going on in the shack or the house. The stables… It's just horses, but my men did the search. Not me. It wasn't my assignment, but…"

"Assignment?"

"You'll search the stables—that's it. If it's clear—you

press that button twice and you get the hell out because I'm blowing the place up. If, on the insanely off chance my guys missed something and there are innocent people on the premises, you press it once and only once."

"And if they're there—then what?"

"Then, I might be able to get you some help. *Might.* But not before I've got proof, maybe not even if I do."

"Cody—"

"No questions. You can't worry about me, brother. You've got bigger things to worry about right now."

Jamison hated that it was true. "You'll stay safe."

"Safe? What do you take me for, Jamison? Certainly not a Wyatt," Cody said with just the tiniest hint of humor. "Now go. And hurry."

That was just what Jamison did.

LIZA NEARLY TRIPPED over the first sign she was on the right track. The metal glinted in the light of the moon—which had been bright enough for her to keep the headlamp off. Occasionally she'd use the beam to check the map, but otherwise it made her feel too conspicuous.

Now she flipped it on and found a little pink tricycle, covered in dirt and pine needles like it hadn't been used in a while. Based on the fact it was early spring, it probably hadn't been.

She tried not to get her hopes up. A little pink tricycle could mean anything. But mostly it meant a little girl had been around here somewhere at some point, and a little girl was what she was looking for.

She turned the headlamp off and looked up. Off in the distance, she thought she saw the hint of lights. Lights.

Slowly, carefully, she moved toward it. The closer she got, the more the trees crowded together—providing excellent cover. But after walking awhile, she nearly sobbed in relief, because through the trees she saw the warm glow of lights dancing in windows. *Windows*.

In the moonlight and starlight, the shadow of a big, beautiful cabin loomed. It had to be what she was looking for. It *had* to be.

Knowing her father, she was sure there would be all sorts of security. Men watching from all angles. Cameras, maybe. Anything was possible because this whole place was very unlike the Sons. They liked their tents and shacks and things you could leave behind, and quickly. They preferred caves for big meetings and "justice" being served because evidence wouldn't be found.

This whole spread before her was very strange—and spoke to a permanence the Sons had never attempted before.

Maybe, just maybe, it could be their downfall.

But that wasn't the point of right now. Now she was solely focused on finding Gigi. She stood behind a tree, forcing herself to slow her breathing, to think rationally.

She'd made it, found her father's place. Now she just had to find Gigi. And avoid all detection by the Sons, and hope Jamison found Cody to stop the explosives.

She knew she should entertain the thought Jamison could fail, but it wasn't possible. *Jamison* and *failure* in the same sentence didn't make sense. She couldn't get her brain or her heart to think it possible.

It didn't matter—because she had a job to do here. A girl to find and protect. And if someone found her or them, she had a gun. She'd defend herself and Gigi.

Yes, a *gun will defend you from a horde of gang members*. Why did she think she could do this?

Because it's the only choice.

The only choice. She repeated that to herself as she turned back to face the house. She searched the dark, seeing a dozen shadows that looked like they were moving toward her.

Her imagination and tricks of the moonlight. She listened to the night. No footsteps. Just the wind and the trees and…

Horses. The distinct sound of a horse snuffling. She must be close to the stables, and Gigi had mentioned a horse. Maybe that would give her some kind of clue, or at least a better, safer vantage point.

Liza moved toward the noise and realized she was ridiculously close to a large, squat building that clearly housed the stables. She reached out and touched the wood. She was at the back, maybe, because there was no door or window on this side.

She used her hands to guide her as she felt her way toward the front. The door into the building had a big chain and padlock on it. Strange.

Dread crept along Liza's spine, but she inched forward, still trying to find the source of the horse noises.

Eventually she came to a high window, the soft nose of a horse sticking out of it. There was something like a door—also locked with a padlock—but the door itself was more like a gate—big bars with space between them.

Liza crouched down and looked through the gate, seeing if she could peer into the stables for any clues. She was too close to the house to turn her headlamp on, so she had to hope moonlight was enough as she squinted into the dark.

At first, it was just moving, melting dark that she couldn't be sure was *actually* moving, or just her eyes playing tricks. But as she watched and her eyes adjusted, she was almost certain she saw something moving around deep in the stables. It could be anything. Other animals. Mice.

She shuddered, squinting through the gate until she was almost certain she saw...

Eyes.

Liza kept perfectly still, watching as the eyes moved back into the shadows. But something was moving closer. She held her breath, adjusted the gun in her grip.

The figure was small. Too small to be a man. Too small to be anything but a child.

"Gigi," Liza whispered, more hope than certainty.

"Sissy?"

Liza nearly collapsed. She swallowed down tears as pudgy fingers curled around the gate, Gigi's dirty face peering at her through the spaces in the bars.

"I'm not supposed to be here," Gigi whispered, glancing warily at the cabin.

Liza tried not to sob as she fell to her knees to put her eye level with Gigi. "I'm not either, baby."

"I want Mommy."

"I know. I know." Liza studied the gate. The height from the ground to the top of the window. "Can you climb up here?"

Gigi looked up, then her mouth curved just a hint. "George will help me."

George? "No—no, don't tell any—"

But Gigi was scurrying away. Liza let out a sigh of relief when she only went over to the horse in the stall.

"Mommy taught me a trick," Gigi said—too loud, far too loud.

Liza pressed her face to the gate. "You've got to whisper, baby. We have to be careful. Anyone could be out here and the only way we get out of here safe is if we're very, very quiet."

"No. It's meeting time. We're all alone until the lights upstairs go out. Then someone comes with supper."

"They're keeping you out here?" Even though all signs pointed to it, she could hardly believe it. Tony Dean was a monster, and she'd been locked in her share of rooms and closets, growing up with him as a father. But Gigi was so sweet.

Silly to think there was any difference between how Tony would have treated her, and how he would have treated Gigi. Daughters were useless, until they weren't. Why wouldn't he treat Gigi just as badly, if not worse?

Gigi didn't respond to Liza's question out loud. It was possible she nodded or shook her head, but it was too hard to see in the dark. Gigi whispered something to the animal, then it seemed to... It seemed to kneel.

Liza fairly gasped as Gigi shimmied up the horse's large body into a sitting position on the horse's back. Liza heard a thud and realized that Gigi was giving the horse a pat as it got back onto its feet. Higher up, the moonlight glinted against Gigi's blond hair and big smile. Her grip was in the horse's mane, and she learned forward and pressed her cheek to the horse.

"Mommy said George would help me escape someday," Gigi said, sadness creeping into her tone.

"Your mommy was right," Liza managed to squeak, ignoring the tears tracking down her cheeks. "Come here, George," she encouraged the horse.

The massive horse made its way close enough to the gate so Liza could hold out her arms. Gigi pulled herself onto the top of the gate without hesitation, like she'd done this before. Who knew, maybe she had. Maybe she and Carlee had worked on this very escape.

Liza couldn't think about that too much right now. She held out her arms and Gigi jumped into them with an easy trust that made tears clog her throat.

Liza hugged Gigi tight, wanting to cry over the little

girl being in her arms again, but there was no time. Liza glanced at the upstairs lights—still on—but that didn't mean no one was watching.

"Daddy said he's going to kill George. When the time is right," Gigi said, laying her cheek against Liza's shoulders and squeezing tight as if to assure herself Liza was real.

Liza didn't know what to say to that. This horse had potentially saved Gigi's life in this moment. "No, we won't let that happen." Somehow, they'd figure out a way to come back and get George.

Now, it was up to Liza to save Gigi. She was here, impossibly here, with Gigi in her arms. Everything was going to be okay.

Gigi being out here by herself was some miracle and Liza had to use that miracle to her advantage. "Listen, baby. We're going to run away, okay. You just hold on to me and be real quiet."

Gigi lifted her head. "What about the others?"

Liza's blood went cold. "What others?"

Gigi pointed back at the stables. "The others. I'm supposed to stay with the others."

Hell.

Chapter Fifteen

Jamison was starting to believe he'd headed in the wrong direction. It was dark and he was tired and maybe he'd lost all sense of direction. Maybe he was walking in circles, destined to cause everyone in his life to die.

He shoved that thought away. Luckily, he had some practice with battling those voices, those doubts. He hadn't let anyone die when he'd been a kid. Under no circumstances would he allow it to happen now.

So, he kept moving forward and didn't allow doubts to threaten. Second-guessing himself *would* get him lost and likely get someone killed. He had to believe in himself, in his abilities. Like he was believing in Cody to do the right thing, and Liza to take care of herself.

Living life or death so often meant constantly *believing* in people. He knew some cops who got too bitter, or too arrogant, who didn't think anyone could ever have their back.

But it was a death sentence when you knew life was on the line. Hope was so often the real difference between life and death.

Not just his or Liza's or Gigi's, but Cody's, too, now.

His brother was involved in *something*, God only knew what. Considering there were explosives involved,

Jamison had a hard time believing it was something within the law. That ate at him, if he'd let it.

And if he let it, he wasn't worrying over walking in the wrong direction.

Hadn't Jamison and his other brothers worked their butts off to give Cody every opportunity away from the Sons? Instead, he was in the thick of things—plotting with *other people* to blow things up.

It just about figured.

He might have let that guilt and irritation fuel his forward progress, but he came up short when he saw lights ahead. The kind of light that came from homes. Warm and glowing dots in the distance.

Homes. It was so weird to think of the Sons in association with a *home*. Cabin, shack, stables. Sure, they'd probably stolen it from someone they'd killed, but it was so unlike the Sons' MO Jamison had grown up with. He had to wonder how well he knew how to fight this new version of his father's gang.

One that put down roots, and potentially sold and traded people. Liza had told him it had changed and in a way he'd understood that power and violence had grown unchecked. He'd understood he needed to look at them differently, maybe even fight them differently, but this new development of them doing "*normal* people" things while also potentially trafficking little girls... It seriously messed with him if he thought too much about it.

So, he couldn't. He had to focus on how to fight it, because whether he was good at it now or not didn't matter. He was still doing it.

He crept closer and closer to the light, pausing every so often to listen. Mostly it was all wind and branches rustling, but the closer he got, the more he thought he heard...whispering.

He moved toward the noise, continuing to pause, trying to determine if the voices were male or female. The Sons only used men for security or outside watches, and they wouldn't necessarily have cause to whisper.

Jamison had to believe it wasn't armed Sons men talking, but he couldn't see the figures yet to tell for sure, so he could only creep closer and closer until the moonlight gave him some clues.

There was a small figure crouched next to a big building, and a larger figure trying to scale a…gate of some kind. Like they were trying to get inside—like *she* was trying to get inside.

"Liza."

The figure bobbled, then fell to the ground, though landing on her feet. "Hurry," she strained to whisper.

He moved toward them both, noticing the way the little girl scurried behind Liza's legs and held on to them for dear life.

"Gigi, it's okay," Liza soothed, putting her hand on the girl's head. "This is Jamison. He's my friend and he's going to help us. I promise."

The little girl vigorously shook her head.

Liza crouched next to the girl as Jamison came closer. "Jamison is one of the few very good guys around. He saved me once. A long time ago. I promise he's one of the good guys. He's going to help."

"You found her," Jamison said stupidly. He couldn't believe it. Here they both stood, alive and well. Now all they had to do was—

"She says there are more inside the stables. More girls," Liza's voice cracked on the last word.

So much for things being easy. Jamison let out a breath. "I found Cody. I just have to get a message to him and we'll stop the explosives." With nerveless fingers,

Jamison pulled the device Cody had given him and hit the button once. It solved one problem, but not the other just as deadly threatening problem. "That should give us time. But we still have to get out of here. All we've managed to fix is the explosives situation."

"Take Gigi. I'll get the other girls."

Jamison didn't even pretend to consider that. He strode for the gate and studied it in the moonlight. "Give me a boost. I'll go over and get them and hand them off to you. I'll be able to get back out easier than you will, especially with your leg, and Gigi will feel safer with you out here."

"Jamison."

"No time to waste." He adjusted his pack and put his hands atop the stall door. There'd be no way or time to get that padlock off, but he wasn't altogether certain he could boost himself back over. Still, better him stuck in here than her.

He pulled himself up onto the ledge. He couldn't get all the way up—it was just a pinch too high—so he instructed Liza to push him the rest of the way over.

He fell, and in the dark he couldn't make it a particularly graceful fall. He landed on his side, jarring his elbow and his hip against the solid dirt ground that smelled like manure. His body vibrated with pain, but nothing was broken—yet.

Unfortunately the thudding, clumsy fall sent the horse into a bit of a panic. It whinnied and reared. Jamison was far more worried about the noise than any potential bodily harm. Nonetheless, he scurried back onto his feet trying to calm the horse.

"Shh. Shh. It's all right," he muttered, holding up his hands. The horse pranced in the small space of its outdoor stall, kicking up smells and noises and the potential for them all to die. "Shh," Jamison continued, stepping a little closer. The horse continued to move nervously, but Jamison managed to get close enough to touch, to reassure.

He gently smoothed a hand over the horse's flank and it settled some. It was likely somewhat used to strange men coming and going. After a few more calming words and soothing pets, the horse calmed completely.

He glanced back at the gate, Liza and Gigi standing there watching him. A lot riding on him and no time to waste.

With the horse stilled, he moved past it and into the dark of the stable building. He hesitated, looking around, but he couldn't even see if there were windows or more gates. He'd need a light, as much as that was dangerous. He couldn't do it without one.

He took the headlamp off his head and held it pointed to the ground as he flipped it on. By keeping the beam pointed downward, he hoped to avoid detection from the outside. Dirty hay was under his feet as he slowly swept the beam around. He found himself in a bigger stall. There was a door, and it was luckily unlatched. Presumably it was how Gigi had gotten into the stall, and to Liza, in the first place.

He slid through the stall door opening and into a long cement hallway of sorts. Around him were all sorts of stalls. He didn't hear anyone or anything, which led him to believe they only had one horse.

And room for plenty of other horrors. The silence was what really got to him. There should be shuffling or moving, breathing or whispering if there were more people back here.

But he was a cop, and he knew his duty. He began to search the stable building like he would any other. He took each room methodically, carefully, keeping his beam of light low and away from anything that looked like a window to the outside. He checked corners and behind doors in every stall.

He doubted Gigi had made up the story about more people being in here, but maybe she was confused. Maybe they were somewhere else. But Gigi had somehow gotten to Liza, and even at four it wouldn't be that confusing to know she'd left a group of people.

Why would Gigi have permission to get out to the horse, though? Special favors for the boss's daughter? Doubtful if she'd witnessed her father murder her mother.

Jamison swept through another stall. He had yet to find a door that was padlocked shut like the outside doors, but he supposed locking the doors to escape from the outside was protection enough.

There was only one room left. It wasn't like the stalls—it had a full door and was toward the back. Like some kind of stable hand's quarters or a manager's office. Jamison crept closer and still heard nothing that give any inclination human beings were trapped inside.

Living human beings anyway. It was possible Gigi had been left with dead bodies. He wouldn't put it past the sons, and if they'd killed Carlee over this, who else might they have?

Still, though his soul recoiled from having to face it, the potential for dead bodies was one he'd live with, because he knew how to deal with horrors. He'd been dealing his whole life.

He would do whatever it took to protect the innocent—he'd made that promise to himself and the world a long time ago.

As he eased open the door and swept his light into the last room, he nearly sagged with relief. For the first time he found something besides empty cement or dirty hay. At least ten girls were huddled in the corner. They winced against the light, holding on to each other and pushing closer together as if they could become invisible if they only pressed together tightly enough.

They had it down to an art form. He hadn't heard them until he'd stepped inside. They'd made themselves so still, so silent, Jamison hadn't heard *ten* girls until he'd been standing practically next to them.

Jamison had to access the cop part of himself that compartmentalized the cold horror away and act.

"I'm not here to hurt you," he said quietly, keeping exactly where he was in the entrance to the stall so they didn't feel threatened. He turned the light to shine on him, rather than them. "I'm not with the Sons. We're going to get you out of here, but you're going to have to listen to me, and you're going to have to be very quiet."

They huddled closer, and he doubted they believed him, but he couldn't exactly force them out, either.

"I'm a police officer. Here…" It took precious time they didn't have, but he couldn't drag these girls out kicking and screaming. Not just because they'd be caught, but because these girls had been through enough.

He shrugged off his pack and unzipped the small, interior pocket. He grabbed the badge he'd shoved into the pack what felt like a million years ago but was only a few days. "Here's my badge." He shone the light on it. "I'm a police officer. I'm going to help you."

Of course, if they were all Sons girls they'd been taught at a young age to distrust police, but he had to hope in this current situation they might change their mind.

No one moved. No one spoke. He returned the badge to its pocket, reshouldered his pack and put the lamp on his head.

"I just need you to come with me. One at a time. I'm

going to take you to the horse's stable outside. I'm going to help you over the gate. There's a woman and the little girl who was in here with you waiting. Gigi? She's already out. Once we're all out, we're going to run."

"They'll kill us if we run," one of the girls whispered.

"Not if I can help it." Jamison knew enough about getting people out of a dark situation that flat out lying didn't often produce the desired results. But neither did he want to give the unvarnished truth to a bunch of scared *girls*. The oldest couldn't be more than twelve, at best. Disgust and horror clogged his throat, but he had to speak.

Put it away. Focus on getting them out.

"They have to catch us first. Would you rather stay here or would you rather try to survive?"

There was nothing but silence. Still, Jamison wouldn't give up. Not until they were all out. "One at a time. Who wants to be first?"

He waited. Too long. Too damn long. But finally one of the girls struggled onto her feet. A few of the other girls told her to stop, but she shook her head. She was one of the older ones.

"I'd rather die than stay here," she said firmly.

Jamison nodded. He wanted to offer a hand, but he figured that would be more threatening. "You just follow me out, okay?"

She nodded, and as he walked back the way he'd come, she followed. He turned off his light as he reached the outdoor part of the stable, then moved forward.

When the girl saw Liza and Gigi, she ran toward the gate and fell to her knees with a sob. "It's true," she whispered. "You're going to save us."

"We're going to try," Liza said, patting the girl's hand that was clutching the bars of the gate. "Let Jamison lift you over. Then I'll catch you."

She nodded, looking back at Jamison. He and Liza worked together to get her over the gate, and she immediately started to cry in earnest.

"It has to be quicker than this," Liza whispered to Jamison as Gigi wrapped her arms around the crying girl.

"I know" was all he said, before he went back in, hoping the next girls would follow.

LIZA WATCHED THE house between each girl Jamison brought out. This was taking too long. The upstairs lights couldn't stay on forever. Eventually someone would be coming with the girls' supper, according to Gigi.

And Gigi wouldn't leave her side.

Liza had instructed the eight girls Jamison had gotten out so far to go hide in the woods. One girl knew a spot where she thought they could all be undetected if the main house flipped on the floodlights. But Liza hadn't been able to get Gigi to go with them, and she'd started to throw a fit when one of the girls had tried to carry her away.

She was in too much danger here, but Liza didn't know what else to do. The girls coming out of the stables had been hurt. So much worse was waiting for them if she and Jamison left them here.

There was only now to save them. Save them they would. Things were going better than Liza could have expected and the lights upstairs were still on. Every second that clicked by, Liza's heart beat harder against her ribs.

Maybe they'd make it. Maybe they'd get every girl out before those lights clicked off. Maybe—

The upstairs went suddenly black. Liza almost couldn't believe her eyes as the entire top story of the cabin in the distance went dark. She froze for a second or two, but Gigi's voice brought her back from that icy precipice of panic.

"The lights went out, sissy," Gigi whispered, fear emanating from every word. "They're coming."

"I know, baby. I know," Liza said. She had to do something. She had to act.

But Jamison said there were two more girls. The lights had gone out, which meant someone was coming. If they were found…

Finally, Jamison appeared with another girl.

"The lights went out, Jamison. They're coming."

"But Jenni is still in there," the little girl he was leading whimpered. She didn't look much older than Gigi. Jamison had to lift her up and practically set her on top of the gate. Liza pulled her down.

"Come over yourself," Liza said to Jamison, trying not to sound as panicked as she felt, for the girls' sake. "Take the girls somewhere safe. I'll get the last one."

"No. Not enough time. Besides, they'll all be more comfortable running with a woman. You start moving. The last one's a little afraid, but her sister here was very brave. She'll follow me now, so we'll meet you. Head for the cabin. Hopefully Cody is there."

Liza didn't want to leave this spot—for that last girl too afraid to leave, for Jamison too brave and good to leave a scared little girl. But the more people were here, the less chance they had of escape. All of them.

"Come on, girls," she said, taking the two little hands in hers. It just about killed her, but she started walking toward where the other girls had gone. She'd get them and start heading for the cabin.

She wouldn't look back, didn't have time to.

If Jamison didn't follow, she'd drop the girls with

Cody and go get him. She wouldn't let him sacrifice himself for...

Wouldn't she do the same?

Shouldn't you do the same?

She looked down at Gigi, who hadn't left her side. No. Like Jamison had said back at the original cabin, if she died, the likelihood Gigi did, too, increased. Gigi was the priority. Until she was safe, nothing else mattered.

She couldn't think about saving Jamison just yet. So, she just had to believe he'd save the last girl *and* himself. Of course he would. Jamison always did.

She urged the girls with her to run, though they both hesitated with the dark around them. Liza heard a door creak open, then slam closed somewhere far off.

Someone was coming.

"Come on. We have to hurry." She wished she could pick them both up, but that wouldn't help any.

She walked, trying to hurry, holding them up when the girls stumbled and keeping their movement forward no matter what. They were doing all right, making fair progress by Liza's estimation when her foot got caught on something and she pitched forward, the girls tumbling with her.

Liza didn't cry out, though falling hurt like hell. Though she was pretty sure she'd twisted her ankle or broken all of her stitches or both. But it didn't matter. Liza struggled to her feet, pulling Gigi and the other girl to theirs, as well.

They were both crying, quietly at first, but the pitch and volume began to increase. Growing louder and louder in the silent woods.

"Hush, now. We don't want anyone to hear us." She knelt and squeezed both girls to her sides, pressing kisses to their temples. "I know it's hard, but we have to do this hard thing to be safe. What's your name, sweetheart?"

The little girl sniffled. "Bette."

"Okay, Bette. I'm going to carry you for a bit. Then it'll be Gigi's turn. Okay? Okay."

Liza hefted the little girl onto her. Her ankle and leg screamed in protest, but she ignored the pain and retook Gigi's hand. It didn't take them too much longer to reach the grove of thick trees where the oldest girl had said she was going to go.

"Where's Jenni?" one of the girls asked. Liza couldn't make them all out in the dark.

"She's coming. But we need to keep moving. Now—"

"Wait."

The desperate whisper came from behind. Snapping twigs and an approaching form too small to be a Son.

"Jenni!" Bette cried out. Liza immediately clapped her hand over the girl's mouth, but the damage was done. The name echoed out through the trees and if anyone was looking for them, they would have heard that.

"We have to run, girls," Liza ordered, hoping they all understood how important it was to follow directions and ask questions later. "As quietly as possible. You're going to follow me. No sounds. Walk as quietly as possible. We'll walk two by two. Make sure you're holding someone's hand so no one falls back. Jamison will…" Liza's heart sank when she realized the girl had come alone. "Where's Jamison?" she asked of Jenni, as calmly as possible for the kids' sake.

Jenni let out a ragged sob. "He told me to run. I don't know… I don't know what happened after that."

"That's okay. That's all right," Liza said, though her throat got tight at the thought of him stuck back there in the stables. "You did just what you should have. Now, everyone, find a partner."

They had to get to safety, and to Cody. Because someone had to save Jamison.

She made sure the girls all had a buddy, and settled Jenni at the back with Bette. She began their walk, Gigi's hand in hers, keeping the pace quick and efficient. She tried not to think about Jamison, but it was impossible. With every look back to make sure all the girls were keeping up, she looked beyond, desperate to see Jamison running behind them.

He'd be okay. She assured herself over and over again. Even if he was caught, he was Ace Wyatt's son. No one would hurt him.

At least until Ace got there.

Chapter Sixteen

Jamison hadn't followed into the woods like he'd promised the girl he would. Like he'd promised Liza he would. Still, he'd known Jenni would follow Liza. No matter how unsure she was of him and his promises of safety, she would follow her sister—the little girl Liza had taken away with Gigi.

So, he didn't feel so bad about staying behind. The girls needed more time to escape. This would have all been for nothing if the Sons men discovered they were missing and immediately found them in the woods.

Then there was the fact it would take him time to scale that gate—too much time. He'd only be found.

So, Jamison stayed, and he waited. With luck, there wouldn't be too many coming to bring the girls supper and he could take them out. It would buy everyone time—including himself.

With time he could potentially fashion something out of his backpack to haul himself over the gate or pick the padlock. But only if he had time.

He heard noises. Footsteps, talking. The clank of a chain, the echoing click of a padlock falling open.

He surveyed the room the girls had been in. Somehow he had to take an undetermined amount of men out before they alerted everyone in that house there was a problem.

More chains clinking, then footsteps coming closer.

Jamison positioned himself in a crouch in the corner of darkness the girls had been huddled in. He held his gun in one hand, considering acoustics and wondering if it would send men from the cabin running out here.

It wasn't his best option, but if it was the last resort, so be it.

If there were too many for Jamison to fight, well, he had a plan for that, too.

They hadn't discussed it, but Jamison was counting on Cody still having and monitoring the device connected to the one he'd given Jamison. He was *counting* on Cody understanding that if he hit the button again, it was an okay to blow it all up.

If it blew up with Jamison in the cross fire, so be it. He'd have done what he came to do.

Saving people meant being willing to lay your life down for them if the situation called for it. He'd saved himself a lot of times, and always been willing to pay a bigger price if necessary. This situation couldn't be any different.

Even if a future with Liza was waiting on the other end, it was just as she'd said. How would he live with himself if he didn't give those girls a fighting chance at survival?

He couldn't.

Jamison listened, focusing on the now. Two sets of footsteps. Two voices.

He could definitely take out two men. Maybe even without firing a shot. Still, he held the gun in one hand, a knife in the other, and kept himself ready to attack.

"Learned to be real quiet, haven't they?" a deep voice laughed, coming closer and closer.

"I guess they're smarter than we thought."

That two men could be so callous about keeping little girls locked in a dank, dirty stable had fury spiking through him. Jamison banked the rage and disgust. Had to, in order to focus.

Two big men entered, chuckling to each other as they hung a camping lantern from a hook on the wall. One carried containers of food, and the other held a lamp, with a gun at the ready in his other hand.

"I guess they are smarter than you thought," Jamison said calmly. "Way smarter."

The man with the food immediately dropped it, presumably to reach for a weapon. Jamison lunged—not at either man, but at the light. He smashed the butt of his gun into the plastic and heard a satisfying crunch and shatter before it went out—plunging them into darkness.

They wouldn't shoot blindly into the dark. He had to hope.

Unfortunately, he hoped wrong. The deafening pop of a gunshot went off, though as far as Jamison could tell, the bullet only hit wood.

"You idiot. You could have killed me," one man said to the other.

"What else am I supposed to do?"

Their arguing gave Jamison time to slip out, his eyes adjusting to the dark as he strode as silently as possible down the stables. He stopped at the stall with the horse. It would make noise, but he could outrun the goons still bickering in the room behind him.

He pulled the horse into the corridor and then gave its rump a hard pat, which had the horse galloping for the front door, where the men had presumably come in.

Jamison didn't give himself time to hope. He just acted, moving through the corridor and then sliding out the door after the horse. He heard the men coming, so he quickly shut the door, pulled the chain through the handles of the door as tightly as possible, then slammed the padlock into place. All by the bright, silver moonlight.

The men no doubt had walkies, and Jamison wished he could have disabled those. But he'd gotten out. Two men were detained, and they wouldn't be able to tell much about which direction he'd gone.

So, Jamison had to move, and quick.

But when Jamison turned away from the door, there was someone standing there. The figure's teeth flashed in the moonlight, and not a second later two men grabbed either arm, liberating both the gun and the knife from his grasp.

Jamison struggled against them, but they had tight grasps, and used their bulk to keep him mostly immobile.

"You honestly think I let idiots like that do anything without listening to their every move?" the voice asked.

A bright light flashed against Jamison's face. Jamison didn't wince at the light, and he forced himself not to tense under the hands of the men who held him down. He had to keep his body loose. It would be his only chance of fighting off the men who gripped him by each arm.

The man in front of him didn't drop the light, so Jamison calmly closed his eyes against it. He didn't have to see to recognize the voice of the man standing before him. "Tony. Good to see you. So to speak, since you're blinding me."

Tony laughed, and Jamison tried not to sneer in response. He'd always hated Liza's father, as much as if not even more than his own. Ace was the leader because he was cold and calculated. He knew how to manipulate, and how to stir up a certain kind of loyalty. He was dangerous because he understood people, and he used that knowledge against them.

Tony Dean was dangerous in the completely opposite way. He didn't care about people. His brain didn't work like other people's—it was incomprehensible as far as Jamison was concerned. Jamison would have called him a sadist, but that would be ascribing his chaos to some kind of order.

No one ever knew quite what Tony was going to do—which was why he was Ace's right-hand man. The machine and the maniac who'd built quite the kingdom for themselves.

"They won't get far," Tony offered, tilting the flashlight's beam down at the ground so it no longer shone in Jamison's eyes. "But I'm impressed. You certainly got them farther than I expected. Then again, Ace taught you everything you know."

Jamison smiled at Liza's father, though he wanted to retch at the comparison. He wasn't Ace, but Ace *had* taught him something. You couldn't escape the Sons.

And since he wouldn't give in to them, there was only one other choice. Destroying them. Maybe the odds were stacked against him, but he wasn't dead yet.

"Didn't he just?" Jamison returned.

The men held his arms—but with the right shifting on his feet and pressure of his elbow against his pocket, he could put pressure on the button Cody had given him.

He managed to click it once before the men tightened their hold and ordered him to stop moving. He let himself relax, counted to five, then gave a jerk and managed to click the button the second time.

It earned him an elbow to the gut, but if Cody got the message, it was worth the pain and loss of breath.

"Tie him up," Tony said in a heavy sigh. "Don't rough him up too much. We've got Ace Wyatt's precious eldest."

Jamison didn't fight the men at his sides as one pro-

duced a rope from the dark. There was no point in fighting when it would only take Cody a few moments to
follow the cue. Jamison hoped.

It took another minute or two. But before Tony's goons
had finished tying him up, the first bright light exploded
from the cabin, followed by a thunderous, deafening
boom and debris flying.

Tony's goons scattered, dropping Jamison's arms and
running away from the light.

But Tony didn't. He held the gun on Jamison's half-
tied-up form. "I guess you should have set that off a
while ago."

"You think so?" Jamison replied cheerfully. "Good
to know."

"You think who your father is matters to me? I'm his
partner. I'm not afraid of Ace. Ace wouldn't mind if I
killed you. He'd probably thank me."

"I wouldn't be so sure, Tony." Tony was clearly all
talk because he still hadn't pulled the trigger. "I'd think
very long and hard before you spoke for my father. You
know how he gets."

Another building exploded—this time the shack.
Jamison had to believe the stables would be next.

It'd probably kill him. He had to let out a breath and
accept that. As long as it took out Tony Dean, too, it
would be worth it.

THEY WERE GETTING AWAY. Liza should feel relief. Hope.
But her stomach was in knots and she couldn't help but
look back every few minutes, hoping to see Jamison
catching up with them.

But he didn't.

Most of the girls didn't make a sound as they hiked
along in the dark. The farther they got away from the

cabin, the more Liza let the pace slow. The girls were tired, likely undernourished no matter how much supper they'd been given, and most of all, terrified.

Liza carried Gigi after a while, Jenni carrying Bette, who appeared to be her little sister. The older girls helped the younger girls. A few times Liza got turned around, but she kept moving forward. She had to believe she'd find the cabin or safety—as long as she was leading them away from the Sons, everything was okay.

Somehow, Jamison would eventually show up. Somehow, she would get the girls to Cody and he would get them all to safety.

Somehow, because her life had always been a series of somehows and she was still here. Still breathing, no matter how much her ankle throbbed or her lungs burned with exertion.

She pushed forward into a clearing, and found her next somehow.

Somehow they'd made it. The cabin sat in the eerie dark of predawn, where it was still dark but the sky seemed to glow.

She'd led the girls to the cabin. She'd saved Gigi. She hugged her sister closer and gathered the girls closer. Relief was a balm, but it was short-lived.

It isn't over yet.

No, no, it wasn't. She couldn't forget that. Even if she wanted to. Jamison missing left a hard weight of dread in her stomach.

Was he trying to fight them off? Was he lost?

Is he dead?

Even though that question kept swirling around in her head, every time it hit her square, she had a hard time sucking in a breath or letting one out.

Cody stepped out of the cabin as Liza brought the

girls into the clearing. He opened his mouth as if to greet them, but as his eyes traveled over the eleven girls, his expression changed.

The girls quickly huddled together, and then behind Liza as much as they could.

"It's all right," she said, looking at Cody. He'd been something like thirteen the last time she'd seen him. Even when he'd spoken to Jamison earlier, she'd only seen a shadow, the hint of a man.

Now she could trace all the similarities to Jamison on his face. His nose wasn't crooked in the same way, and his eyes were lighter—tinged with green. He was more rangy, not quite as broad, but taller.

But, boy, was he a Wyatt. Not only did he have the same appearance as his brothers, it was the expression in them that solidified what she'd begun to accept. She didn't have any doubts about Cody's involvement with the Sons anymore. That look was all cop.

"This is Cody," Liza said. Though she was talking to the girls, she kept her gaze on Cody. Wanted to watch his face and make sure he understood what he was seeing. "He's Jamison's brother. He's going to help us, just like Jamison helped you all out of the stables."

"Let's get you all inside," Cody said. He tried to smile, but he wasn't very good at it. He kept his hands behind his back, though, and stepped clear of the door as if to say to the girls he wasn't a threat. Liza encouraged the girls to go inside, following them like a sheepdog herding its flock.

When she reached the doorway, Cody stopped her. She looked down at his hand on her arm, then gave him a raised-eyebrow look that said "Watch yourself." He might not be with the Sons, but that didn't mean she trusted him.

He didn't budge.

"Sit wherever you like," Cody told the girls as they stood in a group in the middle of the cabin. "You can't do anything wrong in here. You're safe now. Have a seat. Rest." There was a fire in the hearth and a few camping lanterns strewed about. There was also that computer from the bathroom sitting on the counter.

"I'll see what food I can scrounge up in just a moment," Cody continued, his hand on Liza's arm still keeping her from entering.

He nodded at the girls, then closed the door a little bit—leaving it ajar. She didn't want to give him credit, but he seemed to understand the girls wouldn't want to be locked up in another dark place.

"Where's Jamison?" Cody asked quietly, his fingers tightening around her arm.

Liza tried to jerk it away, but he held fast. "Listen—"

"Tell me where he is," Cody seethed.

And because she knew Jamison well enough, she thought she saw something more than anger and a cop on a power trip. Something like fear lurked in Cody's hazel eyes.

"He helped get the girls out, but he…" She swallowed, because she wouldn't believe it meant anything bad. Not yet. "He didn't follow the last one out. He told her he would, but he didn't."

"Liza, are you telling me he isn't… He's not with you? He's back there at the cabin?"

"At the stables. The girls were in the stables. He probably just stayed to make sure we got away. There were men coming and—"

Cody swore and rubbed a hand over his face.

"What? What is it? What's wr—"

Something boomed in the distance, followed by a flash of light.

Everything inside Liza froze as she watched the blaze bloom and grow. "What was that?" she whispered.

"Liza." Cody's voice was careful. Too careful as he slowly released her arm.

"What was that, Cody?" she demanded, giving him a shove. Even though she knew. Even though she knew exactly what it was.

And what it meant.

"He hit the button twice."

"What? What does that mean? What are you talking about?"

Cody heaved out a sigh—irritation, fear, sadness. "I gave him a device. It sends me a message that can't be picked up or intercepted. He hit it once at first, which meant he'd found people in the stables." Cody looked at the door, shaking his head. "Those girls were in there."

"You didn't know."

"I should have," he muttered. "I didn't engage the explosives. I was having a conversation with my superiors about the potential for collateral damage when I got the transmission again—this time twice. That was the signal to engage the explosives."

"For the cabin," Lisa said, more desperate hope than rational thought.

"Liza..."

She didn't wait for him to continue. She turned and started to run back from where she came. Her ankle screamed and she didn't care. Didn't dare worry about her own pain when Jamison was...

"You can't go running into an explosion," Cody called after her. "They'll go off before—" Another boom, more light.

She stopped, looked in horror at what was clearly fire in the dark distance. No. She refused to let this be it. She could get to him. If he'd hit the button, he wasn't stupid enough to be in there getting blown up. No. It wasn't possible.

She didn't get more than a few more strides before Cody grabbed her from behind. She turned and swung a fist at him, but he easily dodged it before grabbing that arm, too, and holding her immobile.

She tried to fight him off, but he held firm.

"You have to stay here with the girls," he said between gritted teeth as she continued to struggle and he maintained his iron hold to keep her in place. "I'll go and—"

"I can't save them, Cody. I've done what I can do. I can't get them to safety from here. You can. You can get men in here or get them out or…something. You have the connections and the computer. You have superiors to communicate with. You have to get them away from here."

"You can't save Jamison if he can't save himself. Liza. He's a trained police officer." There was a pause, and when Cody continued, his voice was flat. "If he didn't survive, there's nothing we can do."

"That's bull." She stilled, then gave up fighting him off, sucked in a ragged breath and let it out. She believed Jamison could survive almost anything, but she also believed she was the same.

She'd needed help sometimes, and Jamison needed help sometimes. He hadn't liberated all his brothers on his own. He'd needed help from his grandmother, from the occasional Sons member who wasn't so keen on hurting kids, sometimes even on strangers.

"Maybe he got out," Cody said, and his tone was almost gentle, perhaps because he had to hope for the same.

"Maybe he'll make it here. But you can't go after him. We don't know what's left out there and there's still one more blast to go off."

She didn't want to hear it. Couldn't accept it. "Stop it!" She tried to free her hands so she could reach out and shake him, but he wouldn't release his grip.

"I can't stop it, Liza. If I could, I would have already done it. The explosives are connected. The third one will go off any second. It gave Jamison time—if he ran away after the first blast, he'll have time to get here. You should stay here and wait for him to show up."

"And if he doesn't?"

"That's why you need to let me go. I'll call my guys to come in and get you and the girls out. Then I'll head out and you stay here and safe. Let Wyatts handle Wyatts."

Wyatts handle Wyatts. Jamison was as much hers as anyone's. Beyond that, her father had been the one in the center of this. Not theirs. "But Ace Wyatt wasn't keeping these girls, was he?"

Cody's expression shuttered, going into full cop mode now. She'd hoped he might loosen his grip on her hands, but he held firm.

"Go inside, Liza. I'll handle the rest."

"Be a good little woman and let the big, strong men handle it?" She thought about stomping on his instep, but he shifted, almost as if he could read her thoughts, so that she'd have to do it with her bad ankle.

"Let law enforcement agents handle it."

"Just what *agency* are you with, Cody?"

He shook his head, refusing to answer.

"That's what I thought." Because Cody might have some cop training, but computers and explosives were something else altogether. He might be on the right side, but that didn't mean he was on the right side of the *law*.

When the third explosion went off, she knew she didn't have time to argue. Cody still held her arms. She just needed to escape. She *needed* to do what she could to help Jamison.

She looked up at Cody, letting all the worry and fear show in her eyes. "Sorry about this," she whispered.

"About wh—"

She kneed him in the crotch, using the moment of surprise and pain to wriggle away from his grasp and run like hell.

She reached the edge of the woods before she felt someone grip the back of her coat and yank hard—hard enough she *fell* backward. She glared up at Cody but got right to her feet. He wanted to try to stop her? *Let him.*

She squared, fists clenched and ready to deck him. She'd fight tooth and nail to have a chance to save Jamison.

He rolled his eyes. Insultingly. "You're out of your mind."

"What does that make him?" Liza gritted out, keeping her fists up and ready. Cody had already let his guard down once. He'd do it again and she'd land a decent enough punch. Again and again, until she got to Jamison.

But in two seconds flat he moved, like a ghost or a ninja, and had both her hands behind her back with one hand and snaked his other arm around her throat.

"It makes him completely insane," Cody said with disgust. "Now, get ahold of yourself and I'll let you go."

"You'll *what*?"

"I'll let you go. I just need you to let me do something first."

"I'm not going to fall for any tri—"

"You've got to stop," Cody muttered. He started grumbling about people who wouldn't follow orders and how this was life-and-death, on and on. But she'd stilled, and as he grumbled, he shoved something up her sleeve.

"There. Now, go ahead on your fool's errand. But when you end up dead, don't come haunting me. I warned you."

She stared at her sleeve. "What did you do?"

"Don't worry about it. Trust me."

"Why should I trust you?"

"I'm assuming because we both love Jamison and don't want him to be dead."

Liza blinked at that, then scowled when Cody made a shooing motion. "Go on, now. I've got to deal with the girls you saved. Just trust that if you find Jamison, I'll be able to send someone to find you both. All you have to do is stay alive."

The girls you saved. Because she'd gotten Gigi out, gotten her safe. Cody had explosives and contacts and would be able to get law enforcement in here to get those girls somewhere safe—so she'd done her duty to her sister.

Now she had to do her duty to the man she'd always loved, who'd saved her once upon a time. Because she'd saved those girls, and she was going to save him, too.

Chapter Seventeen

There was pain. Everywhere. Pulsing, searing, burning. He wanted to float away from it all, but there was something he needed to do. Somewhere he needed to be.

Jamison managed to blink his eyes open, only to find flame. Everywhere.

It was the fire—that clear reminder of what had happened—that had him leaping to his feet no matter how his body and balance protested. He stumbled a little to the left, trying to right himself before he fell over and only just barely succeeding.

He searched the world around him. Everything was on fire—or at least so it seemed. He ordered himself to calm, to catalog. The blast had thrown him some and he wasn't as close to the stables as he'd been. Now that he was on his feet, he could see that the spots of fire were where debris had landed and smoldered.

In one of those spots of fire lay a body. Not too far off from Jamison himself. Jamison took a few stilted steps toward it.

Tony Dean lay completely still, eyes open and unseeing, a gruesome piece of debris sticking out of his gut.

Jamison stared at the body for more time than he had, trying to reconcile…any of what had happened. Tony Dean was dead, and somehow Jamison was alive.

There was no time for contemplating that, though. He had to find…safety. Water. Fresh air. He had to get away from this place because he could hear shouts, see shadows of men trying to put out the blaze.

It hadn't taken down everyone.

Liza's father and surely the men Jamison had left in the stables were dead. Maybe the men who'd tried to tie him up, but maybe not—they'd started running after the first blast. Which would have definitely killed the men who'd been inside the cabin at the time, but Jamison could see at least eight men running around house and shack. Their focus was on putting out the fire, as far as Jamison could tell.

He began to walk, though every part of his body throbbed in painful protest. He moved for the woods. He wanted to believe that everyone would be too busy with the flames to look for him, but he knew the Sons.

He knew what kind of orders Tony would have given his men before he'd gone out to meet Jamison at the stables. Tony had known it was him. It would have been imperative for Tony to spread the message that the person who'd liberated those girls was none other than Ace Wyatt's son.

Someone would be looking for him once the confusion died down.

Jamison had to be gone by that time, and not toward the cabin where Liza had been headed. That could lead the wrong people toward Liza and those poor girls. He wasn't sure how much time he'd been unconscious for, but it couldn't have been that long if the flames and shouts were anything to go by.

Not enough time for Cody to have helped Liza and those girls to safety.

Jamison swore under his breath and had to hope

against hope that his brother would prioritize the girls and not come running after him once he realized Jamison had sent the signal while still on the premises.

Jamison found the woods behind the wreckage of the stables. Some of the trees were on fire. He skirted the line of trees and the fire and moved toward the front of the cabin. He'd go that way—the complete opposite of the direction he'd come.

He tried to bring the map to his mind, picturing where he'd be going if he headed out that way. How he could get to safety and help in that direction. Everything was a little fuzzy—clearly he was more rattled from the explosion and his loss of consciousness than he wanted to admit.

Rattled or not, he had to keep moving. There was no time for stopping to clear his head and *think*. He couldn't afford to be seen or caught. Not in such bad shape. He wouldn't stand a chance in a fight right now.

He made it toward the front of the burning cabin. The explosion had impacted the back side of the house the most, so anyone trying to stop the fire was back there. The front seemed empty.

But there was a road here. A road Jamison didn't remember being on his map—though it was dirt, so maybe that was why. If he was going to go in the opposite direction of where Liza had taken the girls, he had to cross this road with no cover.

Something in his body recoiled from the idea. He pushed it away, chalking it up to explosions and head fuzziness and the odd shakes now racking his body. Just shock or adrenaline or something. He moved forward, feeling as though he was pushing through molasses.

Something wasn't right, but he didn't have *time*. On the next step, his leg gave out and he fell to his knee. He looked down in surprise at the offending limb. It was only then he realized he had his own dagger of debris stuck in his calf and he was just now noticing the pain, the blood dripping down into his boot.

That couldn't be good. Worse when all he could seem to do was stare at the piece of wood, not sure what to do about it.

The sound of an engine brought him out of his reverie. He spotted a Jeep cresting the hill. Also not good.

Jamison tried to jump out of the way as the headlights got closer, but his body wasn't moving at full capacity. The light caught him. Jamison moved to run, but another car came—and men materialized from the woods until he was surrounded.

He stood, breathing heavily, unable to think of one smart action to take.

The door of the first Jeep opened and out stepped his father, the flames dancing across his smiling face. A face all too similar to the one Jamison saw in the mirror.

Jamison actually laughed. It was so ridiculous. So impossible. All the things he could survive and in the end it would still come back to this moment right here.

Maybe it was fitting.

"You're not looking too good, son," Ace said with a smirk.

"And, per usual, Ace Wyatt is unharmed and unscathed. Go figure." There were six men creating a perimeter around Jamison, all with semiautomatic guns pointed at his chest. They wouldn't shoot—unless given the okay from Ace, or maybe if Jamison went after Ace. Then all bets would be off.

No, they wouldn't kill him, but they wouldn't be afraid to hurt him if he ran, either.

Jamison thought running and risking getting hurt might be worth the chance of escape. But if Tony was dead and Ace was here, staying put and keeping Ace busy meant a better chance for Liza and the girls to get away. The longer he could keep his father's attention on *him*, the better for *them*.

"So. Is this how it ends, Dad? Or do we get to have a heart-to-heart first?" Jamison had to work to keep his teeth from chattering.

"Jamison, you underestimate me. It's never the end until someone's on their knees, begging."

"I've never underestimated you. I have had a few fantasies about you on your knees, begging."

Ace laughed. "The sad thing is, even if you could make that happen, you'd never have the balls to pull the trigger. Too much of your mother in you. She had her chances to end me, and she never could."

Jamison didn't explode like he might have years ago. One thing he'd learned about his father was that he only ever brought up Mom when Jamison was actually getting to him.

So, Jamison pushed the old hurt away, let the cold shock of *all* of this make his words lifeless and bored. "You still sticking by that drug overdose story? Or did you want to confess?"

"The thing about you, Jamison, and why you've never been any threat to me, is you're too *good* to understand how the world works. I know you weren't behind this." He waved a hand to encompass the flames. "You don't have it in you. All this collateral damage, death. It'd eat you alive."

Jamison considered all the people who'd been inside the burning cabin, involved or complicit in eleven little girls—*girls*—being held captive in the stables. He had no doubt the whispers Liza had heard were correct. The girls were here to be trafficked—and likely weren't the first group of girls.

"That might have been true once," Jamison replied. "It isn't true any longer."

"Tell me, Jamison, why is it a child's life is so much more precious to you than anyone else's? Don't we all have souls? Don't we all have the capacity to change?"

"You have a choice in everything you do. Children don't." It came out edgier than he wanted it to. His body was shaking against his will and he was beginning to fully understand he couldn't make it out of this situation alive.

That had been fine enough when he'd been sacrificing himself to end something. It wasn't so fine if his father got to do it the way he'd always wanted to.

"Everyone who can walk and talk has a choice, Jamison. I was seven years old when I was left on my own to die, but I chose to live. To lead. Just like you chose the coward's escape, and a sad little life trying to feel important because of a badge."

It might have pricked at his pride some, but not enough to bite. His escape hadn't been cowardly, and it wasn't his badge that made him feel important. It was the fact that some days, he did get to help people. Some days, he was all that stood between a person and harm. Maybe not as many days as he'd anticipated when he'd been going through the academy.

But enough. Helping was always enough.

If things ended here, at his father's hands, he'd saved eleven little girls' lives, and that was a price he was willing to pay. Always.

THE CLOSER LIZA GOT, the larger the flames seemed. Still, she didn't let that slow her steps. Until she saw a body lying still as death. She exhaled shakily, then forced herself to inhale. To calm. She stepped forward, determined to keep it together.

She held her composure and checked to make sure it wasn't Jamison.

It wasn't.

The wave of relief almost took her to her knees, but it was hardly over yet. There was more walking to do. And more bodies on the ground.

The next body she checked wasn't Jamison, either, but still her heart lurched.

It was her father. There were pieces of debris sticking out of him, and part of his body was burned. His eyes were open and unseeing. He was very clearly dead.

She didn't feel sad so much as horrified. Growing up in the Sons meant she'd seen a dead body before. She'd watched men shoot each other. She understood death a little too intimately, and to an extent she'd learned to detach herself from it. Had to in order to survive.

But this was her father.

She'd hated him for as long as she could remember, but it was her own eyes that stared back at her. She could hate him, and what he did, but it didn't make the feelings inside her uncomplicated.

She leaned down and closed his eyes and let out a breath to steady herself. It was good. He couldn't hurt anyone anymore. Not her. Not Gigi. No more Carlees—at least not by his hand. Good riddance.

As she moved to stand back up, she noticed a few things on the ground. Jamison's backpack, for one. It wasn't guaranteed that meant Jamison had been out here. Dad could have taken it off Jamison inside the stables, left Jamison there to die and brought the pack outside.

But Jamison's headlamp was also on the ground a

few feet away, as if it had been knocked off him. Which meant Jamison hadn't been in the stables when the explosion had gone off. They might have taken his backpack from him, but they would have destroyed the headlamp, not moved it out here.

She stood, believing these signs meant Jamison was alive. Desperately needing to believe it. She walked on, checking every body she found, avoiding the cluster of men standing next to the flames of the cabin.

They seemed to be conferring, and if they were worried about strangers infiltrating their grounds, they certainly didn't act it.

Jamison wasn't dead. He couldn't be dead. She would have seen him in the wreckage. She would *feel* it. So, she had to keep looking, keep trying to find him wherever he'd gone.

She crept forward. If Jamison had escaped all these men, he would have gone in the opposite direction of where she'd taken the girls. Too much potential to be followed if he came back to Cody's cabin.

He would have gone this way, hoping if he was caught or followed, they'd have no idea the girls had gone the opposite direction. He would do everything to keep the Sons off her tail.

Maybe she should backtrack. He wasn't dead as far as she could tell, and he wasn't hurt if he was on the move. She should go back to Cody's cabin and let him find her.

No matter how many times her brain urged her to do that, her body could only seem to move forward listening to the crackle of the fire, the conversations of small groups of men. Looking out for bodies, and always seeing Jamison's face a second before she realized—no, that was not him.

She paused as she reached the front area of the cabin.

There were a few vehicles circled in the front drive, all
with their headlights pointing to the same spot.

Everything inside her stilled as she focused on the
spot where all the light was directed.

In the center of it all was Jamison.

And Ace.

Jamison looked awful. Bloody and singed, a gruesome piece of wood sticking out of his leg. Six men
stood around them with very large-looking weapons.
All pointed at Jamison.

Liza swallowed and looked down at her sleeve. Whatever Cody had put there or done, she had no idea. But he
said he'd be able to find them.

They had to be alive for it to matter. Liza crept
closer. There was no way she could take all six men.
She wouldn't even be able to create a diversion. They'd
just kill her. If she was lucky they'd *just* kill her.

"Let's not do this here," she heard Ace say. He sounded
amiable, almost like he was having a pleasant business
discussion.

Cold dread formed at the base of her spine, making it
hard to move or think. She knew that tone of voice. And
she knew the kind of orders that came after it.

Kill him.

But she knew, she *knew*, Ace wouldn't kill Jamison—
right away. He'd torture him first, get his poetic revenge.
Liza stood to her full height, even as her body shook.
If she were there, they'd torture her first. He'd want to
make Jamison watch.

As much as she didn't want to put him through that, it
would keep him alive. She needed time. Time for Cody
to track them however he thought he could track them.
So, she couldn't let Jamison go it alone.

She cleared her throat and slowly stepped toward the

beams of light. "Having some kind of party, Ace? And you didn't invite me?" Her voice was light, even if her hands shook.

Jamison swore viciously. She smiled at him. He didn't smile back, but at least he was smart enough—or maybe just hurt enough—not to go on.

"Ah, the Juliet to my son's Romeo. Touching that you'd want to die with him, Liza. Really."

One of the armed men nudged her into the circle of light. She looked at Ace with a sharp smile. "I take it you've never actually *read* Shakespeare."

Ace inclined his head and one of his men stepped forward and plowed his fist into her jaw. She saw stars, but she kept her balance. She'd been taking blows since she'd been a kid.

Of course, Jamison lunged at the man, idiot that he was, and got knocked to the ground by the butt of a gun.

Liza crouched next to him. "Don't. I can take it," she whispered, letting her fingers drift gently over his temple. He was dirty and bloody, and she wanted so badly to hold on to him. She looked at Ace. She had to keep the attention off Jamison. The more Ace decided to torture her, the better chance they had.

Jamison couldn't take much more beating from the look of it—he was clearly in shock. So, Liza stood, helping Jamison to his feet.

"What are you doing?" he choked out.

She only shook her head at him. "Ace likes watching *other* men beat up women and little girls because deep, deep down he's a coward." She shot Ace another screw-you smile.

"A coward." Ace laughed, but there was a sneer to it. Not so easy to dismiss her when she was poking at his pride. "I see your father didn't knock near enough sense into you."

"My father's dead." She matched his sharp smile with one of her own. "Saw him myself. What are you going to do without Tony to carry out your sadistic punishments you can't stomach yourself?"

He withered, and Liza felt a certain kind of triumph light her up from the inside. She was getting to him—which was quite a feat.

She'd probably end up dead because of it, but it was satisfying one way or another.

"You think he's the only sick bastard ready to jump to do my bidding, Liza." Ace sighed as if she was a particularly dim-witted child. "Surely you didn't think your father was special. I'll replace him once I've killed both of you." He snapped his fingers. "Like that."

"You've had so much time to kill us, Ace. Yet here we still are. Chatting."

"Tie her up. And gag her, for the love of God."

Two of the men grabbed her. She decided to fight them, because it would take more time. When one hit his gun against the back of her head, she didn't just see stars, the world went black for a second. She clung to consciousness, but she stopped fighting.

They tied her up roughly, shoved a gag in her mouth with even more force. Her vision had doubled, but slowly came back to clarity.

Jamison was watching her, murder in his eyes. She realized she'd miscalculated more than she cared to admit, because with that look on his face he was going to get himself killed long before help came.

"You do pose a very interesting question, though, Liza. One, I assume, has kept you both up at night." Ace smiled again. "Many nights. For many years. Is that shadow going to materialize into everything I ran away from?"

Ace moved toward Liza. She refused to let fear grip her because it would show up on her face. When Ace took her chin in his hand, though, she couldn't help but recoil.

He watched her with a glint she knew too well. She'd seen that look so many times over the years on her father's face. A man who enjoyed inflicting pain on people.

She'd never seen Ace actually hurt anyone. Order someone else to kill or torture, yes, but she'd never seen him do the dirty work. She wasn't so sure she'd be able to say the same after tonight—if she'd ever be able to say anything at all.

"You want to know why you both survived as long as you did? Because, Liza, you're less than nothing. No one cares about you, so hurting you doesn't help me any. Or didn't."

He turned his gaze to Jamison, though he kept his hand on her face. "I was waiting for you to have a son, Jamison. So, I could take him away from you like you took mine away from me. I know you don't value your own life, but you would have valued a child's." His gaze returned to Liza. "And it appears you value hers now. That's good to know."

He released Liza's chin and walked toward one of the cars. "Take that stick out of my son's leg, then put them both in my Jeep," he ordered one of his men. "Don't communicate anything over the walkie. Follow my driver."

All Liza could think was, *Please, Cody, hurry.*

Chapter Eighteen

They were both going to die.

Jamison could come up with no other possible outcome of being shoved into his father's vehicle. Hurt, probably as injured as he'd ever been. His father was going to win.

Scratch that. There had to be a way he could save Liza. Had to be. He couldn't give up on her. He'd saved too many people under next-to-impossible circumstances because he'd believed he could. This wouldn't be any different.

One of his father's other goons pushed Liza in on the opposite side. Dad and his driver sat up front and conferred about something, but Jamison couldn't hear.

Maybe once the Jeep got going, one of them could open the door and jump out. They'd maybe die, or be hurt enough to eventually die, but it would be better than whatever Ace was cooking up.

Jamison wasn't tied up like Liza. He'd love to believe it was out of stupidity, but no doubt Ace had some sick reason for the lack of restraint. Maybe to give them hope. Maybe he wanted them to try to escape so he could make the game last. Maybe he knew Jamison just didn't have it in him to fight.

But he'd find a way. Someway.

If there was anything Jamison understood about his father, it was that he liked the long game. Some people grew up suffering, and when they pulled themselves out of it they wanted to help end others' suffering. So, no one had to go through what they had. Jamison understood that one.

Others, like Ace, grew up and out of their desperate circumstances wanting to inflict that pain on someone else—and those people almost always escalated—inflicting more and more of that pain. And then even more.

Still, Jamison calculated the odds. He could disable his father's driver with one well-timed blow, which could cause an accident. Of course, Ace and his driver were buckled—Jamison and Liza were not. Survival wasn't in their favor.

As he went through several other scenarios, Liza inched her way over on the back seat. Despite her hands being tied around her back, she maneuvered herself until she could reach her fingers out to brush against his hand.

He took her hand in his, then tested the bonds. He could untie them. It would give them more of a chance.

Her fingers curled around his and squeezed, and she shook her head.

Jamison knew he couldn't talk, couldn't risk his father overhearing anything, but it just about killed him to keep his mouth shut.

Then she started to…tap his palm. At first he thought she was trying to get his attention, but she already had it. There were pauses between the taps. Hard taps and light taps. Not Morse code…or any code he knew.

But Cody had done that. Cody, who had access to things. Was she trying to tell him that Cody was going to help them?

Liza was here without the girls, which meant she'd gotten them somewhere safe—Cody. Cody had the girls, and Cody potentially had the means to save them. Potentially.

He supposed he had to stay alive to find out. Which meant outwitting his father. He'd be stupid to think it would be easy.

But maybe *with* Liza, it could be possible.

"It's real sweet you two found your way back to each other. Real sweet," Ace said, curling his arm behind the driver's seat and turning his body so he could face them. He smiled genially, like a real father might look at his son and his son's girlfriend.

But he was not a real father, no matter how well he could put on the mask of one.

Liza made a noise, but it was muffled by the gag in her mouth. Probably for the best, because she couldn't articulate something snarky to Ace.

"It's a shame about your sister," Ace said, still smiling pleasantly at Liza.

Liza's eyebrows drew together, but since she couldn't talk, Jamison had to ask the questions. Which was always a minefield when it came to Ace. Still, he couldn't let the information sit there if only because Liza would want answers—and would get them one way or another.

"What do you mean?" Jamison asked, not having to feign confusion.

"I figured you two being here meant you'd figured out she was here." Ace scratched his cheek, seeming to mull that over. Then he shrugged. "She was in the stables. Which means the explosion—which I assume you had something to do with—would have killed her. A real shame you're responsible for the death of your beloved sister, and ten of her closest friends."

Jamison could only stare at his father. He counted his

heartbeats to keep from laughing or smiling or anything that might give away the truth.

Ace thought the girls had still been in the stables. Somewhere communication had broken down and he didn't know.

He didn't know.

Jamison wanted to laugh. He wanted to laugh and laugh and laugh.

Even if they didn't escape, as long as Cody found Jamison and Liza, he'd be able to arrest Ace Wyatt for connections to a human trafficking ring.

Liza turned her head into Jamison's shoulder. She didn't make a noise, but she made some effort to move her shoulders as if trying to convince Ace she was crying. Jamison had a feeling she was laughing like he wanted to.

Jamison ducked his own head, pressing his face into her hair. The absolute worst thing they could do was tip Ace off that they'd gotten the girls out, but it gave Jamison such hope it was a hard thing to fight.

Instead he and Liza kept their heads bent together as the Jeep traveled over bumpy roads—if they were even roads they were traveling over. Jamison couldn't see out of the tinted windows, so he didn't bother trying.

When the vehicle stopped, Jamison didn't have to work to hide his smile any longer. Dread crept over all that hope. Whatever happened before hope won, he was going to endure a heck of a lot of hurt before they succeeded.

Dad and his driver got out, then both sides of the back doors opened and two of Dad's men grabbed each of them, jerking them out of the Jeep on opposite sides.

Jamison bit his tongue to keep from crying out as each tug of his limbs felt like fire, but he would do everything not to give them the satisfaction of hurting him.

Liza was still bound and gagged, but since he was pushed up a cement walkway first, Jamison couldn't see if she was fighting the men who were bringing her forward. He had to concentrate on fighting the pain and dizziness so he could stay on his own two feet. His leg had gone numb, which was something of a relief. He limped through the numbness and squinted his eyes through the dizzying swirl of the world around him.

Jamison recognized where they were, sort of. It was Flynn, and a building he'd been in a hundred times as a child. But it wasn't the rotting structure of an old church any longer. It had been fixed up, remodeled or restored. The outside looked like a modest church that was well tended. A pure white against a grove of old trees. It was like stepping into a picture, especially as the sun was rising in the east, pouring gold over the world around them. Like a promise.

There was no peace to be found here, but he wanted to believe that sunrise was the promise of peace he'd find if he held on.

The man holding him shoved him inside the quaint building, and again it was nothing like it had been when Jamison was with the Sons.

The interior was finished and looked like some kind of shrine. Instead of the ruins of an old church Jamison remembered, the pews nearly gleamed like the wood floor. The altar was sweeping and held a big chair in the middle of it, where a pulpit would normally be.

Ace took a seat on the chair.

There weren't any Christian symbols anywhere, but signs of the Sons. Their patch—a skull amid the Badlands—on a flag hanging from one wall, their motto burned into the wood of the wall behind Ace.

The Srong Save Themselves.

Ace sat underneath it, giving the appearance of royalty, or maybe something larger than royalty. He fancied himself a god, and this would be his church. The Sons were his loyal worshippers.

And the disloyal were punished.

This was something fancier than Jamison had ever seen the Sons put together. It was like Tony's cabin setup—incongruous to the transient, ready-to-move Sons Jamison had grown up a part of.

Had they gotten so bold, so sure they'd never be caught that they'd actually planted roots?

Jamison didn't know whether to be cheered by that, by all it meant for their potential to be caught and brought to justice, or to be scared down to his bones that they were really unstoppable.

No, he'd never believe they were unstoppable. Maybe evil triumphed over good more than it should—but that didn't mean it survived in the same form forever.

There were other sayings burned into the walls. "The strong wear a patch. The weak wear a badge."

Underneath that one were pictures of badges, with specific officers' DSNs either etched into the badge or written underneath. There were red Xs over some.

The police officers they'd killed.

Jamison ignored the white-hot surge of anger and focused on the fact it was evidence to bring them down. He'd seen it now, and if he lived, it could be evidence used to put Ace in jail.

Truly behind bars for the first time ever.

"This is a bit ridiculous, even for you," Jamison said, earning him a jab from the gun the man behind him held.

"This?" Ace asked, gesturing around the church. "This is your chance to beg my forgiveness, son. Your chance to beg. I'd suggest getting on your knees."

Jamison laughed, then spit at his father. He knew the blow would come, so he dodged it and turned to face the two men with guns behind him. They held the guns trained on him, but they couldn't use them. Not without the nod from Ace.

There were *some* perks to being a madman's son.

"You, get him on his knees," Ace said tightly. "You, bring her here."

The first goon came at Jamison, who elbowed him in the nose, sending a splatter of blood across the gleaming wood floor. It felt a little *too* good—the kind of good that reminded Jamison he was indeed the son of a madman.

He didn't like that feeling, didn't want violence to sing through him, potent and deadly, so nothing else mattered.

Because Liza mattered, and she was being led up to his father. The two men moving her forward didn't force her to kneel—they positioned her on his father's lap, like she was a small child.

Or worse.

Ace smiled at Jamison.

Jamison swallowed down the rage and the bile and lowered himself onto his knees. He would kneel. He'd even beg. But he wouldn't give up. Not on saving Liza.

"Good boy," Ace said. He curled an arm around Liza's waist. She raised her chin and fixed her gaze forward but didn't react in any other way.

"I was left to die by my own parents, but I didn't die. I survived, and what I built—"

"In my survival is a loyal community ready to do my bidding. Because I was strong. Stronger than anyone," Jamison intoned. He had knelt, but he refused to look at the floor in supplication. He held his father's steely gaze. "Your speeches are still boring and predictable."

"Every true leader must go through betrayals, Jamison.

I have been through yours. I've waited for retribution, because a good leader bides his time. A good leader, a true leader waits until the time is right, no matter how long."

"Well, since I don't have any sons for you to steal, I guess you'll have to wait a little longer."

"Transgressions must be paid for, Jamison." His grip on Liza tightened and it took every ounce of control Jamison had honed in thirty-seven years to stay where he was and not lunge at Ace. "One of you will pay with blood. The other will pay with failure."

"You're starting to sound more like a cult than a gang," Jamison gritted out.

"Don't worry," Ace said easily. "We can be both. What happens when a strong leader falls, Jamison? Chaos. What happens if you don't return to your brothers? Would they fall apart, too? No. I don't think so. You'd be their thing to avenge. Vengeance for a particular person can't be your motivation. If I only wanted vengeance on my parents, what would I have built? Nothing. I wanted vengeance on the world and I built one of my own."

"It's a big world out there, outside the Sons. All you've built is a...village, maybe," Jamison returned, because if he kept Ace talking, he bought them all time. Jamison had to believe time mattered.

"I don't need the world, Jamison. I only need the loyal. It's a shame that's neither of you." Dad produced a knife and held it far too close to Liza's cheek. "I taught you that the only truth is power. Everything else is a weakness. You didn't believe me. Now I have your weakness right here. What do you think I should do with it?"

LIZA DID EVERYTHING she could to hide her revulsion. Ace's arm was wrapped around her waist like a python. The contact made her stomach roil in disgust.

She could see the barely leashed fury in Jamison's eyes, and she knew it wouldn't last forever. He'd snap if something didn't change. And soon.

Ace had one thing right, she *was* Jamison's weakness, because he'd likely do something stupid before he let Ace hurt her.

Ace pressed the knife to her cheek, and she moved her gaze to Jamison. She knew he wouldn't see it if he didn't *want* to see it, but she did everything she could with her eyes to beg him to stay put.

"You surprise me," Ace said as the knife pricked the skin of her cheek. "Either you've learned some restraint or she doesn't mean much to you at all. Both would make me proud."

"That's what I've always lived for," Jamison returned caustically. "To make you proud."

"I know you fancy yourself above my influence, but don't think there isn't something to you becoming a cop. You and all your brothers. As if that badge will save you from what you really are."

The knife dug harder against her cheek, and Liza did everything she could not to react outwardly to the searing pain.

Then, out of nowhere, both the knife and gag dropped from her face.

"I wouldn't want to muffle your screams of pain," Ace said. This time when he pressed the knife to her skin, it was against her throat.

Fear was ice in her veins, but she focused on Jamison. She focused on the battle light in his eyes, in all the ways he'd tried to save her.

But she'd needed to do her own saving. She'd saved Gigi. She could save Jamison.

She wouldn't shake. She wouldn't beg. She would be strong, the way he'd always taught her to be.

"Don't you want to order one of your morons to do the dirty work for you?" she asked, her voice steady, disdainful.

"Normally I would, since you're less than nothing, but I want Jamison to have the vision of me slitting your throat in his head till the day he dies."

Liza knew she couldn't stop herself from being killed. She was in too deep and death seemed inevitable. But she wouldn't give Ace the satisfaction of having it his way.

He had a knife to her throat and her hands were tied behind her back. Jamison was eyeing the men with guns on him, clearly calculating his own attempt to save her.

If they could act together, it would be more of a fight than a slaughter—but how?

She didn't have time to think up an answer because something exploded behind her, sending her sprawling off Ace's lap and onto the floor—face-first.

She was so dazed it took her a few seconds to realize she was on the floor, people were shouting, guns were going off. She was bleeding—from the cut Ace's knife had made in her cheek, possibly her throat. She wasn't sure. Everything was a blur.

Until someone grabbed her.

Ace flipped her onto her back and she immediately fought back. She didn't have any strategy, just to kick as hard as she could—but she didn't have her hands. She didn't have anything.

He used his body to bracket her legs together. She twisted and fought to sit up, but he held her shoulders down. On the bright side, he couldn't exactly stab her as long as he was holding her down.

"You think you've won," Ace said, moving one hand

from her shoulder to the center of her chest. He held her down with that one hand then, brandishing that awful knife. "But you'll never win."

"That's the difference between you and me, Ace. I don't need to win. Surviving this nightmare is enough for me. I don't need more than that."

"You think you're going to survive?" He laughed. "I'm the survivor."

"Not this time," a man's voice said from behind Ace.

Ace stilled and Liza looked up at the figure. Cody held a gun to Ace's head.

Cody was here. But… "The girls…" Liza whispered.

"Are fine and safe," Cody assured her.

Ace's eyebrows drew together for a moment as he looked at the knife in his hand. As he seemed to put together what that could mean.

"Yeah, we saved them," Liza had the pleasure of telling Ace. "Right under your nose. Want to lecture me some more about strong leaders? We've all been stronger than you, Ace. Now you're going to find out how much."

"Drop the knife," Cody ordered.

"I could slit her throat before you put a bullet in my brain, son. I'd watch the tone you take with me."

"Do it, then."

Liza couldn't hide the surprise or horror that stole over her face, especially as Ace looked like he was just about to do that.

But a gunshot went off, and somehow the knife flew out of Ace's hand, clattering to the ground as the bullet crashed into the opposite wall. Someone had *shot* the knife out of Ace's hand.

When Liza stared up at Cody, he shrugged. "Snipers come in handy now and again. As do explosive experts," he said, giving a vague nod toward the blown-in back of the building. He then inclined his head toward someone. Liza felt herself be pulled out from under Ace, the binding on her wrists being cut as she was set on her feet.

She surveyed the very strange sight. Almost the entire back wall of the church, so to speak, was gone, but there wasn't fire left like at the cabin and stables. Explosives expert, indeed.

She glanced at the interior. Two of Ace's men were tied to each other, lying in a heap. Two others were clearly dead. And Jamison… Jamison was lying on the floor—one of Cody's men patching him up.

Liza practically tripped over herself to run to his side.

"I'm all right," he muttered as she reached out to touch his cheek.

"He's got a head wound that needs stitches, at the very least," the person working on him corrected. Liza was surprised the voice belonged to a woman. All of the people Cody had brought in were dressed in head-to-toe black, armed to the teeth and wore a variety of hats, helmets and scarves that obscured their identities down to gender.

She looked back at Cody, wondering what on earth he was involved in. Then back at Jamison.

"Is Ace still alive?" Jamison asked, his voice a raw scrape that had her wincing at the pain it must have caused him.

"I think so."

"Help me up, then," he said, struggling to push himself up as both Liza and the other woman kept him pressed to the floor.

"Jamison."

"You shouldn't get up," the woman said, though she had wrapped a bandage around his head.

"Have to," Jamison said to the woman.

Knowing he wouldn't give up, Liza gave a nod to the woman and helped Jamison to his feet. He swayed as he stood, and Liza helped steady him, then led him over to Cody.

Cody, who still held a gun to Ace's head, had a look on his face that had Liza grabbing onto Jamison's arm—trying to keep him away from this scene. Ace was lying on his back, smiling up at Cody, and nothing—*nothing*—good could come from this moment.

But Jamison calmly put his hand on Cody's shoulder. "Don't kill him."

Chapter Nineteen

Cody didn't look away from Ace's grinning face, but Jamison knew Cody had heard him. His grip on the gun had changed, and there was a sense of hesitation to him now.

Jamison knew he had to press on that while he could. "I want him to rot in a cell," Jamison continued calmly. His head ached, and his vision was gray and doubled, but he was alive. He'd survive.

Now he had to make sure his baby brother did, too. Really *survive*, not just walk out of this alive.

"If he's dead, it's over," Cody said, his finger curled around the trigger. But Ace would already be dead if Cody didn't have a certain level of uncertainty about killing their father.

Over. It was tempting. To know Ace wouldn't be able to pop up in their lives in the future and wreak havoc. Wasn't that what had held him back from really *having* a life all these years?

But Cody would have to live with it, and Jamison didn't think it was worth it. That weight. Forever.

"Do you want to be like him?" Jamison asked quietly.

Cody didn't answer that, so Jamison continued.

"His second-in-command is dead. He'll be going to jail for a very long time." Jamison turned to face his father. If Ace felt defeated, he didn't look it. Jamison wanted him to *look* defeated. To feel it. To embody it. And a jail cell? Jamison was certain the lack of freedom would do just that. Far more than death ever could. "What did you say happens in the absence of a powerful leader, Dad?"

Ace smiled. "Chaos, son."

Jamison nodded and turned back to Cody. "We got what we wanted. This is over. The Sons will be chaos. He'll rot in jail, and you know it. It's over. Don't make it live on for yourself forever."

"It'll never be over, Jamison," Ace said, all but laughing as he spoke. "Not ever. Not until one of you has the guts to take me out. But you won't. None of you have the courage. None of you have the survival instinct."

Jamison watched Cody's jaw work, but he didn't have to say anything. Cody lowered the gun. "You sound like a man who wants to die, Ace. I don't plan to be the one to give you what you want."

Cody made a signal, and two of the men who'd swept in after the explosion pulled Ace to his feet and handcuffed him.

"Not a complaint," Jamison said, watching his father being led away. "But since you all clearly aren't licensed law enforcement, should you be handcuffing him?"

"We'll take care of it," Cody replied. He still held the gun with too tight a grip, and his gaze hadn't left their father. "It'll be legal by the time we're done."

Jamison didn't know how to feel about that.

"The girls?" Liza asked.

Cody finally turned away from Ace and motioned Liza and Jamison to follow him out through the exploded back wall. There were a line of black cars waiting.

"They've been taken to a medical center. I didn't want

to get Social Services involved until you were both there. Some of the girls could tell us who their parents were and if they were involved in the Sons, but some are just too young. It's going to take some doing, but we want to make sure we don't return any of these girls to parents who might have sold them."

"Sold them?" Liza said on a gasp.

"Unfortunately, it happens. And in the Sons? Anything is possible. But no matter who's in charge now, we took down almost the entire trafficking ring. Tony is dead. Ace will be incarcerated. It's not likely to happen again. Not here anyway."

"You didn't know the girls were there, though," Jamison said as he followed Cody to the cars. "How did…"

"We were investigating the death of Carlee Bright. She has a connection to someone in our group. We hadn't found any evidence of the trafficking. Which leads me to believe this may have been their first attempt. That you two stopped it before it got off the ground."

"We didn't stop anything," Jamison said. The girls had already been captured. He had no idea how they'd been treated in those stables, or for how long. At best he'd kept them from a worse fate, but he certainly hadn't kept them from fear or cruelty.

"Those girls would be dead if not for you two. We would have blown them up." Cody said that flatly, but Jamison knew that kind of misplaced guilt well enough to recognize it.

He squeezed his brother's shoulder. "But you didn't."

Cody nodded. "My men will take you to the girls. Where you can also be checked out. J, you can get those stitches. Liza can get her ankle looked at. The rest of us have a lot of work to do here and at the other explosion site."

It was a strange thing to be told what to do by his baby brother. At Valiant County, Jamison was the ranking officer. To sit back and let Cody and "his men" take care of it was the antithesis to everything Jamison wanted to do.

But Cody had saved him. Not that he couldn't offer his two cents. "There were badges. Pictures of badges— DSNs x-ed out and hung on the wall. It was clearly some kind of hit list. I don't think the blast ruined too much of it. It could be used against Ace."

"My associates will be taking pictures and any other evidence they can find to build a case against Ace. We might not be official, but we know how to get everything into the officials' hands. Tony being dead makes him the perfect scapegoat for a lot of the stuff that carries the chance at a life sentence, and God knows Ace will use that all he can. Ace will get jail time, he's too connected, but I don't think we're going to get him on murder."

"If we put him away for a while, we can build a bigger case while he's inside," Jamison replied.

"I sure hope you're right, because if you're not, we're all in danger. Serious danger. Worse than it was. Bad enough to escape him. Actually put him in jail? We're targets now. I don't think the kind he'll wait on."

"We'll handle it. Whatever comes, we'll handle it."

Cody looked at where Ace was being shoved into a car. "We may have to kill him yet."

Jamison knew it was possible, but it would also be his last resort. And he wouldn't let his brothers be the ones to live with that weight. "We're better than that. Better than him."

Cody sighed, and he didn't have to say the words for Jamison to know what that sigh meant.

I'm not so sure.

So, Jamison would have to be sure for the both of them—for all of them.

Despite forever and always working so hard to be *good*, Jamison wasn't so sure he was, in fact, good. He'd worried for years that the evil inside his father might take hold of him.

But here they were. Alive. Having helped save some innocent lives. He'd take that as a win for today.

Cody opened the back door of a big, military-grade-looking SUV. Jamison paused, studying his baby brother. He shook his head in awe. "What *are* you involved in?"

Cody smiled wryly. "After this? Nothing."

LIZA DOZED ON the drive to Cody's "medical center," which looked like any run-of-the-mill hunting cabin Liza had ever seen, but was a full-blown medical clinic inside. She practically punched a doctor who tried to check her out before she could see Gigi.

She finally let the doctor examine her while Gigi sat curled up on her lap, talking about the pretty unicorn the lady doctor had given her.

Liza tried not to cry and did a pretty good job of it. Gigi dozed on her lap and Liza let the female doctor—well, Liza assumed she was a doctor—fix her stitches and patch up all her other injuries. They gave her crutches to help stay off her sprained ankle.

"You'll need to take it easy for a few weeks."

Liza laughed. "Yeah, you don't have to tell me twice." She looked down at Gigi, who was fast sleep in her lap. "These girls… Were they…" Liza couldn't bring herself to say it.

"Aside from a few bumps and bruises and a little undernourishment, Gigi is fine. She'll recover in no time."

Liza knew what that meant. "But the others?"

"I can't tell you about the others, Liza. I'm sorry. Patient confidentiality. I've taken good care of them, and they're safe because of you."

Liza managed a smile for the doctor, though she didn't feel it. It turned out saving someone wasn't the be-all and end-all she'd always assumed it was. She understood Jamison better now, because saving someone meant they'd been through something awful in the first place.

And that you couldn't take it away simply by saving them. There was some guilt even in a happy ending. Maybe if she focused on the happy, the guilt wouldn't be so bad.

Another woman popped her head in the door. "Cody'd like to talk to you, Liza. I can put Gigi to bed."

Liza's grip tightened on Gigi, and the woman smiled warmly. "You're not going to be able to carry her with your ankle. I'll carry her, and show you right where I'm going to put her. You can sit in bed with her until you're satisfied. Cody can wait. Might be good for him."

Liza smiled and nodded even though it was weird that all these strangers knew her name, and Gigi's. The woman was kind and seemed to understand how much Liza wanted to stay with Gigi.

She didn't know any of their names, but she trusted them. Trusted Cody. He'd saved their butts—all of them. She owed him just as much as she owed Jamison.

They wouldn't think of it like that, though. Neither of them. She had to swallow against the wave of emotion. She was out of the Sons, and that meant she got to have some part of that goodness again. Grandma Pauline. The Knights. The Wyatt brothers. Jamison...

They'd all be in her life again. In Gigi's life.

The woman gathered up Gigi, and then waited for Liza

to get to her feet and balance on the crutches. She led her into a dark room, but there was a night-light plugged into the wall. There were a variety of beds—some that had clearly been pushed in from other rooms. So the girls could be together.

The woman laid Gigi down on an empty bed, then stepped back so Liza could tuck her in.

Gigi didn't so much as shift or whimper as Liza covered her. Liza sat there for a moment, looking at Gigi's sleeping form, then looking around the room. The sisters slept cuddled together in the same bed, but most of the other girls were in beds of their own. All fast asleep.

They were safe. Maybe they'd seen horrors, but they'd survived them.

The woman nodded toward the door and Liza reluctantly followed her outside.

"We've got a monitor. If anyone wakes up scared, we'll send in either you or one of our people they've been introduced to. We want to make this as easy on them as we can, I promise you."

Liza nodded, afraid she'd start crying if she spoke. She was led to another room. She realized the front of the cabin was deceptive, or it had been in the low light of dawn. It seemed to keep going, farther and farther back. Exam rooms and bedrooms and now this room that reminded Liza of an interrogation room.

But Jamison was there—all sorts of bandages on his face, his arm in a sling. He looked up at her, exhaustion dug into every line on his face.

Love slammed into her so hard and painful, that no matter how well she'd held herself together up until this point, she lost it all here and now.

A sob escaped her mouth, and she was completely immobilized by all of it.

Not even a second went by before Jamison's arms were around her. "Shh. It's all right. We're all right."

She shook her head, feeling stupid and foolish and just wrung out. "Sit down. You're hurt," she croaked, even as she held on to him for dear life.

He rubbed his hand up and down her back and kissed her temple. "I'm fine. I'm fine. Come on, baby. You're killing me. It's all right now."

She leaned into him, letting it all pour out. It *was* all right. No matter what they had to face in the future, they could. They would. Because they'd made this all right, and if they could do that—kill her father, put Ace in jail, stop a human trafficking ring—they could do anything.

She managed to pull herself together, let Jamison lead her to a chair at a table. He nudged her into it, leaned her crutches on the wall, then took the seat next to her. Cody sat on the opposite side of the table, a tablet in front of him.

"I wanted to brief you on the future for the girls," Cody said, all business, as if she hadn't sobbed her guts out in front of him. As if she hadn't known him when he was a baby or a pudgy toddler. "We're checking missing persons files first. But the ones we know for sure are Sons girls… We could find good families for them without going through the state."

"How?" Jamison demanded. "They'll need records and to go to school and—"

Cody smiled at Jamison before he interrupted, "By ways I shouldn't explain in the presence of a by-the-book cop."

Jamison winced at that, but he didn't push Cody for specifics. Cody turned to Liza.

"In your case, Liza, the state would likely award you custody of Gigi through the normal channels. You're the closest living relative that we know about, and Gigi knows you. If you wanted—"

"Of course that's what I want," Liza snapped.

"All right. We'll get you in touch with the right people and make sure it goes as smoothly as possible." Cody's expression changed, though Liza couldn't read it. "You haven't asked about the horse."

Liza winced and shook her head. "I don't want to know. Really, I—"

"I got him out," Jamison interrupted. "I didn't know if he'd get out of the blast zone, but I got him out of the stables."

Liza looked at Jamison in complete awe. He'd somehow saved himself *and* George?

"The rescue team I called out to get the girls found him in the woods. Gigi told him he saved her. So, we got him out, too."

Liza laughed. It was all she could seem to do. They were all safe and whole. Even George the horse.

Unfortunately, no matter how thrilled and relieved she was, there were still serious worries that hadn't been addressed.

"What about Ace?" Liza asked, wishing she could doze on Jamison's lap like Gigi had slept in hers.

"He's currently being held at Pennington County Jail. We're working with local law enforcement on state charges. I've also got one of the men in my group working on what we can get going on the federal level."

Jamison nodded. "Now, most important, when can we go home?"

"When the girls wake up, we'll move you. Grandma and Duke agreed to put up all the girls until we get them placed. We're trying to move as fast on that as we can so they don't feel like they're being juggled, but we don't want to overlook anything. Wherever we place them, it'll be permanent. They'll be taken care of well, and not just now, either. We'll keep tabs. Keep them safe. It's what we do."

Liza rested her head against Jamison's shoulder, beyond tired. "I just want to go home."

Jamison rested his arm over her shoulders, holding her close. "Soon, Liza. Soon."

Chapter Twenty

The ranch was chaos, but the kind that made Jamison smile.

Grandma had taken in four of the girls, including Gigi. Three were over at the Knight ranch, being looked after by Duke—and Sarah and Rachel, his two daughters who still lived on the ranch. And best of all, four of the girls had been placed back with the families they'd been kidnapped from.

Regardless of how many were still staying at the ranches, every night everyone descended on Grandma Pauline's dining room for dinner as they were doing right now.

Four of the girls were being placed in their new homes tomorrow, and the parents who'd agreed to adopt them had come for dinner, too. The house was bursting at the seams, and Grandma ran her kitchen like the general she was.

When they sat down to eat, Duke told stories that had them all laughing. It felt like Christmas. A celebration.

In so many ways, it was. A celebration of survival and life and knowing they all had futures to build ahead of them.

Once dinner was done, all the girls moved to the stables. It was now a nightly routine for everyone to pet and coo over hero-horse George, whom Cody had managed to transport to the ranch.

He had the much-deserved life of a hero now.

Jamison and whichever brothers were home were relegated to cleanup—he and Cody were currently handling dishes while Dev wiped down the table and swept up the debris before sneaking out to feed the dogs some scraps.

Cody had spent most of the past three days at Grandma's. As if he was planning on staying right here.

"So, when are you going to tell us about this group?" Jamison asked as Cody handed him a plate to dry.

"Never." Cody grinned, but his smile dimmed some and he went back to the dishes he was washing. "Once this is officially over, I'm kicked out."

"Why?"

"Too much connection. It's a secret group, Jamison. I compromised the secret."

"You helped people. You saved us."

Cody paused in his scrubbing for a second, then shook his head. "It's only ever temporary. We know any mission could expose us and we'll have to move on. It's part of the group." Cody shrugged. "I did my time. I helped some people. Now I'll have to figure out what's next. Seems like Dev could use some help around here."

"You hate ranch work."

"Maybe I'll find a new taste for it in my old age."

"You won't." Jamison chuckled, because he realized that Cody might stick around the ranch for a while, but he'd find something else. He'd found this "group" on his own and done good things…whatever they all were. He'd find a way to do more good things, Jamison had no doubt. "You know, you're not so old the police academy would reject you."

"We'll see."

Jamison could have pushed Cody, but there was no need. It wouldn't be a bad idea for his brother to stick around the ranch. They'd need to keep an eye on things these first few months and make sure the Sons didn't band back together stronger without Ace than they'd been with him.

Jamison doubted it, but they still had to be careful.

They finished the dishes, joined the others until they slowly began to disperse. Grandma and Liza put the girls left with them to bed. Cody had disappeared to his room, and Dev and Sarah were out doing the last chores of the evening.

So, Jamison climbed the stairs. His body still wasn't healed—not by a long shot. But he'd get there.

He walked down the hallway to the door to the room Gigi was sleeping in. The door was open, and Liza was curled up in bed with Gigi, telling her a story.

Jamison watched until Liza finished telling Gigi the story. With an elaborate happy ending that Gigi sighed over. Liza handed her the unicorn one of the doctors had given her, then pulled the blanket up to Gigi's chin.

"Stay till I fall asleep, sissy?"

"Always, baby."

Jamison waited. When Liza finally slid away from Gigi's bed, she didn't act surprised to see him in the doorway. She smiled.

She closed the door behind her and they stood in the hallway. The past few nights she'd spent in the same room with Gigi, not wanting to leave her. They hadn't had a chance to really talk.

They had a lot to talk about.

"Where are your crutches?"

"They're more of a pain than this sprain. I'm fine,"

Liza replied irritably. She gave him an enigmatic sideways look. "How long until you have to go back?"

He frowned in spite of himself. "Desk duty calls." It would bore him to death, truth be told. He might not need to be constantly solving crime, but he liked to be out and active in the community.

And he liked being here, though that had more to do with her and Gigi than anything Bonesteel lacked.

Liza frowned at that. "You're hurt."

"I can take calls. Gage's got my Bonesteel attachment for the time being, which means I absolutely need to go back to work and give him the trouble he's always giving me." He reached out and squeezed her arm. "You'll both be safe here. For as long as you need."

LIZA STARED AT the man she loved, who'd given her the space to all but smother Gigi these past few days. She'd needed that. Some time to focus on Gigi alone. To think about what their new life would look like.

But it didn't look like anything without Jamison in it. He wanted her to stay here. Out of the way and safe. Because he loved her, and he was a man who'd spent his life saving people. So, he thought love was sacrifice.

She'd have to teach him otherwise. She placed her hand on his chest. "I can think of another place we'd be safe."

Jamison stared at her hand, then at her. He looked hurt almost, which didn't make any sense to her.

"Liza…if you want to take Gigi somewhere far away, I'd understand. I could help. But you should wait—"

"I'm not talking about far away," she said, giving him a light shove. "I'm taking about a town with a school, and a very serious police officer keeping the streets safe."

He opened his mouth, but he didn't say anything.

"Unless you're taking back all the love stuff."

He straightened. "I'm not taking back anything."

"Ace is in jail," she said, wrapping her arms around his neck.

"For now," Jamison said, but his arms came around her waist. She could see the worry in him, *feel* it. But he wasn't stepping back.

"Even if he wasn't, I'm on his list." When Jamison tensed, she kissed his jaw. "You know I am," she said gently.

"What about Gigi?"

"It just so happens I have a great role model in keeping younger siblings safe. She'll be safe with me. With *us*."

"You could both disappear. If you gave me time, I could—"

"For how long?" Liza shook her head. A younger her would have been hurt that he could live without her, but the woman she was now understood all too well he was just trying to protect. "You could have sent your brothers to the ends of the earth. You all could have left. But you stayed, because this is home, and because they dictated too much of our lives already. We stay, Jamison. And if we're in danger, we fight. Together."

"I love you. I want you by my side, Liza, but—"

"No *but*s. That's it. We love each other. We'll keep each other safe. And we'll both do everything in our power to keep Gigi safe and happy. What more could a girl want?"

"Well, probably a better place to live than a shabby, empty apartment above the local lawyer's office."

"So, we'll find a house."

He looked down at her, so serious. If she hadn't always loved him, that careful, serious study would have done it.

"If we find a house, we're going to be finding the altar," he said resolutely, something like a challenge.

She merely raised an eyebrow. "You think that scares me?"

"I don't think anything scares you, Liza. But... Realistically..."

"Realistically I faced death about ten times in the past week."

He brushed a piece of hair away from her face, and when he spoke his voice was gentle. "So, maybe we're not in the best place to be making lifetime commitments."

Liza laughed. She couldn't help it. "How many women have you been with in the past fifteen years?"

He straightened, all flustered and indignant. Adorable and perfect. And hers. Always hers.

"I don't see what that has to do with anything we're talking about."

"Not very many, then."

"I didn't say... That doesn't mean..."

"It means you were waiting for me, whether you admitted it to yourself or not. Because you made a promise to me a long time ago, and you, Jamison Wyatt, don't break promises." She let out a sigh, because it was true now, and it would always be true. "Even when you want to. You were waiting, because somewhere deep down you knew we'd find our way back. Just like I did, no matter how little I could let myself hope for it."

"I don't know how it's possible. To be apart for so long and change in a million ways, and yet... I don't believe in any of that stuff. In knowing what we don't actually know. Waiting without realizing. I don't believe in it. But..."

"Here it is."

"Here it is," he repeated, lowering his mouth to hers.

But he didn't kiss her. Not just yet. "I guess it doesn't matter how, as long as we believe it is."

"I do," she said, then pressed her mouth to his instead of waiting for him to get around to it.

Because her future was now, and she'd always been fighting for one with this very good man.

* * * * *

COMING SOON!

We really hope you enjoyed reading this book. If you're looking for more romance, be sure to head to the shops when new books are available on

Thursday 6th March

To see which titles are coming soon, please visit

millsandboon.co.uk/nextmonth

MILLS & BOON

MODERN

Power and Passion

Prepare to be swept off your feet by sophisticated, sexy and seductive heroes, in some of the world's most glamourous and romantic locations, where power and passion collide.

MILLS & BOON
MEDICAL
Pulse-Racing Passion

Set your pulse racing with dedicated, delectable doctors in the high-pressure world of medicine, where emotions run high and passion, comfort and love are the best medicine.

MILLS & BOON

THE HEART OF ROMANCE

A ROMANCE FOR EVERY KIND OF READER

MODERN

Prepare to be swept off your feet by sophisticated, sexy and seductive heroes, in some of the world's most glamourous and romantic locations, where power and passion collide.
8 stories per month.

HISTORICAL

Escape with historical heroes from time gone by. Whether your passion is for wicked Regency Rakes, muscled Vikings or rugged Highlanders, awaken the romance of the past.
6 stories per month.

MEDICAL

Set your pulse racing with dedicated, delectable doctors in the high-pressure world of medicine, where emotions run high and passion, comfort and love are the best medicine.
6 stories per month.

True Love

Celebrate true love with tender stories of heartfelt romance, from the rush of falling in love to the joy a new baby can bring, and a focus on the emotional heart of a relationship.
8 stories per month.

Desire

Indulge in secrets and scandal, intense drama and plenty of sizzling hot action with powerful and passionate heroes who have it all: wealth, status, good looks…everything but the right woman.
6 stories per month.

HEROES

Experience all the excitement of a gripping thriller, with an intense romance at its heart. Resourceful, true-to-life women and strong, fearless men face danger and desire - a killer combination!
8 stories per month.

DARE

Sensual love stories featuring smart, sassy heroines you'd want as a best friend, and compelling intense heroes who are worthy of them.
4 stories per month.

To see which titles are coming soon, please visit
millsandboon.co.uk/nextmonth

LET'S TALK
Romance

For exclusive extracts, competitions
and special offers, find us online:

 facebook.com/millsandboon

🐦 @MillsandBoon

📷 @MillsandBoonUK

Get in touch on 01413 063232

For all the latest titles coming soon, visit
millsandboon.co.uk/nextmonth